Inkbound Inheritance

The Inkbound Chronicles

K.T. Jay

For my husband.

~

You never stopped believing in me.

CONTENTS

CHAPTER ONE

"**N**ora! It's time to start chores! What's taking you so long?" Ida turned the knob to her daughter's bedroom and spotted her scrambling to put something away.

"Writing again?" Ida sighed. "When will you get your head out of the clouds and focus? We need your help on the farm." Ida looked at Nora, whose eyes were strained on the small wooden desk in front of her. "Your brother is waiting for you to start your chores." Ida paused. She opened her mouth, closed it, nodded, and briskly shut the door.

Nora puffed out a big breath. She knew writing wasn't what her family needed, but she couldn't get the stories to stop swimming in her head. She *had* to write them down. The images came so clearly and clawed to be let out. Once she started writing, she had a hard time stopping. The world she created on paper called to her. She could slip in and enjoy the magic. Biting her lip, she stared at the papers.

Not now. She had to help her brother.

Gathering up her work, she ran her fingers across the parchment and could almost feel a pull from it. She tidied them up and left to find her brother.

"Good morning, Nora," her father greeted her from the table as she stepped into the kitchen.

"Morning," Nora muttered.

"Callum is out back waiting for ya."

"Thanks."

"I hear things are a bit behind at the bakery?"

Nora tensed her jaw. "I'm doing the best I can, Dad."

Staring at her, he nodded. "Go find your brother."

Nora swept past him, out the door, closing it as calmly as she could. Callum stood at the wooden fence that separated the farm from the house. She trudged over beside him and leaned her forearms on the fence.

"Mornin'," Callum cheerfully greeted her. Nora never understood how he could be so happy in the mornings. "Did you try the new rolls mum made this mornin'? Homemade butter makes all the difference."

"No, not today," Nora said.

Callum regarded her. "You skipping breakfast? That's not a good sign. You manage some tea at least?" His gray eyes were calm compared to the sky above.

"No." Nora stared at the ground.

Callum pursed his lips. "You skipping tea is a terrible sign. What's going on, Nor?"

"She caught me again," Nora said. "I don't know what to do anymore. The stories won't stop coming, and if I do nothing, it's a nightmare. And once I'm there, in the story, I feel happy. I feel alive." Nora looked up at Callum, his face blurring through her tears.

Callum put his arm around Nora and pulled her into his chest. "It's going to be alright, Nora."

"You don't know that though," Nora cried. "Dad keeps talking to be about how far behind I am in my apprenticeship at the bakery. I know I'm letting mum and dad down, but I hate it here. Fiadh is cruel to me and I can't take it anymore."

Callum rubbed Nora's back to calm her like he did when they were younger. After a moment, he held her out at arm's length, his eyes now stormy. His gaze caught on something and flicked to her shoulder. He eased the fabric away.

Nora winced.

"What did she do to you?" Callum seethed.

"I—I dropped some rolls taking them out of the oven and she...took a rolling pin to me." Nora squeezed her eyes shut, trying to forget Fiadh's furious voice and the shoots of pain from the giant rolling pin.

Shaking his head in anger, nostrils flared, Callum said, "I will do something about this, Nora. I'll tell dad—"

"No, you can't! She said if I told on her she would tell the guards I tried to steal rolls from the case." Nora clung to Callum's shirtfront.

"That's a lie!"

"Who do you think they'll believe? A struggling farm girl or the bakery owner whose family has been here for decades?" Nora's voice strained. She could see the struggle on her brother's face.

"It's not right. I'm telling dad." Callum started for the house.

"No, you can't!"

Ignoring her, Callum kept walking.

Nora turned the other way and ran toward the forest behind their farm.

"Wait, Nora! Where are you going?" Callum called after her.

With tears running down her face, she raced toward the thick wall of trees in front of her. She ran from her parents' disappointed faces, from their questions about her apprenticeship, from her desire to live in her stories and be someone else.Nora made it to the tree line on the edge of her family's property and sprinted into the forest. She ran past the first row of trees, into the looming woods, and kept running until her chest burned.

Once her lungs felt like they were on fire, she stopped and bent over to catch her breath.

Looking up, she tried to get her bearings. The surrounding trees were unfamiliar and seemed untouched. The leaves, still damp from the morning mist, sparkled in the light.

Closing her eyes, she welcomed the warm sun's rays on her face. The fresh smell of rain, bark, and the spring breeze helped douse some of the fire in her lungs.

"Hello there, dreamer."

Nora's eyes snapped open, and she spun around.

"Wha—" Her heart slammed in her chest as she looked at the cloaked woman in front of her.

"Oh yes, sorry to startle you, my dear, but you have wandered into my woods. I couldn't let you arrive without giving you a proper greeting." Her kind, deep blue eyes caught Nora's attention. They reminded her of the rocking sea when her family would travel around Ireland's ports selling goods from their farm. "My name is Celeste. These woods have been my home for decades. What brings you out this far?" She tilted her head.

Nora tried to speak, but the words caught in her throat. What was she supposed to say to a woman in the woods? Who knew if she could trust her or not.

Clearing her throat, she said, "I ran and this is where I ended up."

"What were you running from?"

Nora shifted from one foot to the other and clenched her fists. "I was just . . . running."

"Hmm . . ." Celeste said again, nodding slowly, eyeing Nora's unsuitable running attire of work boots, house dress, and apron. "Perhaps I can help you find what you're looking for."

"Why would I be looking for something?"

"Few venture deep into the forest without reason. What are you searching for?" Celeste asked.

"What do you mean?" Nora clenched her jaw at her incessant questions.

A smile crept across Celeste's face. "I have a special power, you could call it. I can grant wishes, and it sounds like you could use a wish. Correct?"

"Well, I . . ." Nora stammered.

"Or perhaps I am mistaken?" Celeste shrugged and turned away.

"Wait!"

Celeste froze mid-step and brought her gaze to Nora's. It was patient and strangely welcoming for a woman who supposedly lived in the woods.

"If you want, I can help you journey into your storyworlds and make your inkbound desires reality."

"How did you . . . " Nora trailed off, unsure of what to make of Celeste's sudden knowledge.

Nora's deepest desire was to fall away into her stories and to meet the characters she wrote about. To have the adventures they had, the freedom they had. This woman offered her exactly what she had been yearning for all these years. How could she say no?

Her gaze met Celeste's, and she nodded.

"Okay dearie, come over here to the spring and we'll start on your wish." Celeste motioned to a freshwater spring she'd been obstructing from view.

Nora padded across the wet leaves and knelt in front of the spring next to the mystical woman.

Celeste began to recite a riddle or spell, maybe. As she did, her hands swirled above the spring and bubbles formed on the surface while her voice sung words Nora didn't understand.

Entranced, Nora watched the water whirl. Blinking, Nora realized Celeste had been silent for a few seconds.

"Drink from the spring now, child," Celeste directed Nora, her voice cool as the breeze touching Nora's cheek.

Nora dipped her hand in the water and brought it up to her mouth. The water glided over her lips, trickled down her throat, and settled in her stomach, filling her with peace. Confused, she looked up at Celeste.

"Don't worry, dear. You'll see the magic work once you write your first story. Heed my earlier instructions; they contain what you require."

Nora studied her face and thought she saw sadness in her smile. Celeste bowed her head and faded into the forest as if she'd never been there at all.

The muscles in Liam's arms burned as he pushed the bar away from his chest, counting another rep. One more to prove to himself he could.

Shakily, he brought the bar back down to his chest and summoned his strength for one more press.

Re-racking the weight, he thought about the summer of lifting he'd done alongside his karate classes. Would it be enough?

"Hey, stick boy!" he heard behind him. Closing his eyes, he balled his hands into fists.

Just breathe. Breathe and it will be okay. He half believed his own reassurances.

Clive and his rugby friends formed a circle around the slight boy to Liam's right.

Not him.

This was new.

"You going to show us what you can do, James?" Clive leaned against a squat rack and jutted his chin out at James, the one he called 'stick boy.' The rest of Clive's friends from the high school rugby team threw doubtful looks at James. Perhaps James had been a little ambitious when he loaded the bar, so he'd be chest pressing one hundred pounds. He hadn't even successfully pressed eighty yet.

Liam had noticed James in the weight room for about a week. He'd keep to himself, head down, dark hair messy and clothes rumpled. He made Liam think back to himself in this weight room months ago. Insecure and altogether terrified. James' dark blue eyes darted around, his long face tense with worry.

"What are you waiting for, stick boy? Too scared?" Clive scoffed and pushed a meaty hand through his own head of golden hair, brown eyes dark with cruelty.

James swallowed and looked at the five guys surrounding him, not going anywhere. He glanced at the overloaded bar, exhaling slowly. Sliding onto the bench, he ducked under the bar and gripped it, sweat rolling from his hairline to his cheek.

Liam chewed his cheek and watched, wondering what he should do. This would not end well.

James filled his lungs with air, braced his core, and pushed on the bar with all he had.

He pushed and pushed, his legs shaking as he stabilized himself to chest press a weight he'd probably never done in his life.

It didn't budge.

Exhaling, he tried again.

Pushing on the bar, his face turned scarlet and sweat beaded his face. His arms shook with effort but couldn't raise the bar.

Clive and his friends snorted, then burst into all-out laughter. James stopped and pressed his lips together. His face grew even redder. Liam could feel the shame and embarrassment coming off him.

"Stop!" Liam's voice punctuated their laughter, catching them by surprise.

"Oh." Clive's eyebrow arched. "Wizard boy has something to say?"

Liam wanted to smack the stupid smile right off Clive's round, ruddy face.

"Leave him alone." Liam set his jaw and stood taller as he faced the rugby boys.

Clive pursed his lips. "What's that, wizard boy?"

"I said leave him alone," Liam growled. "And I'm not the wizard boy, so knock it off."

"Huh, look at him, boys! He's found a voice apparently. Too bad you're all bark and no bite." Clive tilted his head and the rest of his friends chuckled. "We all know your mom wrote those books about you. Those kids' books. The chosen one! A wizard destined to save the world. But look what happened. You couldn't do it in the book and you can't do it here either. You can't be a hero all by yourself. It's five against one. What are you going to do?"

Liam ground his teeth and clenched his fists.

He was tired of his mom's bestselling book series following him around. Everyone at school thought she'd written them about him so he could have fun stories when he was little. He did love them as a kid. He'd beg her to read them to him again and again. All twenty of them. But now, embarrassment simmered in his stomach. He wasn't a kid anymore. His mom assured him the books were not about him, but no matter how much he shared that with other people, they didn't believe him. People had been calling him 'wizard boy' since middle school, and now in his junior year of high school it had far surpassed the point of getting old.

Tired of Clive and his crap, anger heated his stomach. He knew how much stronger he'd become since weight training and karate for the past several months.

Looking over at James now standing several feet away, shame eclipsing his face, he decided he wouldn't take it anymore.

"Get out of here, Clive. All of you." Liam took a step closer to them and raised his chin. All five of them tightened the circle. They each stood a head taller than Liam, at least, and twice as broad and muscular as him. A muscle in his jaw twitched as he sized them up.

"Are you going to make us?" Clive pushed off from the squat rack he leaned against and sauntered over to Liam.

Liam swallowed and held his glare.

"I don't think so." Clive grinned and someone grabbed Liam around the neck, yanking him into a choke hold as someone else punched him in the stomach, and he doubled over.

Gasping for breath, Liam swung at his assailant and felt his punch land. Seconds later, someone grabbed his arms, then his legs, rendering him immobile and useless. His muscles burned with anger as he strained against the rugby boys.

Out of the corner of his eye, Liam saw the terror on James's face before the boy ran. A fist smashed into Liam's face. He tasted iron, then everything went black.

CHAPTER TWO

"Liam! Liam? Please wake up. Are you okay? Your parents are *not* going to be happy about this." Aubry, Liam's cousin, wrung her hands and gingerly touched his shoulder.

"That's why we're not going to tell them about it," Liam said as her green eyes came into focus.

"What are you talking about?" She shook her head.

Letting his head fall to the left, he saw the weight room machines and squat racks. The musty smell of sweaty boys and blood hung thick in the air. Looking to the right, he noticed the empty room.

Where did James go?

Liam rolled onto his side and groaned in pain. Wheezing, he touched his stomach and flinched. Pulling up his navy t-shirt, he winced at the bruises decorating his torso.

" Liam!" Aubry dropped to her knees and covered her hands with her mouth. Scanning Liam's bruises, she asked, "The same guys as before?"

Closing his eyes, Liam swallowed. "Yeah."

"Liam—" Aubry started.

"Aubry, no. I'm not going to talk to the principal. They'd just bother me even more if they found out. I think they have enough ammunition, don't you?" With an exhale, Liam pushed himself up to sitting and tried to quiet his groans for Aubry's sake. He stared into her green eyes and saw the same worry she'd had every time he'd gotten hurt as a kid. Growing up together, she'd consistently avoided what she loved to call 'precarious situations' that could get her hurt. She settled for being on the sidelines to Liam's countless 'reckless stunts' instead. How did a seven-year-old kid have such great vocabulary? Aubry and her studies.

For every fantasy adventure book Liam read, she would pick up a chemistry, physiology, or math book.

"At least you could—"

"I'm not telling my mom either." Liam set his mouth in a line. "She has enough going on right now."

Aubry opened and closed her mouth, out of arguments. She sighed. "Well at least let me help you up."

"Where's James?" Liam asked, leaning on her more than he'd like to admit.

"Who?"

"James, the boy who went to get you," Liam said.

"Oh, do you mean the scrawny—"

"His name is James," Liam said, scowling.

"Right, yes. James. He came to tell me you were in here and needed help before he ran away. You can imagine how confused I was, since there isn't much help I can give you in the weight room. But I'm glad I came," Aubry said. Her concerned face softened when she looked at him.

"He's okay then. Good," Liam said, half listening to Aubry.

"Yes, but you're not!" Aubry said, waving her hands at his bloody face.

"Help me clean up, will you?" Liam asked.

She rolled her eyes. "You're lucky I keep up my first aid certification." She looped an arm around him and led him to the weight room office.

"Yes, that's the thing I mention I'm thankful for every night before I go to sleep," Liam quipped.

Aubry gave him a side eye and sat him down on a bench while she got the first aid supplies.

"So what happened this time?" she asked from the other side of the room. "How did it start?" She paused, then looked at Liam again.

He stared at the stained grey carpet. "They were picking on James," he said in a quiet voice.

Aubry walked over and squatted in front of him, unwrapping an antiseptic wipe. "So you were standing up for him?" She pressed the cold wipe to the cut by his eyebrow.

Liam sucked in a breath but didn't flinch at the sting. He knew the drill.

Aubry worked in silence for a few minutes, wiping the blood from his face, bandaging his cuts, and handing him some ibuprofen and a glass of water.

He chugged the water and threw the pills into this mouth.

"Did you think you could face them by yourself?" She sat next to him on the bench, scrutinizing his expression.

Sighing, he said, "I don't know. I just . . . I couldn't stand by and do nothing. You should have seen James's face. They were tearing him up." He shook his head, recalling the red mask of shame James had worn.

"Liam, what did you think would happen? Five against one? You can't be a hero alone, you know."

Annoyance burned in Liam's stomach. That was the same thing Clive had said.

"I saved him, right?" He pondered the additional months of weightlifting and karate training needed to confront them without getting injured.

"Liam—" Aubry shook her head.

"Aub, can we stop talking about this now?" His tone came out sharper than he expected, and Aubry recoiled.

"Um, yeah." She cleared her throat. "I'll just clean this up," she whispered as she gathered the bloody wipes and gauze.

Regret bubbled in Liam's chest. *What a jerk. She cleans me up, and this is how I treat her?*

"Here, let me help . . . and then I'd love to treat you to ice cream on the way home." He turned and gave her a half smile, hoping she'd recognize his apology.

He saw the corner of her mouth prick up into a small smile. "Sure, that'd be nice." Tucking her wavy auburn hair behind her ears, she stood straighter as they cleaned up from the day's event.

"Liam? Is that you, honey?"

Liam dropped his keys in the bowl next to the door in the entryway. Shrugging his backpack off, he let it thunk to the floor and winced at the pain in his abdomen.

"Yeah, Mom, I'm home!" he called. The after-school beating and ice cream trip set him back, which meant his mom had probably already started making dinner without him. He hurried to the kitchen to help.

Stepping across the threshold, he saw his mom slowly moving through the kitchen, getting out ingredients for his favorite dinner, spaghetti and meatballs. Her small frame barely filled out the green housedress she wore. She'd pulled back her wispy dark hair into a low ponytail. Looking around his grandparents' Victorian-style kitchen, he admired the parts that had stayed the same these past two years. Gran and Grandad always had tea canisters on a shelf above the tea kettle. The window over the sink had the same lavender, mint, and basil plants on the sill. The same floral mugs hung on hooks above the stove.

Since his grandparents had come to California after his mom got sick, they'd instilled a love of teatime in him. Yes, he was probably the only high school guy in his friend group who liked tea, but he wasn't ashamed of it. At teatime his family came together, ate Gran's delicious baked goods, and drank amazing tea. What better way to spend an afternoon break?

Grandad whistled as he popped out of the pantry, a joyful gleam in his eyes. He slid fresh scones onto a plate and shuffled over to the breakfast nook in the corner where Gran sat with a steaming pot of tea and four teacups and saucers.

"Hi Grandad. Hi Gran. How are you two today?" Liam smiled and walked over to hug his grandparents, relishing how tightly they squeezed him back although his new bruises protested. Amidst many changes, he was grateful some things always stayed the same.

"It's good to see you Liam, dear!" Gran went to pat his cheek but stopped halfway there and gasped. "Liam! What happened?"

Dread pooled in his stomach.

Shoot.

His mom whipped around and frantically scanned him, looking for what had alarmed Gran.

She rushed to him and gently took his face in her hands, scanning the bruising on his eye and the bandage by his eyebrow.

"Liam, what happened, honey?" Worry lines carved themselves into her sallow forehead.

"Oh, that's why I'm late. I, uh, really stupid, actually. I tripped in the parking lot and hit my head on the car door, so Aubry patched me up and I took her to ice cream as a thank you," Liam said, praying and willing his mom to believe him.

Her grey eyes locked onto his and he thought he saw sadness in them before it flitted away. She cocked her head to the side. "Are you sure you're okay?" She slid her hands down his arms and held him out at arm's length.

"Yeah Mom, I'm okay. Really. I promise." Liam forced as much confidence into his voice as he could and even flashed her a hopeful smile.

She nodded. "Okay. Want to help me with this sauce, then?"

Liam looked at his grandparents. Gran raised a skeptical eyebrow as she took a sip of tea. Grandad winked and pushed the plate of scones toward Liam.

"Yes, of course." He snagged a scone before he joined his mom at the stove.

He felt his grandparents' eyes on the back of his head as he cooked. Despite not being entirely sure he had convinced them or his mom of his story, he was grateful they didn't probe further. He could see his mom moving slower and his chest pricked at the thought of her slowly declining from her energetic, adventure-loving self.

She'd gotten the cancer diagnosis two years ago, and it had been a long road. Doctors found a small brain tumor, yet his mother refused radiation therapy. She didn't want to endure the symptoms. They'd all begged her to reconsider, but she was adamant and declined quickly. Liam and his parents moved in with his grandparents so they could help take care of Nora while Liam was at school and his dad was working.

Liam welcomed the extra help and stability his grandparents provided.

"You doing okay, Mom?" Liam asked when he noticed his mom breathing heavier. He'd started stepping up to help his mom cook a year ago when he saw it got too hard for her. He recognized his grandparents' tireless help during the day and wanted to contribute. Recently, Nora would stand for about fifteen minutes before needing to take a break while Liam finished cooking dinner.

Nora braced herself with both hands on the counter.

"I think I need to sit down," she breathed.

Liam came behind to support her and led her to the table. "No problem, Mom, you can have some tea and scones with Grandad and Gran." He helped her slide into the breakfast nook and poured her some tea as Grandad passed her a scone. "You all just rest and I'll finish dinner, okay?" He smiled.

Nora's return smile didn't reach her eyes. She reached for his hand and squeezed. "You're my precious son, you know that? I'm so proud of you, Liam. Thank you." Her voice hitched, and she cleared her throat and blinked the beginning of tears away.

"Always happy to help, Mom," Liam said, squeezing her hand back before turning around to prepare his favorite meal for dinner.

CHAPTER THREE

---◆◇◆---

"You know, books were one of your mother's favorite places as a girl." Gran laced her fingers around her after-dinner cup of peppermint tea.

"Don't you mean one of her favorite things?" Liam asked, standing to clear the table.

His dad had taken his mom upstairs to rest, and Grandad was most likely in his favorite chair by the unlit fireplace, reading.

Gran chuckled. "One would think. But no, Nora would lose herself in stories, books, characters. Then she started writing her own stories, talking about them nonstop."

Liam smiled. "Were any of the stories she talked about related to her books now?"

"In some ways. I've seen parts of them scattered in her series. You know—" Gran shook her head, eyes trained on the last of the tea in her cup— "it's amazing to see all the stories she's created. Coming from a small farm in Ireland, we never imagined that writing could be a viable career option. Her imagination was beyond anything I could ever comprehend." Gran sipped her tea, thinking.

"Ah, looks like I'm just in time for tea." Joseph, Liam's father, stood on the threshold to the kitchen. His dark, sunken blue eyes and messy brown hair startled Liam. His shirt was wrinkly over his tall, muscular frame. Usually, his dad liked to keep himself put together. 'It makes for a good first impression,'

16

he'd said. Anxiety fluttered in Liam's chest. Was something wrong? Was it his mom?

"Come join us, Joseph. The water's still hot," Gran said as she ushered him to the table and served him.

"Liam." Joseph met his son's eyes. "Your—" He cleared his throat. "Your mother wants to see you." He pressed his lips together.

Everyone was still for a beat.

The quiet grew thick.

Gran sniffed, wiping a small tear from the corner of her eye. "Finish up your tea and scone first, and then you can go on up."

Liam sighed a ragged breath. His mom had been sick for two years and he was tired. Tired of hurting, tired of carrying the heaviness of his worry. It hung over him like a giant, weighted cloak. Each time he moved underneath it, something pushed him farther down into the darkness. But he couldn't let it show. He had to be strong.

He gulped his tea and shoved a scone into his mouth.

When he passed his father, Joseph reached out an arm and grabbed his shoulder. They locked eyes, and his dad nodded as encouragingly as he could. One squeeze, and his hand fell away as Liam walked toward the staircase to make his way to his dying mother.

Liam hesitated at the door, unwilling to confront what was on the other side. He wanted to remember his mom as she was before the sickness took her. Back when wonder shone in her eyes whenever she talked to Liam about stories and writing. Her imagination always expanding. Her head always in the clouds.

Back then, she spent so much time in her writing room surrounded by papers, scribbles, notes, and drawings. She'd lose herself to her creations. Her dedication mesmerized Liam. She rarely came out of her writing room, so eventually he started writing with her.

He'd bring his notebook and pencil case into her office and sit in the corner while she worked. Occasionally, she smiled at him. He felt an unexplained sadness in her eyes but ignored it. He was probably mistaking it for something else.

When she needed a break, she would stop and ask about his writing. Those were some of his favorite moments. He'd tell her about his current story project, and she would give him feedback. He relished everything he learned from his mom in the hours he spent with her in her writing room.

Facing her bedroom door, he contemplated what she'd miss. Would she even make it to his graduation next year? She wouldn't be there to talk with him about his literature classes. Or discuss poetry. They wouldn't be able to write together anymore. A sharp pain jabbed Liam's chest.

He was running out of time. How was this fair? He had to spend time with her while he could.

Sighing, Liam knocked stiffly on the door.

"Come in," called his mother's feeble voice.

Liam opened the door.

Sickness filled the room like fog despite the cracked window and moonlight streaming in.

Liam took in his mother's thinning red-brown hair and sunken face from where she lay in bed. She seemed skinnier than he remembered her even at dinner. Was that possible? The brain tumor seemed to drain her life faster each day.

"Come in and close the door, Liam," his mom said with a partial smile.

Liam crossed the room and sat down next to his mom's bed. She reached out a bony hand, palm up. Liam took it gently and tried to stifle a shudder when he could feel her bones. It felt like grabbing a bundle of sticks. His mom noticed and gave him an apologetic smile.

"Liam. You've gotten so handsome," his mom said.

Liam tried to force a smile for her sake. Avoiding her eyes, he looked at the wall of books behind her. Her books. They surrounded her like magical sentinels.

If only some of that magic could heal her.

Liam thought back to the characters he'd read about as a boy. His mind flashed to his favorite. A powerful wizard named Milo who, despite having almost failed many times, continued to come out on top and outwit the villain. He'd often wondered who inspired such a thoughtful and collected character. Everything someone would want in a powerful wizard.

"I have to tell you something before it's too late," she said, barely above a whisper. She took a few breaths.

Too late for what? Liam's chest buzzed with worry.

"Liam, I have a special gift and once I . . . Once I'm not here anymore, the gift will pass on to you. I know the timing isn't ideal, but I must tell you now." She shook her head, glassy gray eyes staring into his blue-gray ones. "I'm so sorry. I didn't think it would happen like this."

Panic rose from Liam's chest to his throat.

"Mom, what are you saying? Are you feeling okay?" Liam felt her forehead for a fever. She felt normal. She grasped his hand gently and brought it back down.

"Liam, I know what I'm saying."

Liam stared at his mom, shaking his head, throat tightening. The flame of life in her eyes flickered dimly, barely holding on. He forced himself to breathe.

"What—what are you talking about, Mom?" He shook his head, trying to make sense of her words.

"There is one more story I haven't finished yet. And I need you to finish it for me." Her intense stare scared him.

"Mom, it's your story. You need to finish it. I can't do it for you. I don't know how. I—" Liam sputtered.

"Yes. Yes, you do." She cocked her head. "Remember what we've been doing together all these years." Her eyes gleamed with nostalgia.

She had been teaching him how to write. But that was different. He'd written short stories and papers for school, even sent in the occasional entry to a magazine. But writing a book was a whole different beast. He didn't know what it took. What was his mom thinking, asking him to do this?

"It's not the same." He shook his head.

"Yes, it is, honey. You can do this. I know you can. Do this. For me. Please." She squeezed his hands.

How could he say no? She looked so small in her bed, so desperate.

"Okay," Liam nodded. "I'll do it for you, Mom."

She exhaled, and it looked like a weight lifted from her shoulders. She bit the inside of her cheek. "There is one more thing." She winced. Taking a breath, she sat up a little straighter. "I have special powers I received as a girl and you're going to inherit them soon."

Her words hung in the air for a couple of seconds. Was she joking? She'd never joked like this before. She must be really unwell. Powers? Did she realize what she'd said?

She opened and closed her mouth, then fiddled with her hands. "I know this is hard, Liam. This isn't how I wanted things to go," his mom sniffed. "I'm so sorry. I'm sorry I'm losing you and you're losing me."

Pain tore through Liam's chest so hard, he curled in on himself and fisted the sheets. He closed his eyes and let his grief and sadness wash over him. He wanted to float away and be someone else, somewhere else. Out of habit, he created a story in his head, something his mom had taught him to do when he felt overwhelmed or scared.

For a moment, he imagined himself as a boy in a magical forest with his friends, the air thick with humidity as birds rose and fell in the cerulean sky. His emotions bubbled up, over and around him, taking his breath away. Calmer now, he looked up; his mom was gone.

Instead, he stood surrounded by a forest. His mother and her sick room vanished. Sunlight warmed his skin; he heard birdsong and distant joyous cries. Leaves underfoot crunched; he wasn't dreaming. More leaves fell from above and he caught one, feeling the rough, crisp edges with his fingers. It felt so real. It all did. The sun, the leaves, the breeze through his hair.

Liam crinkled the leaf in his hand, and it disintegrated into small pieces.

This is real.

Panic gripped him, and he started to hyperventilate. He shook his head to clear the scene. He was imagining. This couldn't be real. He couldn't possibly be in a forest right now. He was in his grandparents' house in California, with his mom.

Closing his eyes, he tried to convince himself he was in his mom's room and not in some forest. He heaved big breaths in and out to slow his pounding heart. He opened his eyes, then glanced at his mother to confirm she was sitting in her bed. She looked at him in terror with her mouth agape.

"How—" she dropped her head into her hands. "It's happening already."

Dumbfounded, Liam rushed to his mother's side. She was scaring him. Did the sickness finally reach her mind? Was he getting sick too? He didn't think brain tumors were contagious, but he'd heard of them causing hallucinations. Surprisingly, it hadn't happened yet, but his mom, always defiant, had fought against the sickness in her brain.

"What are you talking about, Mom?" he asked, taking her hands in his.

"You were there . . . weren't you?" Her eyes bored into him.

Liam swallowed. "Mom, what are you talking about?"

"Liam, I just saw you disappear and appear right here!" She pointed toward the end of the bed where he sat a moment ago, lost in his thoughts.

He stared wide-eyed at her.

She saw that? What is happening? Liam's breath quickened.

"You went into the storyworld. You went to Domhania," she said, looking at him, desperate for him to understand. Liam shook his head again, trying to make sense of what had just happened.

"Mom, I think I was just imagining things, you know, like you taught me. I made up a story in my head and imagined I was there." Liam, checking her face for illness, finished, "That's it."

Then it happened again. This time, his mom faded out of existence. Her hands slipped out of his, and her bed was empty. It lasted mere seconds, and then she was back in bed, like nothing had happened.

"Mom, what the heck? What the heck is happening?" Liam's voice approached hysterical.

"It's okay, let me explain," she begged.

"This is *not* okay, and it's not normal." Liam stood up, laced his hands behind his head, and started pacing. *Just breathe. There must be a logical explanation.*

"When I was a little girl, I made a wish," Nora said, stopping Liam in his tracks. "I wished I could go into my dreams, into my stories. I wanted to be someone else, be somewhere else, and live in my imagination. I met someone in the woods at the edge of our farm in Ireland where your Uncle Callum and I grew up, who told me she could make my desires reality. She sang a song and my wish came true. When I wrote stories, I could travel to the storyworld I created on the paper and experience them," his mom explained, reaching for Liam. He moved over to her and sat on the bed. Taking his hands, she continued.

"Because you are my son, that power is now yours. Because I'm . . . fading, you'll grow stronger and have the power to go there," she told him. Her remaining color faded. She was using the last of her energy to tell him about her power. She looked over at the moonlight glowing from the open window to her right. "On the full moon, the veil between worlds thins, and you can come in and out of the storyworld. Then and only then." She looked hard at him, making sure he heard every word.

"The remaining pages of my last story are in my writing room in a leather journal with a drawing of a pendant on it. You know the one." She nodded, her eyes clear.

He knew. Ever since he could remember, his mom would sketch a picture of a sapphire pendant on any spare piece of paper around her. She repeatedly described the locket, ensuring he visualized it perfectly. He never understood the importance of committing it to memory, but he did as she'd asked.

Liam shook his head, trying to digest what his mother told him. He couldn't believe any of it. How was this possible? How did this work? His mind whirred with questions.

"We don't have much time." His mom's words strained. "You can't make the same mistakes I did."

Liam pinched up his face in confusion. "What do you mean?"

"Don't get lost. Don't get lost like I did." She reached up to hold his face in her hands. They were like ice. The lines around her eyes looked like someone had taken a pencil and drawn them deeper. Her gray eyes weren't a vibrant deep-sea color, but more like washed-out steely silver. Tightness crawled its way up Liam's throat as he noticed these changes in his mom. How could he manage this alone?

"What do I do?" Liam searched her face for an answer. She was fading away in front of his eyes. Her skin lost more of its color; her eyes hollowed out. How was this happening so fast?

"Liam, with this power, you hold a great amount of responsibility. It's up to you to protect the storyworld and look after it for me."

"What— How would I even get there?" He flailed his arms.

"On the full moon. Sit down and imagine it like you just did, then write about it. You'll get there. Be stronger than me. You have only just begun to unlock your true potential, my son. Embrace the powers within you and let them guide you on your journey." She nodded and kissed his cheek, then reached for his hand and squeezed, using the last of her strength. "Can you please get your father?" She sighed, leaning against pillows. Her face grew translucent.

"But Mom, I have so many questions," Liam started. "Does dad know?"

Regret flashed across her face. "No. He doesn't. Not really."

"How can he not know?" Liam asked. "I don't understand."

"I know. I know. I should have told you sooner, but I thought I could save you from it. I can't and now it's too late." She looked down at her hands, knotting them, then back up at Liam. "I need to say goodbye to your father. Can you please call him?"

"Goodbye?" Liam shook his head. *No, this is not happening!* "Not yet, Mom, not yet!" he pleaded with her, grasping her hands as tight as he could without breaking them.

"I'm afraid it's not up to me." She gave him a sad smile. "I've held it back as long as I could. I can't any longer. I'm sorry," she whispered, holding his gaze. In her eyes, he saw all the years they wouldn't have together. All the moments that would never happen. He couldn't bear to look at them.

"Dad! Dad, come quick!" Liam shouted through the door. Panic rushed up from his stomach into his chest. His hands shook, his heart thrumming. He tried to wrap his head around what his mom told him.

"Mom, how do I control it?"

"Writing on paper will make it flow out of you. What you feel, what you think, will help to channel it. You can create wondrous and terrifying things, Liam. Make wise choices. Be better than I have been. Don't forget—"

"Nora? Nora!" Joseph barreled through the door. He rushed over to her and threw his arms around his wife, cradling her head against his shoulder.

"Are you okay?" Tears gathered in his dad's eyes as he gently held Nora's face in his hands. His mom put her hands over his dad's and brought one of them to her lips.

"It's time, my love," she choked out.

Joseph shook his head. "How can I lose you?"

She gently kissed his lips.

Liam felt something tear through him as he watched his parents say goodbye. They held one another's gaze like they were trying to memorize every detail while they still could. Twenty-five years of marriage lived in their gaze. The ups, the downs, the laughs, the cries. Could this really be the end?

After a moment, they motioned Liam over.

All three of them shared their final family embrace. Liam held onto his parents, incredulous at what was happening. He refused to believe it. For a moment, he felt outside of himself, like he was watching a movie. Someone else's life, but not his.

He felt his mom pull away. She leaned back onto the pillows piled around her like clouds. She slowly closed her eyes, a soft smile on her face.

Holding her husband's and son's hands, she slipped away.

Liam and his dad stared at her, not believing the moment they had been living in fear of for months had finally arrived. A cold emptiness formed in Liam's chest as he stared at his mom's still body on the bed, surrounded in white. He waited for her to move and say, 'It's not over yet' like a resurrected hero in one of her stories.

She didn't move.

She looked gray.

And at peace.

From where he sat next to her, Liam's dad grabbed her hand and brought it to his forehead. He held her hand and the bed shook.

Liam realized his dad was sobbing.

He watched his father weep over his mother's body until he couldn't anymore.

He tried to catch his breath, coming in short waves.

No. No! This is not real. This is not happening. He would not believe it.

He couldn't stand to be in her sickroom anymore. The walls felt like they were closing in. Liam ran out and down the hall, heart pounding in his chest.

CHAPTER FOUR

***

Three Months Later

"Yesterday in class, we got to titrate hydrochloric acid into ammonia until we made a neutral solution!" Aubry gushed over the phone Liam held between his face and shoulder as he shimmied the keys into the lock of the bookstore. "It was absolutely thrilling!"

Liam imagined her spinning in a circle in her room, overflowing with enthusiasm. He smiled to himself.

"That's amazing, Aub! Sounds like you're right where you should be. Even though I think you're crazy for taking summer classes," Liam said. Struggling with the old door, he pulled it toward him and finally fit the key into the lock.

"Yeah . . ." Her enthusiasm deflated.

A beat of silence.

Liam sighed. "What? What do you want to say?"

"It's just. . ." She huffed. "I know your mom asked you to finish her last book and you haven't yet, Leems. Maybe you could start writing again?" Her voice hitched hopefully.

Liam shook his head and watched a family of four laugh and walk down the sidewalk of downtown, where the bookshop was located. "You know I don't do that anymore, Aub." Liam opened the flap of his messenger bag and threw the keys in.

"But you could, Liam. Don't you think it's time—"

Liam cut off her gentle voice. "No. It's not. I—" How could he explain it to her? He stopped writing as soon as his mom died because he couldn't bear to do it without her. He didn't know how to. He didn't want to feel the loss of her while he wrote, so he simply stopped. He knew he'd told his mom he would finish her last story, but he wasn't ready for it to be over yet.

He knew he didn't want to take summer courses like Aubry. She couldn't resist getting the extra credits so she could start college even more ahead than she already would. It was their last summer before senior year. He wasn't going to waste it on more school. Instead, he took a job at the local bookstore downtown to stay busy. Although he wasn't writing, but he couldn't shut himself off from books. Everything he'd learned about friendship, family, truth, and love came from books. He had to be near his teachers now that his mom was gone.

Still, he contemplated writing often. He'd get home from his shift at the bookstore and stare at his journal on his desk, imagining what it would be like. Ultimately, he couldn't bring himself to do it. He forced himself not to think about the storyworld his mom told him about before she passed. How could he go there without her? It felt wrong.

"I'm just not ready, Aub. Okay?" Liam pinched the bridge of his nose and closed his eyes as he forced his voice to come out steady.

He heard her gentle sigh. "Okay."

He dropped his hand from his nose and took a breath. Turning on his heel, he headed toward his car parked behind the store.

"Are you coming over tomorrow? I'm helping with that book signing event at the bookstore," he reminded her.

"Yes, how could I forget? You've told me about it every day for like the past month." She laughed.

Reaching his blue Honda Civic, he wrenched the door open and plopped into the driver's seat.

He smiled. "Okay, perfect! So I'll see you tomorrow morning then?"

"Yup, I'll be there. See you then, Leems." Her voice sounded defeated. Liam clenched his teeth, thinking about the number of times he'd disappointed his family the past three months.

"Bye, Aub." Tapping the call off, he let his phone slip from his grasp onto the floor of the car.

Here in his car, he could feel the grasp of helplessness and hollowness brush their fingers against him. Gripping the steering wheel, he forced himself to breathe. To not think of his mom. He felt lost without her.

After staring into the darkness for a couple of minutes, he let his forehead fall onto the steering wheel.

This sucks. I hate this. When will I stop feeling like this?

If his mom was here, she would tell him to write about it. Write a story about someone going through adversity and forge a way through it. *"It helps to give us perspective when we put a character into our situation. Seeing a way through for others is easier than for ourselves."*

After that, he'd made a habit of writing stories anytime he was struggling. Most of the time, he successfully wrote each character through their hardships.

That all stopped after his mom died. Pain pricked his chest, and he took a deep breath. Pushing up from the steering wheel, he leaned his head against the headrest and stared at the car ceiling.

Buzz buzz. His phone hummed from the floor. Letting out a breath, he reached down to grab it.

Will you be home for dinner, dearie? Gran texted.

He shot her a response, telling her he was on his way home. He jammed the keys into the ignition, roaring the car to life.

CHAPTER FIVE

---•◦•---

L iam fell backward onto his bed after dinner. Another meal with his despondent dad and hopeful grandparents.

Since his mom died, his dad had turned inward, not talking much. And even if someone tried to carry a conversation with him, his answers were short and thoughtless. He hadn't stopped to take time off work and grieve. "I don't need to," he'd said when Liam suggested he take a break. So he kept working. Kept moving. Stayed distracted while Liam tried to figure out how to process his mom's death.

He thanked God every day for his grandparents. They'd become his rock. Yes, they'd been quietly disappointed he hadn't started on his mom's last book, but they understood he needed time.

At dinner, his grandparents had asked if he started working on any writing projects lately. His dad didn't make eye contact. Just stared at his plate.

Liam shook his head. "Not yet."

They had forced smiles and nodded at him.

Lying on his bed, Liam groaned at the ceiling.

After a couple minutes, he pushed himself up to sit. What would his mom do if she lost someone? Would she keep writing? Keep doing the thing that connected them even if it threatened to pierce a hole through her heart?

He narrowed his eyes at his leather journal sitting on his desk and thought about the one in his mom's writing room, waiting for him to finish the last story.

Maybe . . . Maybe I could try to write about it like Mom taught me all those years ago?

He missed her. And maybe this would be a way to connect with her? Maybe he could finally try to at least see the notes his mom had left for him.

Blinking, he realized he already stood in front of the door to his mom's writing room. Squaring his shoulders, he took a breath, gripped the cold metal handle, and pushed it open.

It looked exactly the same. Like his mom had just walked out to load up a tea tray before she would be back to continue writing. The left side of the room showcased a beautiful wood-carved fireplace surrounded by emerald tiling. A small blue velvet loveseat bordered with dark wood sat across from a burgundy wingback chair in front of the fireplace. A wooden side table held a stack of classics in his mom's favorite leather-bound form.

The opposite wall boasted nothing but books. Floor to ceiling. Liam remembered the summer his mom asked his dad to install the bookshelves on the wall.

"You're sure you want the entire wall to be bookshelves? From top to bottom?" his dad asked, eying the wall, then his wife.

"Absolutely." She'd beamed.

That weekend, Liam had helped his dad haul plywood back and forth, stain it, seal it, then install it to make the bookshelf of his mom's dreams.

She'd lined up her twenty-book series in the middle, followed by the fifteen other books she'd written as standalone novels or trilogies. As Liam walked over to her best-selling series, the wood floor groaned. He ran his fingers across the books that had made up his childhood. He had reread them again and again, memorizing the adventures the characters went on, wishing he could join them.

Sighing, he looked over at his mom's giant writing desk. Maybe there was one more adventure of his mom's he could help put out into the world. He walked over and sank down into the chair behind the desk and it let out a creak. Liam winced. He imagined the chair scolding him for staying away for so long.

For a moment, he just sat, looking over his mom's giant wooden desk with papers strewn about in messy piles. Pens lay scattered atop papers, and several colored journals were stacked in one corner. His mom liked to handwrite her story ideas and process them on paper before she typed them on her computer. She said it kept her closer to the real world.

How ironic for someone creating make-believe worlds.

After a few minutes of shuffling through her piles, he found his mom's story journal underneath a couple of notebooks.

Its worn leather edges and spine made Liam wonder how many times she'd flipped through this journal. How many places had she taken it with her?

Clipped to the front was none other than the sketch of the pendant he'd memorized as a kid. Focusing on her pencil strokes, he saw the long chain snake down to the oval-shaped pendant with a sapphire set into the middle of it. Silver vines and leaves crested the sapphire, accentuating its oval shape. The back side of the pendant had a symbol of a rose on the left and a snake on the right, with what looked like an engraved string connecting them.

He let out a breath and puckered his lips in thought. Shaking the nervousness out of his hands, he brought them to the cover of the leather journal and opened it to the last page with words on it.

Immediately, he recognized the characters his mom had written about from her twenty-book series, *The Casting of Ancient Magic Series*. The one he knew like the back of his hand. Desperate to read her words, he devoured them on the page.

Conroy stood at a cross section that would change his life forever.

Remember what his father taught him or continue down a path of destruction and power from which he could not return? After revolting against his calling as the Chosen One, he had forged his own path of darkness. The very lives he was charged to steward, he took. Blinded by power, he ravaged villages throughout the land, looking for more power, more lives to take. With each life he stole, he became more ravenous. It was never enough.

Yikes. This is how the last book is going? Liam wasn't sure what he'd expected, but it wasn't this. Yes, his mom's books had taken a darker turn about halfway through when the main character, Conroy, who was supposed to have been the one to defeat the dark ancient wizard, Zadimus, joined forces with him instead. Everyone who read the series was shocked. He figured his mom was looking for a good plot twist.

She talked about hope so often, he was sure Conroy would get a redemption arc in the books. But it didn't look like it was going that way. This was what she'd left for him? How was he supposed to fix this? He wasn't a best-selling novelist. He hadn't written thirty-five books. What was she thinking, asking him to do this?

With a groan, he slumped back into the chair and stared into the empty fireplace, the moonlight streaming in the window giving it a blue glow.

Maybe . . . he had to write something new? Something different?

Pitching forward in the chair, he looked at the empty page next to his mom's words. The creamy whiteness of the paper stared back at him.

"A clean page is full of possibilities. It's the beginning of an adventure. What kind of adventure do you want to go on? Think about that, then write it. Write about your adventure," Liam's mom mused to him one rainy day as he sat in a beanbag in her writing room with a notebook on his knees.

"Okay, Mom. Let's go on an adventure." Running his hand over the blank paper, he touched a pen to it.

He recalled the place he had imagined at his mother's bedside. Maybe writing about the forest and a new adventure would inspire an ending to his mom's story. He was a few months late, but it was better late than never.

He imagined himself immersed in a luscious wood, the crisp air, the birdsong echoing through the trees. Warmth traveled from the paper to his hand and up his arm. Liam raised an eyebrow at his hand.

He took it as a sign he was on the right track. Scratching the pen onto the thick journal paper, he wrote about an enchanted forest with wizards, fairies, and magical creatures. He thought about his mom's books and what he loved about them. He practiced writing about that world so he could write an ending for his mom.

The more he wrote, the warmer his arm felt. Encouraged, he wrote more fervently. Then he saw a golden light emanating from the page. Gasping, he looked around as the golden light grew and traveled to the rest of his body.

"What is happening?" he yelled. He tried to shake it off like it was a swarm of flies, but the light grew brighter until he couldn't see anything. He covered his face. The warmth grew to a burning ache.

And then it was over.

Taking a breath, he tried to slow his heartbeat and smelled pine trees. Voices called to one another. The sound of a rushing waterfall filled his ears.

He whipped his head around and saw tall trees surrounding him.

What the heck? Am I losing it?

He tilted his head toward a bird singing in the distance. A breeze ruffled his hair. Fairies fluttered past his head. His eyes followed their trail of glittering dust floating through the air. They flurried around and then away into the thick forest.

His mouth dropped open. *Is this the place Mom mentioned? It can't be. She was delusional at the end of her life.* His heart slammed in his chest as he racked his brain for an explanation.

He had to make sure this was real. He bent down and crinkled a handful of leaves from the forest floor. They broke apart the way any normal leaf would. Looking up, he found the sun. It was still round and bright like back home, too.

"Hey! Keep moving! Keep up!" A dark-haired boy around his age pushed past him. Not just one boy, Liam realized, but a group of kids his age and younger. He stayed rooted to his spot as the group hooted, hollered, and ran around him. They wore linen shirts, dark pants, and boots. Some of them wore belts holding weapons. Maybe he was dreaming? A type of Renaissance Fair dream? Or maybe it was some variation of a fantasy dream? Liam raised his eyebrows as he scanned the crowd in amusement.

He *must* have fallen asleep.

The ground shook with a far-off rumble. The group sprinted away as Liam noticed a plume of smoke rising into the air from the direction of the tremor. Dream or not, he did not want to stick around and find out where it was coming from.

He followed the dark-haired boy at a distance for a couple of minutes, running away from the horrible rumble as much as he was running to find out where the group was going.

Liam's lungs burned, and an ache bloomed in his side.

Finally, he reached a circle of kids near a cliff, all huddled together. He huffed in relief. Spying some tall trees and overgrowth, he moved to hide in them and stay out of view.

Six boys stood in a cluster and a seventh one approached them from the edge of a cliff to Liam's left. The sky spread out behind the boy in a vibrant cerulean blue with puffy white clouds drifting through it. From his vantage point, he could see a valley of green trees and more cliffs in the distance.

"Alright boys, that was a close one!" the dark-haired teen who bumped into Liam announced. He stood tall and confident, addressing the rest of the group. He wore a sword at his belt and had a strong build. Almost as big as the rugby boys. "Who was the one who bombed the Woodland Boys with rotten mangos?" he asked with a playful smile, seeming to be the leader.

"That was me, sir," a boy in the circle said as he thrust his hand proudly into the air. *Did the boy just call his friend 'sir'?*

"Hilarious, Ben. Remember that for next time. Although, maybe not since that stunt seemed to upset them even more. Barely got out that time," the leader said, rubbing his neck.

"Yeah Ben, what were you thinking?" said someone, shoving Ben.

"Hey! Who's that straggler back there?" the tall, dark-haired and dark-skinned leader jabbed his chin at Liam.

Dread pooled in his stomach. Enthralled by the boys, he hadn't realized he'd poked his head out to get a better look. He was clearly in their line of sight. His mouth went dry.

"Who are you?" the leader's narrowed eyes bore into Liam's.

Should he tell them? He certainly couldn't stay silent. That would be suspicious. Who knows what they might do to him? He had to say something. Why wasn't his mouth working?

Swallowing, he croaked, "I'm Liam."

"Liam, eh?" The leader narrowed his eyes at him, resting a hand on the hilt of his sword. "And what are you doing here following the Stream Kids around?" He walked toward Liam, cutting through the middle of the clump of boys.

All eyes were on Liam.

"Uh . . . I'm sorry, the what?" Liam asked.

"Don't you know who we are?" The leader raised an eyebrow.

"Actually, no." Liam raised his hands in surrender and willed him not to pull his sword out.

"You expect me to believe that?" Laughed the leader, still moving toward Liam, who held his ground. He was about twenty feet away now.

"Why would I lie to you?" Liam tried to hold his gaze and hide the nervousness rising from his stomach.

"You dirty spy!" Liam heard from behind him. With a blow to the head, he flew face first onto the leaf-covered ground.

CHAPTER SIX

———◆———

"What are you doing, Sly, sir?"

"I'm making sure he's still alive. Why'd you hit him so hard, Sunny?"

"I was just trying to test him."

"Well, you went and knocked out our mystery guest. How are we supposed to ask him questions now?"

"At least we know he isn't a wipen or a spy."

"Or feeling very welcome here," murmured Liam.

"Ah!" The two boys standing over him jumped backward.

Liam blinked and felt a colossal headache coming on. He groaned, touching his forehead. He could barely make out two blurry boys standing to his right. Beneath him, he felt something soft like a bed. Apparently, he was lying down. Slowly, he sat up. He seemed to be in a small room with dirt walls and floors. Dried brown roots hung from the ceiling.

Are we underground? How is that possible?

His vision came into focus and he immediately recognized the taller of the boys as the one in charge, the one they called Sly. He stood straight and confident, his complexion the color of an almond. His eyes were a knowing russet color that commanded respect. The boy next to him, Sunny apparently, was a head shorter, with hair so blond it was almost white, like he had taken a dip in the sun's rays.

They were both wearing brown tunics, leather pants, calf-high boots, and leather vests. Sly had knives on his vest and looked ready for a fight. Liam remembered the sword, panicked, and frantically checked if it was in his possession, but it seemed to be missing.

Well, that's a good sign, at least.

The walls composed of packed earth, and with his sight only partially returned, he could make out what looked like a brown square sitting in the corner. He figured it was a wardrobe or something of the sort. Next to Liam, a carved wooden side table held some things that were still too fuzzy to identify. His vision was taking its sweet time coming into focus.

"Where are we? And who are you two?" Liam asked, looking from tall boy to short boy.

"We're in the Stream Kids' secret hideout. And this is Sly, our leader. I'm Sunny," enthused the shorter, younger looking boy, his bright hair flopping in excitement.

Sly shot Sunny a piercing look. "Well, just tell him everything, why don't you?"

"I'm sorry Sly, sir. I was trying to welcome our guest." Sunny motioned to Liam. Sly narrowed his eyes in response.

"I'm sorry about hitting you earlier," Sunny apologized, dipping his head.

Squinting at the two boys, Liam recalled he'd just been in his mom's writing room, and now he was underground in an unfamiliar place with two boys above him. One of which had knives strapped to his leather vest. And the other had just admitted to striking him on the head.

Is this real? Or am I dreaming? Maybe I hit my head in Mom's writing room and this is all my imagination?

Slowly, Liam reached out to touch Sunny, who was closest to him. His fingers bumped the younger boy's elbow and stuck. He didn't vanish. Sunny stared back at Liam, an eyebrow raised, a look that said he was contemplating Liam's sanity painted on his face.

"Uh, you okay there, buddy?" Sunny pursed his lips and took a step back.

Sly raised his eyebrows at Liam.

Liam looked back and forth between them. "So, this isn't a dream?"

Sly swiveled his head toward Sunny. "How hard did you hit him?"

Sunny shrugged.

Sly sighed and put his head in his hand, taking a breath for patience. "No, you are quite awake."

Liam gripped the sheets he was sitting on. They felt real, too. "How is this possible?" he whispered. Squeezing his eyes shut, he thought back to what his mom had told him the night she died. That night wasn't something he liked to think about often. Forcing himself to remember, he recalled her words from the back of his memory. She'd asked him to finish the last pages of her story, which was what he was trying to do a few minutes ago. He remembered her talking about special powers that would bring him to the storyworld when he imagined the world she'd created in her books, but that couldn't have been real. That was the sickness talking.

Fisting the sheets and peeling his eyes open to stare at Sly and Sunny, he thought that maybe *this* was what his mom was talking about. Was this the world she created?

"What's wrong with him, sir?" Sunny eyed Liam, who had been silent for a handful of seconds and slid closer to Sly. "Maybe he's a spy for Conroy?"

"What did you just say?" Liam whipped his head toward Sunny.

The blond-haired boy swallowed and took a step back, wide-eyed.

"Did you just say the name Conroy?" Liam swung his legs over the bed. "Where exactly are we? What is this place called?"

"We already told you, the Stream Kids'—" Sunny started.

"Not that, the name of this land. The kingdom or whatever."

"Um, Domhania?" Sunny offered.

"No way . . ." Liam breathed. He was in the storyworld. Domhania. That's what his mom said it was called.

"You're not from around here, are you?" Sly looked Liam over, noticing his running shoes, jeans, and t-shirt in contrast to their boots, linen shirts with light leather armor on top of dark, thick pants, and weapon belts.

"No." Liam swallowed. He realized there was no point in lying or making something up. Not that he was good at that on the fly anyway. He always ended up stumbling over his words and looking even more suspicious.

Smack!

"Ouch!" Liam yelled and brought a hand up to protect himself from Sunny, who had hit him *again*.

"Hmm . . ." Sunny rubbed his chin. "Well, definitely not a wipen then. A blow to the side of your head would have reverted you to your original form. Which looks something like a winged centaur," Sunny explained.

"What the—" Liam rubbed the back of his head, finding a slight bump growing already. Why hadn't his mom mentioned all the hitting and smacking to him earlier? He didn't remember that in any of her books.

"That's enough talk for now, Sunny. Go tell the others that our guest is alright," demanded Sly with a nod.

"Yes, sir." Sunny retreated through the doorway.

Sly looked directly at Liam, sizing him up. Slowly he started, "I'm Sly. Leader of the Stream Kids. It's my pleasure to make your acquaintance." He held his hand out to shake Liam's. Liam cautiously reached out to take his hand, fearing another "test" that could result in another bump on his head.

"I'm Liam Adams. Pleased to meet you," he said, almost without thinking. Hit on the head or not, he was his Gran's grandson, and she taught him to have manners in every situation. They finished their handshake and Liam looked around at the small room. But on closer examination, "room" wasn't really a proper description. It reminded Liam of a hobbit hole the way the walls were made from earth and dangling roots.

In this "room," there were no windows, but two beds, one of which he was on. His bed was pushed up against the wall on the left side, and he could now see a teapot and cup on a small bedside table set to his right. Upon seeing it, he realized how cold and hungry he was.

How many hours had he been gone, exactly? How did time work here compared to back home? Was he even in the world his mom created? He wasn't sure he believed he was yet.

His heart pounded quicker in his chest. "I don't recognize this place." Liam looked around the room again. Outside, running through the forest, he recognized hints of his mom's descriptions from her books, but he didn't recall reading about this place.

"What do you mean?" Sly asked, his eyebrows coming together in confusion.

"I'm from Central California. The Central Coast, to be exact. One second, I was there, and the next, I'm here in the middle of you all running away from something." Liam shook his head, trying to clear it, but pain shot through him. He groaned again, touching his head. *Dang, I need to watch out for that Sunny kid.*

"Oh, here!" Sly thrust him the cup of tea on the bedside table. "This will make you feel right as rain."

Liam took the warm cup and drank it. The earthy taste was much different than the Earl Grey he was used to back home. The warmth of the smooth china thawed his icy fingers. Just as Sly had said, the tea worked instantly. As soon as the warm liquid slid down his throat, Liam felt the pain dissipating from his head. After gulping it and setting down the cup, the fog in his mind cleared.

"What was that?" Liam asked, rubbing the back of his head to check for pain. He felt normal; the bump he had before was gone.

"That's our special concoction Roya makes when one of us gets hurt," Sly said. "She's our resident potions master."

"Potions?" Liam asked.

Sly stared, waiting for Liam to continue. He blinked a few times and raised his eyebrows.

"You know, potions. It's the study of magical substances and how one can combine them to help or hurt others."

"Huh," Liam said.

"Where did you say you were from again?" Sly asked, tilting his head.

Nervousness rose in Liam's chest. Maybe he shouldn't have told Sly where he was from but thought of a cover story. Would that have protected him?

"Listen mate, we're here to help you. Now that we know you aren't here to hurt us, you can trust us," Sly reassured him.

Liam's mind raced, and without fully hearing Sly, an idea sparked. "Do you have a piece of paper? I really need to, um, write something down."

Sly stared at him for a beat, arms crossed, eyebrow raised. "Sure." Walking over to the desk in the corner, he pulled out parchment paper and a fountain pen. "You sure you're okay, mate? Maybe Sunny hit you harder than I realized."

"Yeah, I'm fine. I just really need to do something." Liam hurriedly grabbed the paper and pen. Taking a breath, he held his shaky hand over the parchment, gripped the pen, and wrote.

He imagined his mom's writing room with her softened chair from hours of her sitting in it. The wall of books he and his dad built for her, polished and clean of dust. In his mind, he saw the wingback chair he'd sit in so he could be close to his mom as they both wrote. Warmth bloomed in his palm and traveled up his forearm to his chest. Hope rushed through Liam as he felt the reassuring warmth, confident he would get out of this crazy experiment.

"What in the—"

He heard Sly's voice but pushed it from his mind. Focusing, he tried to hold onto the real world, his home, so he could go back. He needed to get out of here and sort things out.

Bright light exploded in front of him, giving way to his mom's writing room where Aubry stood, staring at him with a look of terror on her face.

"Aubry?"

"Liam?" she yelled, grabbing for him.

"Help me, Aubry!" Liam lunged for her and they grabbed one another's forearms. "Pull!"

Aubry tugged Liam toward her, trying to wrestle him into his mom's writing room.

"Liam, what's happening?" she screamed.

"Just get me out!"

He felt resistance. Aubry's tugs weren't budging him. He pulled harder and harder, desperate to get home. To get someplace where things made sense.

One more giant pull and Aubry tumbled toward him, knocking him to the earthen floor. The light dissolved as Liam and Aubry fell on the Domhanian ground at Sly's feet.

CHAPTER SEVEN

―◆◇◆―

"**I** — Just— What—?" Aubry sputtered. She shook her head, auburn waves moving around her pale freckled face. She opened and closed her eyes a few times.

"No." Liam sat up and leaned his head into his hands.

"This isn't possible. It's just—not possible. How did this happen?" Aubry's shrill voice filled the room. "Liam, Liam. Explain to me right now in a logical manner what just happened. This—this is not possible. Please tell me there is a logical explanation." She sat upright on the floor, squared her shoulders, and readied herself to hear his reasoning.

"Aubry." Liam shook his head. "You won't believe me."

"Liam, I need you to try to explain this to me," she pleaded. With conscious effort, she ignored everything else around her and just looked at Liam, desperate for his answers.

He let out a long breath. Staring at the ceiling, he started, "I think this place is the storyworld my mom created." He let that sink in first. Staring into her green eyes, he saw her disbelief. Despite it, he kept going. "When she died, she asked me to finish writing the last pages of her story." The words caught in his throat and he ignored the weight he felt on his chest. He recounted the way his writing transported him into this world. "And as soon as I got here, I thought I could get back, and that's how you just saw me. I tried to write myself back home, but

I pulled you in instead." Dread and guilt pooled in his stomach. As Liam spoke, Aubry's face drooped with each sentence.

"I don't know why it didn't work," Liam growled and threw his head back.

"On the full moon, the veil between worlds thins, and that's when you can come in and out of the story world. Then and only then," His mom's voice rang out in his mind.

Grabbing Aubry's shoulders, he stared at her and said, "That's why! The full moon. It must be over. That's why I couldn't get back."

She looked at him like he'd lost his marbles.

Dropping her shoulders, he started counting. "The full moon happens once a month. So we just had one and now we're here, which means . . ." Letting out a breath, he slumped down and covered his mouth in disbelief.

"Liam?" She flattened her lips into a thin line. "Do you mean to tell me we're stuck here for twenty-nine days? Until the next full moon, if I'm to believe that fantasy garbage you just spouted?"

"I'm so sorry, Aub." Liam's dejected expression set something off in her.

"No. No. I simply can't believe it. This cannot be happening. This isn't real. This isn't logical. How do you expect me to believe this?"

Liam shrugged, devoid of words.

"Excuse me, miss." Sly cleared his throat. "I'm sorry to interrupt, but I'd like to come forward and offer that our home is very far from garbage."

Swiveling her head toward Sly, Aubry took in his tightly crossed arms, calf-high boots, leather pants, leather vest atop a cream linen shirt, his built frame, and challenging dark-eyed gaze. She just stared.

Liam skittered his eyes back and forth between them. Neither of them moved.

"Liam?" Aubry whispered out of the side of her mouth.

"It's okay, Aub, he's a friend of mine." That apparently didn't make her feel any better because her eyes got bigger the longer she looked at Sly. Oblivious to her hesitancy, Sly moved toward her until he was standing an arm's length away.

After being under Aubry's stare for a few seconds, a muscle twitched in Sly's jaw and he shifted on his feet. Was he uncomfortable? Liam tilted his head and found himself amused. Liam's minimal interaction with Sly suggested he wasn't a leader easily intimidated.

"Please excuse my lack of manners for not helping you off the floor sooner, miss." Sly smiled apologetically at Aubry, who looked back at him, eyes still wide and slowly slid her hand into his outstretched one. Gracefully, she stood up with Sly's help. For a moment, they locked eyes, still holding hands.

"The name's Sly," he said. "I'm the leader of the Stream Kids. Pleased to make your acquaintance." He smiled proudly and bowed.

Well, that was much warmer of a welcome than I got. Liam narrowed his eyes, thinking about Sunny's blows.

"And I'm Aubry, captain of the Chemistry Club on campus." She squared her shoulders proudly.

Liam rolled his eyes. Leave it to her to think of chemistry at a time like this. "Aubry's my cousin."

"Captain you, say? Well, that's impressive" A warm smile spread across Sly's face. "You'll have to tell me about your expeditions sometime."

Aubry tucked a piece of hair behind her ear and stared at her shoes.

Since when is Aubry shy about her accomplishments?

It was Liam's turn to clear his throat. "Are we going to get back to the matter at hand, or have a staring contest?"

They dropped one another's hands instantly and blushed as they turned to Liam. Aubry busied herself with dusting off her jeans and blue blouse.

Sly swallowed and moved his gaze to Liam. "Right, did I hear you say something about your mom creating this world, mate? And can you please tell me what in the world just happened?" He stuck out a hand and helped Liam off the floor.

"So," Liam motioned with his hands. "I'm pretty sure we're stuck here for a month—"

"Twenty-eight days," Aubry interrupted.

"What?" Liam flicked his eyes to her, annoyed.

"Lunar cycle is twenty-eight days, not quite a whole month. I want to make sure we're not stuck here for two months based on your bad astronomy."

Liam sighed and glared at his cousin. "It looks like we're stuck here for twenty-eight days until the next full moon. I think this place is the story world my mom created in her Middle Grade book series, the one she asked me to finish. She told me she had powers, but I didn't think it was true. And now . . . well, here we are," Liam rambled and raised his hands to the surrounding room.

"What do you mean, this is a storyworld? And *middle grey*? What is that?" Sly asked.

"Uhh . . ." Liam rubbed the back of his neck as he scrambled to think of something to say. How was he supposed to explain their whole life existed because of the imaginative whims of a little girl? That none of it really mattered? Could he really break someone's whole understanding like that?

"He means where you live is another dimension which was created by some-one different from who created our world. We're from a different world, and we need to get back home," Aubry explained.

Liam stared at her, openmouthed. *Not bad, Aubry.*

"Your mum is the one who created this world?" Sly turned, rubbing his chin, returning to their conversation. His brow furrowed as he tried to piece things together. Liam understood the feeling.

Sly stared at the wall for a few seconds, deep in thought. Waiting for him to freak out, Liam stayed silent. To Liam's surprise, Sly just nodded and returned his gaze to Liam, waiting for him to continue.

"Um, well," Liam huffed, not knowing what to believe. He knew his mom wanted him to continue her story, and when she was dying told him about some powers, but she couldn't have been serious. And yet, here he was. "We ended up here by mistake. We just need to get back home. Do you know anyone who could help?" Liam asked.

Thinking again for a second, Sly nodded. "Milo, the wizard who lives in the mountains, should be able to help. Wizards can create things, manipulate the elements, and the like. It sounds like maybe that's what your mum could do if she created a world."

Milo. Liam knew the character from his mom's books. Milo was one of his favorites. A wise wizard who always knew what to do. Knew the right things to say at the right times. There were so many moments Liam wished he could talk to Milo or enlist his help when he was being pursued by Clive and his friends. He was sure Milo would have had a solution. A way to stand up to them without getting beaten to a pulp.

"Wait, you're saying you think my mom was a wizard?" Liam scoffed. Liam reflected on the books his mother had written. She loved writing about wizards, magic, and fairies. He thought about Milo and the other wizards she'd written about, like Conroy, and Conroy's evil master, Zadimus. But there was no way *she* could be a wizard. If she created this world, did that make her a wizard? How did that make sense? It didn't. None of this did. "But how would that work if she's not from . . . here?" Liam made vague gesture to his surroundings. "My mom said she wished for this ability as a little girl and now she passed it on to me. I inherited it from her."

Sly raised his eyebrows. "Inheriting powers sounds like magic to me. There are other options, I suppose. I've heard there are special people who can travel from world to world. Realm Jumpers, we call them. But only certain people have that gift."

"Wait, this is normal? You've heard of this situation before?" Liam gestured again at nothing in particular.

"None of this seems like a likely possibility." Aubry massaged her temples. "I'm still not totally convinced I'm not dreaming or drugged or something."

Clive's face came to mind as he and the rugby boys spitefully called him 'wizard boy.' Anger simmered in his stomach. He'd had no powers to help him when he needed it. He wouldn't allow it to be true. Wouldn't allow Clive's taunts to be real. This whole thing was just a big mess, and he wanted out. Needed to get him and Aubry out.

Liam's head was spinning. "Where does Milo live? If he can get us out of here, we need to see him."

Sly's dark eyebrows slid up his forehead. "It's not somewhere you can go to alone. It's several days' journey there and I couldn't just send you out there on your own."

Aubry crossed her arms defiantly. "We're more capable than you know." She raised her chin at Sly.

"I'm sure you are." The corner of Sly's mouth curved into a gentle smile.

Aubry's expression softened, and her cheeks reddened.

"Where exactly are we again?" Liam took in the room again, waving his arms around, realizing he had never asked. He'd been so focused on getting out of here, he didn't think to figure out where he was besides in the storyworld.

Sly smiled, amused. He took a breath and looked lovingly at the room, eyes alight with fondness. "You are currently in the Stream Kids' hideout, which is inside a tree. Domhania itself is magical and sometimes it gives you what you need when you need it. And no, none of us are wizards," Sly said just before Liam asked. "After Conroy destroyed our village, and killed all our parents, we needed shelter, refuge. We gathered together and wandered the forest looking for somewhere to go." Sadness eclipsed Sly's expression as his dark brows came together and he stared off. Liam could see the heaviness of the memory in his eyes.

Processing what he said, Liam's stomach dropped. "Did you just say Conroy?"

He had only just entered this world and felt like someone had thrown him onto a treadmill, running at full speed. Thinking back to the books his mom wrote, he couldn't recall Conroy destroying villages, or killing kids' parents. In the portion of his mom's notebook he'd read before he ended up here, it said Conroy had gone down a dark path of destruction. But killing parents and creating orphans? That was a whole other level of evil and darkness.

With a sigh, Sly brought his attention away from the wall and back to Liam and Aubry, calm and collected again.

"Yes." Sly's jaw ticked.

Liam brought his hands to his forehead. Did his mom have something to do with this? If she created this world, how could she have let this happen? Did she not have control over the characters here? Her last words in the leather journal seemed soaked with sadness. Maybe she didn't have as much control as Liam thought.

A conversation he hadn't thought about in a while came to mind. *"Sometimes, Liam, there isn't a lot we can do to change people's decisions. We can nudge and encourage, but ultimately, people have the freedom to make their own choices, no matter how hurtful they may be."*

"But you're the writer. Can't you change things? Make things better?" Liam *asked when he noticed Conroy, who was supposed to be the hero in his mom's stories, spiraling down a dark path.*

"I do my best, honey." She gave him a sad smile and brushed his cheek. *"But I can't force anyone to do anything. That's not love."*

Confused by what she meant, he had stayed quiet and went back to his own writing.

"Do you know Conroy?" Sly's hands hung at his sides in fists, but his voice was even.

Aubry looked back and forth between them anxiously.

Liam shook his head. "Not in the way you think. My mom wrote about him in her books. I've read about him before. I just—I didn't know he did all this. He was supposed to—"

"Be the one who brought peace to the land? But he joined Zadimus, a dark wizard, and now feeds on the life forces of adults in surrounding villages."

The look of horror on Aubry's face tightened the knot in Liam's stomach and he winced.

"So every kid here . . . their parents are dead?" Aubry's thin voice whispered.

Sly's jaw ticked again. "Yes."

Aubry took a steadying breath. "And Conroy '*took their life forces*'?"

Sly nodded.

"I'm so sorry," Liam said, grief pooling in his chest as he thought back to the moment he lost his mom. A village of kids without parents, experiencing the same grief he did. But their lives were taken by force by Conroy, not sickness. Liam had to watch his mom fade day by day. Watched her walk feebly toward the end of her life. The Stream Kids didn't have any notice. Their lives changed in the blink of an eye. He wasn't sure what was worse. He pulled back from thinking about it as it made him frustrated and sad all over again.

"And how did this tree become your hideout?" Aubry gently asked, trying to put all the pieces together.

"As we were fleeing the night we lost our parents, I was silently asking for a safe place for all of us. A place we could go where Conroy wouldn't find us. As soon as the thought passed through my head, a door appeared out of a tree trunk. We went inside and found this hideout." Sly half smiled. "It had everything we needed. And if it didn't, it would create a room when the need arose. So that's where you are. The Stream Kids' hideout." Leaning back against the packed earth wall, Sly watched them expectantly.

"How many of you live here?" Aubry hung her head to the side.

"About thirty of us. Ranging from ten to eighteen years old."

"Wow," Liam breathed, caught between wonder at the magic of this world and horror at the atrocities these kids faced because of Conroy. Trees that turned into hideouts to protect you from a murderous wizard—he didn't remember that from any of his mom's books, either. He guessed there were some things in Domhania she must have kept to herself. Each additional part he uncovered felt like another piece of his mom he was unwrapping.

Sly shifted on his feet, staring off, then quickly moved his attention back to Liam and Aubry. "Okay, well . . . now you know where you are and why we live here. I'm sure you're still eager to get back home. But since you're here, why not meet the rest of us, and we'll plan from there?" Sly nodded, and walked out of the room, not looking back to see if Liam and Aubry followed.

CHAPTER EIGHT

L iam and Aubry stayed rooted to their spots, taking a moment to breathe. Liam's head was spinning as he thought of the possibilities. Why did his mom leave him with this? An entire world with people she hadn't told him about. She said it was his responsibility now.

He wasn't prepared for this. Which was why he needed to get Aubry and himself out of here as soon as possible. He promised his mom he'd finish her story, but he didn't have to be *in* the world to do that. What the Stream Kids went through was awful. Maybe if Liam could get back, he could write something that would help them. What, he didn't know.

"Are we just going to follow him?" Aubry asked, pacing.

"What other option do we have?" Liam threw up his hands. "I tried to go back already, and the portal closed on us. The only hope of something changing would be from the wizard."

"How are you okay with all of this?" Aubry pinched her nose as she moved back and forth across the floor.

"I'm not. I'm just as frustrated and horrified as you, but I don't know what else to do," Liam admitted. He hated feeling helpless. He got enough of it at school. "I am sorry, Aub. I didn't mean to drag you into this."

She huffed. "I know it's not your fault, Liam. This whole thing—" she imitated Liam's gesturing from earlier.

Liam narrowed his eyes at her.

Aubry ignored him and kept going. "It's way over my head and I can't believe your mom kept something like this from everyone her entire life. And then just dropped it in your lap when she—" Aubry stopped short and moved to stand in front of Liam. "I'm sorry too. I'm sorry this is all now on your shoulders. It just makes little sense why she would do it this way. It's not logical." Her gaze passed over him as she tried to understand the tangled web of his mom's decisions.

"Not everything is logical, Aub."

"Well, it should be. It makes things much easier."

Liam chuckled.

"Well, shall we get on with this so we can figure out a way to get back home?"

"Yeah, let's figure out where Sly went," Liam said.

Just then, Sly popped his head back through the doorway, brown eyes surveying them. "Are you two going to stay in here? I promise you, the rest of the hideout is much nicer." He winked.

They followed the Stream Kids' leader down the hallway and around a couple of turns to an open room the size of Liam's school cafeteria. Stopping to take it all in, they saw about thirty people, as Sly had said, packed into the main room of the hideout milling about. Some of them were eating at the long tables in the middle of the room, and others toward the front were talking and playing cards. Sly sauntered to the front of the room where a group of two boys and a girl stood.

Liam noticed the girl's beautifully coiled coffee brown hair and how nicely it brushed against her shoulders. She had the same piercing eyes and dark complexion as Sly. She animatedly talked to the two other boys standing with her, captivating them with what she was saying.

Walking up behind her, Sly placed a hand on her shoulder, then brought her into a hug that she allowed with an unamused expression. Liam saw the group of them talking, then saw their heads swivel toward him and Aubry, looking them up and down. Liam swallowed and attempted to hide his nerves, although he suspected his face betrayed him. Aubry had always told him he was an open book. Sly motioned them over and Liam immediately stepped forward and collided with someone walking by. A series of apologies flew from his mouth as heat rose to his cheeks. The other person kept walking as if nothing had happened.

"Liam, Aubry! Come meet my little sister." Sly waved them over.

"This the guy Sunny knocked out?" the taller of the two boys asked, looking sideways at Liam. Black hair stuck out every which way on top of his head. The linen shirt he was wearing stretched tightly over his broad shoulders. A look of disdain smeared his face.

"Yes, Johnny, this is our guest, Liam, and his cousin Aubry. You will do well to not take Sunny's example of knocking around new people out of the blue," Sly warned.

"Well, it's a pleasure to meet you." The shorter and younger looking boy stuck out his hand and smiled. "The name's Fox."

Liam gingerly took his hand and was met with a firm but friendly handshake. Fox's dark almond-shaped eyes stared back at Liam with wonder. Liam felt oddly calm looking into them. He had the same unruly black hair the taller boy, Johnny, had.

"You'll have to excuse my brother," Fox said. "He doesn't do well with other people." Johnny narrowed his eyes. Fox ignored him.

"Johnny and Fox are brothers." Sly motioned to the boys and explained that despite them looking alike and being two years apart, sixteen and fourteen, their height was the easiest distinguishing factor.

"And this is my sister, Juniper." Sly inclined his head toward his sister, who stood a head shorter than him.

Juniper stepped forward and energetically stuck her hand out. Liam grasped it and she shook it while she spoke. "Nice to meet you, Liam. I hear you dropped in from another realm?" Liam looked into her eyes and saw an almost electric gleam. The dirt under her fingernails, dagger strapped to her belt, and mud on her shoes gave Liam the impression she was unafraid and ready for adventure.

"Yeah, we came here by accident and unfortunately can't get back, but Sly thinks Milo can help us." Liam smiled politely.

Juniper glanced at Sly, then raised an eyebrow toward Liam, her eyes gleaming. Before he could say anything in response, she released his hand and shook Aubry's with just as much enthusiasm.

"And like I said, we can't send you to find Milo's castle alone. We'll be coming with you," Sly said.

"And why would we do that?" Johnny leaned back against the table they were gathered in front of.

Sly turned to face him. He raised his eyebrows. Johnny's nonchalance seemed to waver as he adjusted his stance.

"Do you have a problem with that?"

Johnny shifted from one foot to the other. "Why are we jumping up so fast to help this person we just met? And no one has seen the fellow for years. How do you expect us to find him?" he scoffed.

Fox looked back and forth between Johnny and Sly with concern.

Sly pressed his lips into a line before he responded. "Do I need to remind you what's at stake here?" Sly's look made Liam hold his breath. "Milo is the next best wizard we have who can give us some answers. I don't think it's a coincidence Liam here dropped into this world at this exact time." Hope flickered in his eyes.

Sly didn't look at Liam the entire conversation. It was odd to have someone talk about him while he was right there. Especially about powers and stakes he knew nothing about. His head spun. He didn't dare interrupt Sly and ask questions. Not when he looked at Johnny like he would flatten him.

What did Mom get me into? Liam groaned internally.

"Do you think there's someone better for the job?" Sly asked Johnny. "Maybe I could ask Curly to help instead. He said he wanted to go on more missions."

"Curly? Really?" Johnny's face deadpanned, unamused. "You think he could really have your back like I could?"

"Well, he has a better attitude, that's for sure." Sly stared hard at Johnny.

After a beat Juniper broke the silence. "Well, you know I'm game! I've spent too much time inside and I'm tired of playing drubles for the day." She gestured toward the kids playing cards on the long tables.

"Fox?" Sly turned toward him.

"I'm here for you, sir." Fox inclined his head.

Johnny glared at his brother, then threw up his hands, scoffing. "Well, fine then. I can't let you go alone."

"Meet in the Potions Room in ten minutes," Sly said cooly, surveying the group.

Everyone turned on their heels and scattered. Someone pulled Liam backward by the arm and he tripped over his feet, Aubry righting him.

"You two come with me. You can help me gather things. And I'll show you our supply closet." Juniper was dragging him by his arm toward the right corner of the room before he could say anything, Aubry trailing them. Liam was struck again by Juniper's confidence to be so sure of herself to just pull him around.

"Hold on, I have a couple of questions," Liam said, yanking his arm back from Juniper. She turned to look at him, brown eyes crackling with adventurous energy.

"Okay, go ahead. Ask then," she said, crossing her arms.

Liam stared at her, taken aback by her expectant look.

She raised her eyebrows.

Clearing his throat, Liam proceeded with his questions. "Why do the boys call Sly 'sir'? He doesn't seem to be that much older than them."

"I suppose they respect him. They haven't got any parents themselves, so an older person is all they have to look up to," Juniper said.

"What was Sly talking about earlier? What's at stake? And me being here not a coincidence?" The weight of that settled in his throat, making his words tight.

Juniper took a breath and thought for a second. "Conroy has been attacking new villages throughout the land. We think he's looking for more life forces. He started with ours and hasn't stopped."

"Why?" Liam shook his head, unable to wrap his mind around Conroy's motive.

Juniper looked into his eyes like she was searching for something.

Liam shifted on his feet and stuffed his hands in his pockets.

She considered him for a moment more, then said, "Rumor has it when Conroy was a boy, he was supposed to inherit power from another powerful wizard. His parents, who no one has seen for decades, trained Conroy. They kept Zadimus at bay while they trained their son to defeat him. Apparently, it was Conroy's birthright to inherit their power so he could go on training, but they died before he could inherit it. Death doesn't immediately lead to the inheritance of power. A ceremony needs to be performed. And with nowhere to go, he turned to Zadimus, the strongest wizard he'd heard of." She flicked her eyes off him and considered her words. "But no one has seen either of them for a long time. Then Conroy's powers started growing. He was supposed to be the one to take down Zadimus and his recruits, who were draining the land of life force. He'd take it from people, from nature, from animals, all so he could gain power and rule over Domhania. We've been living in fear of him taking over. It's been happening slowly. But if you came here from a different realm, maybe things are changing." She looked at Liam with the same spark of hope he'd seen in Sly's eyes.

"Um, I don't know about that." Liam rubbed the back of his neck. "This sounds like something the people of Domhania need to work through. This really isn't my fight. I came here by mistake and Aubry and I need to get back." He grimaced at Juniper when he saw disappointment dim her eyes. "I'm really sorry about your parents," Liam said. "I know what it's like to lose a parent. It's . . ." He shook his head, unable to verbalize the pang in his chest when he thought about his mom.

"Thanks." Juniper gave him a sad smile.

His heart pounded as he thought back on Juniper's words. What was he going to do against a powerful wizard?

She nodded. "Visiting Milo, the wizard in the mountains, would be your best bet then. He's been around for as long as anyone can remember. He's got to have more memories and knowledge of this place and how magic works. As far as we've heard, he's been in his castle for decades. Wizardry is a bit of a dying practice, so I'm not sure why he would hide away instead of trying to teach more people."

"You're saying it can be taught?"

"Generational magic is a lot stronger, but yes, it can be taught if people are open to it and willing."

Liam looked at Aubry, her interest mirroring his.

"If that's the case maybe Milo could teach me how to use these writing powers to get back home." Is this what his mom meant when she said to save this world and not make the same mistakes? Did she make mistakes when learning her magic?

"C'mon, let me show you something." Juniper motioned to them before she turned and resumed walking.

She stopped in front of a tall wooden door with carvings. It was about eight feet tall and a few feet wide, the color of the wood stain his Grandad used to have in his garage. The surface of the door was decorated with images of people walking through the forest, climbing a waterfall, and swinging from trees. The border was carved with flowers, leaves, vines, brush, and other nature found in the forest.

His Grandad worked on antique pieces to restore them, but this was like nothing Liam had seen before. He stared open mouthed at the detail of the carvings.

"Do you like them?" Juniper asked, staring at Liam.

Liam swallowed past the dryness in his mouth. "I've never seen anything so beautiful carved into wood."

"It's absolutely stunning," Aubry said.

"I spent a lot of time on it. A whole year, actually. I even scrapped a couple doors until I created one that was right."

"You did this?" Liam's eyes widened in her direction.

She jutted her chin out. "Yes, I did." Liam saw color flash under her caramel skin.

"Its. . . it's beautiful."

After a beat, Juniper said, "Well, let's get on with this. Don't want to keep the others waiting." She motioned for Liam and Aubry to stand back, then went up to the door and placed her palms on it. She traced what seemed like a pattern into the space next to the handle. After her graceful hands moved in different circles and flourishes, the door made a creaking sound and opened slightly.

Juniper swung the door open wider and Liam was at a loss for words once again. He eyed the stone walled room from corner to corner and tried to make sense of it in his head. In the middle of the room, a woman hunched over a long wooden table, fiddling with what looked like an extensive chemistry set. She was concocting things with vials, liquids, herbs, and Bunsen burner type machines. Wooden shelves lined the surrounding walls, holding hundreds of jars filled with different dried herbs, books on potions and healing, and mortars and pestles of different shapes and materials. The woman in the room worked next to a boiling cauldron with a flame underneath. On the long table in front of her, a wooden cutting board, and a small knife laid next to herbs in the middle of being prepared.

The ceiling was ten feet high and candle burning chandeliers hung from them like spiders on a string of web.

"Roya! How is my blend coming along?" Juniper yelled across the room to the woman hunched over the long wooden worktable.

"Wait! Don't move a muscle!" Roya's voice demanded. Juniper froze mid-step and held out a hand to Liam and Aubry to do the same. A few seconds of stillness passed.

"Ah, okay. I'm done. You may move now." Roya slipped off her gloves and turned around to greet Juniper.

Liam and Aubry exchanged confused glances.

Light from the chandeliers caught on Roya's silky brown hair piled on top of her head, making it look like she was glowing. Her olive-toned face glistened in a layer of sweat from working above the flames, Liam guessed. She didn't look tired the way her hunched body had suggested when they approached her. Exuberance and delight poured off her. She stood a little taller than Juniper. When she turned, Liam saw Roya was older than everyone he'd met so far. About twenty, he guessed. The smile lines around her coffee brown eyes crinkled as she looked at Juniper and opened her arms wide to hug her.

A pang of longing went through Liam. The way Roya hugged Juniper reminded him of his mom's hugs. Hollowness settled in his chest.

Roya pushed back from Juniper and held her out at arm's length. "Just as beautiful as the last time I saw you," she said and winked, which made Juniper shake her head and smile.

"And this is Roya, the older sister I always wanted," Juniper introduced her. Turning back to Roya she said, "It's a wonder you can still be so sweet after spending all day stuffed in here." Juniper looked around at the giant stone walled room with no windows.

"Ah, I got everything I need around me," Roya said, walking back to the table. Her long tan apron atop a dark green linen dress swished around her legs as she moved. "And who are your friends?" She cocked her head and raised an eyebrow.

"This is Liam and his cousin Aubry. Roya is our resident potions master." Juniper smiled proudly.

"So you were the one who made the tea for me?" Liam rubbed the back of his head, remembering where Sunny had hit him. Twice.

"That would be me." Roya turned and flashed an elegant smile. Her eyes sparkled with kindness and gentleness. "Heard you took quite a blow to the head from Sunny?" Her dark eyebrows stood out against her olive skin.

Liam sighed, trying to keep the frustration from his voice. "Yeah, he thought I was a spy or something?"

"Ah yes, well, you never can tell these days with everything going on. Conroy and his recruits have forced us into hiding, burned our homes, and taken so many lives. Can you blame the kid for being suspicious?"

"I guess not," Liam said quietly, not making eye contact. He saw Aubry out of the corner of his eye, rocking on her heels and interlacing her fingers in front of her. Something she did when she wished she was somewhere else. He understood the feeling. Part of him roiled at the thought of all the atrocities the Stream Kids had gone through, while the other part of him resisted getting too attached. They were going to leave soon, and this wasn't his battle. Heck, if what he'd been led to believe was true this world wasn't even real, right?

"Ah, I see you've met Roya." Sly drifted in, saving Liam and Aubry from the building awkwardness.

"Yes, apparently there are potions in this world now. I guess I shouldn't be surprised," Aubry said.

"You don't like surprises?" Sly cocked his head and stopped to stand next to Aubry.

"Ha! Aubry, like surprises?" Liam scoffed.

She glared at him.

"If you mean surprises that involve carefully planned strategies where every facet and possibility has been thought through, then yeah, she might like them." Liam crossed his arms and raised his eyebrows at his cousin.

"Well then—" Sly flashed her a smile. "Let's get to planning, shall we?"

CHAPTER NINE

———◆○◆———

S ly led their group through an arched doorway from Roya's Potions Room to a table in the Weapons Room. When they entered, Aubry looked around anxiously at the weapons on the walls. In the left corner every kind of medieval weapon imaginable spanned the wall. Bows and arrows, swords, small knives, throwing stars, staffs, and weapons he didn't know the names of.

Are these kids weapons proficient? Liam wondered, taking in the walls.

Cloaks, boots, hats, and leather armor filled the room's far corner, suggesting a dressing area. As he moved closer to the table, the smell of metal, leather, and sweat overwhelmed his senses. Distracted for a moment by the gleaming weapons, armor, and scene that looked just how he'd imagined it would when his mom described armories in her books, his mouth ticked up in a smile.

"Got the map!" Fox came running toward them with a rolled-up scroll raised above his head. He danced over and placed the scroll on the long table.

Aubry and Liam moved in closer. Finally, some information about where they were. The scroll's tan frayed edges smelled like a vintage bookstore full of ancient long-forgotten tomes. Fox flicked the map open. A foot-and-a-half long piece of parchment unfurled on the wooden table.

Hand-drawn landmarks stood out against the worn parchment. Colors popped and Liam couldn't decide where to keep his eyes. The map's upper left showed snow-capped *White Mountains*. Below that a green forest labeled

63

Larksfall Woods and *Fairy Land* caught his attention. It stretched from the right corner into the middle where it touched the rest of the lands and different terrains.

In the lower right-hand corner sat another mountain range, brown and colorless compared to the White Mountains. Jagged mountain peaks outlined a similar looking castle. The label on it read *Zadimus*.

"*That's* where Conroy and his master hide out?" Liam pointed to the desolate-looking castle.

Sly nodded. "That would be the place."

"Best stay away from there," Fox warned.

All throughout the map, a winding river and several waterfalls—one of which was on the road to Milo's White Castle in the White Mountains— ran through the lands.

"Alright. We must head west." Sly indicated a road exiting the map's central base, the Stream Kids' hideout location. The hideout wasn't notated on the map. Instead, it showed a thick forest. *Land of the trees*, thought Liam.

"The road through Fairy Land?" Johnny wrinkled his nose and glanced at Sly skeptically.

"Not there." Fox stared at Sly, wide eyed.

"What's so bad about fairies? Aren't they supposed to be whimsical and nice?" Aubry asked.

"Have you ever met a fairy?" Sly asked.

"Well . . . I've read a lot about them and everyone knows their mystical existence is actually just people misinterpreting perfectly rational scientific phenomena—" Aubry started.

"She's never met one, then," Johnny dryly cut her off, talking past her to Sly.

"Well, we can go through, and you can see for yourself." Sly's eyes gleamed.

"Why don't we head more south and avoid the fairies? For all our sakes? We don't need to get mixed up in their games of dancing and drinking tea until we grow old." Juniper looked up her nose at Sly.

"Excuse me, until we grow *old*?" Aubry gaped.

"It's a figure of speech," Sly said, one side of his mouth rising.

"So we can take *this* road farther south and then circle up to the White Mountains?" Liam asked, pointing to the line on the map, trying to keep everyone on track.

"Yes, we will have to cross the Raven River to get there," Sly pointed out. "Nothing we haven't done before!" His excitement was almost palpable.

"What will you need for this trip?" Roya yelled over her shoulder through the open door.

Sly rubbed his chin. "Probably the usual . . . and some extra Wizard Ward. That reminds me." He snapped his fingers, grinned widely at Liam and Aubry, and quickly turned to face the armory wall. "We need to teach you two how to handle a sword. Or a bow and arrow. Or an axe." He kept looking back and forth between the wall of weapons and his guests as if he was trying to imagine them fighting with each one as he listed them off. "Whatever you want to fight with really."

"Fight?" Aubry's eyes widened.

Sly touched and assessed each weapon on the wall as if the right one for Liam and Aubry would show itself when probed. "You didn't expect us to send you out there without any protection, did you?"

"But—but, I don't know how to fight." Aubry looked back and forth between Sly and Liam.

"Don't worry, I'll teach you." Sly winked. Aubry tensed her jaw.

"Well, that sounds fun to me." Liam perked up. "I was in a medieval sword fighting club, so I already know how to fight with a sword."

"Um, an evil sword fighting club? Should we be concerned?" Juniper raised her eyebrows and looked around at everyone.

"No! No, it's not like that. Medieval is a time where there were knights, queens, kings, castles and the whole bit," Liam explained.

"Everyone has nighttime." Johnny narrowed his eyes at Liam, who blew out a frustrated sigh. Liam realized his mom must not have given them *any* knowledge of Earth's history.

"Okay, the point is Liam has basic knowledge of sword fighting," Aubry said.

"Well, it's your lucky day, my friend, because I studied under a master swordsman and can teach you everything you need to know to take down your opponent." Sly surprised Fox, seizing him in a headlock. Fox struggled, but Sly's hold was rock solid. "And I'm not too bad at hand-to-hand combat either."

"I've been training in karate for the past six months as well," Liam muttered, trying not to think about Clive and his friends. Despite not being physically pushed around since the last time they knocked him out in the weight room, they engaged in verbal battles with him daily.

"Did you say you've been training in *raw tea*? How exactly will that help?" Johnny looked at Liam, unimpressed.

Liam huffed. "No, I've been learning how to fight too."

"Hm," Johnny grunted, crossing his arms as he looked Liam up and down like he doubted it.

Liam glared back.

"C'mon, I'll show you some armor you can borrow." Juniper pulled Aubry's arm and led her to the back of the room.

"You ready to start sword fighting, Liam?" Sly released Fox from the headlock and patted him on the back.

"Sure, why not?" Liam shrugged and looked at the wall of swords Sly was motioning to.

"Excellent." Sly smiled.

Upon further inspection, Liam realized the Weapons Room was a lot bigger than he initially realized. There were swords lining one wall above another table that held smaller things like daggers, axes, and throwing stars of some sort. He previously overlooked a small hallway behind the main room, leading to the Sparring Room. He stood across from Sly holding a longsword, heavy in his hand. Sly was lecturing him on the proper way to hold a sword, the stance one needed for sword fighting, and how to predict your opponent's moves. All information Liam knew, but not wanting to be rude and interrupt, he just smiled and nodded.

"So, when did you learn to sword fight?" Liam asked after he was done.

"It was one of the things my mentor taught me during my apprenticeship at his shop. I helped him make swords for people who would request them, and then he would train me in sword fighting. When we found this place"—Sly motioned to the room—"I thought it would be a good idea to teach the other kids how to defend themselves should they ever get in a sticky situation. Not that sword fighting would really stand a chance against a dark wizard." The muscle in his jaw clenched and Liam felt like Sly's comment was somehow personal and painful. "So everyone here is decent at defending themselves. Would I take every person into combat with me or have them be my second in a fight?" He made a motion like he was weighing his options. "No. That's why I have Johnny and Fox. I know that they won't hesitate when a life is on the line."

"Does Juniper fight too?" Liam asked.

"Oh yes, she can hold her own." Sly nodded. "Enough talking. Let's practice now." Sly stepped forward and jabbed his sword toward Liam, who parried and held Sly at sword point.

"Whoa, pretty fast reflexes, huh?" Sly's mouth ticked up in a smirk.

"I told you, I was in a med—in a sword fighting club in school." The corner of Liam's mouth crept up.

"Oh yeah, the evil sword fighting club?" Sly's eyes widened in mock fear.

Liam huffed. "Let's just say I've had some training of my own."

"Perhaps this won't take long." Sly nodded approvingly.

Liam took a breath, gray eyes narrowing as he readied himself.

With a graceful flourish, Sly lunged forward, his blade slicing through the air. Liam parried the strike with a clash that reverberated off the walls.

They danced across the floor of the training room, exchanging blows and parries, their movements fluid and precise. Liam's agility and fitness from karate and weight training matched Sly's raw strength and lightning-fast reflexes.

Liam kept advancing, willing his sword to strike where he wanted it to. With an arc, he brought his sword down and sparks erupted where their blades met. Warmth pulsed through Liam's arms and he felt power crackle through him, making his arm hairs stand on end.

Sly leapt back in surprise, holding his blade in front of him, looking at it like it was going to bite him. He snapped his gaze to Liam, staring.

"What was that?" Sly swallowed, steadying his breath.

Liam examined his hands, expecting to see a sign of something, but everything looked normal.

"Is that not normal for these blades?" Liam asked.

"No," Sly said, looking skeptically at him.

Was that me? Was that part of the power Mom passed on to me?

"That was unprecedented." Sly's gaze landed heavy on Liam. "Let's go again."

Sly ran at him, catching Liam off balance. With a clumsy parry, he blocked Sly's jab just in time. The strength of it rattled Liam's bones. Sly was stronger than he looked.

But so was Liam. Six months of training wasn't for nothing. Spinning to face Sly, he lunged at him, aiming for his chest as soon as he blocked Sly's previous strike. Catching Sly off guard, Liam grazed the leather chest armor he wore.

Liam sucked in a breath. He really didn't want to hurt him. But Sly didn't stop. Didn't seem phased. Stepping out of the way, he aimed for Liam's back. Bringing his sword out, Liam went to block it, but it was a feint. Sly brought his sword down hard on Liam's, breaking it from his grip and sending it to the floor.

Panic rose in Liam's chest as he stood defenseless in front of Sly. This was beginning to feel like more than just training.

Sly lunged and jabbed at Liam, who jumped out of the way and dodged three consecutive strikes. He thought back to his hours of karate classes, learning to dodge attacks, and silently thanked his instructors while his mind tried to decipher why Sly was still coming at him while he was unarmed.

What is Sly trying to do? Hurt me? Maybe Sly had been playing Liam and wanted to kill him.

"Yield!" Sly yelled.

No. He would not yield. He would not lose this fight. Not like the last time Clive cornered him. He couldn't bear another defeat. But Sly was pointing the sword at his neck and his sword was all the way across the room.

Sly narrowed his eyes and moved toward Liam. Fear rose in Liam's throat. He desperately looked around for something, anything, to defend himself with. Looking over at the sword, he reached for it and willed it to come to his out-stretched palm. He remembered the warmth in his hands a second ago as he held the sword.

Vines squeezed through the wooden floor and launched the sword into Liam's hand, and he brought it up in front of his throat to block Sly's strike. More warmth bloomed in his hands and blue sparks blasted from the impact of the swords, sending Sly backward into the wall of the Sparring Room.

Chest heaving from relief, Liam held his sword in front of himself and stared at Sly. Was he crazy? What was he playing at?

"What the heck was that Sly?" Liam yelled.

"Liam?" Aubry's head poked in from the Weapons Room where she was try-ing on armor. Spotting Sly on the floor, she gasped and covered her mouth. "Is he okay?" She moved toward where he slumped against the wall, still conscious.

"Aubry, don't move!" Liam warned. She froze.

"What the heck was that?" Liam ground out slowly, leveling his narrowed eyes at Sly, who got up off the floor.

"I knew you had it in you." Sly stood and straightened his clothes while looking at Liam with an 'I told you so' expression.

Anger flared in Liam's stomach. "That just a test for me? You almost killed me!" This was ridiculous. He was here to get him and Aubry home, not be Sly's experiment. Liam's breathing picked up and blue power glowed brighter from his hands the angrier he got.

"Liam." Sly held up his hands and spoke in a cautionary tone. "It's okay. I'm okay. It all turned out. I wanted you to see your powers."

"I'm not your guinea pig to mess around with!" Liam was tired of being thrown around and taken advantage of. That was not why he was here. He shouldn't have even been here. He thought back to his mom's confusing last words to him. How she'd abandoned him and left him a mess to deal with.

As his anger fumed, vines broke through the wooden panels on the ground all across the Sparring Room. They tore through the floor and lashed out at the mirrors on the walls, sending glass shards spraying across the room. Tendrils smashed shields and training swords. A chaos of vines danced between Liam and Sly as Liam shook with anger.

"Liam, it's okay! Just breathe!" Sly's voice was laced with worry as he kept sneaking glances toward the door. Well, that was a first.

Serves him right for messing with me like that.

"AHH!" Aubry's voice pierced through Liam's rage. Whipping his head to look at her, he saw vines snake around her legs and pull her to the ground. Lashing at the vines with her arms, she screamed in horror. They didn't stop. They continued to move up her legs to her torso.

"Liam, help me!" she pleaded.

Trying to block out her voice and the anxiety it caused him, he noticed her go silent. Closing his eyes and taking a breath, he tried to tell the vines to stop.

Please stop?

Liam opened his eyes and saw Aubry had stopped screaming because the vines wrapped around her throat choking her. She gasped for breath.

"Aubry!" Anger melted away, replaced by fear.

She collapsed. Her auburn hair spread around her like a setting sun on the horizon.

Aubry was hurt, and it was his fault. He did this. He brought her here and now he was responsible for injuring her.

"Liam, just breathe. Get rid of the vines," Sly commanded.

Liam nodded and slowed his breathing, trying to focus on the ground and the way the wood spiraled on the floor. He focused on the lines and started counting them. As he took steadying breaths, the vines withered and slithered back into the ground under the torn up wooden floor. Carefully, Liam walked over to Aubry, avoiding the holes from the vines of chaos.

"Aubry? Aubry?" Liam called, willing her to move. Sinking to his knees, he moved her hair out of her face and said her name again.

She groaned.

She's alive. Thank God!

"Aubry, can you move?" Sly made his way over, concern deep in the lines of his forehead.

She made a sound, then faced both boys. "I think so."

"Okay, just move slowly," Sly said, putting a hand on her back.

Liam stared in shock. He'd never seen Aubry hurt like this. She always took care of him. Not the other way around. How could he hurt her like this? What did Aubry usually do when he was hurt? He tried to recall, but his brain was a fuzzy mess.

"Ouch." Aubry sucked in a breath and motioned to her ankle.

Sly moved closer and slowly untangled the leftover root wrapped around her. "There we go. You can move now."

Aubry pushed herself up to turn around to face Sly and Liam. Sly didn't meet her gaze, as he was inspecting her ankle. He probed the swollen area. "Tender there?" Aubry sucked in her breath.

"I'll take that as a yes." He raised his eyebrows and looked up at her. They exchanged a long look.

After a few seconds, Aubry swallowed. "Um, yes."

"Aubry," Liam finally said, his throat feeling like someone had dumped sand down it. "I'm so sorry. I don't know what happened. I—" He looked down at his hands, ashamed.

"Hey, it's okay." Aubry reached out and grabbed one of his hands.

Liam looked up at her. "I hurt you with this—this *power*."

Is this what Mom warned me about? Between the portal and now this, this power is starting to feel more like a curse. Liam's thoughts raced.

"I just—I'm so sorry." He shook his head.

Aubry gave him a painful-looking smile.

"Let me help you up." Sly put his arm around Aubry's waist. She slid her arm around his shoulders, and they stood together. "Are you okay?" Sly searched Aubry's face for an answer.

"Yeah, I'll be okay."

Liam saw Aubry wince and doubted that.

"We'll have Roya fix something up to put on that ankle of yours. She's fantastic at making salves and tonics for when we get injured," Sly told Aubry.

"Aubry, I'm so sorry." Liam stood.

Aubry looked at Liam and forced a smile. "I'll be okay." He couldn't help but hear the dozens of times he had said that to her when their places were reversed. She tried to put weight on her foot and jerked it up in pain. "Dang it!" she groaned.

Sly looked at her, helpless. "Do you need me to carry you?" Sly offered.

Aubry blushed. "No, that's okay! I'll hobble along."

Guilt pooled in Liam's stomach. Taking deep breaths, he worked to calm his nerves. What if this made Sly and the Stream Kids afraid of him? Heck, what if Aubry was afraid of him now? What if they wouldn't help him anymore? What if they thought he would hurt one of them? How was he supposed to help them if he didn't even know what he was doing?

"I'll take her to Roya. Liam, can you uh, put the swords back in the Weapons Room?" Sly jerked his head toward the room he was helping Aubry toward. Liam cautiously followed, swords in hand, heavy like the feeling in his stomach.

Mindful to avoid the shredded floorboards, he asked Sly, "Do you know what happened?"

Sly stopped in front of Liam, Aubry in his grip, thinking. "I think your powers are connected to your emotions. I've heard inherited magic runs deep within you and often the only thing strong enough to reach it are emotions." Sly looked intently at Liam, gauging his response.

Liam shook his head, overwhelmed.

A beat passed before Sly aided Aubry's slow movement down the hall to the Weapons Room and onward to Roya's workshop.

Liam sighed, returning the swords to the wall. Trying to clear his head, he walked back to the weapons laden table. He spotted some throwing stars with much sharper edges than the version he brought home from karate class so he and Aubry could practice in her backyard on a piece of plywood.

He taught her to throw them with enough strength but also precision in her wrist to get them to hit their target. He remembered picking up the shiny throwing star, the weight of it in his hand, grounding him, reminding him to plant his feet, breathe, and focus on his target. His star had stuck strongly in the plywood, as had Aubry's right after his.

Returning to the Weapons Room, Sly exhaled, seating himself on a back-wall bench.

Liam followed.

Sly leaned his elbows on his knees and interlaced his fingers. He stared intently at a spot on the wooden floor.

Liam sat, waiting for him to speak.

"Once, I took Juniper with me to try to find Milo's castle." Sly's mouth pulled tight. "We didn't get very far on our own, though. We were young and didn't know what we were looking for. We had no backup, no maps, no training. We wanted answers, and we thought Milo might be able to help."

Leaning against the wall, he intently watched a point on the floor. "We were attacked. By Conroy's men." Sly swallowed. "Juniper got hurt. Bad.

"I had to carry her back here so Roya could fix her up." His gaze drifted, recalling the past. "Since then, I haven't led anyone out that far, let alone allow anyone to venture out themselves."

Liam sighed, trying to swallow past the tightness in his throat. "The difference is, Aubry isn't like Juniper. She doesn't like adventures. She doesn't like excitement. That's never been her thing." Liam shook his head at the floor. "She has a strong mind. She's smart, strategic, and thinks through things." Liam scoffed. "And I got her into this mess and hurt her." Guilt sat like ice in his stomach.

Liam glanced sideways to find Sly studying him.

After a pause, Sly exhaled, his fists clenching. Sly's voice came out low as he said, "I was supposed to protect Juniper. I'm her older brother, and I didn't do my job. Of course she doesn't blame me. She didn't let it rattle her." Despair clouded his gaze. "But I was afraid. Afraid I would lose her too. And now" —Sly looked at Liam— "I can't stop her from going out onto missions or scouting assignments with us. She loves the thrill and excitement of them." He sighed and stared at the floor. "Sometimes I wish Mum and Dad were here so they could tell me what to do." After a beat, he seemed to realize how vulnerable he'd just been and said, "Well, that's enough of that story."

Sly stood up.

"Sometimes people can surprise you," Sly said, a tight smile pulling at his lips. "Roya is healing Aubry right now if you want to talk to her." He stood and smiled encouragingly. "I'll check on the others and give you two a second."

Chapter Ten

L iam found Aubry seated near Roya's workbench inside the Potions
Room. Roya squatted, applying something goopy to Aubry's ankle.
Aubry watched, a disgusted look on her face.

Well, I guess that means she's at least feeling a little better, he hoped.

Roya turned at the sound of Liam's footsteps and flashed a welcoming smile,
unbothered by the questionable substance all over her hands. Liam nodded back
and kept walking toward Aubry.

"Are you doing okay, Aub?" He put a tentative hand on her shoulder.

Her emerald eyes lit up when she saw him. "Hmm, let's see, I'm in a world
that I'm not quite sure really exists, inside a tree, apparently. Vines sprang up
from the floor and attacked me, and now a magical salve is healing my ankle."
She laughed nervously, then fell silent, lost in thought. She looked down at
her ankle. "But yes. This is the second application of the salve and I feel better
already."

Liam looked down at the thick, green, gooey salve. "Doesn't look very com-
pelling, though."

"Well, you see, it is. Roya's been explaining the compounds she's using for her
creations and I've been thinking about the scientific implications of them. I'm
wondering how these are different on a molecular level compared to ointments
back home. Like a sore muscle lotion or something, but apparently she says her

creations have magic infused into them. How does that happen? How is the structure and makeup of them different?" Aubry's wide eyes darted from Liam to the different ingredients on Roya's worktable.

Liam bit back a smile.

"What?" Aubry reddened.

Roya grinned. "Glad to hear you're so interested in my potions work." After applying the last of the goop, she wrapped Aubry's ankle with a tan bandage. "Alright!" Roya stopped to admire her work. "Give it a few minutes and you should be right as rain." Her eyes crinkled with a warm smile, and she walked back to her potions.

Bubbling cauldrons and the sound of Roya cutting herbs filled the space between Liam and Aubry as they sat in silence and looked at each other. Aubry inhaled after a moment.

Oh boy, here it comes. She's never going to forgive me.

"Liam, there's something I want to tell you." Aubry stared at him, gaze loaded. "I don't blame you for what happened. You didn't know what you were doing." She stared pointedly at him and continued with her next point. "We've barely been here a few hours and you seemingly possess powers." She raised her eyebrows like she was still coming to terms with it. "And they spontaneously activated while you were training."

"Well, actually—" Liam started.

"Events unfolded rapidly and you're unclear how your abilities work. How can this be your fault? I mean, how can I logically hold you at fault?" She looked at him like she was waiting for an answer from someone in her debate club.

"Well, thank you, Aub. I appreciate that. You see, it happened because—" Liam rubbed his neck and thought about how to tell her Sly had almost killed him to activate his powers. "Sly was trying to see if I had powers. He was trying to get them out of me and that's what happened." Liam shoved his hands through his hair.

"Interesting." Aubry pinched her lip between her fingers, thinking. "And it worked?"

"Um, obviously."

"Of course." She waved her hand. "So it comes out of you when you fight or feel threatened?"

"I guess so," Liam answered slowly.

Aubry nodded thoughtfully. "That's an excellent piece of information to know."

She wasn't mad. He sighed in relief. He couldn't say the same for himself. He was still pretty ticked at Sly for pushing him like that. He ground his teeth, thinking about it, frustration simmering in his veins.

"Ow!" They heard Roya from the back table. "What the—" Roya raised her eyebrows and yanked her hand back. Three pots of unlit cauldrons were boiling and steaming on her table.

Oh, no. That's me again. I need to get out of here.

Pushing away from the worktable, Liam swept out of the room, Aubry calling after him.

"Liam!"

He heard Aubry's sigh of frustration but kept walking through the hideout, looking for a way out.

The main hall.

But where is the—

Door.

Oh, well that's convenient. He didn't remember seeing a door to the outside on his tour but it didn't matter now he'd found it.

Anger still simmering in his arms, he stomped to the door and wrenched it open, not noticing the scorch mark he left on the copper handle.

Leaves crunched under his feet and he raised his arms to block the sun from his eyes.

He heard another set of footsteps behind him.

"You can't just leave like that," Aubry scolded him.

Liam turned to give her a look and watched her irritation melt away in wonder. Her eyes widened as she took in the lush forest around them. Liam narrowed his, then turned to see what she was seeing.

Pine trees, damp leaves, and the smell of incoming rain wrapped around him. He didn't realize he'd been clenching his fists so tightly until he felt them relax as he breathed in the fresh air. He took a deep breath and felt the anger sizzle away like a hot pan taken off the flame.

"How is this place real?" Aubry breathed, head on a swivel, auburn curls moving with her gaze.

"My mom made it real." Liam joined Aubry in appreciating the beauty of the moss growing on the towering trees, the way the sunlight dappled through the canopy, and the call of birdsong. The sun warmed his skin in the cool air. Tall pine and fir trees tugged at a memory of a trip he took with his parents to Yosemite National Park.

During one of Liam's Thanksgiving breaks, his dad suggested they get out of the house. At that time, his mom wouldn't leave her writing room for days, and it always concerned Liam's dad. She would go from bed to the kitchen to her writing room and repeat the cycle until she couldn't keep her eyes open. His dad often found her asleep in one of those three rooms, and if it wasn't her bed, he would rouse her just enough to lead her back to the bedroom.

After some convincing, his mom finally relented, and they drove four hours from the Central Coast to Yosemite.

When Liam stepped out of the car and into Yosemite National Park for the first time, it took his breath away. In the valley, the mountains rose around them like the earth had stopped halfway before swallowing them. They stood framed by the towering trees. He felt so small looking up. All his worries washed away with the songs of the birds. The crisp October air welcomed them to their campsite. Many trees had begun turning to autumn colors. He remembered seeing one that reminded him of a flame atop a birthday candle. The yellows and oranges so vibrant, they demanded his attention. He couldn't stop staring.

"Isn't it the most beautiful thing you've ever seen?" His mom had hugged him to her side. He saw tears in her eyes as they stood staring in awe of the beauty surrounding them. Standing there with her was one of Liam's favorite memories. He could still remember the warmth of his mom's arm as she held him against her while they soaked in the beauty of Yosemite Valley.

I wonder if Mom thought of that moment when she wrote about this forest.

Liam felt a wave of sadness picturing his mom in the woods with him. The emotion slithered up into his chest and he tried to breathe around it.

"Liam, what's happening?" Aubry's voice warbled with trepidation.

She was looking around at the trees. They drooped like they'd become top heavy and couldn't stand up by themselves. Pine needles and leaves rained down around them like snow. Taking a step toward her, Liam slid his arm around Aubry's shoulders and tried to shield her from the falling needles. Her quick breaths puffed out her hair as she dropped her head closer to Liam's chest.

Was this because of him again? *Can I just get a moment of peace?* Looking around, he squinted. *Please stop.*

After his thought, leaves scattered from under him, leaving him in a circle of dirt. The pine needles falling to the ground froze midair. A nearby bird stopped mid-flight.

Everything fell silent.

Frozen, like it was stuck in time.

All was still.

Liam blinked and squinted, trying to get a grip on what he was seeing.

What in the world?

In his next breath, everything resumed its natural movement, like someone had pressed play on a remote.

Did my thoughts just control time? Liam heard footsteps crunching in the leaves behind them. He suspected Sly and Juniper were probably coming to see if they were alright, and as much as he was still mad at Sly, it would probably be good to ask him about this even newer power he just accessed.

He glanced at Sly and Juniper, about to inquire, when he saw a tall man, cloaked in black, standing behind them instead.

The man's hand moved faster than Liam's brain could process and, what looked like a smoldering ball of solid fire came barreling toward him.

Instinct threw him to the side to dodge the fireball. Thankfully, he saw Aubry dive behind a nearby boulder for cover.

His heart pounded in his chest, adrenaline coursing through his veins.

The man in black walked toward him. His knee-high black boots, pants, linen shirt, and flowing cape draping to the ground made him look like a walking shadow, and it seemed like the edges of him blurred away. His brown greasy hair was slicked back against his head. The angles of his face looked like they'd been cut from stone and his smile sent a shiver through Liam. As the man stepped closer, Liam noticed the undefined details of him were tendrils of grey smoke winding themselves around his feet, ankles, and calves. It followed him with every step and looked like it was part of him somehow.

If this world truly originates from Mom's books, I might know who this is and that might help me get out of this . . . His thoughts soared through his mom's stories, their characters, the magic, and the evils of Domhania.

Liam attempted to envision a similar-looking character but the man's features seemed foreign.

A fireball exploded above his head in the trees as the man advanced towards him. Black shadows undulated around his feet, following him.

In that moment, it occurred to Liam the faces he imagined for his mom's characters were probably different than the faces she imagined.

I suppose that's the beauty of imagination. Although not super helpful in this moment.

The footsteps came closer along with cold laughter. Flaming fireballs licked up more trees around Liam, lighting them with orange fire. He winced at the heat.

Liam's mind blitzed through possibilities. *If I were writing about this man, how would I describe him? Tall, greasy hair, dressed in black like the night sky, a man of shadows . . . oh . . . this isn't good.*

Behind the man, Liam saw Juniper squaring her shoulders toward the stranger.

She must have come running after she heard the explosions.

Her hand rested on a three-foot knife at her belt.

"Conroy!" she called from behind the man.

Liam's stomach dropped, suspicions and anxieties confirmed.

The shadow man, Conroy, stopped, slowly turned on his heel, and faced Juniper.

"So you're protecting him, then?" Conroy cocked his head, the sun shining off his greasy hair. His mouth slid into a creepy half grin. He shot his hands out to either side of him, braced, ready to throw another fireball, Liam guessed. Even through his clothes, it was easy to tell he was strong and built.

Despite Liam's karate classes and weightlifting sessions, he knew his limits and didn't think he would stand a chance against someone throwing fire.

"You're not getting near him," Juniper's firm voice rang out.

The shadow man's cold smear of a smile sharpened. "How do you know it's him I want?"

Juniper's steady face faltered at his question, and Aubry's scream echoed in the trees.

Liam's heart slammed in his chest and he looked to where Aubry hid and saw the grey tendrils curling around her feet, dragging her out from the boulder. Clawing at the ground, she fought to resist the shadow tendrils, but they pulled her harder, slamming her head into the ground and raking her face across the leaves and dirt.

Without thinking, Liam dashed over to her. Her scream echoed in his mind. He would *not* let anything happen to her. Not again. He could not let Conroy, gone bad, take her.

Flames flew at Liam's head again and he leapt to avoid them. Blazing heat swept across his face as he dodged another fireball.

"Don't be so eager, prodigal son. Your turn will come soon enough." The man cloaked in shadows smiled maniacally as he moved his hands to control the tendrils of smoke and shadow to bring Aubry closer to him.

What is he talking about?

Liam pivoted and ran toward Aubry again. A fireball landed in front of him, forcing him to stop. The flames curled around him in a circle, trapping him inside.

"No! Aubry!" Liam yelled, desperation pounding in his chest.

Through the flames, Liam saw Juniper throw something at the man.

An icy laugh grew from Conroy's chest and raised the hairs on Liam's neck. "You're unaware what you're getting into, aren't you?" Fire smoldered in Conroy's hands.

Liam, heart racing, scanned his surroundings for something to use as a weapon.

"I felt you and your magic all the way across the country. Your magic and your blood." Conroy cocked his head toward Aubry, now suspended in the air, tendrils laced around her body, restricting her movement. She wriggled against them frantically. "It's amazing the lengths we'll go for those with our own blood."

"Juniper!" Liam bellowed.

Something blue glinted in the sunlight as Juniper threw it at Conroy. It landed next to his feet with a cold thunk. He scoffed and made a move toward Juniper, but the vial exploded and a thick cloud of blue smoke engulfed him.

For a moment, he faltered and grabbed his abdomen like he was struggling to breathe. With a wave of his hand, he moved the air to dissipate the blue smoke.

While he was down, Juniper unsheathed her sword and ran at him, ferocity shining her in eyes.

Springing upright, Conroy flicked his wrist and roots sprouted from the ground and wound around Juniper, tripping her and sending her sword flying.

"Stupid, kids," Conroy sneered. "Let's get out of here, shall we?" he said to Aubry.

Her high-pitched scream pierced Liam's ears. Tendrils shot up to her mouth and cut her off, depriving her of air.

"Aubry, no!" Liam moved to jump over the flames, but as he did, they turned a green color and licked out at him, burning his right side. Crying out, he dropped to his knees.

White-hot pain laced up his arm and shoulder, making him dizzy. He forced himself to keep his eyes on Aubry.

In two steps Conroy was next to her, wrapping his black-clad arm around her. She struggled against the smoke and shadow tendrils, whimpering. With a swish of his cloak, Conroy surrounded them in shadows, there was a flash of light, and they disappeared.

"No!" Liam bellowed, vision blurring. As soon as Conroy left, the flames vanished, but the damage was done.

Liam groaned. He'd been burned before, but this was agony. The flames had felt hotter, and the pain pulsed into the rest of his body, making him weak. His head pounded. His nerves were on fire. He gasped for air. Convulsions took over his body.

"Liam!" Sly's voice punctuated the air as he joined them.

Liam moaned. "What's happening?" Sweat dripped down his face, his back. He saw a blurry Juniper and Sly sprinting toward him.

"Wizard's fire. Hold on, Liam," Juniper pleaded with him. "It's a powerful fire that burns hotter, deeper, and affects your nervous system. The pain is supposed to be debilitating," she quickly explained.

He tried to force himself to stay conscious, but white spots dotted his vision and he could hardly see. He felt arms on either side of him lift him. He tried to help, but his muscles seethed in protest. Pain radiated, and he groaned.

He couldn't move anymore. He tried to fight it, but pain consumed him. He was burning from the inside out. Aubry was gone. He couldn't do anything. He felt helpless. Gasping, his lungs spasmed, and he gave in to the pain pulling him under.

CHAPTER ELEVEN

———◆◇◆———

F or the second time that day, Liam woke up in a bed that was not his own. As he drifted in and out of consciousness, sounds droned around him like white noise. He thought he heard voices murmuring, the distant clinking of silverware, and clattering pots. Slowly, he remembered what landed him in bed this time. A sharp-angled face and a disturbing smile flashed across his memory. Fear. Fire. Burning. Pain. Aubry's scream. Aubry.

Opening his eyes, he looked over at his arm to find it covered in bandages. He moved his fingers and groaned as pain radiated through it.

"Liam?" a warm, caring voice asked.

He saw Juniper seated opposite him. A sheen of sweat glistened her face. Her coiled hair fell more limply around her face and her clothes were dirty, like she hadn't changed since the attack. Her brown eyes met his, and she approached him.

"Liam, are you okay? How are you feeling?" She knotted her hands together.

Fear, pain, and Aubry's scream stained his memory. He remembered the terror in his cousin's emerald eyes. The desperate look she gave him as the smoke curled around her. "Aubry?" he croaked, his voice like cut glass.

Juniper's face fell. A cold ball of fear formed in Liam's stomach.

"Where did he—" he started, but pain wrapped around his throat and vocal cords. A whole-body spasm trembled through him. Gritting his teeth, he let out a frustrated groan.

"Here." Juniper grabbed a cup from the bedside table and brought it to his lips as she helped him lift his head to take a drink. Unlike the last potion, this one burned as he swallowed. He coughed and sputtered the potion on himself and Juniper's hand.

Quickly, she grabbed a glass of water from the side table and helped Liam wash the burning potion down.

"Roya said you should remain still for a little while. You've been burned by Wizard's Fire. It burns through your skin and the magic seeps into your veins, which makes it painful to move. It attacks your body the more you move." Juniper wiped her hand, tossing the rag onto the side table.

Letting out a breath, he felt the fiery pain slowly dissipate from his throat and chest. Enough that he could talk without spasming.

"Even with the potion?" he asked.

Juniper nodded. "Potions are powerful, but magic is more powerful. Roya's potion helps speed up the healing process, but the side effects from Wizard's Fire take a couple days to fully wear off." Juniper held up the rest of the potion Liam hadn't sputtered all over them and tipped it into his mouth. She followed it with the water again, and he gave her a grateful half smile.

"They can't all be winners." Juniper smiled sadly as she placed the cup back down. "You really scared us." Her forehead creased as she looked at his arm, nimble fingers making sure the bandage was secure.

"*You* were scared? Aubry was the one kidnapped by Conroy." Saying the words out loud left a gaping hole in his chest. Conroy had Aubry. He'd kidnapped her. "What will he do with her? Where did he take her?" Anger sizzled in his chest.

Juniper broke eye contact, and her mouth twitched.

"What? What does he plan to do?" The seriousness in his voice drew Juniper's gaze back to his. Her dark eyes looked far away—eclipsed by so much. She was silent for a beat. "Juniper, please tell me. She's like my sister. I'm going to find her and rescue her from that cocky little shadow jerk."

Her eyebrows bunched together. "He most likely took her to his castle where he and Zadimus stay. And I know what you're thinking, but even if we knew for sure she was there, you can't just walk up to it and rescue her. It's not that easy."

"I don't care. I'm not leaving her there." His voice was approaching a growl. "It seemed like Conroy knew I had powers, and they might have even drawn him here, but why did he take *her*? It doesn't make sense."

Juniper stayed silent for a moment. "I've heard he's been looking for a vessel."

"A vessel?" Liam sat up on his forearms, pain spiking for a moment, then dissipating to soreness. "For what?" His heart sped up thinking about Aubry cold, afraid, and alone in Conroy's compound waiting to be used for one of his sick dark spells. He *had* to get to her.

Juniper pushed her lips into a thin line. "For a spell." She crossed her arms and studied him before she went on. "He needs a vessel in order to absorb the rest of his power," she said, almost like she was trying to figure something else out. "How are you moving right now?" She narrowed her velvet brown eyes at him.

"How would a vessel help him do that? Aubry isn't magical." Liam shook his head, trying to sort out the mess. None of this made any sense. Aubry disliked fantasy and similar fiction. Anything with imagination really.

"He said something about her blood. Do you remember that?" Juniper stared hard at him.

"It's amazing the lengths we'll go for those with our own blood," Liam remembered Conroy said when he looked at Aubry. "What did he mean?"

Juniper sighed. "He needs her blood for a sacrifice. She'll be the sacrifice he uses to claim the fullness of his magic. He'll perform a spell, make a sacrifice, and then his magic will have the full breadth and power it should."

"A sacrifice?" Liam sat up straight and raised his voice.

Juniper looked at him, perplexed. "How are you already sitting up? You shouldn't be able to move so quickly after the Wizard's Fire."

"I really don't think that's important right now. I need to get to Aubry!" Liam swung his legs off the bed to stand up. Juniper shifted to block his way. Her head came up to his nose, so she tilted her face up to meet his.

"Liam, I know you're really upset right now, but you can't save her by yourself."

"The hell I can't!" He glared down at her.

Instead of flinching like he expected, she raised an eyebrow and smirked. "You want to be a hero, huh?" She stared back at him, an intrigued look on her face.

He made to move, but she gently placed a hand on his shoulder, holding him there. He froze. Her touch extinguished the heat of anger he'd felt rising a moment earlier.

The candlelight from the side table cast a warm glow on the side of her face, distracting Liam. Her brown coils framed her dark face. Her skin looked smooth, and he wondered if it would feel as soft as it looked. He stared at her and willed himself to breathe.

What was he doing? This wasn't the time for distractions. Shaking his head, he resumed his thoughts about saving Aubry. "Don't you understand the urgency of this?"

"Liam," Juniper said and left his name there to hang in the inches between them. Her brown eyes stayed glued to his stormy gray ones as she took him in.

He shifted on his feet.

"I know how serious this is. I know what Conroy can do. We've all watched him destroy our village and take our parents, remember?" The brightness in her eyes dimmed.

Well, this is making me feel loads better about Aubry right now.

"We won't let that happen to Aubry." The promise in her eyes made Liam feel like he could believe her.

"You won't?"

"No. We're going to help you and you're going to help us."

"I am?"

"I saw what you did to the forest." Juniper's gaze pinned him in place. "And what you did to the Sparring Room."

Liam thought back to the day before. He remembered his anger toward Sly in the Sparring Room. Hurting Aubry. He remembered standing in the forest with her, thinking about his mom being gone, and the trees drooping—before the fire burned through the trees. He swallowed another wave of shame and guilt. "Conroy said something about sensing my magic." He pressed his lips together.

Juniper nodded again. "You have magic. And if it's strong enough for Conroy to feel it and come after you and Aubry, then it's powerful. Come to think of it, he probably didn't want to risk kidnapping you if he found he couldn't hold you."

"And how am I supposed to help you?" Liam crossed his arms. He'd dragged Aubry into this, and now she was gone. They just wanted to get home. Would they ever be able to? Would Liam see her again? He shuddered.

"Let me check on something. Stay here." She pinned him with a look and he obeyed as she took a step back, giving Liam space. Her boots thumped on the packed earth as she walked to a bookcase in the corner. Reaching into one of the shelves, she rummaged through what sounded like clinking bottles.

Crossing his arms, Liam stared after her, wondering what she was looking for. After a few seconds, she almost reverently pulled out a dusty bottle with indigo liquid in it. Walking back over to him, she thrust it in front of his chest.

Liam eyed it and then her. "What do you want me to do with this?"

"Drink it." She nudged it closer to him.

"And what is it?" He raised his eyebrows.

"It's a *Witmus* potion. It will confirm if you're a wizard or not. You see, everyone has a spectrum of magical abilities inside them. Some people have so little they never see any traces of it. But it's not out of the ordinary for magical things to happen. Take this hideout for example. People with a particular aptitude can learn minor spells . . . but the big magic, the kind that can turn the tides of war, for better or for worse, that comes from wizards. And they are few and far between. I have a feeling you're a wizard, based on the fact he came for you two, and that you're now standing after just being blasted with Wizard's Fire only hours ago. That stuff puts grown men out for a couple days. If you drink this, it will tell us if you really are a wizard. It's a rare potion because the ingredients are so hard to come by, but I'm willing to use it on you instead of fighting you like Sly did." She rolled her eyes. "Anyway, you want to know, don't you?" Juniper stared at him, challenging.

Of course he wanted to know, and she knew he did. This would confirm what his mom told him on the day he lost her. He was still struggling to believe he had powers. Conroy taking Aubry had convinced him this place was real, but he wasn't sure that he was a wizard like everyone thought. He needed to know.

"Fine." He took the bottle from her, unstopped it, and drank. Going down, it tasted different from the other two potions he'd ingested up to this point. Initially, it tasted like a cold, late night in winter when rain loomed in the distance. And then he tasted smoke, incense, and black tea. Not an unpleasant taste compared to the last potion.

Juniper's eyes widened as she watched him and took a step back, covering her mouth. Following her gaze, he saw his torso glowing the same color the potion had been. As the indigo glow grew, Liam felt power shimmer through his limbs, like something was calling him. Like something dormant was waking up. It felt warm, welcoming, and hopeful. Holding up his hands, he turned them over and saw the indigo hue underneath his skin.

"Woah," he breathed. Astonished, he smiled at Juniper.

She stared back as a smile crept up her face. Then she nodded at him, enthused. "You do have powers. And you are a wizard," she said and pulled him into a hug.

Liam froze. He was hugging her. Or she was hugging him. His breath caught, and he wasn't sure what to do. He'd just met her, but her joy was contagious. He didn't want to make it awkward and just stand there while she hugged him, so he lightly and respectfully hugged her back, forcing himself to breathe and not think about her warm colored skin or how the way she'd raised her eyebrow at him earlier made his anger simmer away into something else he wasn't sure of yet.

"This is amazing! Maybe we have a chance," she mused as she pulled away. "C'mon, we have to join the others and tell them. We'll make a plan. C'mon!" She yanked him outside, grinning.

Liam's heart started pounding with Juniper's hand in his. He felt simultaneously nervous and excited. The way she looked at him over her shoulder with her eager brown eyes and smile sent a shiver down his spine. In that moment, all he could think about was how to make her smile like that again.

CHAPTER TWELVE

———◆◇◆———

"I'm sorry, Liam." Sly's forehead knitted together as he crossed his arms, looking at him. Juniper had left them and rushed out, looking like she needed to do something important.

Liam and Sly stood in the Sparring Room that bore no trace of his chaotic vines. Out of the corner of his eye, he saw one of the last floorboards replace itself and knit back together, returning to its original condition. He remembered what Sly had said about the hideout becoming what the kids needed. Apparently, it repaired itself too.

In the center, instead of a map, the long wooden table held weapons haphazardly laid about like someone had thrown them down in a rush.

"I really am," Sly said, bringing Liam's attention back to him. Refocusing his attention, he saw Sly's eyebrows come together in a sad line. He could almost see the weight of responsibility Sly held in his eyes. Underneath all the joking and sarcasm, Sly carried a heavy burden silently. Liam sighed and figured if they were going to work together, he needed to forgive him. And he guessed he could see where Sly was coming from. He was a stranger from another realm who dropped into their world. Sly needed to protect the Stream Kids and find out who Liam really was.

"Sly, how old are you?" Liam asked.

Sly looked at him suspiciously. "Eighteen. Why?" He mirrored Juniper's defiant stance from Liam's earlier conversation with her.

"It's just . . . you're awfully young to be leading so many kids." Liam took in his tired face. For a moment, it seemed like Sly let Liam see how tired he really was. But then he raised his gaze to meet Liam's, and the walls went back up.

"I'm the oldest one here, besides Roya, and she doesn't want to be a leader." Sly crossed his arms and stared hard at Liam.

His gaze made Liam squirm. "I didn't mean anything by it. It just seems you have a lot going on."

Sly eyed Liam. "You don't look very old yourself. Seems you have a lot going on, too. Guess we have that in common."

Liam nodded as he sat in the reality of Sly's words. He paused, processing the day's events. He'd written himself into this world on the full moon like his mom said he'd be able to. He'd found a way to tap into his powers and hurt his cousin in the process. Apparently, Conroy was trying to absorb as much power as he could by taking life forces from other people, and he'd just kidnapped Aubry for a spell to help him do that. Did Conroy know about his mom? Was he aware she created this world? Is that the power he was after? If so, why not take him? Why Aubry? And what did Sly mean by his earlier comment about his entering Domhania not being coincidental?

"Why do you think I'm here?" Liam studied Sly's expression. Sly didn't flinch or squirm. He had his emotions shielded from his face. It irked Liam.

How is it so easy for him to hide what he's thinking?

Taking a breath, he stared back at Liam with an even expression. "I think you're here because Domhania needs you."

Liam scoffed. "Why would Domhania need *me*?" He just found out he was a wizard, yes. But he knew nothing about his powers and had only hurt people thus far. Juniper seemed to think he could help, but he was doubtful. He was untrained, unknowledgeable. He was much more confident in his medieval swordsmanship than anything remotely associated with magic, and he'd only been doing that for six months.

Sly studied Liam. "Look at the state it's in." Sly waved his arms. "Conroy is destroying villages, taking life forces from more people by the day, and transforming into something darker each time he does. Your mum's the one who created this world. Don't you think that's significant? If you've inherited her magic, you can do something about this. About Conroy. Maybe you can turn things around."

Liam shook his head. "She didn't have as much control as you think. She told me once, 'you can nudge and suggest, but you can't force someone to choose something.' How am I supposed to turn things around? I was supposed to *write* the story. I can't do that from in here."

Sly crossed his arms and leaned back on his heels. "So you're going to give up?"

"No, I will not give up. I'll find Aubry, rescue her from that crazy wizard, then get her out of here." He narrowed his eyes at Sly.

"And what about Domhania?" Sly stared down his nose at Liam.

"What about it? First, my mom tells me about this magical world she created, tells me to finish her last story, then she dies. She told me to take care of Domhania. To not make the same mistakes. What does that even *mean*?" He pushed his hands through his hair, at a loss. "And then, as soon as I get here, I get knocked upside the head and then we get attacked by a fire throwing wizard and almost die! Aubry gets kidnapped!" Liam's face heated with latent anger and exhaustion. He felt anger and power flicker in his hands and he looked down at them, expecting them to be glowing. They looked the same as always. Huffing, he looked up. How was Sly putting all this on him?

Sly's face was calm and pensive. "No one here is a stranger to hard days, mate."

Liam froze, noting the children next door watching him.

Of course not. Liam sighed and the anger simmering in his stomach cooled. This whole time, he hadn't wanted to take on Domhania's problems. Didn't think they were his. And now Aubry was gone. Milo could supposedly help them return home, but now Liam hoped he could help them rescue Aubry, too. And help him figure out these powers. Maybe Liam *could* help in some way? He asked Sly and the Stream Kids to help him rescue his cousin, so shouldn't he return the favor? He was desperate, and it seemed they were too.

He thought back to one of his mom's books where Milo was training a younger wizard. *"If it's within our power to help those around us, we need to rise to that responsibility. Why else would we have been given our powers? Not to uplift ourselves, but to uplift those around us."*

Liam sighed as something shifted in him.

"Listen," Sly started. "I understand what you're feeling."

Did he?

"I understand what it's like to have responsibility thrust on you when you don't feel ready for it. To be responsible for lives you don't know you can protect. It still scares the heck out of me most days." Sly's calm and unmoved expression had given way to vulnerability. "One thing I learned is I'm not alone. And you won't be either." Liam nodded, and Sly squeezed his shoulder.

Boots shuffled in, scraping the wooden floor. Juniper, Johnny, and Fox joined them and quickly walked over to Sly.

"Sly, there's been an attack nearby at Cloverton Village. We just got a message from Duncan. If we're going to leave, we need to go now. They're getting closer to the hideout." Johnny stared at Sly, eyes wide with anxiety.

Liam's heart pounded. "Who are *they*?"

Juniper winced and glanced at Liam but stayed silent.

"*Who are they*?" Liam asked again, more forcefully this time.

Sly puckered his lips and said, "Conroy and his army."

CHAPTER THIRTEEN

L iam leaped toward the doorway. "They've got Aubry. We *need* to rescue her." Sly's forearm met Liam's chest, keeping him from running out of the room.

"Listen mate, you can't just run out there. You won't even know where you're going, let alone what you're doing." Sly's steady voice rubbed on Liam's nerves.

"She's not with them," Juniper said.

Liam's gaze snapped to hers. "What do you mean? How do you know?"

She sighed. "Duncan told us in his message. It's only Conroy and his men. No girl, no one with red hair."

Seeing the empathy in Juniper's eyes doused some of his anger. Uncurling his fists, he exhaled, clenching his teeth together.

"Fine." Liam rolled his eyes to the ceiling and silently asked for patience he didn't have.

Sly nodded once and slowly lowered his forearm from Liam's chest. "Johnny, you and Fox pack up the weapons and food," he ordered. "Juniper, gather what potions we need from Roya, and Liam, come with me." Sly raised his eyebrows at Liam while the others scurried off to carry out their orders. Putting on the demeanor of a general, Sly turned on his heel and swept to the corner of the Weapons Room with the armor. Liam was constantly surprised by how quickly

Sly transitioned from an eighteen-year-old boy enjoying time with friends to a Stream Side Kids leader burdened with responsibility.

It must be exhausting.

"Since we know you can handle a sword, choose one," Sly said, facing the wall of swords. Liam moved to stand beside him.

"Yeah, but I don't think it was my sword that won me the match," Liam said thinking back to his fight with Sly.

A cough sounded behind them and Liam swung to look at Johnny, but his face was neutral as he pulled axes off a wall and strapped them to his back. Liam narrowed his eyes, then turned back around.

"You're getting more interesting by the second, Liam. Sword fighter and now confirmed wizard." Sly looked impressed. One side of his mouth turned up into a smile. He motioned to the wall. "Take your pick."

Liam surveyed the swords on the wall. He found one that resembled one he trained with back home. This sword had a green hilt and swirls around it with gold-colored plating on the end. He reached out and took it from the wall, the metal warming in his hand. Taking a couple practice swings, he tested its balance. It felt perfect. Like it was made for him. Liam stared at the sword, then looked around the room at the hideout.

Is this from you?

Nothing happened. He wasn't sure what he was expecting. Of course, the hideout wasn't going to respond. Inanimate objects didn't do that. Averting his eyes from Sly's perplexed expression, he looked at his chosen sword again. Liam had been inspired by his mom's books to learn sword fighting. Never mind that it was an attempt to impress her, but it was surely coming in handy now.

Knowing what Liam knew now, he wondered if she thought about Domhania every time she wrote. Is this where she'd been coming for years as she was writing? It hadn't occurred to him until now his mom could have walked through these forests too. Liam wondered if she ever interacted with the characters she wrote or if she just stood off to the side and watched their lives play out.

"Oh, that's a good one, mate. Brilliant choice." Sly's comment shook Liam from his thoughts.

"Oh yeah. I like this one." Liam smiled sadly.

"Now let's make sure you're protected." Sly walked over to the corner of the room. Different types of armor decorated the wall. Leather plated, metal, gold, bronze. After a minute, he found a chest plate covered with leather and held it out toward Liam. It was impressively lightweight and soft under his fingers. Sly helped him strap it on and added shoulder and forearm armor as well.

"This is fairy-made. Great artisans. It's a real bugger trying to make a deal with them, though. These will protect you well." Sly clapped Liam's back, then stepped back for a look. "You look like a warrior now."

A warrior. No one had ever called him that before. Were they really going to war? With Conroy and Zadimus and their men? He didn't sign up for this. He didn't know if he really had a choice in the matter anymore. Not with Aubry kidnapped. If that was what it took to get her back, then he'd become a warrior.

Fox hauled over knapsacks loaded with enough food to last a week.

Is this really going to take that long?

Imagining Aubry held captive for an entire week with Conroy made Liam shiver. He had to get to her as soon as possible.

Juniper gently set down two sacks full of potions, salves, and powders. Sly dug through the two bags of weapons Johnny gathered. Liam watched quietly and intently, considering the situation ahead. Using a sword in his club at school was one thing, but arming themselves for war was a different matter. The seriousness of the situation solidified in Liam's stomach like a rock.

Do you really think I'm ready for this, Mom?

Juniper stepped forward and reached for a bow and arrow, strapping it onto her back. Johnny jammed his hand into the bag and pulled out a sheathed sword, which he took with a grunt and stiff nod, adding to the axes already strapped to his back. Fox pulled out throwing stars and tucked them in a leather pouch on his belt. Sly stuck with a sword. Resting his hands on his own sword, Liam looked around at the group and felt equal parts fear and determination take root.

There was something in his bones, an expectancy. Suddenly his mother's cryptic message from her deathbed resonated in his head again. *"Don't get lost. Be stronger than me. Protect the storyworld."* He still wasn't sure what she meant, but he *was* gearing up to protect the storyworld. So much for thinking all he had to do was write the end of a story.

He didn't think he was lost. Although he accepted he might be about to get lost. Be stronger than her. How? He shook his head at the thought of his mom. He sighed and wished yet again she were there to tell him what to do.

Despite her not being alive, her presence lingered in Domhania, as if intentionally marked for him. The way she'd described the forest in her books inspired by their trip to Yosemite, the way the leaves burst with color.

Johnny loudly cleared his throat and stared unamused at Sly, hands lazily resting on the belt at his waist. Fox looked up at Sly with an expectant expression.

"Everyone ready, then?" Sly looked around the circle at their crew and took a breath. "When we're out there, I want everyone to remember we're in this together. We have one another's backs. No matter what. Am I clear?" His intense stare bored through each person.

Everyone mumbled their own type of "yes."

"Good," Sly said. "Let's be on our way, then." Brushing past everyone, he seemed to glide across the floor toward the main door.

Liam felt a sense of gladness as he looked at the dirty Main Hall, now home to many kids he had met, knowing he was fighting for them. A sense of gratitude welled up in him for having landed near the hideout. He didn't want to think about what would have happened if he had been writing about Conroy's castle during the full moon.

He gripped his sword and stepped into the forest.

The sting of the crisp air stirred something in Liam for the journey ahead. Sure, he hadn't intended to end up here, but here he was. Aubry needed him. He wouldn't abandon her. He tensed his jaw, thinking about where she could be in Zadimus's castle. He couldn't bear to think about it. Shaking his head, he cleared the thought.

A chill breeze wound around him as the group waited patiently. Walking over to Sly, Liam nodded.

"Onward, everyone!" Sly shouted into the trees and they made their first steps on their journey to find the wizard in the mountains. Johnny and Fox fell in behind them and Juniper brought up the rear.

After a few moments of just the sound of their boots crunching through the forest, Liam couldn't take the silence. "So how long exactly will it take us to get to Milo's and figure out a way to save Aubry?"

Sly looked sideways at Liam and chewed on his question. "We're hoping not more than a week."

"What?" Liam blurted. This confirmed his fears from earlier. "Aubry's going to be in that castle for a *week*? By herself?" He shoved his hands through his hair and told the helpless feeling threatening to swallow him to go away.

Sly nodded and kept walking. "It'll take a couple of days to get to Milo's castle. From there I'm expecting it to take a couple days to come up with a plan and prepare to rescue Aubry." Sly swallowed. "Then it will take time to enact our plan."

"And remind me again why we aren't going to rescue her now?" Liam stared at Sly, chest heaving with his frustrated breaths. Leaves swirled on the ground around Liam's feet.

Glancing down, Sly cleared his throat. "Because we can't just barge unprepared into the most powerful dark wizard's castle. We don't know the layout, who is guarding what, and even if we could get in, we don't know where they're keeping her. Milo is a wizard himself, so he'll have a better idea and can advise us on how to run a *successful* rescue mission."

Of course. They needed to be strategic and measured, just like Aubry would want them to be. What was with all this anger that suddenly seemed so close to the surface? Was it a side effect of his magic? He needed to get it under control so no one else got hurt.

"And if Milo takes a liking to you, maybe he can help you figure out how to use your powers." Sly looked sideways at Liam as they walked.

They traveled in silence for a while. Liam's thoughts buzzed, jumbling and banging into one another. He tried to focus on the sun warming his face, the smell of pine, the birdsong.

"Sometimes, when things don't go how I think they're supposed to, I remind myself of what has gone right. Of what is true. Of what is good. Maybe that could be helpful for you too?" Fox had matched his stride to Liam's, catching up to him. He delivered his words with an air of wisdom and wonder that fourteen-year-olds sometimes have. Fox's dark eyes searched his, and Liam saw concern and hope.

Gratitude welled in his chest. Even after facing so much tragedy, Fox still held onto hope and shared it with others.

Liam smiled. "Thank you, Fox. I'll try that."

Fox smiled back, hope shining in his eyes.

"I'm sorry about what happened to your parents." The words spilled out of Liam, and he instantly regretted ruining the hopeful moment with memories of loss.

"It's okay. Our parents didn't die the same way everyone else's did," Fox said matter-of-factly.

Liam's eyebrows came together. "What do you mean?"

"They died years before Conroy killed everyone else's parents."

Watching Fox, he didn't see any falter in his step or a drop in his mood. Liam wondered if this contributed to Johnny's cold demeanor. Fox talked like he was having a normal conversation about the trees in the forest or the flora and fauna around them. Clearly, Johnny did not feel the same way Fox did.

"Mum and Dad had gone on a trip to see one of the waterfalls in the area for their anniversary. Apparently, a dragon had wandered closer than it was supposed to and . . ." Fox trailed off.

Liam didn't need him to continue. Both parents at once. While they were supposed to be on a pleasant trip.

"We moved in with our uncle, but—" Fox looked over his shoulder. "He never really did anything for us except remind us how much of an inconvenience we were to him. So Johnny has been taking care of us and providing for us ever since. He'd do odd jobs here and there, trying to get whatever money he could. He thinks I don't know, but—"

"How are you holding up there, Fox?" Johnny grumbled from right behind them, giving his brother a flat stare. Fox's eyes widened, and he glanced away, flushing.

"Fox here teaching you some history, huh?" Johnny's nostrils flared as he stared down Liam.

"Um," Liam started.

I think this is the most he's ever said to me since I got here.

Johnny huffed and moved away from them.

Okayyy. . . Note to self, don't talk to Johnny about his past. Let's think about something good and something true.

"Sly, is that what I think it is?" Juniper said bleakly from the back of the group.

From the front, Sly held up a hand, signaling for them to stop and hide behind the trees lining the path. Straining to see what they were talking about, Liam saw what looked like a type of carnival up ahead. Different colored tents decorated the clearing of trees where people cooked food, danced, and sang.

"What's wrong with that?" Liam looked around at everyone's faces marked with trepidation.

"Fairies," Fox whispered, shifting nervously.

"I thought we were going to avoid them?" Liam said.

"They're out farther than they're supposed to be. Must be getting more confident. Or reckless." Sly pressed his lips together and scanned the area.

"Reckless or confident, is there really much of a difference?" a cool voice asked behind them. Liam turned to find a girl who looked about the same age as Fox, but about the size of Liam's hand, floating in the air, suspended by blue sparkling wings.

Wings. Liam smiled despite the worried looks from the Stream Side Kids. A fairy. He was looking at a fairy right in front of him. Flowers wove themselves through her long pale hair that spilled down her shoulders to her hips. She wore a light grey tunic on top of a blue skirt that floated through the breeze like water. Her blue eyes matched her skirt and sparkled with a look that enticed Liam, making him take a step toward her.

"Stop." Sly's arm swung out in front of Liam's chest, stopping him like a bar of iron. Shaken out of his trance, Liam noticed Johnny's grip on his sword, Fox's hands resting on his pouch of throwing stars, and Juniper's bow now at her side.

"What are you—" Liam gaped at them.

"You can't trust them," Sly said, not taking his eyes off the blue fairy and her pale golden hair.

She cocked her head. "I don't think we're the ones you need to worry about not trusting." Her icy blue eyes cut a look at Johnny. His knuckles whitened on his sword. "Isn't that right, Johnny?" She looked at him like she was getting ready to pounce on her prey. Johnny folded his arms and touched his chin like he was trying to recall something but was coming up empty. He glared at her, nostrils flaring.

"Us fairy folk don't have such flippant memories like you humans do. When someone wrongs another, it is necessary to correct the action. How about we take something of yours like you took something of ours?" One of her golden eyebrows arched as her eyes bore into his. Gracefully, she lifted her arm and flicked her finger, and Fox glided toward her.

"No!" Johnny bellowed, drawing his sword.

Sly gritted his teeth and drew his sword, silver blade gleaming in the sunlight dappling through the trees.

"Ah, ah, ah." She waved her finger. "Don't act so fast. We just want to have a little fun. Come and join us." She raised her hand in the air and Johnny lunged at her with his sword. She snapped her fingers, and she and Fox disappeared, Johnny's strike slashing through air.

CHAPTER FOURTEEN

---•◦•---

"She took him!" Johnny growled. "We have to go in there." He spun around and started toward the fairy camp.

Sly stepped in front of him. "What was she talking about?"

Johnny stood eye to eye with Sly and glared. Johnny was stockier than Sly, but Sly was taller, faster, and more trained.

"Did you steal from the fairies?" Sly asked in a voice that left no room for lies.

"What?" Johnny looked offended.

"Did you steal from the fairies?" Sly bellowed.

A long silence ensued.

"... It was a job, about three years back, before you all knew us. They needed mortal muscle and I fit the bill. Things went a little sideways when the target's defenses were stronger than they realized. When the dust cleared, the other fairies were gone, and I was stuck with the bag of gold. That money fed us for two months." His eyes flitted away from Sly's for a second.

"So you stole someone else's gold?" Sly gaped in disbelief.

"I was just doing a job, and I figured since the fairy leading the raid had expired, my contract had been voided . . . apparently Seraphina didn't agree." Johnny grimaced, annoyed.

Sly let out a breath. "And now here we are." He shook his head.

"I had to provide for my family," Johnny retorted and pushed his chest out to stand up straighter.

"You could have asked for help."

Johnny narrowed his eyes.

"Well, let's go get Fox, then. What are we waiting for?" Liam looked back and forth between them. Slowly, they both turned their heads toward him.

Sly exhaled and squeezed the bridge of his nose. "We must be careful. We need our wits about ourselves. Fairies like to play games and speak in riddles. If we're not clever, they can enchant us and delay us for days on end."

"What do you mean?" Liam flicked his gaze to Juniper's.

"You must remember what is true. What is real." Juniper nodded at Liam.

What is true, and what is real? Here in this storyworld? What was true? What was real?

"Don't eat anything," Sly ordered.

"Don't drink anything," Johnny muttered.

"Just stay with me and you'll be okay." Juniper nodded encouragingly.

For the umpteenth time, Liam wondered what he'd gotten himself into.

"Once we step over this boundary, we're at the mercy of the fairies. You're going to feel like a fog has come over you. Just breathe and keep—"

"My wits about me. Right," Liam finished for Sly, who nodded, staring straight ahead at the fairy camp.

"You wanted to be a hero, right?" Juniper bumped Liam's shoulder and raised an eyebrow at him. "Here's your first chance."

Liam swallowed as he gazed into her challenging brown eyes. He could do this. He had read all his mom's books and remembered the parts with fairies in them. Liam took a deep breath, trying to steady his nerves.

They moved toward the invisible barrier at the border. The air around him felt charged with a crackling energy, and he could sense the faint presence of a fog like Sly had mentioned. The blood in Liam's veins felt like it was vibrating as he stepped closer to the boundary line. Juniper's words echoed in his mind—remember what was true, what was real.

Sly looked at each of them, nodded, then led them forward. As they crossed the invisible threshold into the heart of the fairy camp, Liam felt a strange sensation wash over him. The air felt thick and humid. Faint voices hummed, piquing his curiosity and beckoning him deeper into the forest. The colorful tents and twinkling lights blurred.

A thick mist rose from the ground, enveloping them, clouding Liam's thoughts and senses. He gripped his sword tightly, heart pounding in his chest. Shadows flitted at the edges of his vision, and he fought to push back the disorienting effects of what he assumed must be the fairy magic.

Sly led the way, his sword drawn and head on a swivel. Johnny followed closely behind, jaw set in a grim line. Juniper moved gracefully beside Liam, her bow at the ready, scanning their surroundings.

Seraphina appeared before them, wings shimmering in the dim light like sapphires. She regarded them with an enigmatic smile, eyes glinting with mischief and something darker beneath the surface.

"You've come to play, I see." Seraphina's voice rang like a melody laced with hidden threats. Liam felt a chill run down his spine as she circled them, movements graceful and hypnotic.

"We're not here to play games," Sly stated firmly, grip on his sword unwavering. "We're here for Fox. Release him now."

Seraphina's laughter tinkled, like shards of glass in the air. "Oh, dear mortals, always so serious. Where's the fun in that?" Her gaze settled on Liam, making his heart pound. "You, young one, carry the blood of the ancient ones. The power of your mother flows within you, waiting to be unleashed."

Liam's heart raced at her words, a mix of fear and excitement coursing through him. He glanced at Juniper, who gave him a reassuring nod.

"What do you want from us?" he asked, trying to keep his mind clear amidst the swirling magic. The tents and dancing people he'd seen a second ago came in and out of focus, like they were a mirage.

Seraphina's smile widened, revealing pointed pearly white teeth that glinted in the dim light. "Perhaps you can offer something to me in return for your friend."

Liam felt a surge of defiance.

"What could we possibly offer you?" Sly glared at her.

The fairy's eyes gleamed with hunger. "A trade, of course. A simple exchange of information. Are you willing to pay the price?" She tilted her head.

Sly stepped forward, his voice cold and determined. "We will not bargain with you, fairy. Release Fox now or face the consequences."

Seraphina's laughter echoed through the camp. "Oh, brave mortal, always so quick to threaten. Very well, if you insist on playing this game." She snapped her fingers, and Fox materialized beside her, floating in the air, eyes wide with surprise and confusion.

"Fox!" Johnny cried out. "Are you alright?"

Fox nodded, his expression tense. "I'm fine, no thanks to her." He nodded to Seraphina, who smirked in satisfaction.

"Remember your place, mortal," she purred. "Fox is safe with me for now, but our time together is far from over."

Sly clenched his jaw as he glared at the blue-winged fairy floating around them. "What do you want?"

Seraphina's smile widened as she circled them, wings casting shimmering shadows on the ground. "I want a challenge. An opportunity to test your wits and strength. If you succeed, Fox goes free. If you fail . . ." She let the threat hang in the air, eyes glinting in amusement.

Liam swallowed and looked at Fox's scared face as he hung in the air. He couldn't let Seraphina win, not if it meant risking their lives and the safety of his friends. *His* friends? He'd only just met them, but he felt an urge to protect them. He squared his shoulders and met her gaze, trying to project an air of confidence he didn't entirely feel.

"What kind of challenge?" Sly asked, voice steady.

Seraphina's eyes gleamed with delight. "A test of courage. You must navigate through the Veilwood, a place where reality twists and illusions reign. Find your way to the heart of the forest before sundown, and Fox will be released."

Seraphina's offer hung in the air for a few seconds as Sly considered. He looked side-long at Johnny and glared at him. Johnny quickly looked away.

"We accept your challenge," Sly declared. Sly and Juniper exchanged wary glances, but nodded in silent agreement. Juniper tightened her grip on her bow.

Seraphina clapped her hands together, the sound like a crack of thunder in the still air. "Very well, mortals. The challenge begins now."

With a wave of her hand, the surrounding mist thickened and shifted into a swirling vortex of shadows and light. The ground beneath their feet trembled, and Liam felt himself drawn forward.

He plunged into the twisting mass of magic, his friends close behind him. The world twisted and contorted, reality warping into surreal shapes and colors that made his head spin. The trees became bloated creatures with long, thin fingers that came to needle-like points. Shrubs transformed into hounds with razor-sharp teeth, dark, matted fur, and red eyes. They snapped and growled, then lunged at Liam. He screamed, and they disappeared like mist. Shadows danced at the corners of his vision, bearing resemblance to his family, except each person wasn't quite right. The shadows distorted their features. A drooping mouth, eyebrows crunched together, gashes on their faces. Liam shuddered and tried to look away. Mist rose and whispered taunts and half-truths.

"Your mother never really wanted to be with you."

"What do you think you're doing?"

"You're out of your depth."

"You could never amount to what she wanted you to be."

"Do you really think you're strong enough to save your cousin?"

"You're destined to hurt people."

"Destined to be abandoned."

Liam's breaths came quickly with each taunt. Each struck him, calling out his own doubts. His chest squeezed as he considered each one. Forcing himself to steady his breath, Liam desperately grasped for what he knew to be true, his mother's teachings echoing in his mind like a guiding light in the darkness.

"You can write your way out of anything, Liam."

"Remember, the heroes in the stories didn't think they were strong enough either, and look at all they accomplished."

He focused on each step, each breath, as they navigated the shifting landscape of the Veilwood. Blinking to clear the warping images around him, he searched for his friends. Reaching out, he found an arm. Juniper. She grasped him back.

She had a pained expression on her face, like she had experienced her own distortions. She swallowed, tried to force a smile, and nodded at him to keep going. The rest of the group led the way ahead of them.

Time seemed to bend and stretch, the minutes feeling like hours as they pressed forward, determined to reach the heart of the forest before sundown. Though it was midmorning when they came upon the fairy camp, darkness descended on the wood, sending a chill through the air.

Time must be different here. Liam looked around, searching for the sunlight he'd seen moments ago. The images of dark trees with spindly hands and gaping mouths twisted and shifted, giving way to a glimpse of sunlight for a moment before the darkness of the forest swallowed it up again.

He breathed a sigh of relief. The sunlight was still there. He knew that was true. That was real. He realized the fairy magic messed with his mind, changing what he perceived unless he concentrated on seeing through the fog of false images.

"We need to keep moving towards the thickest part of the forest. That's the centre," Johnny said, eyes trained forward, axes gripped in both hands.

As they ventured deeper into the twisting maze of illusions, whispers filled the air, words indistinct. They made Liam's skin crawl. Though he couldn't make out what they were saying, the whispers left him feeling hollow and helpless. Shadows darted around them, taking on twisted forms of different creatures, from serpents to deformed woodland creatures to wyverns that seemed to swoop down on them and blow fire. Juniper screamed. Sly turned, his sword drawn. Johnny lashed out with an axe, and it passed through the wyvern.

This isn't real. The wyvern isn't really here. Liam's breath heaved. He shook his head to try and clear the images. He reminded himself where he was, what time of day it was, and what their goal was.

Suddenly, a figure materialized in their path, its form shifting and changing with each step it took. Its eyes gleamed like hot coals its voice dripped with venomous sweetness.

"Welcome, brave travelers, to the heart of the Veilwood," the creature hissed, its voice echoing through the twisted trees that loomed overhead. "I am the Guardian of Shadows, and only those who prove themselves worthy may pass."

Liam's mouth went dry as he sucked in breaths, trying to focus on the Guardian of Shadows, its dark, shadowy form flickering like a dying flame in the darkness. He felt his fear crackle through him, waking up his powers. Blue sparks spurted from his palms. He willed himself to be calm. He couldn't let his mom down now. "What must we do to prove our worth?" he asked, voice steady despite the rising tide of fear within him.

The Guardian's eyes gleamed malevolence as it spoke. "You must each face your deepest fears and confront the shadows that lurk within your own hearts. Only then will you be granted passage through the cursed forest. Refuse to confront them, and your little friend becomes one of Seraphina's pets."

Johnny clenched his jaw and stepped forward. "We accept your challenge, Guardian."

"Very well," the Guardian hissed, its form pulsing with dark shadows. "Let the trials begin." With a wave of its shadowy hand, a breeze swept up, clearing the air of fog to reveal a path in front of them. Liam's heart pounded with a mixture of apprehension and persistence. To emerge victorious, they would have to confront their innermost fears head-on. He wasn't entirely sure what that meant, but it was too late to turn back now. And they couldn't abandon Fox.

Johnny stepped up to Liam and put a hand on his shoulder, and leaned close to his ear so he could hear over the whoosh of the changing forest. "The fairies take your darkest memories and twist them into futures you fear," he explained.

Liam looked at Johnny, who nodded once and dropped his hand.

Johnny stepped up to the path surrounded on either side by thorns reaching up from the ground. An image materialized in front of him.

A young Johnny and Fox stood alone at their parents' gravesite. Fox had tears running down his face and Johnny had his arm around his brother, face set in a grief-stricken expression.

From there, it morphed into Fox and Johnny in a small stone house, a measly fire burning in the fireplace.

A tall, full man lumbered into the room.

"What are you boys still doing here? I told you I didn't want to see your faces today." The grown man looked related to Johnny and Fox, his shiny black hair standing out against his forehead in the firelight.

"We were just heading to bed, uncle. We'll get out of your way," Fox submissively answered.

"Leave it to my sister to dump you two useless brats on me." Their uncle glared at them.

Young Johnny's hand curled into a fist, but he clenched his jaw and stayed quiet as he ushered Fox into another room.

The image changed into Johnny's cloaked figure sneaking out the window from their room and heading through the forest into town. The darkness of night wrapped around him, concealing him as he moved into the center of town.

His eyes darted around him anxiously, but he walked with purpose to a dark alley behind the pub.

"You bring me what I asked for?" a scratchy voice asked from the shadows as rain started to fall.

Johnny made his way to the voice and produced a sack, extending his arm. The man in the shadows snatched it. He fumbled with it for a couple seconds, then smiled greedily at the contents inside.

"Knew you were a good pick." The scratchy voiced man grinned at Johnny, who looked ready to bolt.

"And my compensation?" Johnny asked, making himself stand taller.

"Yeah, yeah. Here you go, kid." The man lobbed a brown sack at Johnny.

Johnny caught it and looked inside. "This is less than half of what we agreed on." He narrowed his eyes.

"You complaining, kid?" The man stepped into the moonlight, a knife glinting in his hand.

Johnny shook his head and stepped back.

"Good. Now get!" He spat.

Johnny wiped his face and walked away.

"Did that really happen?" Liam whispered to Juniper on his right.

Juniper stared at the image. "Fox told me things were bad when they were growing up, but I didn't know it was this bad." Concern creased her forehead.

The image wavered again and twisted into a scene where Fox was lying in bed, sick and dying, Johnny at his side.

"Told you he wouldn't last." Their uncle crossed his arms from the doorway.

Slowly, illusion Johnny took a breath, forcefully wiped his tears, and stood to face his uncle. He'd grown since his first memory and now towered over his uncle by at least four inches.

"Get out of here! Get out now! I don't want to see you in this room again!" Johnny shook with anger as he bellowed at his uncle, who looked at him, stunned. After a beat, his uncle opened his mouth as if he wanted to yell back but then backed slowly out of the room in silence. Johnny slammed the door, then walked back to Fox and cried over his body.

The illusion twisted and shifted again, showing Johnny older than he was now, standing at Fox's headstone alone.

Current Johnny curled his fists and shook. "No. No! That will not happen. I won't let you get in my head!" Johnny yelled to the image. He took a step through the illusion, and it started to waver and dissipate like mist in the wind. Johnny stilled, his shoulders rising and falling rapidly. Continuing forward, Johnny emerged on the other side of the path, his shoulders squared and his gaze steady. He looked back at Sly, Juniper, and Liam with a scowl that told them even though they all knew his story now, it wasn't an invitation to talk about it.

The Guardian of the Shadows' dark form flickered into view a few feet from Johnny. His ash-colored face looked displeased. Turning his head, his dark lifeless eyes traveled to Sly, and he motioned for him to step up to the path next.

Liam took a shallow breath and looked at Juniper and Sly.

Sly stepped forward next and rolled his shoulders, readying himself. A light mist formed, then swirled into an image.

Sly was setting the table in what appeared to be his home. Two adults swept in the door and gave him a big hug.

"How was your trip?" Sly asked them.

"It went well. We have something for you," the man said. He was tall and long-faced like Sly.

"Are those your parents?" Liam asked Juniper.

She nodded silently.

Liam looked sideways at her, noticing her eyes get shinier. He turned his head back toward Sly to give her some privacy.

The woman who looked like Juniper with her coiled brown hair and bright eyes reached into her cloak and brought out an oval shaped pendant with a sapphire set in the middle of it. She held it out to Sly by a silver chain.

"What is it?" Sly looked at his parents, then to the pendant.

The woman, Sly's mom, smiled. "It's a very special pendant that I need you to keep safe. I trust you can do that?"

Younger Sly nodded eagerly. His mom smiled, then moved to secure it around his neck.

"Mum, Dad, you're back!" Juniper came in from the hallway and squeezed each of her parents like she hadn't seen them in a while. "I missed you."

"We missed you too, sweetheart." Their dad smiled and hugged her tightly back.

The four of them sat down at the table together, to talk about their parents' most recent journey.

The scene drifted away like a breeze pushed it through the air. In its place a dark image came together.

Sly kneeled on the ground in front of Conroy, who stood triumphantly, clutching the pendant in his hand. They were in a village that had been burned around them. People ran, trying to escape the fire and the men chasing them.

"You couldn't stop me then. You think you can stop me now? You thought you could save all of them and spare their lives?" Conroy cocked his head and stared pityingly at Sly. "How adorable. Instead, you're the reason they will all burn. Your failed leadership has led to this. And now, you'll watch the results of your failure. I think we'll start with someone you know."

Sly made to stand, but two guards held him down. He fought against them, but they were stronger, and tied his hands behind his back. Two more guards moved into the image, dragging Juniper with them. They shoved her to the ground, her hands tied in front of her, face bloody and bruised.

"Not my sister! Take me instead! Please!" Sly pleaded, struggling in anguish to get up.

"Begging." Conroy tsked and looked down his nose at Sly. "The great Sly, Leader of the Stream Side Kids begging. Never thought I'd see the day, but it's much too late for that now." Conroy took a breath, smiled, and turned on his heel toward Juniper, a bright blast of magic consuming her.

"No!" Sly's raw scream rang through the air. The real Sly let out a yell at the same time as the illusion.

"Sly, I'm here! You're here! This isn't real!" Juniper yelled.

The Guardian of the Shadows' laugh echoed through the dark forest.

He's enjoying this. How sick.

Sly closed his eyes, shook his head, and opened them again. He stood tall, chest heaving, and looked back to his sister safely at the beginning of the path. He nodded, sweat dripping down his forehead. With a fierce determination burning in his eyes, he stepped forward, weakening the hold of the illusion until it shattered like glass around him. He joined Johnny on the other side. They nodded at one another, then toward Liam and Juniper.

"Remember, Liam." Juniper turned to him.

"Remember what is true?" Liam finished for her.

She let out a breath and nodded solemnly. "Yes." She grabbed one of his shoulders and stared into his eyes. "See you on the other side." She squeezed, then her hand fell away. Liam instantly missed it.

Juniper stepped up next, hands trembling slightly at the illusion that awaited her.

The same scene that played for Sly materialized for Juniper, but from her perspective. Younger Juniper walked out from the hallway to greet her parents. She watched her mom tell Sly about the pendant and how he needed to keep it safe.

As she watched, an icy voice whispered, "They didn't trust you. They forgot about you."

Liam watched Juniper intently and saw her tense her jaw. The image swirled into a memory from what looked like the Stream Side Kids hideout.

A select group met in the main hall. Juniper stood to speak up.

"Oh Juniper, sorry I forgot you were there," the blond-haired boy who was leading the meeting stared at her, blinking.

The unfriendly voices came back and whispered, "See, this is just the beginning."

Images twisted and swirled, then created a future based on Juniper's fear.

Sly, Johnny, Fox, and several other Stream Side Kids gathered around a long table in the main hall, chatting after a recent mission.

Juniper sat away from them by herself. No one paid her any attention.

"Great mission, Sly." Someone clapped him on the shoulder and plopped down next to him at the table.

"Really couldn't have done it without you," Johnny mused.

"You're the only leader we'd ever want." Fox beamed at Sly.

The Juniper in the illusion slid down the bench closer to the group. "Tell me about this mission, Sly." Juniper looked at her brother expectantly.

Sly slowly turned to look at her, gave her a once over, then looked away. The rest of the group followed suit.

"Do you want me to ask Cook to make some celebratory cake?" Fox asked after a moment of awkward silence.

"That would be delightful, Fox. Thank you." Sly smiled at him.

"Sly, did you hear me?" Juniper sharpened her tone.

He looked at her blankly. "I'm sorry, remind me of your name again? I'm not one for forgetting, but today it seems I have." Sly inclined his head apologetically.

Juniper stared at him, stunned. "Juniper," she whispered.

"Right," Sly smiled suavely at her. "Glad to have you with us, Juniper." He reached out to shake her hand.

Juniper stared down at it, swallowed, and shook it.

Liam watched the scene in disbelief. He couldn't imagine Juniper being forgotten. Even in the short time he'd known her, she'd made a significant impact in his life. Without her, he wouldn't know he was a wizard. His chest ached at the thought of her feeling alone and forgotten. He longed to step forward and comfort her.

The icy voices swirled in the air around Juniper. "You are insignificant. Nothing. Not to be remembered. You make no difference in the world around you."

Tears spilled over Juniper's cheeks, and she clenched her hands into fists at her sides. She closed her eyes, her breath hitching. Liam willed her to remember the words she had just spoken to him.

"Remember what's real, Juniper!" Liam couldn't help himself from calling out to her.

With her eyes still closed, she took a breath, opened them, and squared her shoulders to face her fears. The illusion flickered, its hold over her weakening with each passing moment until it dissipated into nothingness. Juniper walked forward and hugged Sly.

Johnny, Sly, and Juniper stood at the end of the path, looking back at Liam. Finally, it was his turn.

CHAPTER FIFTEEN

—◆—

T he Guardian of the Shadows swung his head toward Liam, a twisted smile creeping up his gray face. Everything around Liam darkened, and one of his memories unfolded before him.

His fifteen-year-old self and his mom stood shoulder to shoulder in front of a table with pieces of books around them. Their first book binding class.

"Here Liam, let me help you," his mom said. She could see he was getting frustrated. Her nimble fingers threaded the spine, and she showed him the technique to use. Those days her smile was wider, the light in her eyes brighter.

"There you go. Now you try." His mom handed the book back. He mimicked his mom's motions and made messy stitches.

"Books are amazing, aren't they?" she asked him with a far-off look. "They're an adventure and a portal to find yourself. You can be anyone you want, do anything you want." She flicked her gaze over to Liam.

"What would you be Liam?" she touched his cheek tenderly. He scrunched his eyebrows together, pondering his answer. He never got to tell her that day.

Her hand dropped from his cheek to his hand, her grasp tightening. She wobbled and slowly sunk to the floor.

"Mom?" Liam yelled. "Mom!" He shook her, but her eyes rolled back into her head. From there scenes blurred together. Other people in the class jumped into action. The image swirled to Liam riding to the hospital in the ambulance with her. Liam's dad holding him, telling him everything would be okay, tears spilling down his face. Doctors telling them she had a brain tumor. Then the last memory he had of her, slipping back into the pillows on her bed while he and his dad said their last goodbyes.

The memories faded and a figure of his mother materialized in front of him.

She stood tall, strong, and healthy. Her cheeks were rosy with life, hair glossy and chestnut brown. She smiled at Liam, her kind eyes filled with love and understanding. She held out her arms, happy to see him.

The image was so lifelike, it took Liam's breath away. He wanted to stare at this image of her forever. He wanted to be next to her. To soak in her features so he wouldn't forget them. Liam moved forward, and her smile turned into a scowl. She looked him up and down and disappointment flooded her features.

"What have you done, Liam? I asked you to take care of this world and look at what it's become. Death and destruction. How could I have thought you were up to this task? I told you to be stronger than me. I was wrong about you. You really aren't ready for this." His mom shook her head and backed away.

"Mom," Liam said, shame settling in his chest. He felt a surge of emotion threatening to overwhelm him. He tightened his jaw. He would not get emotional. He tried to withdraw from the feelings that threatened to overcome him and felt his arms tremble. No matter how strongly he wanted to hide his pain, he couldn't stop the eruption of grief that pulled at him. All at once, tears pricked his eyes, and once they broke through, he had no strength to stop it.

Through the blur of tears, he could see an orange glow emanating from his hands. All he could hear was his own heartbeat and the heavy breathing coming through his mouth.

He didn't hear the screams of his new friends as they took cover. He didn't hear the sharp crack of fire that had begun in his palms and exploded out from him, the flames shooting in all directions. All he saw was his mother, suddenly backlit by the same orange glow he noticed in his hands. Agony spread through his chest, down his arms, and blasted out from his palms. He couldn't control it. It was too much for him. His power felt like a live wire, and he was powerless to stop it. Liam heard a scream and felt his throat go raw. It was coming from him. His mother's image faded away and the flames flourished around him. But he didn't stop. It felt good to let go; it felt good to have no restrictions; it felt good to let it all burn.

But as he did, the fear, pain, and sorrow seemed to harden, like a heavy cloak pulling him underwater. It felt like his chest was burning.

"Mom," Liam whispered raggedly, longing to see her image again.

Flames blasted from him, licking up the dried leaves on the ground and devouring the trees. Everywhere Liam looked, he saw fire. Felt anger. Pain. Grief. Chaos.

"Enough!" bellowed the Guardian of the Shadows. His grating voice cut through to Liam.

"Boy with the blood of the ancient ones, stop this now or you'll destroy the entire forest!" hissed Seraphina, her voice devoid of mockery for the first time.

"Remember what is true, Liam!" Juniper's voice rang out above the roar of power in his ears.

What is true. What is true?

"Be stronger than I was," his mother's voice whispered in his ear. Latching onto her words, he gave a final yell and fell to his hands and knees, spent.

Gripping the charred leaves on the ground, he forced himself to breathe. He was with his friends. In Domhania. A world his mom created. He was in a forest. Clenching his jaw, he focused on his breathing, forcing it to slow.

In and out. In and out.

With each inhale, he tried not to focus on the smell of ash and burnt forest. Tried not to think about what he'd done. Why he hadn't wanted to stop.

In and out.

Breathe.

"Liam?"

He stayed on all fours and looked to his left to see Juniper's face.

"You're okay. We're here with you. Remember where you are." Her pleading eyes grounded him. Calmed him. The color of his favorite cup of tea.

She brought her hand to his back, and he froze. Warmth and reassurance radiated from her touch. It anchored him, bringing him back to himself.

Juniper smiled at him. "See, you're okay."

He nodded, entranced by her eyes.

"Be gone, Guardian. I'm no longer in need of your services." Seraphina waved her hand. Its form flickered and wavered, fading like a wisp of smoke in the wind. With a bitter laugh, the Guardian vanished into the shadows, leaving them standing in the clearing of ashes at the heart of the Veilwood.

Finally, Liam looked around and saw he'd scorched the forest. For about thirty feet in every direction, leaves, logs, and trees smoldered and crackled. He looked down at his hands, black with soot. Sitting back on his feet, he sagged with the weight of what he'd done.

"The ancient power in you is stronger than you know, Liam." Seraphina examined him from a safe distance. "Take your Fox and leave this place now before I decide to punish you for burning our home." She glared at Liam, her slight fairy face cold with disdain.

With a snap of her fingers, Fox appeared out of thin air and landed unsteadily on his feet. At the sight of him, Johnny hurried over and hugged him. Fox's shorter and thinner arms wrapped around him.

"Yes, yes, displays of affection later. Leaving now." Seraphina's tone hardened. She pointed to a pathway that materialized to lead them out of forest.

"Let's go, everyone." Sly motioned with his head. Liam wearily stood up, dazed by the sudden rush of power he'd just experienced. Juniper held out her hands to steady him. Sly lead them out of the forest, down the path Seraphina pointed to. Squinting, Liam could see a spot of light at the end.

Daring a look back at Seraphina, Liam took in her chilling pursed lips and cutting ice-blue eyes framed by long, golden hair.

"We will meet again, Liam." She said it like it left a foul taste in her mouth.

Taking a breath, he looked away and sincerely hoped he wouldn't see her again.

Their group walked in silence, following Sly on the path and into a clearing bathed in the warm glow of the setting sun. As they approached the clearing, the air seemed to still, the oppressive weight of the forest lifting off Liam's shoulders. He felt lighter with each step.

Sly came to a stop once they were several feet from Veilwood and safely in the sun-bathed meadow. His eyes trailed over each of them. Liam exchanged grateful smiles with everyone. No one mentioned Liam's fiery destruction, but it couldn't mean anything good. Anxiety tightened his chest.

He looked down at his hands, feeling a connection to something ancient and powerful stirring within him. As they stood on the edge of the Veilwood, a voice echoed in Liam's mind, a whisper of guidance from his mother. *"You have only just begun to unlock your true potential, my son. Embrace the powers within you and let them guide you on your journey."*

Embrace the powers within him? How could he do that when they exploded out of him and scorched everything in a thirty-foot radius? His powers up to this point, had been purely destructive and harmful. How could he embrace that?

"Our journey is far from over," Sly said. "There are more challenges ahead, I'm sure, but we'll face them together."

Liam saw his friends nod in agreement, their eyes shining with a shared sense of determination and camaraderie.

Their support left Liam ashamed. He didn't deserve it.

"That detour forced us to travel through the old Stream Side Village," Sly said as he rested his gaze on each person for a moment.

Johnny stiffened. Fox stared at Sly, eyes widening. Juniper pressed her lips into a line.

"I know it's been two years since we've been back, but it's our only to get to Milo's castle." Sly's voice held a confidence Liam didn't see in the others. "And I think we can all agree that finding Milo and allowing Liam to master his powers would be the best course of action."

Guilt bubbled in Liam's stomach and he looked down at his soot-covered hands again, the image of the scorched forest flashing in his mind. He swallowed, and balled his hands into fists so he didn't have to look at them.

"Let's move out." Sly nodded and lead the way to the village they had once called home.

CHAPTER SIXTEEN

———◆O◆———

"**H**ere it is," Juniper said from the back of the group. Liam startled and sucked in his breath.

He wasn't sure what he expected, but as the village came into view, horror crept its way through his body. They'd made it to the main road of Stream Side village, where houses lined both sides. Charred remains replaced the homes that should have been there. The fire left only outlines where buildings once stood. Others still stood, their walls blackened and mostly burnt away, like skeletons of a former life.

Looking at the leftover char on his hands, Liam swallowed his guilt. He and Conroy were more similar than he'd realized. If Conroy got lost, he could too. He shook his head and kept going.

As he looked down the street at the rows of charred houses on either side, he saw a glimpse into the pain and destruction Conroy had caused: houses that once held happy families, lives burned away, leaving nothing but pieces of memories. He scanned the lots, seeing half standing living rooms, leftover heirlooms, and bedrooms. Only part of the stories, part of the lives that once filled these homes.

As Liam walked, his boots sent ash swirling in the gentle wind. It scratched at his throat, dried out his mouth, and stung his eyes. "It looks like this just happened yesterday," Liam said. Nature hadn't overtaken the fallen homes, contrary to Liam's expectations for a village deserted two years ago.

"Wizard's Fire," Juniper explained hoarsely. "And Conroy used his power to suck the life force from the land. So, nothing can grow."

Dread dropped like a stone in Liam's stomach. It was like a permanent reminder of what Conroy had done. All the lives he'd taken. Was that his intention? The hairs on Liam's neck stood up.

Juniper struggled to catch her breath. Johnny's became shallow. Fox walked stoically. Sly's eyes scanned from house to house like he was looking for something.

They walked in silence, their boots kicking up parched ground and ash.

Finally, Sly stopped and looked at a house on the left. Stone steps led to the bottom half of a charred blue door, the top looked like it had been blasted away. Shattered windows framed the doorway. The burned roof caved in. Liam swore he saw the walls shudder in the breeze, like they were barely standing. Sly froze in front of the dilapidated house, struggling to steady his breathing.

Juniper walked up next to Sly, grabbed his arm, and squeezed. "We can do this," she whispered. "We *have* to do this." She looked up at him with watery eyes.

He stared straight ahead and nodded ever so slightly. He took the lead and went up the stone steps, following them to the door. Sly reached out for the blackened handle. Nudging it, the half door swung open easily. Sly stepped inside and Juniper followed.

They moved into the house and disappeared from view. Liam didn't move. Johnny and Fox stayed where they were, frozen, silent.

After several seconds, Liam couldn't take it and his curiosity got the best of him. He walked up the stone path.

He wanted to be there with them, so they didn't have to be alone. He wished someone had been there when his mom was telling him her secrets, so he didn't have to bear the burden by himself.

Hesitantly, he walked into the house, stepping on ashes and burned wood, and shuddered. It looked worse on the inside. Liam looked into Sly and Juniper's past life, which Conroy had destroyed. The extent of the pain he'd inflicted and continued to boiled Liam's blood. Resentment flared in him and he felt heat in his palms. He widened his eyes as he looked at his hands, and took a careful breath.

Conroy wasn't here. He was here with his friends. Now was not the time to have an outburst.

Inhale, exhale.

The warmth dissipated from his hands, and Liam sighed.

Taking a moment to look around, he saw a little hearth with some blackened chairs and an antique loveseat.

Juniper brought her hand up to her mouth shakily. Sly looked around and grabbed his sister's shoulder. Liam stood silently behind them, not knowing what to do, but not wanting to leave them alone. A minute passed, then Juniper reached up to Sly's hand on her shoulder, grabbed it and said, "Are you sure you want to keep looking?"

Liam thought he should say something, but the words caught in his throat. So he watched. Watched as Sly and Juniper gingerly stepped through their burned house and poked through the rubble. He watched them disappear around the corner and felt stuck, not sure if he should give them space or follow. He chewed the inside of his cheek, then followed. Rounding a corner, he walked down the hallway and found them in a bedroom off the kitchen and living area. They stood there for a moment, just looking. Sly moved to touch the burned bedpost.

"This is where she told me more about it." Sly's dark hand came up to his chest and rested on something hidden beneath his shirt.

"Told you more about what?" Liam asked, unable to stamp down his curiosity.

Sly's head snapped over to him. "Her pendant." Sly fished it from underneath his linen shirt.

Liam stared at it, stunned.

Sly held a silver pendant with a blue gemstone in the middle, hanging on a sliver chain around his neck. The same pendant Liam's mom had sketched again and again since he was a boy. The same pendant she made him memorize. The same pendant from Sly's memories in the Veilwood Forest. The same pendant drawn on a paper clipped to the front of his mom's writing journal. The *journal* that had brought Liam into Domhania.

"How did you get that?" Liam trained his eyes on the pendant and moved closer to Sly, hand outstretched. His mind whirred.

The pendant I memorized my whole life is real. What does this mean?

"My mother gave it to me. She warned we couldn't let it end up in the wrong hands. The hands of someone evil, or death would consume the land." Sly looked back and forth between the pendant and Liam.

"What does that mean?" Liam asked.

"I have an idea, but I'm not certain." Sly bit his lip. "She trusted me with this and I —" Johnny and Fox ran into the room, breathless.

"They're coming!" Fox's voice wobbled in fear.

"What? Who?" Juniper asked.

"Conroy and his men. It's them," Johnny said, voice shaky.

"Why are they here?" Juniper's face fell.

Sly looked at them. "Liam's power? Conroy must have felt something. He must have been watching. Waiting. Are you guys ready for this?"

No! Liam wanted to say.

Juniper stood up. "Let them come." She drew an arrow and placed it in her bow.

The sapphire gem glinted in the dim lighting as Sly hid it underneath his shirt. "Everyone get ready. We don't know how this is going to go." As he spoke, the far wall trembled.

Liam stared hesitantly at the wall. He grabbed the hilt of his sword to steady his hand. His heart pounded in his chest. Conroy was back. The memory of the fire consuming him filled his mind followed by Aubry's screams. He closed his eyes and willed the images away.

"Let's go! We need to get out of this house so they don't pin us down," Sly ordered and led them out of the small room. All nostalgia vanished from his face. He wore his leader hat now.

"I don't know if we have time for that!" Johnny warned.

Sly leaped over a pile of burned wood to lead them out the front door. He paused and leaned against the remaining wall around the doorway to the house. Juniper followed, and the others fell in line. Liam crouched behind the blackened antique loveseat.

Crouched, Liam hoped no one saw as he tried to steady his breathing. He didn't think hyperventilating would be helpful at a moment like this. His ears started ringing.

No. No. Get it together. With his gaze fixed on the floor, he counted the burn marks. He listened for birds singing but heard none. He anchored his rapid breaths to Fox's steady breathing beside him. *In and out.* The pattern eased the weight on his chest, but the ringing persisted. He squeezed his eyes shut, willing his hands to stop shaking.

Not here, not now.

He felt a gentle, reassuring pressure on his shoulder. He latched onto the realness of it and the ringing in his ears faded.

Focus on what's real. Breathe in, breathe out. Liam exhaled and looked up to see Fox's steady eyes on him, nodding. Liam nodded back and swallowed.

From his position, Liam watched Sly peek out the windows. "They're surrounding the house, but there's a break in the guards to the left. Juniper, you and I are going to go right and distract them while the rest of you go left and find cover in the trees," Sly instructed.

"Sounds good to me." Juniper gritted her teeth and adjusted her grip on her bow and arrow.

"Johnny, you lead the others," Sly said. "Now." He and Juniper silently moved out the door to the right in their crouched positions.

Johnny motioned for the rest of them to follow him out and to the left. Liam took his sword from his belt and held it in front of himself. Following close on Johnny's heels, they moved along the side of the house until they got to the end of the row. Johnny held up his hand for them to stop. Soot rose with their steps and burned Liam's lungs. He held in a cough.

Shoop!

A knife landed to the right of Liam's head and stuck into the wall. He stared wide-eyed at it.

"Get down!" Johnny yelled. They crouched low to the ground and ran for the trees. "Don't run in a straight line!" Heeding his directions, Liam lunged and sprinted in a zig-zag pattern. Fire burned past him and hit a nearby tree. His heart pounded as he sprinted behind Johnny and Fox. Johnny ushered them behind a giant tree at the edge of the forest. Fox soundlessly took cover. Liam slid in behind the tree, breathless, and bent over to catch his breath.

"Are they still coming?" Fox looked worriedly at his brother.

Peeking out, Johnny quickly drew his head back as a fireball flew past, barely missing his head. "Yup, definitely still coming!"

"Hey! Firehead! What are you doing over there when I'm all the way over here?" Sly's voice came from in front of the tree.

The fireballs stopped.

Liam peeked from behind the tree to watch.

Conroy slowly turned to face Sly. The Dark Wizard's face gleamed with sweat. Dark hair plastered to his head, he remained dressed in black, the same as when Liam last saw him. When he'd kidnapped Aubry. Anger flared in Liam. Conroy's men wore similar dark clothes and armor. Conroy's gaze slid to Sly and fire blazed in his hands as he twisted them by his sides.

"I thought I was putting up a pretty good fight. You knackered?" Sly said.

Liam gritted his teeth as Sly taunted Conroy, remembering the Wizard's Fire.

"Tired?" Conroy's nasty smile rose on his face.

"A man of your age *must* be knackered."

Conroy scoffed. "How old do you think I am?"

Liam figured he was in his twenties.

"Mmm . . . at least forty, I would guess."

Conroy lobbed a fireball at Sly leapt out of the way into a roll. He shot back to his feet, and an arrow sailed through the air and lodged into Conroy's shoulder at the seam of his black leather armor.

Conroy yelled. His head snapped to where the arrow had come from, up in a tree, and he launched a fireball at it. Juniper's scream rang out as the fire licked the bark and rushed up the tree. Liam's breath caught as he watched her quickly jump from branch to branch, Conroy shooting fire at her as she descended.

Sly ran full speed at Conroy and tackled him to the ground. Sly rained punches down on Conroy over and over. One of Conroy's men ran forward and ripped Sly off him, slamming Sly to the ground.

"Stay here!" Johnny commanded with a hard look. Drawing his axes, he ran to help Sly, who had rolled onto all fours and attempted to stand. One henchman helped Conroy up as Johnny approached.

Liam saw another of Conroy's minions to his left, trying to sneak up on them. The fear in his chest raged with every step the man took, and he couldn't help but want the man far away from him. He closed his eyes as the fear took over. Wind whipped through his hair and he heard a yell.

Opening his eyes, Liam saw the man fly backward. The strong wind whipped through Liam's clothes and hair, ripping the henchman off his feet and sending him flying ten feet away.

Woah. Liam looked at his hands in disbelief. *Was that me?*

Fox stared at him openmouthed, then motioned for him to follow as he ran behind a tree closer to the action.

Conroy stood face to face with Johnny and Sly. It was two on two.

"You know why I'm here. Let's just cut the niceties and get to it, why don't we?" Conroy stepped forward and eyed the blue pendant shining in the sun. Sly stepped back and Johnny stepped in front of him.

"You'll have to go through me first." Johnny held up his axes, one in each hand.

Conroy raised his eyebrows. "That shouldn't be a problem." He lifted his arm, and another arrow sailed through the sky and into his forearm. Conroy growled in pain and cradled his arm. "Someone needs to take care of that girl!"

"With pleasure!" Another one of Conroy's henchmen turned to run to where Juniper stood, and she sent another arrow through the sky. It landed in the man's abdomen. The tail end of the arrow sticking out of the man's stomach smoked, slowly engulfing Conroy and his remaining men. Sly grabbed Johnny and ran toward his sister. The two of them met up with her and sprinted into the cover of the forest, joining Liam and Fox.

Liam saw the arrow's smoke engulf the two men, reminiscent of Juniper's failed attempt to overpower Conroy at the Stream Side Kids' hideout. Again, with a flick of his wrist, the smoke disappeared.

Liam looked over at Fox, whose eyes widened with fear. "Let's go!" They ran through the forest, twigs cracking under their boots. The footsteps behind them grew louder the deeper they ran into the forest.

"If you won't give it to me, I'll just take it from you." Conroy's voice boomed around them. Dark shadows exploded and slithered toward Sly and Johnny. They slashed at them with their weapons, to no avail. It curled up and around their legs like it had Aubry's.

Liam's stomach dropped. *No!* He would not watch the same thing happen again. Quickly, the shadows coiled around their torsos and looped their necks. Sly and Johnny's hands flew to their necks to pry the shadows away, but they couldn't get a grip on them. They gasped for air as Conroy stepped toward Sly, his eyes on the pendant.

Narrowing his gaze on Conroy, Liam felt anger and hatred boil up for the man who'd killed so many, kidnapped his cousin, wounded him, and now threatened to kill his friends.

If his power had come out through his anger before, maybe he could use it now. Recalling how he'd felt in the Sparring Room at the Stream Side Kids' hideout and in the forest at Veilwood, Liam let his anger flare, directing it at Conroy.

The ground trembled and Conroy stumbled, looked around, then settled his gaze on Liam. He used his anger, and vines shot from the ground, wrapping around Conroy. First one foot, then the other. Instead of fear, Liam saw amusement in his eyes.

The jerk. He's enjoying this.

"Very good little, Liam. Show me what you've got."

He would not let Conroy make a game out of hurting his friends. Out of taking their families. Sly and Johnny gasped for air. His vines had done nothing to distract Conroy.

Liam gritted his teeth and dug deeper into himself for his powers. He tapped into the buzz he felt moving toward the surface of his skin. It felt raw and unbridled. Using it, he shot his hands out at Conroy and wrapped vines around his legs again.

Conroy laughed.

The shadows released Johnny and Sly and they dropped to their knees, sucking in lungfuls of air. The darkness moved toward Liam like a shadow. It reared up and shoved him to the ground, knocking the air out of him. Liam's focus shattered. Conroy tore himself from the vines.

"You want me to take you first, then?" Conroy stepped toward Liam, shadows curling from his hands. "You can join your cousin." His cruel smile ignited another level of rage inside Liam.

How dare he.

Liam summoned more vines from the ground to wrap around Conroy's legs. They started out small, Conroy kicking them away. But they grew thicker and thicker, stopping his stride toward Liam.

Conroy waved his arm and scorched them. They shriveled to the ground. He pulled himself up tall and set his gaze on Liam, commanding the shadows hovering by his sides.

Liam scrambled to get away. Dark gray tendrils looped around his legs and torso, keeping him on the ground. His heart pounded as more of the smoky shadows wrapped around him. A cold hopelessness dripped into his veins when they reached him. Each piece of skin they touched felt like icy water dragging Liam into its depths. The shadows crept closer to his chest, taking his breath away. He felt like he was drowning in a frozen river. The shadows closed around his chest and pulled him face down into the dirt. Dust settled in his mouth as he gasped, trying to breathe while the shadows pulled the air from his lungs.

Is this how I die?

Conroy's arrogant face swam in Liam's vision. He couldn't let this vile man win—the supposed Chosen-One-turned-villain in his mother's books. She wanted Liam to fix this, and he was going to keep his promise to her. He couldn't give up. Aubry still needed him.

Liam forced his lungs to expand and fill with air. Pain shot through his chest, and he groaned past it. Tapping into the power that ran in his veins, he channeled it and broke his arms free of Conroy's shadows.

Sitting up, he slammed his palms onto the packed earth. The ground shuddered and Conroy faltered, confusion wiping the delight from his face.

Narrowing his gaze on Conroy, Liam pressed his palms harder into the ground and imagined what he wanted to happen. He willed the earth to obey like he'd willed the fire in the forest.

Conroy's eyes slid to the ground. A line appeared in the dirt, opening. Faster than Conroy could react, the ground crumbled away and swallowed him.

Liam fell onto all fours, spent.

He heard shouts and saw blurry figures. Juniper's face came into focus.

"Liam! Are you okay?"

He tried to shake his head, but his body wouldn't obey. He was so tired. So heavy. "Is he—"

His arms gave out, and Liam's shoulder hit the ground, dirt settling in his mouth.

CHAPTER SEVENTEEN

"Do you think he'll be okay?"

"I don't know. I've never seen anyone do that before."

"I think he overextended himself."

"I'm sure he'll be fine."

Liam woke to voices above him. Letting out a groan, he pushed himself up from the floor.

"Liam, you're okay." Juniper bent down, her smile filling his vision.

"Yeah, I think I am," Liam said, feeling around for injuries. No new bumps on his head or burns on his skin. Just heaviness in his limbs.

He could barely see Sly and Johnny a couple of feet away in the dim light. Liam put his hand up to feel the wall he was sitting next to. Bark. It felt like tree bark.

"Are we . . . inside a tree? Again?"

Sly raised his eyebrows. "Different tree, but yes."

"And do you just have express ownership of the inside of all the trees in the forest?" Liam looked at the Stream Side Kids.

Sly chuckled. "No mate, this one was all you." He smirked.

"What?" Liam stared at him.

"After you uh . . . had the ground swallow up Conroy," Juniper started, "we carried you and tried to find somewhere safe. While we were walking, you pointed to a tree and told us to try it."

"We thought you were delirious." Johnny eyed Liam skeptically.

"But when we got closer to it, a door appeared out of nowhere," Fox enthused from where he was sitting on the other side of Liam.

"It's like you knew what you needed. Or the tree knew, and here we are." Juniper motioned around them.

They were truly inside the trunk of a tree. It looked like someone had hollowed it out all the way to the top. The surrounding walls of the trunk came in and out like ripples in the water, with just enough room inside for all of them to pile in.

"What happened? Why did I . . ." Liam couldn't bring himself to say faint.

"We think you overextended yourself when you used your powers," Juniper said, pulling some food from a sack and handing Liam an apple.

Fox eagerly reached for the food, then passed it to his brother.

"I'm guessing you've never done that before?" Juniper inclined her head toward Liam.

"No."

Sly nodded. "Quite a lot of power to output at once. You exhausted yourself. Nonetheless, thank you. You saved our lives."

"You're welcome," Liam said, meeting Sly's look of gratitude, feeling a pang of unworthiness. "You would have done the same thing."

"Heh. If I could wield magic." A corner of Sly's mouth slid into a smile.

"Did you make it away with the pendant?" Worry beat in Liam's chest until he saw the gleaming silver chain at Sly's neck.

"Got it right here." Sly touched a bulge beneath his linen shirt.

"All right, then. What are we waiting for? It's still light outside. We should gather everything up and find camp by the river," Johnny said.

Liam stood and swayed into Juniper.

"Woah, you okay?" Juniper steadied Liam, looking at him with her beautiful brown eyes.

"Yeah, I'm okay," Liam breathed, staring at her.

"Okay," Juniper drew out the word and cracked a smile.

"Alright, let's keep moving. Don't want them to get any ideas and try to find us." Sly waved them over. "Liam? Will you do the honors?" Sly motioned to the part of the trunk Liam assumed was the door. Regrettably, Liam stepped away from Juniper and slipped his hand into a latch that served as the handle and pulled it open.

One by one, they filed out. Liam watched them leave, then looked around the inside of the tree. He wanted to remember every detail. The inside of the bark, the way the trunk rippled around them. Taking a breath, he nodded and closed the door behind him. It dissolved, blending into the tree bark, like it had never been there. Slack-jawed, Liam stared up, taken aback by its massive size and thought back to a memory.

He'd brought his mom scones and a teapot for teatime, which was strictly upheld in their Irish-influenced household. He knocked on the door and turned the knob, expertly balancing the tray on one arm.

On the wall by her desk, a giant cork board displayed pictures of a forest, hollowed out trees, character sheets, and notes he didn't understand. Pieces of string stretched from one picture to the other, creating a web.

"Oh hello dear." She smiled warmly at him. "Trying to finish up this last plot hole." She came to stand on the other side of her desk and started cutting a scone in half. Liam poured cups of steaming tea while rain pattered steadily on the window outside.

"What are all the pictures of trees for?" asked seven-year-old Liam.

"Oh, those are quite exciting. They're going to be magical trees that open and let people inside when they need help." His mom beamed.

"Don't you ever get lost in all that, mom?" Liam motioned to the mess of string and papers on the wall.

She laughed. "Oh yes, dear, but that's all part of the fun. You get lost, and then you adventure to find your way out again." She took a bite of scone. "It's like when you read a book. You get lost in the story, the characters, and you imagine yourself as part of the world." She gestured wildly with her arms, eyes sparkling. "You run away for a little while into a story of your own." She brushed his cheek. "You should try it with a story of your own."

"Could you help me with it?" Liam asked.

"Write something and I'll take a look." She winked at him. "For now, I've got to dive back in." She stood, giddy as she walked back to her board of madness.

On that day, he'd started writing stories to bond with his mom.

He'd furiously write about animals, fairies, adventures, anything his seven-year-old mind could think of. He would fill up a couple pieces of lined paper and then run his story to his mom, waving it in the air.

"Mom! Mom! I wrote another one." He jumped up and down.

"Wonderful, dear! Let's see." She held out her hand for the papers and read through them, glasses on the tip of her nose. Liam waited on pins and needles. His mom nodded and it filled Liam with pride.

When she finished reading, she looked down at him over her glasses. "This is a great story, Liam. You thought of this all by yourself?"

He nodded profusely.

"I'm very proud of you." She embraced him. "Keep going dear. You have the makings of a book!" She handed it back, smiled, and returned to her work.

As Liam walked through the forest his mom created, he thought about the strings on her cork board. What strings had he found so far that could help him understand what she wanted him to do in Domhania? Help him understand his purpose?

Conroy, his powers, the openings in the trees, and the pendant. What did they all mean? How were they connected?

The farther he got into this world, the more confused he felt. He thought being here would bring him closer to his mom, but he'd never felt so distant from her. She had so many secrets—an entire world she kept from him and his dad. He'd expected more answers by now, but instead, he only had more questions.

The setting sun dipped below the fig trees, casting a golden glow on the ground. The sound of rushing water sent a feeling of relief through Liam. They'd finally made it.

"The river's up ahead. We'll stay here for the night," Sly said over his shoulder. Silence hung in the air as tiredness from the day set in. They approached a clearing in the trees, and Fox and Johnny scouted out a place to start a fire and cook dinner.

"Is there anything I can do to help?" Liam asked as everyone broke into jobs.

"Do you know how to start a fire?" Johnny asked, dumping an armful of wood onto the ground, sending dirt flying.

Liam wavered on his feet. "Well, I could try?"

Fox and Johnny exchanged a look.

"Why don't I help you out? Starting a fire requires more than just good intentions." Johnny arranged the wood into a triangular structure. As he methodically placed the logs, Liam noticed long raised scars along his arms that shone silver in the twilight.

"So, how are you doing?" Johnny's question startled Liam. He had said little to Liam since he had arrived in Domhania, and when he did, it was usually something skeptical, leaning toward condescending.

"You mean how am I doing after being chased by a fire-throwing wizard?" His voice had an edge he didn't intend.

"Huh. Yeah, I guess so," Johnny said stiffly, not taking his eyes off the wood.

"Well, I'm glad we got away. I still don't understand why he wanted to talk to me."

"I think he was after Sly's pendant, so it's not just you," Johnny said.

Liam waited, but he didn't go on. Instead, he stopped to show him which sticks to pick up for kindling and found some good-sized logs to carry back. Handing the sticks to Liam, he went to gather additional logs from the woods. The ones Johnny found were all about the same size of his muscular arms. Liam stared at him wide-eyed as he carried the logs back like they were nothing.

"So, you, uh, build fires often?"

"A group of us used to have bonfires together when we all lived back in Stream Side." Johnny cleared his throat.

"That sounds fun," Liam said wistfully.

"Yeah, it was." In the dwindling light, Liam could barely see Johnny, but he thought his eyes and mouth turned down.

"The tent is all set up and ready to go," Fox enthusiastically announced. Johnny forced a smile at his younger brother, Fox's positive energy unyielding.

"Why don't you show Liam how to start the fire? I'm going to make sure Sly has everything he needs." Not meeting Fox's eyes, Johnny hurried away to find Sly.

Juniper, in the process of rolling over some logs they could use to sit on in front of the fire, smiled at Liam, and he returned it.

"Okay, let's light this fire!" Fox bounded over, struck a flint he pulled from his pocket, and the fire sparked to life. Liam thought the embers looked like fireflies congregating at the base of the wood before they coalesced into orange flames.

It wasn't long before they all sat around the fire, eating Fox's cooking. They fell into silence while everyone became lost in their food and thoughts.

Unable to bear the silence Liam asked, "So . . . what's the plan for tomorrow?"

"Well," Sly said, "we're going to wake up bright and early. We'll cross the river, and it should be about half a day's journey to Milo's castle."

"It'll only take four hours to get to the mountains?" Liam asked, astounded, eager to shorten the time Aubry was stuck in that castle all alone while Conroy prepared to use her as a sacrifice. Liam's stomach roiled at the thought.

"Yeah, the lands around here change pretty quickly," Sly said. "And once we find Milo, we can ask him more questions. About your journey, purpose, powers, or anything else you wish to ask him."

Liam nodded, staring into the fire. Was he that close to finally getting some answers? Exhaustion settled in his limbs, the pop and crackle of the fire almost lulling him to sleep.

"Before we sleep, we need to put up some protections. Liam, would you like to help me?" Sly asked, standing and brushing dinner crumbs off his legs.

"Sure." Liam stared blankly at him.

"Since we don't have magic like you, Roya made us some warding potions. Protection potions, if you will. I want to teach you how to use them." Sly motioned for him to follow as he started toward the tent.

Opening the flap in the tent, Liam heard what sounded like glass vials clinking against one another. After a few seconds, his eyes adjusted, and he saw Sly in the back of the tent.

The inside of the tent brought Liam up short. On the outside, it looked like a simple canvas tent, but once inside, he could see three huge sections to it. Sleeping quarters on the far right with bunk beds, a sitting area in the middle, and another sleeping area on the left.

Sly stood in the middle section of the tent at the back, digging through a shelf with ropes, weapons, books, vials, and herbs.

Liam smiled, impressed and delighted.

"Come hold these for me, would you?" Sly held a vial out as he kept his head down and inspected the contents of the shelf.

"Sure." Liam stepped deeper into the tent and grabbed a vial about the size of his palm. The green liquid inside shimmered different shades of green. Flecks of yellow green and dark green seemed to jostle as he turned the container in his hand. The way they moved reminded Liam of pine trees blowing in the wind. "How does this work?"

"As you've experienced, Roya can make different potions for different things. She's infused these with a confusion and repellant blend. We'll spread it around the border of our camp to ward creatures and others away." Sly looked up at him. "And hopefully keep Conroy and his men away, too."

"I ki—I took care of him." Liam furrowed his brow at Sly. Liam hadn't really thought about the fact he'd been so angry he'd taken a life earlier that day. It was difficult for him to say what he did. Had Sly already forgotten?

Sly scoffed. "You think Zadimus' apprentice hasn't had worse than the ground opening up to swallow him?"

Liam stared, not sure what to think. Worse than the ground swallowing him whole? He'd seen Conroy fall into the ground. He thought they had eliminated him, leaving only Zadimus. He took a breath to steady his erratic heartbeat. The relief he hadn't killed someone and the regret that maybe he should have tried harder to do so tore him. Conroy still had Aubry and roamed free to hurt whomever he pleased.

"Conroy's powerful in his own right. I've seen him come back from things like that." Looking up, Sly stopped once he noticed Liam's face. "Hey, mate." Sly clapped a hand on Liam's shoulder. "We're almost to Milo. He'll be able to help with Conroy. We'll figure this out, I promise."

"Yeah," Liam said, looking at the vial in his hands. "I *have* to figure this out. For Aubry."

Sly stared at him for a beat, Liam not meeting his gaze.

"In the meantime, I need you to drink this." Sly held out another vial with a greenish swirling liquid in it.

"What's this one?" Liam finally met Sly's gaze.

"This one is *Camomage*, a protection potion for you. Roya made it when she found out you have powers in case we needed to be stealthy, but I think it'll be best to use now so we don't leave Conroy a magic breadcrumb trail straight to us." Sly held it out and Liam took it.

He sighed. *Another potion.*

"Drink up, and then we'll line the camp with the protection potions," Sly said.

Doing as he was told, Liam slipped the protection vials into his pocket, unstopped the one he was supposed to drink, and tipped it into his mouth. Pine and rosemary danced on his tongue as he swallowed. Liam's arms rippled, and it looked like a second skin settled into place all over his body. The sensation faded as the potion's magic fully activated. He stared down at himself. He looked completely normal.

"Okay, let's line the camp quickly so we can get some sleep. We've had a long day."

Tell me about it. Liam lumbered after Sly.

"It's simple. Just unstopper the vials and trace a line around the camp. If they don't connect perfectly, it's okay. They stretch to one another to close the distance. Thank you, Roya." Sly smiled into the darkness.

Liam remembered his mom writing about similar potions now that he thought about it. Before Conroy went off the rails, he used them to deceive his pursuers by adding it to their drinks. He escaped without a scratch. The village singers sidetracked the men chasing him, and they joined the performance.

"What was your mom like?" Liam asked, pouring his potion at the border of their camp. "And your dad?"

Sly smiled, the orange glow of the flame behind them barely illuminating his face.

"They were always happy to see us. Every time we walked through the door, whether returning from a chore or after playing at a friend's house, they would turn around, have a big grin on their faces and open their arms wide to welcome us home. They made us feel special. Made us feel loved, important, and worthy. Dad was the quieter of the two. Mum was the loud, excited one."

Liam thought about his dad's resolute support. He came to every sword fighting competition, encouraged him for every writing contest, and went with him on hikes when he couldn't persuade his mom to join. His dad was a constant in his life. After his mom passed, his dad distanced himself. Liam would catch him drifting out of conversations. He'd miss competitions, forget to come down for dinner. His grandparents told him everyone grieved differently, and his dad needed time. He wondered how much time.

Sly's deep, smooth voice brought Liam back to the story. "He enjoyed reading, preparing arrows, sharpening tools. Quiet activities. But he enjoyed us standing next to him as he did the activity. Just our presence was enough."

"They sound great." Liam smiled.

"They were. They ran the bakery in town. A family business, you could say." Sly got quiet and stepped to the side to pour another vial on the ground. They'd made it halfway around the camp. "Juniper stayed at the bakery and learned all the tricks of the trade from them. How to make rolls, tarts, croissants, cakes, pastries . . ." His smile slipped into something more somber. "I wanted to try something different, though. I apprenticed with the town's sword master. He taught me everything he knew." He sighed loudly. "But I always think back to all that time Juniper got to spend with our parents, and I kick myself a little. All that time, I could have been with them . . . And then I remind myself that I got more time with them than some." The muscle in his jaw tensed as he stared at the leaves on the ground.

Liam thought back to what Fox said about his and Johnny's parents dying years before everyone else's did.

After a couple beats, Sly cleared his throat. "Let's finish this up. Halfway done. You go that way, I'll go this way, and we'll have it finished," Sly instructed. Sly pointed to Liam's right before walking in the opposite direction.

Guess that conversation is over.

Sighing, Liam finished with his side of the campsite, emptying his remaining vials. Before he poured the last drop, he froze. A few feet in front of him, leaves rustled. Two glassy eyes in the shadows of the brush stared at him. Liam covered his mouth to quiet his breathing.

That couldn't be... What did Sunny call it? A wipen? Before he could second guess himself, the figure moved from a crouched position to his full height.

Yup, that's definitely a wipen. A winged centaur towered over him, its muscular chest and arms even bigger than Johnny's.

Liam commanded every fiber of his being to freeze and not make a sound. His breath stopped in his throat. He'd never seen anything so huge, magical, and menacing at the same time.

Well, maybe Conroy. He's pretty terrifying. But even he wasn't as large as this wipen. It's hooves clomped on the forest floor as it stepped closer to Liam, now only a couple feet away.

This potion had better work. Fear pounded in his chest.

Liam watched the wipen scan the forest, probably looking for them. Sunny said the wipens were spies for Zadimus and Conroy.

Please go away, he repeated in his mind. A few sniffs, and the creature stilled. Liam watched as the wipen's skin shifted over itself, bubbling up, and transformed into something else entirely. In place of a winged centaur, a small rabbit rubbed its ears.

Oh, my gosh. Sunny wasn't kidding. The wipen had changed its form at will. With a few more ear rubs and nose twitches, the rabbit scampered into the forest.

Yanking his hand from his mouth, Liam bent over, hands on his knees, and thanked God for Roya and her amazing, magical potions that had saved his life yet again.

He had to tell Sly. They were looking for them. And they were close.

Chapter Eighteen

"Sly!" Liam scrambled back to where he'd last seen the Stream Kids leader. The last of his potion formed a glowing line on the ground to connect with the rest of the protection spell.

"You good, mate?" Sly surveyed Liam over his shoulder.

"No, not good," Liam panted.

Sly raised an eyebrow, waiting for him to continue.

"Wipen. Over there." Liam swung his arm behind him unceremoniously. The memory of its skin bubbling up and shifting into a harmless-looking rabbit flashed through his mind. "It changed. Into a—a rabbit, and then just—went away."

"It's gone then?" Sly asked after a beat.

"Yes."

Sly nodded, looking unaffected. "Means the potions worked." He slipped the empty glass vials into a leather pouch at his belt, then stood tall and proud. "Roya never lets us down."

Liam gaped at him. "That's it?"

"What's it?"

"That's all you're going to say? Nothing about Conroy and Zadimus's wipen spies? Sunny told me—"

"I remember what Sunny told you," Sly said calmly. "But from what *you* told me, they don't know we're here thanks to the cloaking potions around the camp and the one cloaking you. We'll be okay for a night." Sly nodded like the matter was done.

Liam blew out a breath, deflated, releasing the latent anxiety in his limbs.

"Let's get some rest tonight so we're ready for the long journey tomorrow." Sly nodded toward the camp.

"Okay. Right behind you," Liam said. A weight of exhaustion replaced his anxiety. He didn't know how Sly and the Stream Kids lived like this. They'd gone from Aubry being kidnapped to discovering Liam had powers to running into fairies in the Veilwood Forest and confronting their darkest memories. They'd fought Conroy and his men, and a wipen was looking for them. Liam's nerves felt frayed. And Sly said it was okay and they should sleep.

Annoyance at Sly's calm demeanor flared in Liam again.

I guess he's just used to this life of close calls and encounters with monsters. With a huff, he followed Sly back to the tent.

Liam wasn't sure how long he'd been flowing along the river in his mind before he drifted off to sleep.

Inhaling, he smelled sweet grass and felt the soft blades on his face. He was allergic to grass, but this wasn't itchy at all . . . this felt different.

An odd sound caused him to open his eyes. Bubbling water. Sitting up, he saw a river in front of him.

A pasture of springtime grass, a few inches high and swaying in the breeze, surrounded him. The crystal-clear water winked in the golden sunlight. The light from the sun ran over Liam's arms in patches as it peeked through the tree he sat beneath.

Slowly, he turned, taking in this new, peaceful place. He hadn't been here before, he was sure. Even so, it felt familiar. A gentle breeze bent the tall grass, caressing his cheek, and seeming to whisper, "You're safe here."

Are you sure about that? *Liam stared at the grass skeptically.*

His memories took form in front of him. His mom's face sunken with sickness. Her bony hands, light as feathers. Her urgent voice as she told him about Domhania. The last conversation they had.

His dad's desperate voice rang through his ears. He saw his parents' last embrace and watched his mom slip away from them.

Aubry's terrified face as dark shadows curled around her. His hands burned with white hot fire. He doubled over, gasping for breath, heart pounding.

He let out a hollow, raspy groan as the pain tore through him like a blade.

He brought his arms around him to hold everything in. To hold himself together.

But it was too late.

This wasn't right. It wasn't supposed to happen this way.

Liam collapsed from his knees onto his side. He felt empty, as if someone had scraped out his insides, leaving only a shell. Numbness crept over him.

He squeezed his eyes shut, willing it to be over. Willing the nightmare to stop.

Sunlight spilled in through a slit in the tent and shone on Liam's face. He groaned. Blinking, he stared at the brown canvas wall.

Sitting up in his bottom bunk, he looked around in the dim, gray light, and saw a cot across from him with a still body on it. He blinked, forcing his eyes to focus. He hung his head into his hands, closed his eyes, and took a deep breath.

Images from his dream came flooding back. Losing his mom, her cold frail hands as she said goodbye. Magic trees, fighting, training, fire flying by his head, pain burning through his arms. Aubry's scream. Shadows curling around throats. Anger, frustration, loneliness.

He swung his feet out of bed. Though the ground didn't move, Liam felt like it was crumbling underneath him. A heavy, stifling weight settled on his shoulders, making it hard to breathe.

I need air.

Dazed, he shoved on his shoes and an overshirt. Quietly, he walked out of the tent into the crisp forest air. The gentle morning sun warmed his face. He took a breath and felt his chest loosen.

Tall pine trees towered above, raising green needles up to the sky. Birdsong floated through the air, and chipmunks skittered around the shrubs and trees, looking for food to collect. Liam took in this small moment of stillness. He let the beauty of the nature settle itself around his wounds and bring him comfort.

"Ah! There you are. Sleep well?" Fox's arm brushed his as he walked out of the tent and over to the fire.

Liam followed and saw Juniper sitting on a log, repairing one of her arrows. Fox looked over his shoulder for Liam's answer, and he nodded. Taking a seat next to Juniper, Liam scanned the campsite.

"Sly told me what you saw last night," Juniper said. "The potions work. No one will find us today." She focused on her arrows, black hair pulled behind her head, coils sticking out, reaching for the cool morning air. She didn't even look up to check if they were safe, just trusted they would be.

Liam wished he had half the faith she had, but didn't think he could bring himself to that level. Not with all that had happened the past few days. Liam nodded silently. Fox passed him a tin plate of hash, and Liam's stomach growled as the aromatic spices filled his nose. Fox poked at the rest of the food on a skillet in the fire, avoiding a boiling teapot hanging above the flames.

How in the world could Fox make something that smelled this good in the middle of the forest?

"We're heading out when they come back, so eat up," Fox said and poured him a steaming cup of tea. Liam ate and drank and thought about last night, followed by his dream. The wipen and his broad frame towering above Liam transforming into a forest rabbit. His dream with a peaceful meadow, tainted by dark memories. He shuddered.

Thinking back through his mom's books, he'd never read about a wipen. She'd obviously left a few things out. He sighed and shook his head.

"Good morning, Liam!" Sly bellowed as he approached their campsite, clearly unbothered by last night's wipen.

"Morning, Sly." Liam nodded, annoyed by the excitement in Sly's steps.

"Johnny!" Sly yelled. "Come help me pack up the tent. I know everyone thinks I can, but I can't do it myself."

Johnny rolled his eyes as he followed Sly, tearing his gaze away from the forest beyond the perimeter of the camp.

At least someone else is concerned about the wipen.

"Okay, everything's ready." Sly and Johnny walked back with packs on their backs. Liam hung his half full mouth open. "You're done already?" He saw a space of orange, red, and brown leaves on the ground like nothing had ever been there.

"It doesn't take long. Once you've packed one tent, you've packed them all." Sly smiled triumphantly.

Liam shook his head. It was just one unbelievable thing after another here. Each of them picked up a knapsack and helped Fox clean the dishes.

"We'll cross the river today. Although I doubt any of you need a reminder, since I *know* you've been looking forward to this part of the journey the most." Sly smirked.

They crowded beside Sly on the riverbank to inspect the crossing.

A few boulders jutted out from the water, offering something to cling to. The boulders were spaced apart, which meant they'd need to jump to each of them. The rushing water didn't look very welcoming. Liam looked for a bridge or path across the river. He saw nothing and sighed. Crossing by the boulders seemed to be their only option.

"The trick is to keep your eyes on your footing," Sly instructed. "Oh, and if you fall, there *is* a waterfall a bit of the ways down, so you want to avoid falling down that," Sly added.

Liam pressed his lips together. *Of course there is.*

"Sly!" Juniper scolded and smacked him on the arm.

"What? It's true!" He held up his hands and looked at her innocently.

"Don't worry, we'll be right behind you." Fox smiled encouragingly at Liam. Liam did not smile back.

I just wish one thing would go right on this journey. Please let this be the one thing.

"You can do this," Juniper said, brown eyes looking into his as he tried to assemble a more assured expression on his face.

"Yeah, I got this." Liam rolled his shoulders, voice more confident than he felt. He needed to live up to these powers. He couldn't let them know how afraid of them he was.

I'm going to cross this river like a gazelle, and show them how capable I am. It will be the best crossing they've ever seen.

All the training his karate sensei had made him do wasn't for nothing. After months of balance and agility training, he was sure he could do this.

Never mind the fact that none of my training involved a roaring river and wet rocks.

"Juniper, you follow behind Liam so you can direct him if he needs help," Sly said, putting on his leader hat.

Liam narrowed his eyes in annoyance. He didn't need a babysitter. He turned to tell Juniper as much when the breeze picked up and blew her dark hair up around her like a cloud. Her chest rose and fell as she took even breaths. She was so calm, and so full of excitement as she bobbed on the balls of her feet. His annoyance melted away as he watched her.

This was going to be fine. The Stream Kids crossed the river all the time. They knew what they were doing.

"Just watch me, now!" Sly yelled over his shoulder from where he was standing on the bank.

The closest boulder to the bank stuck out above the waterline to the left. The river rushed against its massive side, spraying it with water. It looked to have an outcropping big enough for a single foot. The riverbank was a couple of feet higher than the water level, giving Sly a bit of a height advantage. Sly swung his arms back and then forward to give him momentum and leaped onto the boulder. His right foot landed perfectly in the crevice and he hugged the boulder, finding spots for his fingers.

Of course he made it look easy.

"See what I did? Where I put my hands and feet? Do the same thing now." He raised his voice so Liam could hear him above the rushing river. Sly watched him from a squat atop the giant rock.

Taking a couple of deep breaths, Liam dropped his hands by his sides. He swung them like Sly did, got a running start, and leaped. His foot found the correct spot and he hugged the rock, but his right hand slipped down the face, cutting his palm open.

Liam grunted but refused to let go.

"You got it, mate." Sly said. Liam inched to the other side of the boulder so he could move to the next one. Sly stood poised, ready to jump. Hugging the boulder, Liam looked over his shoulder to watch Sly.

Sly launched himself to the next boulder diagonally to the right. He landed the jump and scurried to the top.

See, this is easy. I can do that.

Liam told his heart to stop beating so fast and took a steadying breath. Little by little, he turned around back to the boulder to face Sly and make the jump to join him. There was no room for a running start. He could only just manage to stand on the boulder's ledge. Cold, wet rock pressed against his back as he glanced down at the crystal blue water rushing by, bubbles forming around his feet. Liam tilted his head, listening. He heard voices rise above the sound of the raging water, ethereal and mesmerizing. Focusing on the words, he realized they were singing a song.

"Come join us in the water.
We have treasures you want to know.
Slip with us into the water,
And we will make sure that you get home.
Don't fear us in the water.
We are here,
You are not alone."

Scanning the water, he looked for the source of the song.

"Liam, what are you waiting for?" Sly yelled from the top of the boulder.

"Didn't you hear that?" Liam motioned to the water.

Sly frowned. "What are you talking about?"

Attempting to look back at Juniper, Johnny, and Fox, Liam glanced back but only saw the gray, wet boulder.

"How could you not hear that?" Liam gawked at Sly.

"Liam, we don't have time for this. Let's talk when we make it to the other side." Sly waved him over.

Pressing his lips into a thin line, Liam searched the water again. This time he saw a hand made of river water reach up and stroke his boot.

He gasped. *There* is *someone there.*

The hand reached farther out of the water, giving way to an arm, a shoulder, and then a woman's kind face. She smiled up at him. Something in her eyes said he could trust her. She wouldn't hurt him.

"Come join us in the water. We have something to show you." She beckoned him, her voice filling his mind.

Slowly, he nodded, a smile pulling at his lips.

"Liam, what are you—" Sly yelled.

But Liam didn't hear the rest because he launched himself off the boulder into the water.

CHAPTER NINETEEN

———◦———

L iam gasped as the force of the river took his breath away.

Maybe this was a bad idea.

Panic gripped his chest. Pumping his arms, he fought to get above the surface. The water churned at his feet, and he struggled to kick himself forward.

"Liam! Grab my hand!" Sly leaned out as far as he could from the closest boulder without falling into the water himself.

Coughing around the water seeping into his throat, Liam thrashed and pumped his legs, barely moving toward Sly's outstretched hand. Sly's warning about the waterfall came to Liam's mind and made him move his arms faster.

"Don't panic! Don't fight the current. Work with it. Use your powers, Liam," the sweet voice said in his mind.

Despite his panic, a sense of peace overtook him. Doing as she said, he stopped thrashing and willed the water to calm. He let his head slip below the water. Instead of pulling power from a place of anger, he pulled power from a place of peace, borrowing from what the voice made him feel. The blue water glided over his skin in a caress, like it was telling him it would be okay.

"Oh, and I almost forgot. Breathe," the voice said.

What? Underwater? And die? No, thank you. Liam's heart rate ticked up again.

"Trust me, Liam," the voice said, sounding almost like his mom.

His chest burned with a lack of oxygen. He could try breathing and if it didn't work, he could drown. Or maybe kick himself up back to the surface. His chest screamed for air as he debated with himself.

Okay, on three. One, two, three. He took a breath. Wincing, he expected his lungs to burn, but coolness ran through them. *I'm breathing. Underwater!*

A woman materialized in front of him. Underwater, she looked like a normal person.

Brown hair billowed with the swirls of the current. Her dark brows, rosy cheeks, and full-lipped smile framed her oval face. She wore a white dress and instead of legs, she had a blue tail shimmering with scales.

"There you are. All good. See?" He heard her voice but her mouth didn't move.

Am I really hearing her? Liam thought.

"Of course you can hear me. You're an ancient one. Or at least you smell like one," she said.

Apparently, she could hear his thoughts and communicate through them. She called him an ancient one like Seraphina and The Guardian of the Shadows had. He tried to talk back to her with his mind.

"Who are you?"

She smiled warmly. *"I'm Nerina. A water nymph."*

The current pulled at them, but they didn't move. Pebbles, moss, and grass lined the bottom of the river. In the distance behind Nerina, Liam thought he could make out other figures. More water nymphs? Muffled voices from the surface tore his attention away from them.

"Your friends are looking for you. We haven't much time. Someone sent me to deliver a message. A message from the source of your magic. The same power that now hums through you and lives in your blood," Nerina said.

"You mean my mom?"

She smiled kindly. *"No. Nora was not the origin of your powers. There is one greater than her who bestowed them upon her. Celeste. Though your mother kept the details of these powers from you, she was preparing you your entire life. Remember her teachings, Liam. You can do this."* Nerina reached out and gently squeezed his hand. *"Now you must return to your friends. We will meet again one day. Be careful."* She brought up her hand in a small wave.

"Wait!"

She faded away, becoming part of the water.

Frustration burned in Liam's stomach. *Why did she have to be so vague and leave so quickly?* He fought to keep himself calm. *Why are people constantly leaving me in the dark?* He felt the water around him churn in small whirlpools. First his mom, then Sly with his suspicion about his powers, and now Nerina.

Liam clenched his fists. The water around him warmed and the grasses at his feet tangled in the whirlpools he created. He had to get out of here. He pointed his palms at the river bottom and shot himself out of the water so fast he broke the surface and launched to the other riverbank, landing on his back, knocking the wind out of himself.

Real smooth, he thought, wheezing.

After catching his breath, he rolled onto all fours. He sat back on his heels, pushing the sopping hair back from his forehead.

Footsteps thumped behind him.

"Oh my gosh, you scared us half to death!" Fox said, bending over with his hands on his knees. Johnny raised his arms behind his head and looked up toward the sky, also panting.

Juniper dropped from above and landed next to them.

"How did you—" Liam looked at the trees and realized Juniper had climbed one on the opposite side of the riverbank and hopped from branch to branch to get to this side.

"Wow. That's impressive." He raised his eyebrows in wonder. Juniper smirked.

"What the heck was that?" Sly stomped over, eyes blazing.

Liam recoiled.

"Liam. What. Happened?" Sly gritted his teeth, chest rising and falling quickly.

Why is he so upset?

Liam swallowed. "Um, I heard a voice singing. She started talking to me. Then she reached out and invited me into the river with her." Hearing himself say it out loud made him realize how crazy it sounded.

"So you hear a random voice and decide to just go jump into the river that could take you away and smash you to pieces at the bottom of a waterfall?" Sly waved his hands.

Liam grimaced. Guilt settled in his chest. He remembered what Sly had told him about almost losing his sister on a mission. And here he was, voluntarily jumping into a river.

"I'm fine. She knew my mom and gave me a message. She showed me that my powers can control water. And—" Liam smiled. "I can breathe underwater."

Sly stared, stunned.

"Sorry, you can what?" Juniper blinked.

"Breathe underwater," Liam said more quietly. They all stared at him. Were they still mad? Think he was a freak show? He couldn't tell.

"Wow," Fox said, face lighting up. "That's amazing."

Liam laughed. "Yeah. I thought so too."

Johnny raised his eyebrows, looking mildly impressed.

Sly just stared. "She knew your mother? What did she say about her?"

"Um, that her powers are in my veins. And she told me the name of the person who gave my mom *her* powers," Liam said.

Sly raised his eyebrows, waiting for Liam to continue.

"Celeste." Liam looked around, gauging their reactions.

"Hmm," Sly looked up at the treeline. "Haven't heard of her."

"So you met a water nymph, huh?" Juniper stepped closer. "What was she like?"

Liam smiled at her interest. "She was beautiful and had a tail instead of legs."

Juniper nodded. "In the water they have tails, but when they walk on land, they have legs." She sighed. "I've always wanted to meet one."

"Well, if she ever comes back, I'll introduce you," Liam said.

"Good." Juniper bumped his shoulder with hers, and his face warmed.

"Let's get you out of those wet clothes, mate." Sly dropped the bag strapped to his back and dug through it.

Liam watched Sly and the rigidness of his shoulders—likely directed at him and his water adventure.

"Here." Sly stood and thrust some dry clothes at Liam. He took them.

"Thanks." Liam searched Sly's face, anxiety pricking his chest.

Sly exhaled and shook his head like he was clearing his thoughts. "I'm glad you're okay. And now we know you have another power." He grinned tightly. "Another thing Milo can teach you to use."

"Yeah."

"Well, I'll leave you to get dressed." Sly nodded once and grabbed everyone, leaving Liam to change.

"Alright, is everyone ready to go?" Sly asked. Liam spotted the group gathered where the forest met the riverbank. A wall of trees towered behind them, green with moss. An errant breeze made Liam shiver. The mossy ground softened Liam's steps as he drew closer. Raising his face to the warmth, he took a moment to gather his bearings.

He'd been thrust into this world a couple days ago and continued to be left in the dark. And yet, Sly had taken him under his wing, training him. He hadn't written Liam off when he'd asked for help rescuing Aubry, or ostracized him because of his powers, even though none of them understood them yet. Liam realized this journey was also a benefit to Sly. To protect the Stream Side Kids and stop Conroy from killing more people, Sly needed Liam's help.

Based on what he'd read in his mom's journal, it was obvious things with Conroy had gone terribly wrong. And now this message from Nerina ignited his curiosity even more. He wanted to meet Celeste. He *needed* to meet her. If she was the woman who gave his mom these powers, she must have some answers. She could tell him how he was supposed to finish this story. Maybe if he went back into the water to ask Nerina…

No. Aubry needs me. They had to keep moving and find Milo so they could rescue her.

"Why don't you lead the way for a bit?" Sly looked at Juniper.

Liam saw the flicker of a smile as Juniper nodded at her brother's suggestion.

"Okay, let's roll out everyone!" Juniper marched into the dark forest looming in front of them. Everyone fell into step behind her.

Johnny rolled his eyes at her command and motioned for Liam to go first. Sly brought up the rear, avoiding eye contact.

As they trudged away from the river, the moss on the trees and ground disappeared. They walked for an hour and Liam noticed the trees change from dark redwood trees to bare, pale trees. After another hour, his breath came out in white puffs. Juniper rubbed her hands together and tucked them under her arms.

"Um, how did it get so cold all of a sudden? " Liam asked. The trees looked like skeletons with their lack of branches and leaves.

"I've heard it's always winter at Milo's castle. Not sure why . . ." Juniper offered.

"So I take it we're getting closer?" Liam asked.

She nodded. "Yes. If you remember the map we looked at earlier, each location in Domhania has its own environment. This one happens to always be wintry." She stopped and turned around to face the group. "Let's put on more layers." Dropping to one knee, she dug around in her bag. Following suit, Liam put on a hat, warmer overcoat, and gloves. Rubbing his hands together, he jumped in place to warm himself up.

"It won't be long now until we reach the mountains. Just a couple more hours," Sly said, pulling on a furry hat that covered his ears.

"And then we can take the trail that leads up to the castle . . . at the top," Johnny said, blowing on his hands.

"Sounds easy enough," Fox said. His eyes widened, and then he pointed ahead of them. "Look!" He beamed. "Snow!"

Fox took off through the trees. Liam looked around at the group. No one else moved. He couldn't let Fox run off by himself. Liam jogged after him toward what looked like a clearing. The closer he got, the thicker the snow became. Liam's feet sunk deeper into the white powder with each step and he grinned.

Growing up in Central California didn't lend to many snowy winters. It never snowed in the Central Coast where they lived. Mountains were an option, but his mom's dislike of cold and the snow left little opportunity for Liam to see it. This blanketed white clearing was exactly how he'd imagined a wintry forest to be. Liam smiled, silently thanking his mom for the snow. The clean blanket of bright powder stole Liam's gaze. Why wouldn't his mother want to bring him to places like this? He chased Fox. The snow unveiled newfound beauty in the trees, ground, and mountains above that Liam didn't see before.

Coming up on Fox and the clearing, Liam stopped to catch his breath. Fox jumped and danced like a little kid, then flung his arms out to the side and let himself fall back with a soft thump into the fresh snow and moved his arms and legs.

Tilting his head, Liam saw Fox making a snow angel. He chuckled. Footsteps approached from behind. Johnny planted himself next to Liam, crossing his arms and rolling his eyes. Juniper smirked.

"Having fun, Fox?" Sly laughed.

Smack!

Icy wetness exploded on impact at Liam's shoulder and sent snow into his face.

"Hey!" Liam shouted. Fox's completed snow angel gleamed on the ground, while Fox ran to hide behind a nearby tree. "I can see you, Fox!"

"No, you can't!" Fox yelled as he attempted to conceal himself.

"Let's not do this right now, Fox." Johnny frowned. Something bright flashed through Liam's peripheral, then a snowball smacked the side of Johnny's face.

Liam covered his mouth, trying to hold back a laugh. Fox peeked out from a tree, then took cover again.

"Really, Fox? Are we ten?" Johnny huffed and wiped the snow off his face.

Smack!

A snowball hit the back of Liam's head and seeped down his back. "Hey!" he shouted, looking for the culprit as he tried to scoop snow out of his shirt. He could see a flash of Juniper before she disappeared behind a tree. Liam narrowed his eyes and grunted.

"C'mon, we're not doing this, right? This is childish." Johnny looked back and forth from the two trees Fox and Juniper were hiding behind.

Smack!

A third snowball hit Johnny in the back of the head, this one thrown by Sly.

"Okay, I guess we're doing this. You're going to regret it," Johnny warned.

Bending down, Liam grabbed a handful of snow and pushed it into a ball. Johnny motioned to Liam to explain his plan. They crept closer to Fox and came around each side of the tree, snowballs cocked in their arms.

Liam motioned, counting to three, and they jumped around the trunk to attack. Liam launched his snowball and, a second later, one smacked him in the face, the cold stopping him in his tracks. He wiped the snow from his frozen face and saw Johnny doing the same. Fox and Juniper faced them, snowballs in their faces. Juniper had climbed through the trees and formed an alliance with Fox. It was two on two.

"Okay, time to stop messing around," Sly said behind them. As they turned, Sly launched two snowballs at Liam and Johnny. Liam yelped and wiped it from his face. Sly held an arsenal of snowballs in his non-throwing arm.

"Oh, it's on!" Johnny yelled and ducked behind a tree for cover while he made more ammo. "Liam! Come help me!"

Liam dove for cover and quickly helped Johnny make snowballs.

"Can you use your powers on snow?" Johnny asked, making snowballs as fast as Liam had ever seen.

"Um, I haven't tried it, but since snow is frozen water, I suppose it could work?"

"Great, I need you to make a wall of snow to protect us, then direct these snowballs at the rest of them." Johnny moved fast, panting. Liam stared, unsure about what side of Johnny he was seeing right now. Not wanting to ruin this rare good mood and think too hard about it, he nodded.

"Yeah sure, I'll give it a go."

"Great." Johnny focused on his snowball ammo.

Okayyy. This is weird, but we'll give it a go. I can manipulate snow. Easy.

Liam closed his eyes, and a snowball knocked him in the forehead.

"You're going to need to hurry up with that wall," Johnny said.

"I'm working on it," Liam muttered.

"Work faster."

Liam huffed to himself and took a quick breath. He focused on the cold air in his nose, his frozen fingertips, Fox's laughter. He remembered the easy pull of the water, the calm feeling. He pushed that feeling into his hands and willed the snow between them and their attackers to form into a wall. For a second, nothing happened. Then, slowly, a small knee-high mound formed.

"We're going to need more than that!" Johnny yelled over the sound of snowballs assailing them.

Liam narrowed his eyes at the snow and used some of his annoyance at Johnny to will the wall higher. It grew inch by inch. It wasn't enough. He thought about Johnny's barbs and the way he rolled his eyes at Juniper's command. Annoyance bubbled up in his chest and pushed more power into the wall. It shot up ten feet into the sky.

"Woah!" Johnny startled, gaping up at the wall of snow. He smiled and looked sideways at Liam. "Now *that's* a wall."

"Hey, that's not fair!" Fox's muffled voice said from the other side of the wall.

"Liam, that's amazing!" Juniper yelled.

"No cheating!" Sly said.

Liam grimaced. "Guess I don't quite have my control down yet."

"Grab some snowballs and let's make them regret this." Johnny smiled. Liam lifted the corner of his mouth. It was odd to see Johnny so invested, but he liked this side of him. He wasn't belittling Liam which was an improvement.

"Are you just going to stand there, or help?" Johnny motioned to the snowballs.

Now that sounded more like Johnny. Liam pulled on some of the annoyance and some of the calm feeling he remembered from earlier. He let the sound of everyone's voices having fun fill him up and steady him. He motioned to the pyramid of snowballs Johnny made in record time and willed them to find their mark on Sly, Juniper, and Fox. They rose up, then floated around the wall and away.

"Ow!"

Liam and Johnny snuck a peek and watched the army of snowballs berate everyone else from all sides. Juniper raised her hands in front of her face. Fox tried running away, but a dozen snowballs pegged him down. Sly unsheathed his sword and slashed at them, hitting about half.

"Do you yield?" Johnny yelled.

"Yes, okay, I yield!" Fox cried, face down in the snow, arms protecting his head.

"Fine!" Juniper said from a squat, the last of the snowballs smacking her in the back.

"I will never yield," Sly said, panting and looking around for more snowballs to slice out of the air.

Johnny looked sideways at Liam.

Liam nodded and a dozen more snowballs rose up and flew at Sly, who stared them down with a fierceness Liam didn't think was appropriate for snow. Sly let out a battle cry and cut through two snowballs, whipped around and sliced three more. The rest came at him all at once. Snow dripped down his face, soaking his clothes. He glared at Johnny.

Johnny raised his eyebrows, challenging.

"Okay fine, you can be the winner." Sly raised his hands, sheathed his sword and flicked snow off himself.

"I told you you'd regret it." Johnny smiled smugly.

Not like I did anything.

"I would say you had an unfair advantage." Juniper raised an eyebrow as she joined them.

"I was just using the resources available to me. Not my fault if none of you were smart enough to do it yourselves." Johnny shrugged, his face stoic and bored once again.

"Well, I don't like to *use* people." Juniper raised her chin.

Johnny glared at her.

"Okay, so now that we've had our fun, it's time to get moving up this mountain," Sly interrupted.

"I don't know if I'd call that last part fun." Fox frowned at his brother.

"Sorry." Liam grimaced.

"It's not your fault, Liam." Juniper looked sideways at Liam with a look he didn't know how to interpret.

It was though, wasn't it?

"If we're done arguing, I'd like to keep us moving." Sly turned and walked up the beginning of a trail. From his spot, Liam saw a vaguely delineated trail straight up the steep slope of the mountain.

I really hope we aren't going that way. We've had enough close calls for a lifetime.

If he squinted, he could see what looked like a white and gray castle at the top of the mountain. Thick clouds drifted over it, obscuring the image, and Liam wondered if he had really seen anything or was just willing an image of a castle to be there.

"Okay, let's start on the trail, then." Sly took the lead.

This was it. This was what they'd been working for the past few days. Milo. Answers. Training for his powers. A plan to rescue Aubry.

Liam gripped the straps of his pack tighter, took a deep breath, and followed Sly up the trail, hoping it led to more clarity.

As each minute ticked by, the snow grew thicker the farther they walked. It crept higher and higher until snow wrapped around their ankles. Liam worked to pull his leg up high enough so he wouldn't face plant in the cold. Snow stuck to his pants, seeping through and freezing his legs. Cold air burned his throat and lungs. It felt like the air turned more bitter with each step.

How is it still getting colder?

Liam's cheeks ached. Pulling his hat further over his ears, he wished he had more layers.

The five of them trudged through snow up to their shins now, steadily rising the longer they walked. After a mile or two, they had to pick their legs up almost as high as their chests to take a step forward.

"Um, is this normal?" Liam chattered, looking around at the Stream Side Kids.

"Well, I couldn't really tell you, mate. Haven't exactly gone this way before." Sly grimaced, knee to chest height to take another step.

"I thought you said you'd tried to visit Milo in the past." Liam worked to steady his shivering body.

"We didn't exactly get this far," Sly said.

Great.

CHAPTER TWENTY

H ours later, when Liam felt frozen to the bone and about three quarters
of the way up the mountain, something ice cold smacked into his cheek.

"Ow!" He held a hand to his face and brought it down to see what it was.

Water?

"Who's throwing more snowballs?" Another one flew at his head, ice cold
pain prickling his temple.

Sly yelped, touching his face. The others frantically looked around, trying to
find the source. All at once, ice pellets berated them. Liam yelled in pain. Icy
nails pierced his skin and clothes.

"Run!" Juniper yelled. Liam ran as well as he could in four-foot-high snow.
A strong, bone-chilling wind picked up and thrashed through Liam's clothes
and hair.

The strength of the wind pushed Fox to the edge of the trail drop off. Johnny
grabbed a fistful of Fox's shirt, pulling him back. Fox clung to his brother's arm,
wide-eyed.

"What's happening?" Liam yelled over the whipping wind.

"I don't know but we just have to keep moving!" Sly yelled hoarsely.

"I don't know if I can," Liam replied. His head pounded from the cold, and
the wind blurred his vision. Pinpricks of pain studded his face, and he felt blood

warming his skin. Liam held his arms up against the cold and ice pellets. Warmth blossomed in his forearms and blood seeped through his jacket.

"Any more of this and we'll be thrashed!" Juniper yelled, barely audible above the wind and flying ice pellets. "Liam, can you use your powers?"

"I can try," Liam said. He controlled the snow, but that was just snowballs. Maybe he could make a wall like before. It would need to be smaller and more mobile.

I can do this. They're counting on me. Commanding his aching hands to open, he took a breath, trying to ignore the sharp pellets pricking his face, and stuck his arms out to redirect them.

Nothing happened.

C'mon! Work!

In the water, he felt peace. During the snowball fight, he steadied himself with this friend's laughs. Now he felt pain, but he needed to find peace. Blocking out the sounds of his friends' screams, he focused.

Closing his eyes, he thought back to a lazy Sunday afternoon in his mom's writing room. While she scribbled away at her desk, he buried himself in a fantasy book on the loveseat in front of the fireplace.

He struggled to hold the image in his mind as he felt the pellets slice through his skin. His friends yelled, pulling him from his focus. He gritted his teeth, trying to block out the chaos.

He tried again and thought about a warm spring breeze blowing in from the open window gleaming with golden afternoon sun. He sat in his memory of being with his mom. No rush. No agenda. Content to be in one another's presence.

Warmth bloomed in his fingers. Relief came over him. This warmth he knew as his powers. More screams from his friends and the warmth sputtered out.

Focus.

Inhaling, Liam tried to call forth the magic that everyone kept telling him rested in his veins. He still wasn't sure what that meant, but now wasn't the time to think about that. Taking the peace from his memory, he opened his eyes and let the power course gently through him. Ice pellets moved around him like he held an invisible shield. Everyone else scampered behind him to stand in his protection.

As soon as they were covered, he took the lead up the rest of the trail. Liam's arms shook with the effort of producing the shield. He hadn't used his powers for this length of time before.

"Ow." Liam groaned as an ice pellet got through his shield and stung him on the neck. He willed more power into the shield. He couldn't let it fall. He needed to protect his friends.

Letting that thought solidify, he trudged on through the snow. As his steps faltered, he felt a forearm on his back supporting him, and it filled him with renewed strength as someone urged him to keep going through the onslaught of chaos. His muscles screamed in protest. They wanted to shut down from the cold. From the injuries he'd sustained. He willed his powers to keep flowing. To keep protecting them. Step by step, the group moved together. The forearm on his back never faltered.

After what felt like hours, they made it to the top of the trail. As soon as they stepped on the stone landing, the pellets stopped.

Thank God. Liam exhaled and dropped his arms, heavy with fatigue. Red clouded his vision and he wiped it away. His gloved hand came back covered in blood. Liam stifled a shiver. Looking around, he saw Juniper, Sly, Johnny, and Fox had the same needle-like cuts with strings of blood decorating their faces. Liam tried to gulp away his horror. Resting against the wall of the mountain, Liam wondered how much farther they could go. He followed the path with his eyes and saw it wrap around the mountain to the east. They couldn't stop here. They had to keep going. What if the pellets came back? He started up the only trail available.

As they rounded a corner, they stopped in front of a tall white gate standing twenty feet high. Liam took a breath, curiosity drawing him closer to the gate. He looked harder and saw snowflakes and creatures twisted in the iron.

"Wow," Liam said, looking up. "It's beautiful." He glanced at Juniper, thinking back to the carved door she'd shown him at the hideout.

"Don't look at me," Juniper said.

Liam stepped forward and touched the gate.

It unlatched and swung inward a few inches. They stood unmoving in front of the gates. The snow around them cast silence in the air.

Liam bit his lip and stepped forward.

CHAPTER
TWENTY-ONE

———◆◇◆———

H e waited.

Nothing happened.

Another step.

Still nothing.

After the ice pellets, he expected some kind of obstacle. He took a few more steps into a beautiful courtyard with a fountain in the middle. With the water off, snow piled inside the gray stone tub. He looked around at the shrubs decorating the circular courtyard. Behind the shrubs stood white rosebushes that, despite the cold, let out an intoxicating perfume.

The rest of them walked around the courtyard, admiring the big white iron fence that bordered it. Liam saw something of a walkway seeming to lead to the entryway of the castle. He followed it, boots echoing as he approached the castle doors. He gasped up at them.

"Liam, is it?" a deep voice asked.

Liam jumped and spun to his right. A tall older man wearing dark blue robes walked from behind a pillar, eyes curiously running over Liam from head to toe. The old man's eyes were a deep blue, like the ocean on a dark night. Pepper colored stubble decorated his long face and matched his hair.

"Yes, that's me." Liam clenched his fists by his sides, readying himself should he need to fight.

The old man inclined his head. "Pleasure. My name is Milo. And you thought it wise to see yourselves into my courtyard uninvited?" He gestured with his arm at the courtyard and the rest of Liam's friends.

His courtyard? This is the man, the wizard, who's going to finally make this place make sense. I hope I didn't mess this up already.

Milo's indiscernible face curbed Liam's excitement. "We're so sorry to barge in like this. I just touched the gate, and it opened. I didn't know what else to do." Liam frantically tried to make their case so Milo wouldn't strike them down. Liam wasn't sure how friendly he was prone to be, though the accounts his mom had written in her books were pleasant.

If this week had taught him nothing else, it was that his mom had left some things out, and things had gone wrong when she tried to change them in her books. Things like Conroy rejecting the prophecy and choosing a path of darkness. Milo held up his hands.

"It's no matter. You were meant to be here. The gate knew it. Therefore, it opened for you."

"And what happened to us on our way up? Did you set some sort of trap or something?" Sly asked from behind Liam.

Milo chuckled. "A man's got to defend himself any way he knows how when he's living all by himself now, doesn't he? Let me take care of that for you." Milo waved his hand and everyone's injuries knitted themselves back together, and the blood on their faces and arms disappeared.

Liam stared open-mouthed at his hands and his friends' faces.

Sly recovered first. He cleared his throat. "I suppose that's reasonable. But why suddenly make the winds stop?"

Milo smiled. "And throw a group of teenagers off the side of my mountain? That wouldn't be very welcoming now, would it? And speaking of, who are the rest of your friends here, Liam?" Milo looked at Liam and waited for an introduction.

Liam's brain tried to catch up. He couldn't believe he had just met Milo—the Milo from his mom's books. The wise wizard Liam would read about when he needed wisdom and answers. And that he'd miraculously healed him and his friends with a gesture.

When he was younger, he'd imagine Milo's words were for him as he read them. Liam learned so much from Milo when he was growing up. Lessons on doing the right thing, resilience, and kindness. He wasn't sure what he expected. Milo seemed to almost anticipate their visit. He wasn't surprised, but pleased.

"Yes, um, this is Sly. He is the leader of the Stream Side Kids. And this is his sister, Juniper. And Johnny and Fox." Liam motioned to them in turn. "They're brothers. Part of the Stream Side Kids as well."

"Hmm," Milo said, taking them all in and nodding politely. "It is a pleasure to meet all of you. Please do come in." He gestured to the door of the castle and the wooden door with an iron handle popped open.

Liam gasped. First the healing and now the door. If Milo could do that, did that mean *he* could do that too? Or were his powers different?

"Are you all hungry?" Milo asked knowingly.

Fox nodded profusely.

"By all means, let us go inside and warm up by the fire." Milo led them through the door.

When they stepped over the threshold, Liam stared after Milo and followed him deeper into his castle.

As soon as Liam stepped inside, warmth, the smell of old books, and a burning fireplace greeted him. A thick woven rug ran from the doorway to the main room. Patterns twisted and turned on the faded red threading, looking like it had welcomed many sets of cold, travel-weary feet.

"Please take your shoes and overcoats off at the door," Milo instructed. Five hooks curled up from the wall. They placed their jackets on them and stepped out of their boots. Looking up, Liam inhaled, admiring the stone vaulting twenty feet above his head. Wood paneling lined the walls in the entryway and main room.

The group walked past Liam, leaving him gawking at the ceiling until his mouth dried up.

"Coming, Liam?" Juniper laughed, motioning him to join them in the main room. Clearing his throat and flushing, Liam followed his friends into the rest of the castle.

Once through the entryway, the room opened into a vast space with a fireplace, a grand mantle, and a spiraling stone staircase. Scattered across the wide mantle, glimmering stones, delicate spindles, and whirring wheels gave off sparks and sounds that didn't quite belong—sometimes the chirping of a bird or the rush of a waterfall. Bright liquids fizzed and swished inside glass vials. Piles and piles of books accented the mantle's chaos.

Milo walked to the fireplace and sat down in a wide, comfortable looking chair. The red leather surface looked worn but sturdy, and Liam could see geometric patterns carved into the wooden armrest and delicate wooden legs. Other chairs clustered around the fire and Liam had the feeling many wise friends had gathered here over the years, talking over great problems and unwinding deep mysteries together.

Blowing on his hands for warmth, Liam sank into a chair and continued to take in the room. Rectangles of gray light entered through a few tall windows, but Liam's eyes were drawn to the enormous fireplace. Heat and light bathed him and worked on the deep chill that clung to his bones from walking outside for so long.

Off to the right, an archway opened into what looked like the dining area. Behind the sitting area, a grand bookcase filled with cloth-bound books stood tall against the stone wall. Liam itched to take one of them into his hands and feel the paper. Smell the ink.

It's a shame books back home aren't made that way anymore.

"Ah yes, those are some of my books."

"Some?" Liam asked. Books stretched across the walls in bookcases ten feet high.

"Yes, this just scratches the surface. This is my collection of books on nature. My library is upstairs," Milo said.

Liam looked toward the grand stone staircase, arching high to a dim second floor.

"Don't worry, you'll get to see it soon enough." Milo looked at Liam, eyes sparkling.

"You, uh—you're probably wondering why we're here," Liam started and waited to see Milo's expression. It was unchanging and open, inviting Liam to continue.

"Well, we're here because . . ." Liam trailed off.

How was he supposed to explain? How was he supposed to tell this man he'd just met that on his mother's deathbed she'd informed him he would be inheriting her powers and was supposed to protect this world? How Conroy had kidnapped his cousin, and planned to use her as a vessel for some kind of spell? And that he had powers he didn't really know how to use?

His thoughts were a giant ball of knotted yarn, all tangled with one another. He didn't know where to start or which string to pull on first. He'd let himself get lost in the castle's grandeur, but the reality of his situation came crashing back and a tightness formed in his chest.

"We are partly here because of this pendant," Sly said, his eyes moving from Liam to Milo. Sly reached under his shirt and pulled out a sapphire pendant on a silver chain. Milo's gaze went from Liam to the pedant, eyes widening in interest.

"My mum told me to protect it before she died. To not let the wrong person get their hands on it. I was hoping you would know what it does?" Sly explained. He scooted to the edge of his seat, holding out the pendant for Milo to see.

Milo squinted and leaned forward.

"Hmm, I haven't seen that pendant in quite some time. An old piece of history, one could say," Milo replied pensively, eyes trained on the necklace.

They waited for Milo to continue.

"What you're holding came into our world via a Realm Jumper. It's called *Mortivita*. But some have called it the Pendant of Life and Death. Only a wizard who knows how to harness the power in that pendant, and a powerful one at that, would know how to wield it. I wonder how your mother came to have it?" Milo sat back in his chair, rubbing his chin.

Sly dropped the pendant against his cream-colored shirt.

"I'm not sure, sir. She wasn't a Realm Jumper, if that's what you're thinking. She told me to protect it and keep it from getting into the wrong hands. What exactly does it do?" Sly's eyebrows came together as he leaned forward, like he was waiting to catch the answer from Milo's mouth.

"It gives the holder the ability to take and give life at will. The person who wields its power could syphon life from a living person, animal, or nature, and keep it for themselves. On the other hand, one could donate life to any living thing they desire. The captured life forces would live in this pendant until the holder uses them. A very dangerous power, indeed. Your mother was smart to keep it hidden." Milo showed no sign of emotion as Liam and the rest of the group shivered and shifted uncomfortably in their seats.

We're in way over our heads. They'd been traveling with something that could take life away at will. *This mission is way more than I bargained for.*

Sly blinked, and the others stared at him in disbelief. Liam could think of a million reasons an evil wizard would want to get his hands on this pendant.

Conroy had been killing people throughout Domhania, but this would give him the power to take even more life. So far, he'd only taken life force from adults. *Would this allow him to take life from children as well?* He shook the thought away. He wouldn't let Conroy get close enough to this pendant to find out.

Thinking of what he would do with the pendant, his mom came to mind. Her pained, gaunt face as she gripped his hands for the last time. What would her eyes look like to have life in them again? Would she smile at him? Would she be proud of him?

Guilt soured his thoughts. Aubry came to mind and his mouth tasted like acid as he thought about what Conroy could do to Aubry with the pendant. Is that what he planned to use on her? Liam stared at the gleaming blue jewel, heart pounding. They had to keep it away from Conroy at all costs.

"We think Conroy might be after it," Sly said to Milo.

"Ah, yes. This pendant would give him the very power he seeks to possess. I'm sure if he gets his hands on it, death will consume the land," Milo said. "Does he know you have this pendant?" A slight wrinkle formed between his eyebrows, his first sign of any distress.

"Yes, he does." Liam's grave voice filled the room as the tension rose.

Milo nodded slowly, the small pinching of his eyebrows disappearing. "We need to make sure it's kept far away from him. Do you know if he was following you?" Milo's eyes trained on the pendant.

"Not that we know of, sir," Sly answered. "We had Liam take a *Camomage* potion so Conroy couldn't sense him and follow us. He seems to feel Liam's power."

"Good. We wouldn't want to have unexpected guests now, would we?" Milo looked around at them. Liam took in Fox's pale face and Johnny's stony expression. Juniper stared at Sly, who was fully attentive to Milo's every word.

Liam sat dazed, still trying to wrap his head around the power of the pendant Sly nonchalantly wore around his neck.

Silence hung in the air. Liam remembered their earlier encounter with Conroy and his men. He held back a shiver, thinking about the licks of fire and electricity Conroy struck him with, the shadows creeping around his friends, so close to taking their lives. The ground swallowing Conroy.

"Do you think he would still be after us?" Liam asked Milo. "After I uh . . . after the ground opened up beneath him?"

"Hmm," Milo surveyed him for a second. "One would hope the earth taking Conroy would be enough to stop him, but even I don't know the full extent of his powers. I would advise you to keep your guard up and act as if he's still after you. I don't doubt he is."

Dread settled in Liam's stomach as he nodded.

"And my cousin. I was told you can help us rescue her from Conroy. She's been with him for a few days now and we need to save her." Liam sat on the edge of his chair, clutching his knees to keep them from shaking. The room got warmer.

"One of you is with Conroy, you say? A young lady?" Milo asked calmly.

"Yes." Liam's throat tightened. *Why isn't he more alarmed?*

Liam noticed his friends eyeing the fireplace.

Milo nodded slowly. "Well, this situation is more pertinent than I thought." Milo looked straight at Liam. "Yes, I will help you rescue your cousin. I believe she has more time, which we will need since I hear you have powers. I can sense the rawness of them. Before we organise a rescue, we need to get your powers into a more predictable place."

"You're telling me we have to keep waiting to get her away from him?" Liam stood up and felt sweat roll down his forehead.

It's so hot in here.

This was Milo the Wizard's advice? He should have a plan. Some sort of strategy. Why was he just sitting there like they were chatting at tea?

"Liam," Juniper said in a warning tone.

Milo continued to look calmly at him.

"Liam, mate?" Sly clapped a hand on his shoulder.

"What?" Liam raised his voice, annoyed. What could they possibly need? He was trying to figure out a way to save Aubry.

Sly glanced at the fireplace. Liam followed his look and saw the fire had grown and reached into the sitting area. Juniper, Fox, and Johnny backed away from the fireplace in distress.

"Did I—Is that me?" Liam looked back at Sly, panicked.

Sly nodded, lips in a line.

Liam shook his head and forced himself to breathe. Did he almost burn down the sitting area and his friends?

What's going on? I need to get a grip. Rubbing his hands down his pants, he tried to remove the sweat from them.

In. Out. Breathe. He focused on Sly's firm grip on his shoulder, the ticking and whirring of objects on the mantle, and his feet planted on the ground. The tightness in his chest loosened and the fire died down, back to a normal size. Sly released his shoulder and nodded reassuringly.

"I think you all are hungry, correct?" Milo asked them, eyes twinkling again like their conversation about death and destruction never happened.

"Yes sir, very much sir." Fox nodded.

Milo chuckled.

"Very well. Come with me this way into the dining room and we'll continue to get to know one another." Milo stood up, dark robes swishing as he walked through the arch into the dining room.

CHAPTER
TWENTY-TWO

———◆◇◆———

O n either side of the stone archway, bronze sconces bathed the room in warm light. Similar dark-colored furniture decorated the dining room as the main room, and worn tapestries hung down the stone walls. Liam's steps clicked as the floor turned to marble. The scent of lavender, frankincense, and spices filled the room.

In the center a long wooden table sat with twelve chairs tucked around it. A large horizontal window spanned the back wall, its view giving way to mountains and a valley below. To Liam's left a beautifully carved walnut buffet with plates, goblets, bowls, utensils, and anything else needed to enjoy a feast sat against the wall. A shiny teapot grabbed Liam's attention. Longing bubbled up as he realized how long it had been since he sat at his grandparents' table drinking tea with them.

"Please take a seat." Milo gestured to the table. With a flick of his wrist, Milo summoned six golden plates, which shimmered into existence, along with full utensil settings gleaming in the candlelight.

Mouth agape, Liam looked over to the buffet and saw fewer plates there than before. His head snapped back to the table as he made the connection.

No way.

Milo sat at the head of the table. Liam sat on his right, wanting to be close to ask more questions. The rest of the group filled in the empty seats.

Milo waved his hand and a glistening white teapot, adorned with green leaves and vines, floated to the table, dispensing hot tea into each teacup. Liam watched in awe as the tea filled his teacup and steam rose, curling up toward the ceiling. Sitting across from Liam, Sly mirrored his shocked expression. Liam looked up at Milo, who had an amused smile pulling at his lips as he gestured to the milk that appeared on the table. Liam shook his head in disbelief, and a splash of milk fell into his magical cup of tea. Swirling it with a spoon, he breathed in the sweet aroma of Earl Grey; lavender and vanilla wafted about him like mist. He took a sip. A comforting warmth flowed through his body. With a cup of his favorite tea in hand, he started to relax.

Milo waved his hands again and presented steaming bowls of stew in front of each of them. Liam's stomach growled and he snatched his spoon. Tipping a spoonful into his mouth, the rich broth, vegetables, and meat almost pulled a groan of satisfaction from him. His belly warmed with each bite. For a couple minutes, they ate in contented silence, with Fox loudly finishing first.

"That was amazing." Fox leaned back in his chair. His eyes widened like he'd said something he shouldn't have. "Don't tell Cook I said that!" he warned Johnny, who smiled ever so slightly.

"So." Milo leaned forward. "Would you like to tell me why you're here, Liam?" he smiled kindly, eyes warm and welcoming and knowing.

Liam finished his last bites of stew, then set his spoon down. He slid his hands onto his legs, squeezed them into fists, and took a breath.

"Well, I already told you, we need your help to save my cousin and maybe you could help me . . . I don't know . . . not burn anything down accidentally," Liam said.

"That is what you are doing here now, but why are you in Domhania to begin with? This is not your home, not even your realm," Milo said.

Liam huffed internally. He thought they'd already been through this.

Keep it together this time.

"Well, you know I need to save my cousin. We came here by mistake. We got stuck and can't go back to our world." Liam drew his eyebrows together as the ball of yarn tumbled in his mind again.

"And how is it you came to be here?" Milo asked.

"Well..." Liam looked down at his clenched fists and thought back to his mother's gaunt face, frail hands, and confusing words. "I was told I had to finish my mom's last story. She's a writer," Liam explained. "As I was writing in her journal, I got pulled into this world. I know it sounds weird, but she created Domhania and told me that now I have the power to come here, I need to take care of Domhania for her since she's . . .she's gone." Liam swallowed the lump in his throat as the words tumbled from his mouth.

A faraway look came over Milo's face. "Your mother, you say?" he asked, gaze lingering on the windows. "What was her name?" His voice held the slightest bit of tension. One of the first Liam noticed from Milo, who seemed so calm.

"Her name was Nora, sir," Liam answered.

Liam heard Milo's quiet intake of breath and saw his chest rise ever so slightly. When he made eye contact with Liam, his eyes were shiny.

"Your mother was Nora?"

Liam nodded.

Milo exhaled and leaned back in his chair. All his elegance melted away like Liam had snuffed out his spark by confirming his mom's name.

"What's wrong, sir? Did you know her?"

"Yes," Milo breathed. "I knew your mother quite well." He looked pained to admit it.

"How did you know her?" Liam asked, his hunger for information moving him forward in his chair.

Milo surveyed the room and drew himself up tall again. "I think that was an excellent dinner, don't you?"

"What?" Liam asked.

"That's enough talking for tonight." Milo cleared his throat, and the warmth left his voice, replaced by a tone of finality. "I will show you all to your sleeping chambers. It's safest for you here. My wards in the castle walls will keep Conroy from sensing you here. And tomorrow, Liam, we will talk more about these powers of yours."

"But I don't—" Liam started.

Milo's look stopped him. His eyes held a deep hurt that scared Liam.

Had his mother done something to Milo?

"Follow me this way and I will show you where you'll sleep." Milo gracefully pushed up from his seat, robes swirling as he made his way out of the dining room.

Liam stood up and looked at the dirty dishes left over from their devoured meal. He took one last gulp from his teacup, finishing it.

"Don't worry about those. They'll clean themselves up," Milo said over his shoulder. Skepticism tickled the edges of Liam's thoughts, but he had seen so much today, he supposed he shouldn't be surprised.

Milo led them out another archway on the far side of the room that opened into a dark hallway where yet another circular stone staircase led up to the second floor. Milo's shoes clicked and scraped against the stone as he climbed the stairs. When they reached the second floor, their footsteps softened on a thick emerald rug running down the length of the hallway. Scenes of flower fields, towering mountains, and cascading waterfalls in colored glass artfully filled the windows on Liam's right, each directly across from a door.

"Gentlemen, you will be in these three rooms." Milo gestured to the first set of doors on the left. He walked down a few doors and gestured once more. "Juniper, these will be your chambers. You will find everything you need. Beds, linens, and everything necessary to wash up. There are also fireplaces since the castle can be quite chilly at night. I trust you know how to light them. Get some rest. Tomorrow will be a long day. We'll catch up more and begin training."

"Training?" Johnny crossed his arms with a skeptical expression.

"Yes," Milo said. "Training. You said Conroy's after the pendant and has captured Liam's cousin. We must create a plan to rescue her and train all of you accordingly." Undeterred by Johnny's skepticism, Milo continued, "Good night, all of you. I will see you in the morning." Turning on his heel, Milo and his richly colored robes vanished into the darkness down the hallway.

Liam let out a long breath.

This wasn't turning out the way he'd imagined it would. Milo seemed to know his mom but didn't want to talk about her. Had something happened between them? Did they not like each other? Why couldn't Milo just tell him?

Sly said Milo would know more, but he clearly wasn't willing to share. All Liam had were unanswered questions, a dark wizard chasing him, a kidnapped Aubry, and a gaping hole of disappointment in his chest. He pushed his hands through his hair, telling himself to breathe. Commanding his anger and frustration to simmer down.

"Psst."

He turned to see Juniper watching him, concerned. They were the only ones left in the hall.

"Liam," she whispered. "Are you okay?" Her eyes searched his.

"I don't know." Liam shook his head and tightened his jaw. "No." He tried to breathe. No, he was not okay. He didn't know how to be okay. "I just know I'm tired. And I want today to be over. I don't understand why he wouldn't talk to me."

Juniper nodded. "I thought it was weird too."

"We traveled all this way, and he refuses to talk about my mom and what she told me?" Liam shook his head, letting out a frustrated sigh. "Sly said he would know more. What if this was all for nothing?"

"I think he's hiding something." Juniper concentrated on the wall behind Liam, thinking.

"Really?"

Juniper nodded. "His reaction was so strange."

"What do you think he's hiding?"

"Well . . ." Juniper frowned. "He's been up here in the mountains doing nothing while Conroy has been out there killing people for so long. I thought maybe we'd encounter a decrepit old wizard, which would explain why he hasn't been helping. But he seems fine." She shook her head. "It just doesn't add up."

Liam didn't remember Milo ever holing himself away in his mom's books. "Yeah, it doesn't."

"I'll figure more out later. See you in the morning, Liam." Juniper smiled and walked away.

Liam's stomach jumped a little at her parting smile.

What could Milo be hiding?

CHAPTER
TWENTY-THREE

---◆◆◇◆◆---

T he next morning Liam woke up in another new bed. This time, he felt nestled in a cloud. Letting the thought take him, he imagined himself floating, comforted by the soft warmth around him, slipping away, his disappointment dissipating. In his mind, he saw flickers of green pastures bathed in warm light with quiet streams running beside it.

Then, the emotions hit him, deep and visceral.

His mom's sick face, tears running down her sallow cheeks, hugging her for the last time, his dad shaking with sobs, being pulled into the storyworld, getting attacked by Conroy, finding the castle, Milo's disregard. His stomach twisted and his muscles tensed. He shot up in bed, gasping for breath.

Pushing his hands through his hair, he groaned. The drapes around the four-poster bed shone with navy velvet and iridescent stars, like strips of the night sky hanging around him.

The weight of disappointment settled in his limbs as he stared up at the fabric. Remembering his interaction with Milo from the night before, he clenched his jaw. Regardless of his kindness in feeding them and letting them stay the night, it didn't change the fact they'd come all this way for answers and Milo seemed to be hiding something.

Why?

Looking out the window, Liam watched a snowbird fly away from him, toward the valley. He imagined dipping and diving, free like the bird instead of twisted up and confused like a tangled ball of yarn. Sucking in a ragged breath, he pushed against every desire to stay in bed.

Surprisingly, the bathroom had running water. He hadn't bothered to look last night, and instead fell into bed. A wardrobe hugged a wall and Liam made his was over, hoping it had something for him to wear. He grimaced thinking about putting his disgusting clothes from the trek back on.

Dark-colored wood carvings decorated the wardrobe's front, and gold fastenings hung down for the handles. Pulling it open, he found clean trousers, shirts, and overcoats hanging like they'd been waiting for him. Liam reached in and touched a linen shirt, the soft fibers comforting to his fingertips. He wondered if the castle knew what he needed like the Stream Kids' hideout had. He pulled out a dark brown pair of trousers and a linen shirt and got dressed.

Morning sun shone through the different colored glass in the windows and danced along the wall out in the hallway. Remembering where Milo walked away from them last night, he followed the hallway, hoping to find the dining room. After a few minutes and a couple of turns, he found a stone staircase that looked familiar. At least, he hoped it was. Everything looked different in the sunlight.

When he reached the bottom, laughter echoed off the walls, leading him to the rest of the group in the dining room. Sly, Juniper, Johnny, and Fox were seated around the table watching a joyful Milo when Liam peeked around the corner.

"Liam, come sit down. Milo was telling us a funny story about when he was first learning how to use his powers." Juniper motioned him over to the table. Liam sat down next to her. Scrambled eggs, sausage, fruit, biscuits, and—one could not forget—a pot of tea sat in front of him. Liam quickly dug in as Milo continued his story.

"I stood in the middle of the woods at our camp. The day's lesson was to extinguish a small campfire by manipulating the surrounding water. By now, I had done this dozens of times when I was near a river, but this was out in the middle of the woods. I did not know where I was going to get water from. My mentor told me I needed to find and use the surrounding water.

"I nodded, though I wasn't sure what he meant. He wasn't the mentor you question. And at that moment he waved at the fire and it erupted into a chaos of flame spreading around the camp and, before I knew it, a few trees caught fire. Many a time, my mentor thought the stress of survival was the way to get me motivated and I can't argue he accomplished that.

"With the threat of a full-on forest fire should I fail, I closed my eyes and felt for moisture around me I could draw from. That day, the dry air and fire consumed any remaining atmospheric moisture. My senses shot out to the forest floor, and just over a ridge I sensed a clearing with dozens of puddles. With the heat of the flames licking closer to me, I pulled on as many of the puddles I could focus on and summoned them. Now, I wasn't as precise back then, so I pulled as much as I could towards the fire. With my eyes still closed, I heard the hiss of the fire fighting back, not wanting to be extinguished. The puddles kept coming. When I opened my eyes, there was a smouldering pile of what looked like mud and smoke . . . and then the smell hit me. Turns out, the puddles weren't actually puddles. A dairy farm sat over the hill and I had tapped into the moisture stores in all the manure left in the field . . . and glancing from myself to my mentor, I realised we were both covered in it.

"'Well . . .' my mentor said, wiping a lump of brown substance off his face. 'I can't fault you for being resourceful. It looks like our next lesson today will be laundering.'"

"I really hope you learned how to master that spell," Sly said between laughs.

"Oh yes. That one and many more," Milo assured him.

"So, how old were you?" Liam asked. Milo looked startled.

"How old was I? When what?"

"When you started learning magic," Liam said. Milo seemed to relax after he clarified his question.

"I started pretty young. My parents noticed I would make things happen without meaning to when I got sad or upset or happy or excited. They took me to one of the well-known local wizards and he started training me. I was about six. And from then on, I would train with him every day. My parents had more peace of mind, knowing I wouldn't blow the entire house to pieces."

Liam nodded, thinking about how terrifying it would be to watch a young boy blow up a house.

"And today," Milo said, "we're going to see what kinds of powers you have up your sleeve, Liam."

Everyone turned to stare. Juniper wiggled her eyebrows up and down at Liam. Sly sat back in his chair, amused. Fox directed his full focus to his plate of food. Johnny looked up for a second, his face stony as ever.

"I'd like some answers first." Liam stared at Milo. He would not let him act like last night hadn't happened. Like he hadn't avoided his questions.

Milo pressed his lips together, took a second to think, then dipped his chin. "Very well."

Liam loosened his jaw, and a little flame of hope flickered inside him.

"How are we going to save Aubry?" He knew that every second he spent in the castle on this quest meant Aubry was trapped with Conroy and Zadimus, suffering an unknown fate. Liam breathed through his nose at the thought. He couldn't get angry again and risk burning the dining room.

Milo nodded as if he'd expected Liam's question. "Like I mentioned yesterday evening, you all will need a bit of training first. Raiding Conroy and Zadimus' castle is not something to be taken lightly."

"Respectfully, sir, we've all had a fair share of training and know how to hold our own." Sly sat up straight, confident eyes on Milo.

The wizard raised his eyebrows and thought a moment. "I don't doubt your abilities, young man. I merely want to make sure you are prepared to fight against a powerful wizard who has powers and tactics at his disposal that will differ from anything you've fought before." Milo looked at Sly kindly.

Sly's eyebrows came together. "We've experienced his shadows and fire. What other tactics does he have?"

"My sources have told me he's using magic-imbued weapons. Much more deadly when struck by one. I see it as my responsibility to make sure you're prepared for that." Milo looked down his nose at Sly in a rather fatherly manner.

"We brought some potions of our own to combat certain injuries," Juniper said.

"Ah, very good. I would like to look at them and make sure you have enough with you. We never know what we're going to encounter once we get to Conroy and Zadimus' castle. We want to be as prepared as possible," Milo said.

"Then we will talk strategy? Do you have a layout of their castle and the weak points?" Sly asked, putting his elbows on the table.

"You *have* done this a few times before, haven't you?" A playful smile crept up Milo's face.

Sly nodded. "You could say that. Never to the dark wizard's castle, but we've had to run a rescue mission or two ourselves."

Johnny grunted in agreement as he finished his tea.

"Well, we can have a quick look at the map here," Milo said and snapped his fingers.

The food platters moved aside to create space for a map that appeared in the center of the table.

"Now we're talking." Sly smiled, drinking in the map with his eyes.

"To show you that yes, I have some semblance of a strategy, here is a simple map of Zadimus and Conroy's castle. We'll study a more complex one after we've done some training," Milo said.

Liam stood to get a better view of the map. He had little experience looking at the inner workings of castles on old pieces of parchment paper, but he recognized symbols like entrances, passageways, and exits. Sly studied it with an intense expression that told Liam he was already strategizing.

Milo sipped his tea and finished his breakfast for a couple of minutes before he interrupted them. "That should suffice for this morning. We'll reconvene later to form a concrete plan. Does that make you feel more at ease?"

Sly looked up at Milo, nodded, and sat back down. Liam and the group followed suit.

"You also said you knew my mom?" Liam jumped in. The conversation had gotten away from him. He needed some answers.

Milo swallowed and turned to face Liam.

"Yes, I knew her. We spent a good deal of time together when she would travel to Domhania." Milo's taut voice struck Liam as odd.

"Did she talk to you about the prophecy that went wrong? Did she explain how to fix it? She was trying to help Conroy not reject his responsibility as the chosen wizard and the one to bring peace to the land. I found her journals. I thought that's what she needed me to do. To finish the story and change things, but now I'm seeing that's not as easy as I thought it would be. I'm not sure how much influence her writing had on this world." Liam's thoughts ran into one another, trying to make sense of everything he'd been mulling over for almost a week now.

"She talked to me about the prophecy." Milo paused. "When we last spoke, it hadn't gone wrong yet. She didn't know that would happen." He seemed to choose his words carefully.

Liam glanced at Juniper. Maybe he *was* hiding something.

He took a breath and told himself to trust Milo. He needed to trust *someone* to give him answers. In his mom's writing, she always depicted Milo as a kind and wise wizard, like *she* trusted him.

If Mom trusted Milo, maybe I should too? He needed Milo anyway if he wanted more clarity.

"So, how do you think I can help fix things? I'm stuck here and need to save Aubry. If I can help save lives while I'm here, I want to do what I can." A sense of responsibility rose in Liam.

A memory from months ago flashed across his mind: Clive and his friends ganging up on James and the feeling of agitation, then defiance, then determination as he stepped up to the rugby boys and told them to leave James alone. Conroy was just another Clive taking advantage of people who couldn't protect themselves.

Liam looked around the table at Sly, Juniper, Johnny, and Fox. He knew they could fight. They'd made it this far. They weren't helpless. But he remembered how easily Conroy's shadows had slithered around their throats, inches from taking their lives to be his. He couldn't do nothing. Until now, he'd been here to rescue Aubry. The rest hadn't been his problem. But now, he realized it was. Domhania was his inheritance. His responsibility. And he couldn't let Conroy tear apart the world his mother lovingly created.

Once again, Milo's words came to him. The words he'd read in his mom's book over and over again: *"If it's within our power to help those around us, we need to rise to that responsibility. Why else would our powers have been given to us? Not to uplift ourselves, but to uplift those around us."*

"I can help you learn how to use your powers. Gain more control over them. That's where we can start. You're going to need them against Conroy. My understanding is that you made a first attempt, but he will be ready now. We need to make sure *you're* ready. I won't send you to his castle unprepared," Milo said.

Liam shifted in his seat. "How long will it take?"

Milo raised his eyebrows. "As long as you need to understand your powers and gain control over them. Normally, it takes years for a wizard to master that."

"*Years?* You know we don't have years, right?" Liam's heart thudded.

"We will use the time we have wisely," Milo said with his aggravating calmness. "I imagine you'd like to get started as soon as possible?"

"Yes."

"Let's venture to the training courtyard, then. We'll begin there." Milo inclined his head.

"And what about this pendant?" Sly asked. "We need to keep it away from Conroy. What do you propose we do with it?" Sly held out the pendant, candlelight casting a golden hue on the silver.

"It will be safe here for now. I've put a charm on it to make it undetectable. I made sure of that yesterday when you showed it to me," Milo said.

"You? While we were talking?" Sly gaped.

"Yes," Milo said simply.

Sly looked shocked for a moment, but quickly regained his composure and became Sly the confident leader once again. Liam didn't understand how he and Milo could do that so quickly. It irked him.

"While Liam and I train in the courtyard, the rest of you are welcome to go downstairs into the Alchemy Lab and Armory. My friend will be there to help you." Milo cracked an amused smile.

"There's another person here?" Johnny bristled.

"Oh yes, I need help from time to time. And she's made herself quite helpful. Her name is Willow. She is a Winter Fairy. She will help you train, as she's fought against Conroy and his men," Milo said, gracefully standing up from his place at the table.

"Excuse me? You have a *fairy* in this castle?" Johnny curled his fists, face flushing.

Uh oh. Not good.

"Yes. She is quite helpful, like I've said," Milo's calm voice promised Johnny.

"We just had a nightmare of a time getting my brother back from fairies that kidnapped him. I'm not about to ask one for help," Johnny growled.

"Are you so close-minded to think that every fairy kind is the same? That none of them might be different?" Milo tilted his head, gently challenging Johnny.

Johnny pressed his lips together, face still red. He looked unconvinced.

"Listen mate, Juniper will be with you two if anything goes awry." Sly stood and stepped closer to Johnny, trying to diffuse the situation. "This is different. Milo is here to help us." Sly gazed at Johnny like he was silently commanding him to calm down and think clearly.

"Johnny, it'll be okay," Fox piped up.

Johnny flicked his glare to his brother. Fox stared back and nodded slowly.

After a few seconds, Johnny let out a long breath, flaring his nostrils. "Fine," he said through gritted teeth and crossed his arms, giving Milo a hard stare. Milo looked calmly back at him, a slight smile forming in the corners of his mouth.

"C'mon, let's go figure out how to fight Conroy and his men." Juniper motioned with her head for Johnny and Fox to follow as she made her way to the Alchemy Lab downstairs. How she knew where it was, Liam didn't know.

"I'll be going with you, if that's alright," Sly said, looking at Liam excitedly.

"Yeah, that's fine." Liam nodded, thankful for the offer. He wasn't sure he wanted to be alone with Milo.

"On to the training courtyard for us then," Milo said, turning around, sage green cloak swirling around him.

"Where's that?" Liam asked.

"Past the living area, down the stairs, out into the open courtyard. We will start outside. Much safer that way. Just watch out for any rogue 'puddles.'" Milo winked at Liam and made his way out of the dining room.

For the first time, Liam was going to intentionally use his powers, with the guidance of an expert. He felt excitement tingling under his skin. Or was that part of his magic?

His childhood dreams were finally coming true. He was staying in his favorite character's castle, he had powers, and he was going to learn how to use them.

I'm doing this for you, Mom, Liam thought, wishing she were there.

"Okay, let's go." Liam took a breath and followed his new teacher.

CHAPTER TWENTY-FOUR

———◆◇◆———

S tanding at the edge of the training courtyard, Liam took a breath and focused on a spot across from him covered in vines and flowers.

Nature.

It had always been grounding for him. He got that from his mom. When he was little, she'd take lunch breaks with him in their garden and teach him the names of the plants, how to care for them, and what healing properties they had, if any. She kept a vibrant kitchen garden with rosemary, cherry tomatoes, cilantro, green onions, peppers, and various fruit trees. In the springtime, Liam loved sitting in front of the plum tree watching the bees pollinate the beautiful blossoms that would one day turn into mouthwatering, juicy, purple plums. His mom would tell him that when she would get stuck after being in her head all day, she would go outside, run her hand over the leaves, tell them hello, encourage them, and listen to the wind whisper through the trees.

"If you close your eyes, you can hear the breeze telling you to shh. To just be still. To let the sun soak into your skin, let your feet curl into the grass, and breathe in the life all around you."

He tried it. She was right. From then on, when he needed a moment to himself, he'd go into the garden and sit. Just be. Just listen.

When his mom got sick and they moved into Liam's grandparents' house, he realized his mom got her love for gardening from her dad. The garden behind his grandparents' Victorian house was larger than the one he'd grown up in. His grandpa cultivated a rose garden, kitchen garden, aromatic garden, and a small fruit tree grove. The first time he'd seen it, his mouth hung open and his mom laughed joyfully at his astonishment.

"It's amazing, isn't it?" his mom had asked him.

"It's perfect," Liam said.

Pulling his attention back to the present, Liam traced the green vines and purple flowers with his eyes and urged his breathing to steady. Urged himself to be present and not let his anxiety bubble up.

Focus on breathing in the life, the stillness, he told himself, recalling what his mom told him when he was young. This was uncharted territory. He'd surely dreamed of having powers when he slept, but that wasn't reality.

As a child, he longed for the abilities of the characters in his parents' storybooks. He used to dream about going on magical adventures into unknown lands. Wasn't this what he always wanted?

"Wait!" Milo bellowed, pulling Liam out of his thoughts. Milo's arm hung in midair, pointing towards the floor, and Liam realized he almost stepped on a delicately placed pile of sticks. He pulled his foot back.

"What are all these things?" Liam looked around the courtyard at several small stone circles. The one he nearly stepped on contained branches and sticks. The rest circled to the left. Rocks and pebbles lay piled near a circle filled with plants and flowers. A stone pedestal held a mini waterfall. An outdoor fireplace crackled and spit, and a table of potion looking materials, much like Roya's, finished the circle.

"These," Milo gestured to all the stations, "are the different areas in which we will test these powers of yours." Liam looked at Sly, who backed out of the way.

"What am I supposed to do with them?" Liam exhaled and commanded his nervousness to stay at bay. He never liked tests. They always felt like they were judging if you were enough or not. Twice, the pressure caused Liam to have panic attacks before tests in school. This wasn't a math test; this was much bigger. What if he couldn't do what Milo asked of him? Couldn't do what his mom thought he could do?

"You will stand at each of them and try to summon your powers," Milo explained, walking over to Liam, green cloak billowing behind him.

"But I don't even know how to get them to work consistently. How am I supposed to just do something?" Liam tried to keep the annoyance in his voice minimal. Something about Milo kept rubbing him the wrong way. Shouldn't he be thankful to this wizard who welcomed them into his house, fed them, clothed them, and gave them a place to rest?

But he wouldn't talk candidly about his mom. The whole reason he came to Domhania was because of his mom. Juniper's words about Milo hiding something sparked more doubt in his mind. The Milo he stood in front of differed from the one he'd read about, this one more evasive.

"That is why it's called a *trial*. We are going to see what works." Milo's calm demeanor against his annoyance encouraged Liam to take a breath and relax.

Just a trial. It'll be okay.

Liam sighed. "Okay, I'll try." Liam held his hands over the stick pile and waved them around foolishly, like he was a stage magician performing a trick.

Milo cracked a small smile. "If you'll give me a second, I'll explain how this is going to work."

Liam dropped his hands to his sides, clenching and unclenching them, waiting for Milo to continue. Sly had moved to lean against a half wall behind Liam and kept surprisingly quiet.

"Now, when you step up to the unique elements, I want you to close your eyes and look inside yourself. Focus on what you feel. You have power in your blood." Milo stared intently at Liam as if looking for something. Milo paused before continuing. "Power is in your veins. If you take a moment and clear your mind, you'll feel the pull of it. It pulses, waiting for you to use it. To wield it.

If you really focus, you can feel a tug. A yearning. The power wants to be used. Think of it like moving something heavy."

Liam stared at him in confusion.

"You start small, turning on your muscles bit by bit. The heavier you lift, the more strength you need to pull. Today, start with the light weights." Milo smiled, the corner of his eyes wrinkling, and gestured to the sticks on the ground.

Light weights. Okay. He could do that, right? Panic prickled in his chest. The last time he used his powers, he'd hurt people. He'd put others in danger. Aubry, Sly, Conroy, the woods. Glancing back at Sly, he shot him a worried glance. Sly returned it with a thumbs up and excited smile.

At least one of us is excited about this. Just look inside myself and focus on what I'm feeling. He could do this. No problem. Liam planted his feet in front of the stick pile and closed his eyes. He held his palms up.

Inhale. Exhale.

Milo said he'd be able to feel the power in his veins. He imagined himself in his childhood garden, soaking in the sun, listening to the breeze. He forced his mind to still so he could focus on feeling the power inside him.

What do I feel?

A hum. A hum of power. It glowed and called to him. He felt a pull. A restlessness similar to how he felt after not working out for a while. Similar, but deeper. It felt like the restless power shook itself off, ready to be used. He felt it in the air, crackling like electricity. Felt it all around him, presenting itself to him like the warmth from the sun's rays in the garden.

The desire to use it rose into his chest, taking shape like a glowing ball. *Light weights*, he reminded himself.

Calling forth a small amount of power, he opened his eyes and felt it warm his arm, then his fingers, as he directed it at the sticks. Imbuing his power with some of his will to give it direction, he imagined the sticks moving into a teepee formation.

Astonishingly, they moved. A little unsteadily, but they moved.

Glancing up at Milo, he saw him nod.

Finally! He'd used his powers successfully. Hurting no one. Relief coursed through him.

Maybe I can *do this.*

Liam turned to the worn wooden table piled with potted plants whose blooms reached for the morning sun. Vines curled around the table and dropped off the sides. Taking a few steps closer, he focused on the plants that had yet to bloom. Holding out his hands, he tapped into the hum he felt in his muscles. The call of his magic in his blood. Light weights.

Narrowing his eyes at the vines on the table, he pushed his power toward them, calling them to bloom. Flower buds slowly grew along them, becoming bigger and bigger. The buds opened to reveal purple flowers that proudly stretched their petals.

Liam smiled, and he turned to Sly who had stepped off the short wall and stared, his mouth parted.

Turning to the next element in the circle, Liam felt his power welling up, awakening to his summoning. Warmth traveled up his hands and arms, motivating him to keep going. The little tabletop waterfall flowed and bubbled. He remembered how it felt to be in the water, letting it flow around him. Letting it calm him. He saw a flash of his mom's smile in his mind. Flicking his hand at the waterfall, he sent water curling into the air to form circles that spun and transformed into mist.

Turning, he faced the second to last station in the training courtyard—fire. Liam felt a lick of fear in his chest. He tried not to remember Conroy hurtling fireballs at him. Tried not to remember the way the Wizard's Fire burned his flesh and shot pain through him. Milo calmly observed Liam, his face set with neutrality, and nodded.

Liam swallowed and hesitantly waved his arms in front of the fire. Looking for the light weights, he took a breath, trying to find his power flowing through him. Instead of the soft stream it was before, it jumped and skipped inside him. Anxiety pricked his chest.

What is happening? He felt a hollowness in his chest that slowly expanded.

His breath quickened, his chest tightened. He heard his mother's voice the last time she told her she loved him. Felt her frail hands. Saw his dad wrap her in his arms. Saw Aubry's terrified face when he'd first brought her here, then again when Conroy took her. He saw the vines from his anger wrap around Aubry and hurt her. Saw the Wizard's Fire coming for him, his destruction of the forest, Conroy's shadows curling around Sly and Johnny. He felt his arms shaking with effort as he tried to control his powers. Mentally, he tried to push back against his thoughts and memories, but it felt like holding up a cardboard shield and the fears were a concrete wall falling on him.

No! He would not fail! Anger at his mother bubbled up. Anger for leaving him and dumping everything on him—a world she created, powers, her request to take care of a world he knew nothing about. Frustration at Milo's elusiveness with information he craved reared its head. He balled his hands into fists, willing them to stop shaking.

"Liam! That's enough!" Milo commanded.

Liam gasped and his eyes shot open.

Every element hung in the air. A hurricane of water formed as shredded plants littered the table. The sticks lay broken in pieces. Stones pulverized the flowers, and the fire grew out of the chimney into a long snake-like loop that circled around the rest of the elements. Pure chaos.

Liam's breath caught in his throat.

Suddenly, the fire snaked its way over to the potions, lit the table on fire, and exploded in a purple light. The force knocked Liam off his feet, sending his head slamming into the stone floor of the courtyard.

Dazed, Liam blinked, trying to get his eyes to focus. Turning his head to the side, he saw a blurry image of Sly on the ground a couple feet away, clutching his side.

"Sly!" Liam yelled. The volume of his voice sent a sharp pain through his head. Scrambling to his hands and knees, Liam moved toward Sly, who was pushing himself up into a sitting position. Sly clutched at a dark spot on the bottom of his leather vest near his hip. Blood.

"Are you okay?" Liam crawled closer to Sly.

Sly pulled his hands away from his hip and Liam saw what looked like shrapnel made of stone and sticks protruding from Sly.

Liam's stomach dropped.

Not again. Not Sly. Dread pooled in Liam's veins.

"Milo! Help him. Please!" Liam turned to plead with Milo, and the world tilted a little. He braced himself on the floor to keep from falling over.

Milo nodded and gracefully raised his hands from the other side of the circle, causing everything to stop as if frozen in time.

The fire sputtered out, the rocks slowly floated back to their pile, and the shredded plants and flowers limped to their table. The sticks dropped into a sad pile, and the water whooshed into the small fountain it had started in.

Liam's shallow breath brought him back to himself.

Am I destined to create chaos? Pain? Disaster?

Milo approached the boys, kneeling on the ground. "May I get a look at your wound?" the wizard asked Sly.

Sly nodded and grimaced, removing his hand again.

Please let him be able to do something. Please!

"Not too bad. I can fix that for you, if you don't mind?" Milo offered.

"Please. Be my guest." Sly grimaced, still trying to play it cool.

Bringing a hand up in front of Sly's hip wound, Milo took a breath and trained his eyes on the blood. A couple of seconds passed and one by one, the sticks and stones fell away.

Liam stared, wide-eyed.

The wound repelled the rocks, sticks, and other shrapnel. The grime and dirt dissipated, and nothing but Sly's flesh and blood remained. Milo turned his hand counterclockwise, and Sly's blood stopped flowing. His skin knit itself back together and the only remnants of a wound was the blood on Sly's sand-colored tunic.

"There. That should do the trick." Milo's gaze glittered over them and he smiled at his work, satisfied. Milo turned to Liam, seriousness eclipsing his expression. "I have only ever seen a demonstration like that once before. Many years ago. This is far bigger than I thought. Liam, come with me inside. I need to talk to you." Milo stood and brushed past him, up the stairs, and out of the sunken courtyard.

Liam stared after him for a second. He'd just watched Milo heal Sly.

Right in front of his eyes! Had Sly ever seen anything like that before? His awe momentarily replaced his shame.

Liam looked at Sly to ask him, but Sly stared back at him, shaking his head, the same wonder in his dark eyes.

"You okay, mate? I saw you hit your head pretty hard," Sly said.

Liam stared. "I just injured you from an explosion and you're asking me if *I'm* okay?"

Sly shrugged.

Liam shook his head, the pain making him groan. "I'll be okay. You?"

Sly sat up straighter and twisted at the hips, checking for pain. He smiled. "Right as rain."

Liam forced a smile, and shame creeped into his stomach. "I'm—I'm so sorry Sly, I—"

"Listen, it's okay. It's not your fault," Sly said.

"It's not my fault? How could you say that? This is *all* my fault." Liam argued, careful to keep his voice down, his head ringing from hitting the ground.

"You don't know what you don't know. You'll figure this out. You gotta give yourself a break. You've been through a lot." Sly clapped him on the shoulder and it sent a jolt of pain into Liam's skull, making him wince. "Ah, so you did hurt yourself?" Sly raised an eyebrow at Liam, who grimaced. "Let's get you up." Sly helped him stand, steadying him when Liam wobbled.

"Really, I'm okay," Sly said.

"Okay," Liam said, trying to get his vision to stop spinning. "Sly?"

"Yeah?"

"Thank you." Liam smiled sadly.

Sly nodded. "You got it, mate."

CHAPTER
TWENTY-FIVE

O nce back inside, Sly went to find Juniper in the Alchemy Lab to give Liam and Milo some space. Liam sat on the antique couch in Milo's living area with a cup of tea in his hands, staring into the fire.

Milo studied Liam from his tall-backed crimson chair.

"What—" Liam cleared his throat. "What happened?"

Milo exhaled. "What were your thoughts while you were out there?"

Annoyance burned in Liam's stomach. Clenching his jaw, he forced away the tightness in his throat. "Why does that matter?" Liam asked quietly.

Milo raised his eyebrows, and his blue eyes twinkled with gentleness. "It matters a great deal. Remember when I said your emotions and thoughts influence your powers?"

Liam sighed, not looking at Milo.

"Today you saw the result of that. As wizards, we must tame our emotions and thoughts to maintain control. If we fail to learn," Milo paused. "You saw the beginnings of what could happen."

"The beginnings?" Liam asked, dread cold in his stomach.

Milo nodded thoughtfully, staring at Liam.

"My mom," Liam said, staring into his cup of tea. "And Aubry. And Conroy. How he hurt her. How *I* hurt her with my powers. How Conroy came after Sly and Johnny. Everything." Liam looked up at Milo, feeling heavy from his confession.

Milo nodded.

Liam dropped his head and stared at the dark-colored tea in his cup. Earl Grey, his favorite. Although now he had no desire to drink any.

"Fear," Milo said. "What are you afraid of?"

Liam pressed his eyes closed and gripped the cup harder to keep his hands from shaking. He hadn't talked to anyone about this since his mom passed. Instead, he stuffed it down and tried to ignore it all. He cut himself off from writing and anything that reminded him of his mom.

"Why are you afraid?" Milo asked after a beat.

Somehow, with Milo being more removed from the situation, the words fell easily from Liam's mouth. "Because I'm failing!" he shouted, looking up at Milo. "I'm failing my mom! And she just dumped this on me. At the last second! She had her whole life to tell me. And did she? No! All that time we spent writing together, she could have told me, so I didn't have to figure this out myself. So I didn't have to flail and try to understand what she wants me to do." He set the teacup down, covered in tea he'd spilled over himself in his anger.

"And then she tells me it's my turn to finish the story? Which apparently means protecting people in a world she created? Protect them from Conroy? How can I do that if I hurt people I care about when casting simple spells? And I got Aubry kidnapped, and she's God knows where." His voice broke as he thought about Aubry cold, afraid, and alone, because he'd dragged her with him. "I don't—I don't know what I'm doing! I'm not cut out for this. How could this be the last thing she did before she died? How is this what she left me?" Tears stung Liam's eyes, and he forced them to stay put.

"That is why," Milo said, "you affected the elements in that way. There's a power inside you, Liam. Power without direction. Much power that requires sorting. Our emotions are linked to our powers, and the grief and fear you are feeling have a hold on you."

Liam stared up at Milo, resentment beginning to burn in his veins.

"What is something good?" Milo asked.

"What?" Liam scrunched his face up.

Why does he have to be so confusing all the time? It's exhausting.

"What is something good that you remember about your mother?" Milo asked, voice thick with emotion.

"I don't want to think about her right now," Liam said.

"If you don't think about her, and you don't confront this, it will consume you."

"So what if it does?" Liam asked, throwing his hands into the air. Anger laced with exhaustion boiled in his stomach.

"Then you will go down a dark path. This is not my first time dealing with a young boy wrought with grief who had powers beyond what he could imagine." A faraway look rose up in Milo's eyes. Sadness crashed in them like the ocean on a dark night.

"What do you mean?" Liam asked.

"My son," he said, just above a whisper.

Liam stared intently at Milo, willing him to keep going.

"My son he—" Milo stopped and swallowed. Liam could see the pain on his face, the anguish, but Milo continued.

"He was a lot like you. He had powers, and when he was young, I taught him. They were chaotic. He struggled to control his emotions and confront what he felt and deal with it properly. His magic was chaos." Milo got up from his seat to stare into the fireplace. The golden flames cast shadows on his tired face, accentuating the lines around his mouth and eyes.

"All my life, I have lived by the motto that I use magic to do good and help other people. And my son he—he was so consumed by grief and anger, he just wanted to destroy. I worked so hard to try to get him to work through it. But he refused. So he left, and he joined one of Domhania's evil warlocks. The most powerful of them. My son wanted more power, more control, so he didn't have to deal with his grief. I tried everything I could to keep him here, but he left." Milo stared into the fire, hands shaking at his sides from the weight of what he shared.

"Who is your son?" Liam asked. "What was his name?"

Milo turned to face Liam, tears in his eyes. He pressed his lips together to keep them from trembling.

His expression startled Liam. Milo, always collected, was coming apart.

"His name . . . his name is Conroy."

CHAPTER
TWENTY-SIX

---◆◇◆---

"Conroy?!" Liam stared in disbelief. "Conroy the wizard who tried to take out my friends? The wizard who kidnapped my cousin? Who tried to kill me and the Stream Side Kids? That's your son?" Liam stood, flailing his arms.

"Yes," Milo said gravely. "That's my son." His eyebrows knitted together and his hands balled into fists.

"How could you let him leave?" Liam asked.

"Like I said, I tried to get him to stay, but he would not."

Liam paced in front of the fire. "So you have an evil son? And he's decimated entire villages, murdering people? Creating orphans? And now he wants something with my cousin, me, and this pendant?"

"Yes. His goal is to claim what he thinks to be his birthright. That way, he would be the most powerful wizard to exist in Domhania."

"Okay, but what did my mom do about this?" As he said it, Liam realized she didn't have as much control as he thought she did. She could guide people along a path and nudge them, but the ultimate choice was theirs, just like she'd tried to explain when he was younger.

Anguish clouded Milo's face. He stood silent for a while.

Liam stared at him, waiting. "Milo?"

Milo sighed and his gray-brown hair fell into his face. "She tried to teach him the way of compassion. Tried to impart wisdom on him. But he was young and when she was gone, he grew angry."

"What do you mean?"

Milo stared at the ground, like he was trying to figure out how to go on. "She was not here . . . She was not able to be here."

Liam shook his head. "I don't understand what you mean." He stepped closer to Milo and saw tears in his eyes. Liam froze, shocked.

"Nora," Milo said her name with a surprising tenderness. "She wasn't able to come back." He swallowed. "Once you die here in this world, you cannot come back. She told me that's how the magic works."

"She died here? How?" Liam croaked, swallowing past the lump in his throat.

Milo closed his eyes and inhaled. "She died—from an illness." Milo opened his eyes to stare at Liam as he struggled to piece everything together. "Nora, my wife, Conroy's mother, died when she was training Conroy, our son, as a young boy. Something went wrong."

"What?" Disbelief slammed into Liam's chest. His breathing sped up and his chest tightened. The dark hole of fear from the courtyard returned. He shook his head and brought his hand up to his forehead.

What is he saying? He can't be saying what I think he's saying.

"My mom was married to you? And had a child?" The room spun and he steadied himself on the arm of the couch.

"Yes," Milo said.

Liam looked up at him with fire in his veins.

"It was before you and your father. Before her family out there," Milo said. "She left me messages somehow, even after she died here."

The fire dimmed in Liam and turned to coldness. He didn't know his mother at all. He knew she could be disconnected, distracted, consumed by stories. But this was a new level. She had a whole life before him and his dad? A different life here in Domhania?

He thought about all the hours she spent writing in her study buried in words. She must have been looking for a way back. Back to the family she missed.

Was he not enough for her? He wasn't magical, he wasn't something from her imagination. A fiery sensation rekindled within him, starting from his stomach and spreading through his chest and arms. The flames in the fireplace grew bigger and hotter. Conroy was the Chosen One. She wanted to be back with Conroy?

Milo glanced at the fireplace with wide eyes. Liam's hands curled in fists.

"I saw what you did with Sly just now . . . why couldn't you do that for her? You're a wizard! Isn't that something you can do?" Liam seethed.

"She—she was in the middle of the birthright ceremony to give Conroy her power. She didn't finish. And when she stopped the ceremony, something went wrong. I think she stopped because she sensed the evil tendencies in Conroy's heart. I don't think she wanted to give him the rest of his birthright magic. So she didn't. But the ceremony is delicate, and when she stopped—" Milo shook his head, despair filling his eyes. "She became ill, as did Conroy. I was still learning at the time and only had enough power to save one of them. They immediately began aging, as if years were passing before my eyes. I tried at once to reverse the magic on them but all I could do was merely hold the tide. But the moment I let go, their clocks would turn until there was nothing left. It would take my whole focus to push back the time that threatened to take their lives away.

"She asked me to save our son. A young life has more years and is stronger than adult lives near the end of their lifetime. It broke everything inside of me to not be able to save her. I wasn't strong enough. After I wove a spell to heal Conroy, I tried to save her, but I couldn't." Tears rolled down Milo's cheeks. Liam saw the agony in his eyes. The calm demeanor he exuded cracked and fell away to expose what was underneath. Regret, pain, anguish.

Liam needed answers. Needed to understand. "What do you mean, you couldn't?"

Milo's shaky words were no comfort. "I tried everything I could."

Liam couldn't take this. Conroy was responsible for his mom's death here. Conroy was the reason she wasn't able to return. And someone as powerful as a wizard couldn't save her? He couldn't accept that as an answer. Because Milo failed to save her, she lived each day with Liam and his dad empty, longing to go back to the storyworld she was locked out of. If she had been saved, maybe things would have been different. Was Liam a lesser version of the first son she had been ripped away from? Her heart was in Domhania and when she couldn't come back, she became lost. Absent from her life in the other world. Always searching for a way to return. Is that why she always wrote?

And he was right next to her, oblivious to it all.

The room was suddenly too small and too hot. He needed to get out. Needed to leave this world. Needed to get Aubry away from Conroy and this place. He couldn't stand to be here a moment longer. He was done with all the politics and tangled stories from Domhania. He was finding a way out, even if he had to do it himself.

Before he could register it, his legs marched out the front door of the castle. Marched past the courtyard, past the bushes, and out the white iron gates, the bitter cold biting into his skin, a welcome shock.

Stopping at the mountain drop off, his vision blurred as he looked over the valley below. A surge of white fiery anger and grief bubbled up in his chest.

He let an angry scream tear through him. It echoed over the mountain. He flung his arms out wide and pushed all his pain, anger, and frustration into it.

He screamed until his voice felt raw and he felt like his insides had been scraped out.

The tall trees below shivered and splintered. Snow barreled down the side of the mountain, creating an avalanche for the valley below. Rocks flew through the surrounding air like a tornado had torn from where he stood on the mountain, down into the valley. A semicircle of trees below lay decimated, not even the stumps remaining.

Breathing heavily, Liam sunk to his knees, spent.

Is that because of me?

Looking around at the destruction, a thought took hold of his mind. Forcefully pushing up from the snow-covered ground, he stomped over to the eastern side of Milo's castle. After a few minutes, he saw what he was looking for. A door.

After Juniper had put the thought in his mind that Milo could be hiding something, Liam looked for maps of the castle. Both Milo and Conroy's castle. Luckily, he had found some in the Armory. After comparing the maps, he saw the same symbol and some sort of passageway on the edge of both maps. Now he would test his theory.

Snow fell heavily, but Liam's anger burned in him, making him oblivious to the cold. He approached the side wall of the castle and found a tower. Bright white stone stretched to the sky and ended at a dark pointed roof. Running his hands over the curved wooden door, he found the circular symbol next to the door handle. Tapping into some of his available anger and surge of power, he willed the door to open. He felt a click beneath his hand as he grabbed the handle, then turned. It opened inward into a dark room.

Let's see if this works.

CHAPTER
TWENTY-SEVEN

L iam entered the room, trailing snow in, and closed the door to the bitter
elements. Lit torches on the wall brought life to the small circular room.
In front of Liam, he saw what looked like a large mirror that stood taller than
him, inlaid into the stone wall. The rest of the room was empty.

This must be the way.

Stepping forward, he saw the mirror-like surface swirl and shift into an image
of a dark stone castle surrounded by shadows. He took another step, and the
image changed to Aubry lying on the floor of a cell, auburn hair splayed around
her. She looked unconscious. Her torn clothes were dotted with blood. Was it
hers? Panic pounded in Liam's chest. He *had* to get to her.

"I'm coming Aubry," he whispered to the image and tipped forward into the
glassy substance of the portal in the wall.

Darkness consumed Liam, and then he fell, twisting and turning over himself
down a dark hole. As quickly as it started, it stopped, and he slammed into
something hard, taking the brunt of the fall with his forearms. Pushing himself
up from what he supposed was the ground, he blinked and tried to get his
bearings. Similar looking ensconced torches flared to life around him. He stood
in a room that looked identical to the one he'd just come from at Milo's castle,

save for the darker stone almost the same color as Conroy's shadows. Liam swallowed the fear that rose in his throat. He hoped the shadows weren't in this room. He had no idea if they operated independently of Conroy or if they were a part of him. He'd come here with very little information, he realized. But he couldn't let his doubt stop him now.

Forward is the only option. He needed to get in, get Aubry out, and go home.

From what Liam remembered of the maps, this doorway sat below the kitchens in the basement. Milo had told them Conroy would probably keep Aubry in the dungeons even further under the castle, underneath the basement. The guards would use warding magic to protect the dungeons and steer people toward other parts of the castle. Liam figured wherever he felt a push coming from, he'd go in that direction. He took a breath and thought that it would have been smart of him to bring some of the *Camomage* potion that cloaked him from Conroy.

He took a steadying breath. *Stop overthinking and just get it done.*

He knew that would be Aubry's advice to him. Stop thinking and mulling, and just do the thing.

Okay, Aub. I'm coming.

With a last look at the circular room with the portal on the wall, he faced the door, willed some of his power into the handle to unlock it, and stepped through into what he hoped was an empty, unassuming hallway.

Inching the door open, he turned his head right and left to check for observers, but saw, thank God, a dark, empty hallway. He quietly closed the door behind him and watched it shimmer and blend into the dark stone to match the rest of the ordinary hallway.

Well, that could be problematic. Pushing his anxiety away, he decided that was a problem for later. He knew he had to go around the kitchens to the left and then down further into the dungeon somehow.

Which way are the kitchens?

At his question, he felt a hum from his power underneath his skin.

Of course! He could use his powers to find where he needed to go. Where did he feel like he was being pushed away from? Looking to the right, he felt nothing but coldness. He shivered.

Looking left, he felt dread and an instinct to avoid that way at all costs.

That's where he needed to go.

Turning left, he cautiously made his way down the long, dark hallway. Head on a swivel, he watched for shadows, people, or anything that looked like it might hurt him, but he encountered nothing.

So strange.

After walking a couple minutes, he came upon a turn in the hallway, leading him to the left. He felt more resistance. It reminded him of when he and Aubry were little and would shove one another's shoulders to see who was stronger. Calling forth the memory of him and his mom in the garden, he imagined the sun on his skin giving him life. Giving him power. He used that and visualized a shield around him. Some of the resistance dampened but didn't dissipate altogether.

He pushed on, feeling resistance like walking through water. Coming upon another turn down a dark hallway he stepped forward and his legs slipped out from under him. He landed hard on stone, then slid down what felt like an incline. Hurtling through darkness, he had enough wits about him to not scream for fear of someone hearing him.

"Oof." Liam wheezed as he landed. Dry spikes clawed at his clothes, and it smelled like a a barn. Letting his eyes adjust, he saw he'd fallen a couple of stories onto a pile of hay at the end of a hallway. Torches hung on the wall every couple feet and stretched into darkness, leaving Liam to only guess what lay at the end.

The urge to escape, to turn around, to run, was overwhelming. Liam told his thoughts to slow down.

It's okay. I'm not in imminent danger. He froze for a few moments to see if anyone had heard him fall. Silence stretched out in front of him.

He pulled himself out of the straw and walked down the only path available. The echo of his steps off the stone floor and walls made him cringe. As he went, he noticed the hallway interspersed with metal bars in addition to the torches.

Is this the dungeon? Had he found it already?

Uneasiness came over Liam, but he kept going. He tried to keep his boots from clicking too loudly on the stone floor, but it sounded like an explosion to his ears. Someone must have heard him by now.

As he made his way down the hall, he peered into the barred rooms that were indeed cells. A few were empty, but the others held people slumped on the ground or against the wall.

None of them stirred when he passed. He took a breath.

Please let them still be alive.

Moving past each cell, his heart pounded.

What if she isn't here?

He came to the end of the cell block and noticed a reddish-brown smear on the ground.

Aubry!

Liam ran. He didn't care anymore who heard him, he had to get to his cousin. Heart thudding, he came up to the bars of the cell, gripping them. They were like ice. His breath puffed out into vapor. How long had she been down here in this cold?

"Aubry?" Liam whispered.

The body on the floor didn't move.

"Aubry. Please wake up," Liam pleaded.

Be alive. Be alive!

"Mmm," she groaned.

"Aubry, please let that be you," Liam said.

"Liam?" a small, pained voice croaked.

"Yes, thank God, Aubry! I'm here. Can you move?" Liam sunk to his knees and reached through the bars to her.

Aubry moved her head to look at Liam, and he had to force himself not to gasp. Her eyes filled with a mix of pain and relief. Her face was bruised purple and black. Her cheeks looked like someone had hit her again and again. Purple half-moons puffed out under her eyes and dried blood crusted her hairline. Every breath she took appeared to be a struggle, her chest rising and falling with visible effort.

The sight of his cousin in such a battered state ignited a fire within Liam's chest, fists clenching at his sides in helpless fury. He could feel the anger building up inside him, threatening to spill over like an overflowing cauldron of boiling emotions. The need for vengeance burned brightly in his eyes as he met Aubry's gaze, silently promising retribution for the unspeakable horrors she'd endured.

Aubry managed a weak smile through her swollen lips, her voice barely above a whisper. "I knew you would come," she rasped, her words laced with gratitude and agony. The vulnerability in her expression struck deep.

"What did he do to you?" Liam ground out from behind his teeth. "He'll pay for this."

"Well, well. What do we have here?" a sharp voice rang out behind him.

Snapping his head around to look over his shoulder, he saw Conroy standing several feet away dressed in black, covered in dark leather torso armor, calf-high boots, and a black cloak. A man dressed in shadows.

Liam's stomach dropped, and then anger brewed as he remembered what Milo had just told him. As he thought about what he'd done to Aubry, to his mom, to his family, he narrowed his eyes at Conroy, breath coming in heavy.

"Not happy to see me, *brother?*" Conroy sneered.

Liam shot to his feet, new energy sizzling through him, and flung his anger at Conroy. A small fireball flew from Liam's hand at the dark wizard. Curling his fingers, Conroy turned Liam's attempt to attack him into smoke that floated away into the icy air of the dungeon.

Conroy cocked his head, darkness rising in his eyes. "I'll show you what it looks like to really use magic, *brother.*"

Conroy circled his hands, forming ice spears from the air and pulling stones from the ceiling above them. Rotating his hands, he made an ice studded rock ball and hurled it at Liam. He jumped out of the way, pressing himself into the narrow wall of the dungeon hallway.

Aubry cried out as the stone smashed through the bars of her cell and rained rock down over her.

"Aubry!" Liam yelled.

Conroy smiled and ignited fire in his palms, cocking his arm back to throw one at Liam. He launched it.

Liam pushed off the wall into the other side of the hallway and moved, the fireball singing his sleeve.

Not again. Not the Wizard's Fire again.

Conroy lit another.

It hurtled toward Liam, a tail of smoke following it through the air.

Liam had seconds to do something before the fire burned and incapacitated him. Desperately looking for something to use, he saw a pail of water inside the cell next to Aubry's. Pulling some of the humming power from his veins, he flung the water to meet the fireball hurtling towards him. The water extinguished the fireball just in time, drenching him.

Conroy inclined his head. "Very good, little brother." He smiled. "Let's see what else you can do with water, huh? Did Mom give you some of her powers too?"

"Liam, it's a trap! Leave," Aubry said weakly.

Liam didn't have time to figure out what she meant. Water rose from every pail in the dungeon's hallway and turned toward Liam, twisting through the air like whirlpools. The tails of water rushed at him like a dozen snakes and slammed him into the bars of Aubry's cell. The water held him there, crashing down on him like a wave from the ocean. It flooded his eyes, his mouth, his nose.

"Hey!" Aubry shouted. Something flew out of the cell towards Conroy until it hit an invisible shield a couple of feet in front of him and dropped to the floor.

The water drowning Liam fell away, and he dropped to his hands and knees, gasping for air.

"I'm not going to kill him right now. Don't worry, little Aubry." Conroy grinned wolfishly.

Aubry stood, holding herself up against the bars of her cell, arms shaking like it took all her effort.

"I thought it would be fun to play with him before I used him up." Conroy flicked his fingers at his sides and shadows moved from the walls to the ground and slithered toward Liam. He scrambled back, and his back met the cold, hard metal of the bars. He had nowhere to go. He'd seriously underestimated Conroy. Why did he think he could do this alone?

He glanced at Aubry to apologize for failing her. She looked past Conroy, disbelief creeping up her face. Following her gaze, Liam saw three figures moving through the darkness.

Conroy noticed them staring, narrowed his eyes, and snapped his head around to find Milo coming down the dungeon hallway, hands raised, navy cloak flowing behind him, his faded brown hair pushed back from his face. The serene countenance he usually held seemed to be cracking.

"Come to save your new little project, *Father?*" Conroy's said.

Milo flinched. "Conroy, your battle is with me. Not with Liam. Leave him out of this." Milo fought to keep his face calm.

"Oh, on the contrary. Did you know that this boy holds quite the power? Power that is the rest of my birthright. Power that is rightfully *mine.*" Conroy glared at Milo, then slid his gaze to Liam. Desperate desire glinted in Conroy's eyes.

"Conroy, there is another way. The boy is as much your mother's child as you are." Milo stepped forward, reaching toward Conroy.

Conroy scoffed. "Oh Father. How little you understand. I've grown since you've known me." Liam watched Milo's features soften as he looked at Conroy like he could see the little boy he'd lost all those years ago. Conroy's pale face held none of the warmth that Milo's had. Liam tried to picture Conroy as a boy running around in the castle with Milo teaching him how to use his powers. He couldn't.

He couldn't see this man dressed in darkness and shadows running around with any glee in his face. All he saw was lust for power, anger, destruction.

How could Conroy have come from serene Milo? And his mom? He shuddered at the thought. Conroy's short dark hair, dark clothes, and dark demeanor were the opposite of Milo. Serenity, albeit a little unsteady currently, flowed around Milo while darkness surrounded the edges of Conroy.

Liam didn't foresee this going well. He pulled himself up against Aubry's cell.

"Ah, I see you're ready to come with me then? Ready to live out your true purpose?" Conroy flicked his gaze to Liam again.

"I'm *not* going with you." Liam glared.

"Taking the hard route, are we? Very well." Conroy stepped back and sent fire and stone at Liam. He tapped into his anger still simmering and threw his hands up to block them, but the stone continued to hurtle at him. He spun out of the way, but not fast enough. A piece of rubble tore open his arm and set his sleeve on fire. He cried out as the fire burned through his clothes. He could not let it reach his skin again. If it did, he'd be useless in this fight. Remembering the water in a pail in Aubry's cell, he reached for it with his magic, urging it to douse the fire. Like a snake, the water rose up and slithered over to Liam, putting out the Wizard's Fire just before it reached his skin.

Milo ripped a gust of wind through the air and wrapped it around Conroy, like a rope. Conroy batted it away like an errant breeze.

Focused on Milo, Conroy shot dark vines up from the ground that snaked around Milo's legs and forced him down. With Milo down, Conroy spun around and sent tiny ice spears at Liam.

Liam brought his hands up, shot fire at the spears and melted them before they could impale him. Before Liam could catch his breath, his stomach dropped as he saw shadows undulating across the floor to encircle his ankles. He tried to step out of the way, and use the air to dissolve them, but they moved faster, gripping him hard.

Focusing on the ground, Liam willed roots up through the stones. They shot up around Conroy like fingers and lunged for his legs. Before they could reach Conroy, he scorched them away with an amused smile. It distracted him long enough for Liam to twist free from the shadows. Relief flooded Liam, only to be ripped away by dread a second later when the shadows reached for him again and pinned him to the bars of Aubry's cell. Icy coldness flooded his limbs and raced for his chest, feeling like a weight pressed down on him, draining his strength. The shadows coaxed his breath away, making it hard to breathe.

"Liam, no!" Aubry yelled hoarsely and tried to peel the shadows away from him. She yelped and pulled her hand back.

"I'm sorry, Aubry. I'm sorry for the failed rescue attempt," Liam apologized, looking into Aubry's tired and puffy eyes.

"No! You're not giving up! Try harder Liam. I know you can do this," she cried, wiping frustrated tears away.

He didn't know if he could. He was so tired. Tired of failing. Tired of not knowing how to use his supposedly special power. His mom couldn't even stop Conroy, so how could he?

Maybe he could make a door, like he made in the side of the tree when Conroy chased them through the forest. Sure, he had been practically unconscious then, but that meant he should be able to do it now all the more, right?

The shadows were at his wrists and ankles, and he already felt weaker because of them. If he was going to try something, he needed to hurry while Conroy was distracted fighting Milo. Feeling the hum of power in his blood, he answered the call to use it and reached inside himself. He visualized a door coming into existence on the stone wall next to the cell. Saw the golden edges of it shimmer and take shape.

Yes! It's working!

He brought the image to mind, and it materialized. In an instant, it sputtered and the image was gone. He felt a snap inside of him, like someone had slapped a hand over his power.

"You think someone as inexperienced as yourself can get through my wards and make a portal out? How sweet is that?" Conroy said as he threw fire and dodged Milo's ice pellets, turning them to water.

Wards. They were stopping him. He couldn't make a way out.

They were stuck. Trapped. He couldn't get them out of this.

The sound of clattering echoed from the other end of the hallway. Something blue glowed, then dimmed.

"Sly, they're down here!" Juniper's voice bounced off the stone walls. Liam almost laughed with relief.

Conroy narrowed his eyes and turned, sending fire from the torches at them.

"Juniper, look out!" Sly dove in front of his sister and pushed her out of the way. Liam's heart pounded.

Juniper and Sly stood up unscathed. Liam sighed. Maybe they could get out of here. Maybe they had a chance?

Liam looked back at Aubry. She hung onto the bars of her cell, looking helplessly at Liam. The shadows holding him in place hadn't moved. He took a breath and pushed past the darkness of them, looking for the golden sun of his power. Iciness pierced his hands like the shadows were tightening their grip on him. He pushed against them and met bitter cold frostbite at the edge of his fingers. He groaned and pushed the pain from his focus. He took as deep a breath as he could, looking for the power he inherited from his mom. Looking for her hope. For her belief in him. Deep inside him, he felt a small, warm flicker. Small or not, he would take it. Finding it, he grabbed on and looked for the lock on Aubry's cell. Seeing it next to his left wrist, he sent power at it, and golden light balled, disintegrating the lock.

"Aubry." Liam nodded at the open cell. She spotted it and eagerly staggered to the open door. She gently pushed it open wide enough for her to slip through. Once outside the cell, she took a breath, and tears fell down her face.

Liam swallowed. It hurt seeing her like this. Seeing her relief. He hated that she'd ever had the thought that she wouldn't make it out.

"Liam." Aubry turned to face him, wiping her tears from her dirty, bruised face. "I'm so glad you came to get me. But you shouldn't have." Her glassy eyes searched his and she stepped closer to him. "He wanted you here. He wants to take your power from you."

"What? Why?"

"He kept saying it's his birthright. And you stole it?" Aubry looked at him, confused.

"Aubry, there's so much I need to tell you, but we have to go, now," Liam said, pulling on the shadows still wrapped around him.

"Yes, we need to get out of here *now*." Sly slid up next to them. He looked at Liam, then Aubry. When he took in her state, he balked, bringing a hand up to cover his mouth. "What happened, love?" Sly stepped closer to Aubry and gently touched her cheek. She winced, and he pulled his hand away, looking hurt. "I'm going to get you out of here, okay?" Sly promised and pushed her hair from her face, taking in her injuries. The longer he looked at her, the more pained he looked. "Drink this now and get out of here," Sly commanded, handing her a vial of gray swirling liquid that looked like the surface of the portal Liam had come through to get here.

"What is that?" Liam asked.

"A potion Milo taught us to brew. It'll take us back to his castle," Sly explained. "Aubry, you take this first and we'll be right behind you." He shook his head as he looked at the dried blood on her forehead. "Willow will be there right away to tend to your wounds."

"But Liam—" Aubry looked at the shadows holding him in place.

"Don't worry, we'll get him out of here too," Sly promised, cupping her cheek gently.

"Go, Aubry!" Liam said. He couldn't stand to have her here a moment longer. She'd endured enough on his behalf. Enough for a lifetime.

She nodded, tearing up, and tipped the potion into her mouth. She shimmered and faded as she looked back and forth between Liam and Sly. Then she was gone.

Sly looked at Liam. "Okay, now we need to get you out of here."

"You came after me," Liam said.

Sly nodded.

"I'm sorry. I'm sorry I dragged you all into this."

"Escape now, apologise later. How do we get you out of this?" Sly asked, eyeing the shadows.

"I want to try something," Liam said.

"You better try fast." Sly's mouth twitched.

Liam nodded and went back to the garden he'd imagined in the training courtyard earlier with Milo. He breathed in peace. Breathed in the golden warmth and used it to cover the shadows, the same way he'd used it to unlock Aubry's cell. Gold power bubbled out of him and wrapped around the shadows. Liam felt resistance but kept going, adding more weight to his power. With a burst of light, the shadows withered away like weeds scorched by the sun.

"Ah!" Conroy cried out. He stopped fighting Milo and bent over like he was in pain. His cold, dark eyes found Liam, and he glared.

"Liam, now!" Sly passed him the potion, and he drank it. His skin tingled, and he his hand shimmered and disappeared as the scene before him faded away. Sparks of power flew between Milo and Conroy. Juniper slid behind Conroy, slicing his back, then downed her potion.

Milo dislodged a giant piece of the wall and brought it down on top of Conroy, who raised his hands and broke it into pebbles.

Conroy smiled darkly. Liam realized he'd been playing defensively. A long sharp vine shot through Milo's back. The pointed end split through his abdomen, and he cried out in pain.

"No!" Liam yelled.

Milo fell to his knees.

Liam shimmered and faded, and once again felt himself falling, tumbling and turning into darkness.

CHAPTER TWENTY-EIGHT

---◆◇◆---

L iam's chest heaved, burning with traces of power as he crashed into the cold stone floor. The tingle of power quickly turned to pain. He'd overexerted himself. Tiredness pulled at him, making his limbs heavy.

A groan pulled him out of his daze.

"Milo!" Liam turned around. Milo kneeled, sucking in ragged breaths. Liam looked around for help. They were sitting on the stone floor of what Liam guessed was Milo's Alchemy Lab. The cold gray stones spread across the floor and continued up the walls. Aubry sat slumped in a wooden chair, a fairy girl pressing a cloth to her forehead, cleaning her up, the smell of herbs thick in the air. The bowl of water the fairy girl held swirled red with Aubry's blood. Liam's stomach clenched.

Juniper and Sly appeared out of nothing, sweat slick on their foreheads. Aubry sat forward and blanched as she took in Milo on his hands and knees.

"We need to heal him!" Juniper yelled, rushing toward Milo. Liam scanned her, then felt a slight relief. She looked uninjured.

"Help me with him!" Liam looked at Sly as he pushed himself up from the ground. They got on either side of Milo and pulled him to his feet.

Milo groaned. Liam winced. The sharp vine Conroy impaled Milo's abdomen with stuck out of him on either side of him.

Crap, crap, crap. This is not good. Liam buzzed with anxiety and panic, heart pounding in his ribcage. Liam stared wide-eyed at Sly, breathing heavy and nodded a thank you.

Sly returned it, adjusting his grip around Milo.

"Let's get him into a chair." Liam tried to keep his voice steady. Sly and Liam carried Milo, legs dragging, shimmery navy robes snagging on stones and caking with dust.

This cannot happen. He will be okay. He must be, Liam thought over and over. He'd only just met Milo. Only just begun his training. Without him, he didn't know what to do.

Liam tightened his grip around Milo's waist as blood drenched his robes.

So much blood. Swallowing, Liam reminded himself to breathe and put him down gently in the chair. *Just keep breathing. Everything will be okay. He will not die. He will be okay.* His mom's face flashed in his mind, concave and devoid of life. Shaking his head, he forced it away and focused on placing Milo down.

"Hey mate, how are you holding up?" Sly looked at Milo.

Milo sighed in response.

Sly winced. "You need to keep talking to me. And don't close your eyes, you hear me?"

"Ah, giving me orders now, are you?" The faintest of smiles pulled at the corner of Milo's mouth. "Although, I suppose that's what you know how to do best, being the leader of your people and all."

Sly smiled tightly. "That's right, keep talking."

Johnny and Fox rushed in as Liam and Sly stepped back from Milo.

"Is everyone—" Fox stopped as he scanned the room and saw Milo in the chair. The blood drained from his face.

Johnny placed a hand on Fox's shoulder. "Let us know if you need something," he murmured, pulling Fox back against the wall out of the way.

"Tell us what to do!" Liam begged Milo, staring in horror at the branch and the blood spilling down the front and back of his robes. He balled his hands into fists to keep them from shaking. Never in his life had he been surrounded by so much blood than he had these past few days. Never had he seen so much pain, so much suffering.

Milo nodded, eyes half closed. "There is a recipe there for healing. You need to follow the instructions so I can drink it." He nodded at the table in the center of the room. For the first time, Liam looked around the Alchemy Lab. Vials, wooden boxes, hanging cloth bags, herbs, and dried flowers lined the walls. A wooden table in the middle, much like Roya's at the hideout, held books, bowls, utensils, measurement devices, cups, and quills. How was he supposed to know how to use any of that?

"I'm on it!" Juniper yelled.

"What about this branch?" Sly stared at Milo and the branch sticking out.

"You have to take it out," Milo wheezed.

"How are we supposed to do that?" Liam swallowed, trying to keep his panic at bay for Milo's sake.

"You want me to pull it out, mate?" Sly asked.

Liam turned and stared wide-eyed at Sly like he'd lost his mind.

Milo shook his head, "Liam. Liam has to take it out with his powers. You can make it disintegrate."

Liam shook his head. "I don't know how to do that!" He shoved his hands into his hair.

What in the world is he talking about? All I can do is make chaos. He saw it!

"You can. Use your good memories to help you," Milo said, head drifting back.

"Oh, no you don't," Sly said, tipping his head back up.

"Liam, I saw what you did to Conroy's shadows. If you can make those wither away, you can surely make a vine disintegrate." Juniper walked over to place her hand on Liam's shoulder and nodded encouragingly, her coils bobbing.

Liam stared into her calm brown eyes that reminded him of his favorite cup of Earl Grey tea. He saw her belief and took some of it for himself, using it as his anchor.

He had to try. He had to try, or Milo would die. He would not let him die. Turning to Milo, he nodded. His dim blue eyes urged Liam to try. To believe in himself. They needed him to. It would not end this way. He wouldn't let it. Liam reached out his hand, took a breath, and closed his eyes.

He slowed his breathing and tried to think of something good. These past few days had been full of pain and disappointment. He swept that aside and dug around for something good to latch onto. He remembered the Yosemite trip he took with his parents when they hiked to the top of a waterfall together. He remembered the breathtaking view of the valley below. The village of trees, the birds' songs. The blanket of peace nature wrapped around him. With this, he focused on the branch sticking out of Milo and willed it to disintegrate into nothing. Warmth spread from his chest, along his arms, and down his fingers.

Milo groaned. Liam inhaled shakily but kept going.

He remembered birds soaring—*think of the branch slipping away*—the stillness of the moment. He exhaled and remembered the breeze through the trees whispering, "be still."

He willed Milo's pain away. Believed the branch could disintegrate. He pulled at the golden power that rested deeper beneath the surface of his consciousness. It was tired and exhausted, but he needed just a little more. For Milo. Planting his feet, he grounded himself and latched onto it, pleading with it to heal Milo. To save him.

Peeling an eye open, he watched the branch go from solid to something dimmer.

It's working! Liam called forth his power, pushing it to Milo. Heaviness crept into his limbs. He clenched his jaw, pushed past it, and commanded more power to wrap around the vine to burn it away like he did Conroy's shadows. Milo groaned again. Liam pushed on. He kept pouring power out until he didn't feel resistance from the vine anymore. Finally, it disappeared like steam into the air.

I did it! The room tilted. He put his arm out on the chair to steady himself.

He smiled at Sly. They both flicked their gaze to Milo, staring with their mouths open at the hole in Milo, devoid of any tree branch.

Liam stared at Milo, who was still breathing heavily and losing lots of blood. Without the branch to hold it back, it poured from him, soaking his clothes and dripping onto the floor, making his navy robes black.

Liam frantically looked for something to soak up blood with. As he turned his head, dizziness unsteadied him. Sly passed Liam a large piece of cloth.

Liam took it and kneeled to press it to Milo's side, the floor grounding him.

"You're going to be okay. Hang in there," Liam said, trying to convince himself as much as Milo.

Milo forced a weak smile, his blue eyes losing more color.

"Here! I got it!" Juniper ran over with a vial of earthy green colored liquid and handed it to Milo. He tried to grasp it, but his hand shook too much.

"Here, Sly, tip his head back." Juniper motioned with her head and brought the vial to Milo's lips. She tilted it into his mouth, and he drank.

They stared at him, waiting.

The cloth stopped filling with more blood. Looking up at him, Liam willed the bright blue back into Milo's eyes. He had to be alive. He *had* to.

"Are you okay?" Fox breathed from behind them.

Milo nodded ever so slightly.

"I will be. This slows the bleeding and speeds up the healing process. Now I need to rest. Thank you. You've all done well. Please take me to my sleeping chambers."

He's okay. Relief made Liam's limbs even heavier.

Milo's eyebrows came together as he looked at Liam. "I'm going to be alright. You did well." He brought the back of his hand up to Liam's cheek and gently brushed a tear away Liam hadn't realized was there.

Liam let out the breath he was holding, sat back on his feet, and looked to the ceiling, a wash of gratitude coming over him.

"Thank you." Liam looked at Milo, the blue seeping back into his eyes.

"Thank *you*," Milo said.

Liam shook his head. "This is all my fault. You told us what to do, how to save you. You came for me. Thank you."

Milo dipped his head.

Releasing the cloth from Milo's side, Liam attempted to wipe some of the blood from his hands. He held back a gag when he looked down and realized how much blood covered his hands and clothes. The sharp tang of it forced him to breathe through his mouth.

"Would you boys mind helping me to my room, please? The potion is working, but not that fast, I'm afraid. I need time to recover." Milo sat up straighter and winced.

"We've got you, mate." Sly slid his arm under Milo's again and reached around his torso to lift him up. Liam threw down the bloody cloth and got on Milo's other side. This time, Milo helped them so they weren't dragging him across the floor.

Progress, thought Liam. *It's all going to be okay.*

"We'll clean up in here," Johnny said, looking at the bloody cloth, floor, and disheveled potions table, his face stoic, as always. Liam figured he'd seen his fair share of bloody rags since Conroy and his men had attacked their village. He shuddered at the thought.

"Thank you." Milo nodded weakly, a small smile pulling at the corners of his lips.

Liam hoped they could do something about the smell of blood. Otherwise, he didn't know if he'd be able to stomach coming back in here.

"Can you tell us where to go?" Sly asked Milo.

"Yes, I can direct you," Milo said.

Following Milo's directions, Sly and Liam ambled Milo up one flight of stairs and then another to his bedchambers. Liam pushed through the pain and fatigue, telling himself Milo had it worse. He would see to it Milo was safe and resting before he could sleep himself. Milo's room resembled Liam's. A four-poster bed, fireplace, bathroom, but his room also housed a mini library as well as its own potions table in the corner. Thick rugs layered the stone floor, padding their steps.

"Do you want to change out of your bloody clothes?" Sly asked after they set Milo on the edge of his bed.

Milo snapped his fingers and instantly wore new blood-free clothes.

"Well, that must be nice." Sly chuckled.

Milo smiled weakly. "Just a party trick I'm afraid. Shame it doesn't work as well on sharpened foliage."

Sly looked at the giant fireplace at the foot of the bed, cold and unlit. With a flick of his wrist, Milo brought a flame alive.

Sly turned back and raised his eyebrows.

Milo smiled. "You all get some rest now too." He pushed the covers back and lay down.

Liam stared at him for a beat. He looked so small in the great bed.

Should I just leave him? Shouldn't someone watch over him?

Milo stared back, the blue in his eyes seeming more faded than before. "I'll be okay."

"Liam," Sly called from the doorway. "Are you coming?"

Liam blew out his cheeks and followed Sly out the door, leaving Milo to heal.

CHAPTER TWENTY-NINE

———◆○◆———

L iam numbly followed Sly out the door.

He kept his eyes on the back of Sly's brown leather vest and trailed behind him through the castle's twists and turns. He tried not to think about how small and gaunt Milo looked lying down. A heavy fear rose in his chest.

What if Milo dies too?

Helpless in bed, unable to move, slowly slipping away into the last sleep of his life? Choking on the thought, he sucked in a breath and turned around.

Sly's hand grabbed his shoulder, gripping him in place.

"Where you going, mate?" His eyebrows pulled together as he searched Liam's face for an answer. He seemed to find it. Nodded. "He's going to be okay."

Sly let go.

His confidence and steady gaze gave Liam something to hold on to. Something to keep him from slipping into the sea of fear he felt brushing against his ankles, threatening to pull him under. He never had a brother, but he imagined this is what it would be like. Someone there to help keep you from drowning.

"How do you know?"

Sly shrugged. "Because I know what I saw. You healed him. The potion worked."

Liam chewed the inside of his cheek and nodded.

"I'm sure he's been through injuries like this before. Most wizards have. And he's a strong one. I can feel it. It's hard to explain, but I have peace about it, and I know he's going to be okay," Sly said.

Liam tried to swallow the lump in his throat.

Sly held out his dark hand. Liam shook it. Sly pulled him in to clap him on the back.

"It's going to be okay. Even if things don't turn out how you think they should."

"Thanks," Liam said as they pulled apart and walked down the hall. He wasn't sure how Sly could have that perspective after what happened to him and his sister. They watched their parents die. Both of them. Their town was decimated. All the kids became orphans. How were things okay? He rubbed his eyes, pushing the thoughts away.

Thankfully, they'd made it back to the Alchemy Lab. Now that Milo wasn't at death's door, he needed to check on Aubry and make sure she was okay.

"Before we go in there, I need to know." Sly turned to him, hands on his weapons belt. "Why did you go by yourself?"

Liam met his gaze, then looked away, shame heavy on his shoulders.

"I just . . .I needed to get Aubry out. I couldn't take being here anymore." Liam swallowed, thinking about what Milo had told him about Conroy, his mom, and his powers.

Sly studied him. "What happened with Milo after the training courtyard?"

Why does he always have to be so clever? Can't he just once not ask the hard questions?

Liam sighed and looked up at the ceiling. "Milo told me he was married to my mom, and Conroy is their child. When he was young, she was doing a birthright ceremony to give him her powers but stopped. Conroy almost died, but my mom told Milo to save him. He could only save one of them, so my mom died here and could never come back because of it. Now Conroy believes he's the rightful heir to my mom's power, and he wants to take mine from me." Liam let the words tumble out so he could get it over with as soon as possible. Unfortunately, it didn't lessen the sting he felt. Crossing his arms, he stared at Sly, giving him an *'are you happy now?'* look.

Sly pursed his lips and slowly nodded. "Well, I can see why you wanted to run away."

Liam narrowed his eyes.

Sly held up his hands. "I'm just saying that's a lot to take in."

"Each time I grasp something here, something new pops up and I feel like I'm unraveling all over again. I just needed to rescue Aubry and get out of here," Liam said, dropping his arms.

Sly shook his head. "You can't be a hero on your own, mate."

"Apparently not. If you wouldn't have come after us, I don't know if we'd be alive right now," Liam admitted.

Sly made a brotherly grab for Liam's shoulder. "Next time, let us know before you want to go on a rescue mission?"

Letting out a long sigh, Liam nodded. There was no way he would risk himself and Aubry like that again. He looked down and saw he still had remnants of Milo's blood on his hands. All because he thought he could do this on his own.

Maybe Clive was right. Like Sly said, he couldn't be a hero alone. Curling his hands into fists, he bit back the feeling of failure and resentment rising in him.

"I need to go see Aubry now," Liam said, stepping away from Sly's grip. Grasping the handle to the Alchemy Lab with an unsteady hand, he prayed Aubry had improved. He'd never forgive himself if she hadn't.

Inside the Alchemy Lab, Juniper bent over Aubry, holding a cloth to her forehead. Willow hovered above the ground next to them, her wings glittering in the candlelight. Johnny and Fox were gone, but the blood smeared across the floor earlier had disappeared, like Milo hadn't almost bled out in the potions room. Herbs and tea eclipsed the metallic tang in the air.

Sly slid into the room after Liam.

A teapot and six teacups sat on the table in the center of the room. Four cups contained tea, while two cups sat empty with crumbs at the bottom. Liam looked up and around at the castle ceiling. He guessed the castle really did know what they needed and took its job of tending to them seriously.

"Aubry?" Liam's heavy voice echoed off the stone walls, coming back to him hollow. In a few steps, he was across the room, at her side. Bruises still decorated her face, but Juniper had cleaned up all the dried blood. His cousin's chair sat pushed against the wall so she could lean her head against it. The effort it took her to look at Liam and open her eyes looked exhausting, but there they were—those green eyes he'd had in his life since childhood. They were still there. Still open. Still alive.

"Aubry, I'm so sorry." Liam's voice shook, and he gently grasped her hand. The shadows under her eyes spoke of sleepless nights. He didn't want to think about what Conroy did to her during those long hours. She still wore the same shirt she'd come into Domhania wearing. Liam noticed all the rips and slashes in the fabric, her skin raw underneath. He swallowed down his dread and tears.

"Liam." Aubry gave him a small smile. "You're okay?"

"Yes, I'm okay. I should be the one asking you that. I'm so sorry this happened to you. It's all my fault. I shouldn't have brought you here. Into this mess. Into my mess. It hurts me to see you like this." Liam's eyes glistened. "I was supposed to take care of you."

"Since when?"

"Since I'm a year older and you're like a little sister to me," Liam said, annoyed he had to explain himself.

She chuckled, then sucked in a breath, curling in on herself. "Liam, how long have I been taking care of you after your fights at school?" She looked at him through her grimace of pain.

"Every week for almost three years. But that's not the point—"

"The point is—" Aubry pinned him with her stare, and he stopped talking. "The point is, we take care of each other. That's how family works."

Liam stared into her green eyes and saw something in them he hadn't seen before. "When did you get so wise?" he asked.

Aubry looked to the ceiling. "Somewhere in the time Conroy was telling me you and him are brothers and your mom is *his* actual family. It didn't take long to realize he didn't really understand what family means. He kept asking me to tell him your weaknesses, but I kept telling him all the ways you're strong. That you're brave. That you're ten times the man he is even being a teenager."

Sitting in a moment of disbelief, Liam took in his cousin's state. Her bruised and beaten body made his skin crawl. "But you had to go through this because of me."

"Do you know how many times I had to watch you get bloody at school? How many times I wished it was me, just once, so you didn't have to go through it again?" Her voice broke as she stared at him, eyes glassy.

Liam shook his head.

"And I'd do it again for you." Aubry's gaze didn't waver as she stared into his watery gray eyes.

"Can I hug you?" Liam asked softly.

Aubry smiled. "Gently."

Liam let go of her hand and slowly brought his arms around her, careful not to squeeze too hard.

"Love you, Leems."

"Love you too, Aub," Liam whispered before he pulled back and let her rest against the wall. "Juniper," he said, wiping his tears and still looking at Aubry. "Have you got any of that healing potion?"

"She took some right before you came in," Juniper said from behind him.

"How long will it take to work?" Liam turned to face her.

"Well, she isn't a wizard, so she won't heal as fast as you. And uh—" Juniper sighed. "He did a number on her. It's going to take a couple of days. She needs to rest. Can you two help me take her upstairs?"

Sly smiled tightly and moved toward Aubry. Liam got the feeling Sly didn't enjoy seeing her like this any more than he did.

Liam nodded a thank you to Juniper, who just stared back. Turning on his heel to help, he wobbled, and the room spun and tilted.

"Woah," Juniper said, coming to his side, supporting him. "I think you need to rest, too. You've expended too much of yourself and you're just learning how to use your powers. Best let Sly take her up. I can help *you*."

Liam saw Juniper's face swirling and looked at Aubry to make sure she was okay. She flushed and smiled as Sly scooped her into his arms. His gaze held something in it for her, and Liam saw the same in Aubry's. She rested her head against his chest and closed her eyes, a smile pulling at her lips. He guessed she would be okay.

"Alright," Liam mumbled, his mouth feeling heavy. His whole body felt heavy now that he thought about it.

"Let's go. Time for some rest," Juniper said, leading him out of the Alchemy Lab.

CHAPTER THIRTY

---◆O◆---

"Here you go," Juniper said, ducking out from Liam's arm and leaning him up against the wall outside his room.

"Thanks," Liam said, trying to focus on her eyes. The way the light from the sconces flickered lit up her face, making it glow. Warmth bloomed in Liam's chest.

Juniper narrowed her eyes. "Why did you go off by yourself? Why didn't you ask us to go with you?"

Liam sighed. He'd been having such a pleasant moment admiring her face. Why did she have to be mad right now? He'd just talked to Sly about this, and the world wouldn't stop spinning. "Do we really have to talk about this now?"

Juniper pursed her lips. "I suppose not." She stared at him for a beat, the softness of her features melting away. "Don't do it again." She pivoted on her heel and left Liam in the dimly lit hallway.

Liam grunted after her in annoyance and pushed the door open to his room. Shuffling over to his four-poster bed draped in navy velvet curtains with shimmering silver stars splashed across them like the night sky, he looked down at his hands and gagged at Milo's blood still on them.

He shuffled over to the bathroom to find a claw footed club filled with steaming water and a floating bar of soap. Looking around, he saw no one who could have filled the tub on his behalf.

The castle again. He mouthed a thank you and peeled off his grimy, bloody clothes. The hot water rose around him as he lowered himself into it and commanded his muscles to relax. Water curled around his aching body. He waited for the relief to come. His mind wouldn't stop whirring. The tension in his neck and shoulders hardened like stone. He'd been in such a heightened state of stress for the past few days, and he wasn't sure he knew how to make his mind slow down.

Grabbing the lemon scented soap, he scrubbed hard at the blood on his hands and arms. Scrubbed at the grime on his body, thinking that maybe if he scrubbed hard enough, he could make the guilt, regret, and pain of it all go away.

In one day, he'd found out his mom had a whole life here before him, and he apparently had an evil half-brother. How was he supposed to deal with that? How was he supposed to sort through everything swirling around in his head?

He scrubbed harder.

First, he lost his mom before his eyes. He couldn't get the image of her lying back against the white pillows, eyes closed, not breathing, out of his head. He saw the dark half-moons under her eyes, sallow skin, her once rich dark hair faded with sickness.

The last time he saw his mom.

Still.

Lifeless.

He pressed the weight of his hand to his chest as panic pricked in his sternum.

So many times, he'd watched her while she slept. Making sure she kept breathing while she was sick. Recalling the last memory he had of his mom, he saw her lie back like she was sinking into a cloud.

How could she really be gone?

The thought punched him in the chest, adding to the knot of anxiety. He took a breath, trying to loosen the growing ache inside him.

Everything had been different since she'd been gone. He hadn't been able to show her pieces of his writing. He couldn't bring her a tray of tea and scones every afternoon, signaling it was time to talk about their current reads. It had been months since he'd seen the spark in her eyes when she told him about her writing. Three months of her gone.

And he'd almost watched Milo die today.

His throat tightened. In his thoughts, he saw Milo's pale face, blood dripping down his clothes, his navy cloak turning black, his ragged breathing. He'd first read about Milo in his mom's books and seeing him here felt like a sliver of closeness to her. His mom created him. Knew him when she was alive. Loved him. He'd been afraid to lose his connection to his mom as Milo sat in that chair in the Alchemy Lab, dying.

Then he had turned to Liam, telling him he could save him.

How was I able to do that? It doesn't make sense. Aubry got hurt because of him. He'd hurt Sly. Milo had almost *died. Am I destined to have everyone around me die?* Fear of losing more people hardened in his stomach and buried itself there.

Conroy wanted his powers now. His mom gave birth to Conroy. Pressing his palms into his eyes, he begged the thoughts to stop. He didn't want to think about any of it. He hated how the weight of them pressed on him like a boulder, squeezing the air from his lungs. He couldn't hold the weight of everything.

His mom, Sly, Milo, Aubry, Conroy, helping protect this world. His mom asked him to do something he didn't even know how to begin to understand. He had no idea what he was doing. Nothing was in his control. How could he help when he couldn't even fully control his abilities? More than anything, he wished he could talk to his mom.

Closing his eyes, he urged a memory forward.

His mom's face appeared, handing him a waterproof book while he sat in the bathtub. He must have been six or seven years old. Bubbles floated on the water, making Liam feel like he bathed in clouds.

He remembered his mom helping him bathe and reading to him out of the waterproof book. He recalled something about a baby dolphin and its mom. His mom smiled. An ache bloomed in his chest.

She's not here and she won't be here to help me. Tears finally broke free and ran down his cheeks.

So much lost. No more family Christmas gatherings where she shared poems she'd written for each person.

A sob broke free as he scrubbed harder at his hands and arms, pulling him out of his memory and back into the present. He was alone in the bathing room. He was alone where he could let it all out, with no one watching. He let go of the sobs he'd been holding in for so long. The anger. The grief he'd pushed away these past three months. Slowly, it rolled out of him, along with warm tears down his cheeks.

All he had left were memories. Memories of her face, her laugh, her walk, her voice. He wanted the time back. How cruel he'd been robbed of time with her, when he had so many hopes and dreams for it. Dreams of writing with her, dreams of making her laugh, making her proud.

Pain tore through his chest and he gasped for air through his sobs.

How is this fair? How is this real?

His body shook like it was rejecting the very thought of accepting his new reality didn't include his mom.

He punched the water. Again, this time harder. He smacked it so it sloshed in the tub. He took his anger out on it. Mini whirlpools formed, creating waves like he'd seen on a stormy day at home. His grief poured off him and into the water, lifting it out of the tub and into the bathing room, drenching everything in sight.

With a pain-laced bellow, Liam let go of his emotions, exhausted. The water dropped to the ground, flowing over the tiled floor.

Sitting back against the tub, he panted and glared at the two inches of water left in the tub. Shivering, he gripped the sides and wrenched himself out of it.

Padding across the wet floor, he yanked the towel from the counter and dried off. Anger burned up in him. Anger at his mom for leaving him in this situation with no guidebook or map. Anger at Conroy. Anger at Milo for taking parts of his mom that he never got to have. Parts of her that stayed here in this storyworld while she clawed to get them back.

He was angry she had a whole life here he didn't know about, that she never talked about. Who was she? Did he even know her? How did she create this world? Why had she created it?

All questions he would never get the chance to ask her. Why had she kept this part of herself hidden? Why didn't she let him in?

His anger and resentment bubbled up, wrapping around him like a dark cloak. With another bellow, he felt a wave of emotion go out from him into the room.

The doors of the wardrobe flew open. One side broke off its hinges and clothes launched into the air.

Liam's anguished cry rang through the air as the clothes floated to the ground. A loud crashing noise reverberated off the stone walls. The glass in the windows shattered and exploded into the outside air. Harsh wintry wind blew through the room, putting out the fire in the grate that had grown with Liam's outburst. The furniture was strewn across the room. The bedsheet twisted on the bed. Clothes littered the floor. Wood from the wardrobe splintered and sprayed shavings on the ground.

Another mess. Liam sighed. *Another mess I'm not going to clean up right now.* He shook his head. *Mess after mess. When will it stop?*

A hollow pain replaced the tight knot in his chest, and an icy feeling dripped down into his stomach. He slid down to the floor onto his knees, bent over, dropped his head in his hands, and sobbed.

He sobbed for all the moments he wouldn't have with his mom anymore. He sobbed for his dad, now alone. His dad, always there for Liam and his mom, the rock of the family. He sobbed for the loss of future hugs, future conversations, future tea times with his mom. He sobbed for the pain Milo must have felt when she died in this storyworld. He let all his helplessness seep out of him. It tore through him and felt like he was bleeding out.

He looked at the destruction around him and thought it appropriately mirrored how he felt inside. A complete mess, with no energy to sort it out.

Exhaustion settled on his shoulders. He felt like someone scraped out his insides. He was hollow, with nothing left inside of him. He looked to his right and saw his bed was, thankfully, still habitable. He fell into it. Reaching down, he picked up the sheet from the floor and clutched it around him.

He felt flat. Like he was part of the bed. Like nothing of him existed anymore. He had leaked it all out into the room and out the windows. Letting the thought take him, he closed his eyes and floated away into tiredness. Into the sadness that wrapped around him like a heavy coat.

How am I supposed to go on like this? I don't know how to do this.

Numbness pulled him into sleep.

CHAPTER THIRTY-ONE

---◈---

*I*t was dark and quiet. Something soft tickled his face. Liam opened his eyes. He heard what sounded like water flowing down a river, sliding over rocks. He pushed himself up to sitting. Emerald green grass surrounded him and smelled like the sweetness of spring when the sun warms the Earth and the flowers bloom. He inhaled. The golden sun warmed his skin where it peeked through the willow tree above him. Long tendrils of branches swayed in the gentle breeze. They moved like fingers wagging in the wind. The grass butted up against a stream in front of him. When the breeze brushed his cheeks it whispered, "You're safe here."

Narrowing his eyes, he looked around to assess for threats.

Am I really safe here? *He didn't believe it last time. Why was he back?*

This time, he sat up and hugged his knees. He sat and waited to see if it was true—if he truly was safe here.

He inhaled, watching the wind sway the tall grass in a graceful dance.

What would life be like, *Liam wondered*, if I swayed gracefully like the grass, trusting everything would be okay?

He rested his chin on his knees and matched his breath to the grass.

He found a shard of what he realized he'd been searching for.

Peace.

"Are you sure that's a good idea? I don't think we should wake him," a voice whispered.

Liam still heard the rustle and whisper of the willow tree's leaves against one another. He focused on that, hoping he could stay there longer.

"Yes, I'm completely sure. He is already waking," a deeper voice than the first one said.

No. He didn't want to be awoken. *Let me stay in the green grass by the stream.* The voices pulled at him, urging him to wake up.

"Is he okay? Is he hurt? Was he attacked again?" the younger voice asked.

"No. He was not attacked," the deeper voice replied.

Scuffling and dragging sounds pulled Liam fully from his dreamy state. Prying his eyes open, he noticed a spot of black hair by the door, and a tall figure robed in navy blue waving its hands around, standing in the center of the room.

He blinked repeatedly, questioning the reality of what he was witnessing as the furniture rearranged itself. The wardrobe doors reattached themselves, and the clothes on the floor rose, shook off the debris, and found their rightful place on the hangers. The wood shavings from the broken furniture returned to the proper pieces. Starting from the bottom of the frame, the glass from the window reappeared and rebuilt itself.

Liam sat up and stared at the room, open-mouthed.

Everything was in its rightful place. Everything that his panic, anger, frustration, and grief had destroyed was restored.

Milo turned from the window to face Liam. A warm smile pulled at his lips and amusement twinkled in his eyes.

He's alive! He's alive and walking and using magic. Thank God! thought Liam. He couldn't bear to lose another person. Especially someone who could help him with his magic. Someone who knew so much about his mom. Someone he had a burning desire to understand.

Liam looked past him to Fox standing in the doorway, who mirrored his own flabbergasted expression.

"How did—" He looked around frantically to find something out of place. He found nothing. "That was you?" Liam asked.

Milo dipped his head.

"I wish I knew how to do that." He sat back against the headboard.

"You can," Milo said.

"I can?" Liam raised his eyebrows. "Did you see this disaster I created? How can you possibly say I can do what you just did?"

Milo stared at Liam for a beat and nodded. "It is inside of you. You can do everything I'm able to."

Liam scoffed.

Milo's eyebrows drew together. "Looks can be deceiving." Milo clasped his hands behind his back.

Liam studied the wizard before him, clothed in robes the color of the night sky.

"Are you okay, sir?" Liam asked. He looked alright and had just used magic, so that had to count for something. His dark circles and deep lines were more noticeable today.

"I'm on the mend." Milo smiled gently. "As is your cousin, I hear."

Aubry! Liam jumped out of bed and threw clothes on. "Is she doing okay?" he asked as he hurried around the room looking for his boots, then realized Milo had returned them to their proper place in the wardrobe.

Milo nodded. "Yes, Juniper has been taking great care of her and administering healing potions every few hours."

"Is that how you're better so quickly?" Liam asked.

"I am quite a few years older than her, and a wizard, which helps with the healing process. Though I'm sure you have some experience with that?" Milo dipped his chin and raised his eyebrows, amused.

Liam blinked. He guessed he did.

A few days ago, he was just a normal high schooler who lived with his family in his grandparents' house in Central California. He worked at a bookstore, and he could only access the worlds within books by reading them in a comfy spot on the couch, with a blanket and a steaming cup of tea.

Now he had written himself into a storyworld his mom created. How inconceivable was that? And he had powers he still didn't really know how to use. There was an entire world here with real people, genuine problems, and authentic emotions.

It was the adventure of a lifetime. Something he'd dream about after reading his mom's books. Maybe that's what his mom had sent him on? An adventure? Had that been the last thing she did for Liam before she passed? Not leave him in the lurch, but leave him a world and an adventure to go on? An inheritance of magic?

Maybe it was time to bend a little like the green grasses in his dream.

Could he do that? He'd been trying to hold on to everything so tightly, grabbing for anything that seemed close or remotely attainable. What if he'd been holding onto the wrong things?

"Liam, I would suggest you try a little of the breakfast before you see Aubry. It's nothing like Cook's, of course," Fox quickly clarified, redness creeping up his face. Liam followed Fox's line of sight and saw a tray of food on the bedside table, complete with a pot of tea.

Liam bit back a smile and nodded.

He stuffed his feet into his boots. They felt heavy. The weight of the past few days, the past few months, took a toll. His joints and muscles ached. He circled his arms to get the kinks out.

"With some practice, you'll learn how to work those out quicker, too." Milo smiled knowingly. He still stood in the center of the room. He stared into Liam's eyes. "I want you to know that you *can* do the things you want to. We simply need to work on it together. One cannot expect to master something the same day he discovered it."

Liam sighed. "I suppose you're right."

"You will train with me, then?" Milo's eyebrows rose slightly and a faint smile tugged at his lips.

Liam held back a smile. Milo's easy amusement intrigued him. "Yes, I'll train with you."

Milo's smile spread across his face.

"And you'll tell me more about my mother and her time here?" Liam said.

Milo's smile shrunk ever so slightly. He considered it.

Liam held his breath, willing him to say yes. He needed to know more about his mom.

Milo nodded. "Very well. I believe I can do that."

Liam smiled. Milo attempted to smile back, but it looked pained.

"I'll let you tend to your cousin now." Milo inclined his head. "Promise me you won't give up." Milo's sea-blue eyes shone in the candlelight, pleading, the same way his mom's gray eyes pleaded with him the last time he talked with her.

The fear that had burrowed in Liam's stomach stirred. He pushed it down. "Okay. As long as you help me, I won't give up."

Milo nodded, satisfied. "Don't battle the darkness alone, Liam. Remember that. You are not alone, no matter what the darkness whispers."

Liam exhaled heavily under the intensity of Milo's stare. He nodded.

"See you soon." Milo turned on his heel and glided out the door, Fox following close behind.

CHAPTER
THIRTY-TWO

---◈---

*K*nock, knock, knock. Liam rapped gently on Aubry's door, hoping she was awake. He wasn't sure what time it was. Milo's castle didn't have any clocks. He wondered how he kept track of time.

The door opened to Juniper's bright expression, which fell a little when she saw Liam in the doorway. "Thought you might come by," she said tightly.

"Of course I would. She's like my sister."

Juniper nodded once and dropped into stillness.

"Uh, can I come in?"

"Liam? Is that you?" Aubry's voice called from inside. It sounded less weak than yesterday. Liam's heart rose in hope.

Juniper huffed and yanked the door open so Liam could go inside.

Liam shot her a glance as he stepped into Aubry's room. Juniper ignored him. She stepped out and closed the door behind her. Liam glared at where he imagined her through the door and made a mental note to deal with her later. Right now, he needed to talk to Aubry and make sure she was okay.

Stepping into her room, he took in the same four-poster bed draped with curtains that sat in his. Hers were an icy blue compared to his dark navy. Aubry smiled from where she sat in front of the flickering fireplace, a tray of breakfast and tea in front of her.

"Come join me. There's enough food here to feed five people." She motioned him over and he sat down opposite her. The tray overflowed with toast, eggs, sausage, fruit, grilled tomatoes, yogurt, and potatoes.

He looked up at her and raised his eyebrows.

She laughed. "They must have thought I'd be ready to eat like a small army when I woke up this morning." She winced, and Liam hurried to her side.

"Are you okay? What's wrong?" He scanned her face, seeing what looked like salve on the gashes on her forehead and cheek. Her bruises were less dark and more purple today. She wore a navy silk robe that covered her legs and arms. He hated to think about the wounds hiding underneath.

"I'm still healing is all." Aubry gave him a sad smile. "Juniper and Milo said it would take a couple of days. But I am feeling better after drinking all those healing potions."

"Good," Liam nodded. "Aubry." He waited until she was looking at him. He took a breath to muster up the courage to ask a question he wasn't sure he wanted to know the answer to. "What happened after Conroy took you?"

Aubry looked at him and took a slow breath. "He took me back to the castle and started asking me questions about you and your mom. He started talking about powers and birthright and his inheritance being stolen. I was so scared and confused." She shook her head.

Liam reached for her hand.

"I was a bit hysterical, as you can imagine." She grimaced. "He was trying to reason with me at first. But I kept telling him I didn't know anything, and he got angrier and angrier." She looked into the fire. "Then he started using his magic on me to get me to tell him what he wanted to know. He didn't believe I didn't know what he was talking about." Her eyes glazed over.

"You don't have to tell me if it's too painful, Aub." Liam squeezed her hand gently, trying to keep his fury at Conroy at bay.

She shook her head and looked back at him. "No." Her voice hardened. "I need to. I can't let him have this power over me." Taking a breath, she sat up straighter. Bravery and determination hardened her features. "He used his magic and went inside my head somehow. Looked through my memories. He apparently didn't find what he was looking for, so he started to physically hurt me. He kept asking me for your weaknesses and would talk about the bullies at school. I guess he saw my memories. But I told him you never backed down from them."

Liam looked at the ground. So many bullies. So many beatings.

"And then finally, he let me go to sit in the dungeon, saying he'd found your weakness after all." Aubry looked at him, worried.

Panic flooded Liam's chest. "What did he find?"

"He wouldn't tell me." Tears gathered in Aubry's eyes. "I'm so sorry, Liam."

"Don't you dare apologize," Liam said, reaching up to wipe an escaped tear away. "You're so strong, Aubry. So strong," he whispered. "I'm going to make sure he pays for this." Liam clenched his jaw. He would never forgive Conroy for this. For hurting his cousin. His sweet cousin who never wanted to come on this blasted adventure.

"Liam, I don't want you to seek revenge. That won't help anyone."

Liam stood up and started pacing. "It kills me he did this to you," he seethed.

"How will more vengeance make this situation any better? Do you really think that will help?" Sitting back in her chair, she looked at him in disbelief. "I expected better from you."

He exhaled, feeling like she punched the air from his lungs.

"And what would better look like?" Liam threw out his hands, then placed them on his hips.

"Doing something your mom would be proud of." Aubry set her face and stared at him.

Liam rolled his lips and looked away into the fire. What *would* make her proud? She'd told him to finish the story. Clearly something had to be done about Conroy who had chosen wrong time and time again no matter how his mom had nudged him. Nudging would not work anymore.

"He wants to take it from you," Aubry said, the shadows under her eyes standing out in the daylight streaming in through the window behind her. "Your power. He believes it's rightfully his."

"Then I need to train. I need to learn how to use my power so I can fight him. Milo will teach me." Liam frowned, thinking about the work ahead of him.

Aubry nodded. "So, it's all really true? He's your mom's son? Milo is his father?"

After a beat, Liam nodded and exhaled heavily before continuing. "Before I failed to rescue you, Milo was telling me about my mom. She created this place, as you know." Liam looked around at the room. "She created Domhania, and she and Milo fell in love. They were married."

"What? What do you mean, what about your dad?" Aubry sputtered.

Liam shook his head. "Milo said it was before him. She had a whole life here. Before us."

Aubry stared at Liam, gaping.

"Oh my gosh," she said.

"My mom died here."

"She what?" Aubry's voice echoed off the stone walls. She sat forward in her chair.

"She tried performing a ceremony with Conroy. It went wrong and—" Liam's voice caught.

"Hold on a second," Aubry said. "You're telling me your mom gave *birth* to Conroy?" Aubry stared at Liam, eyes running over him, processing what he said. "That means you're half-brothers!"

"Yeah, I know." Liam wiped a hand across his face. "Haven't really processed that yet, because . . . well, I went to rescue you and you know how the rest of that story goes," Liam said with a tinge of disgust.

"The way you used your powers in the dungeon . . . you're learning now?" Aubry asked.

"Yeah, so apparently, emotions and thoughts control my powers, and Milo said anger and grief are powerful chaos magic. It can be very detrimental. So that's been fantastic." Liam crossed his arms.

Aubry shook her head. "Liam, that sounds dangerous."

Tiredness settled on Liam's shoulders. He just wanted to curl up with a book in front of the fireplace and go to sleep. And maybe pretend for a couple hours his life was different.

Aubry reached a hand toward him. Liam returned to his seat and slipped his hands around hers.

"Liam, I'm here for you. You can talk to me about this. You brought me here for a reason, didn't you?" Liam stared straight ahead, not looking at her as she spoke. "You can't do this all by yourself."

"That's not what my mom told me." Liam chewed the inside of his cheek.

"Your mom was dying. She was on her deathbed, Liam. She wasn't able to tell you everything," Aubry's gentle voice reminded him. "She did the best she could. And she told you at the last second and yes, that sucks, and that was horrible. And she probably should have done that better. But this is what we have right now, and we have to deal with it." Her voice rolled into a confidence that poked at Liam's fear. "But you're not alone. I'm here with you. You can't do this alone. It's eating you up."

Liam flinched at her frankness. But she was right. He'd tried to do this by himself and too many people had gotten hurt. He needed her help. He thought back to his dream and the grasses that swayed in the wind. What would it be like to bend a little?

Liam leaned forward, elbows on his knees, head in his hands. He took a shuddering breath. "I guess there is more I should tell you . . ." Sighing, he pushed up from his knees, back against the chair.

Aubry nodded and sat back, ready to listen.

"I need to see if she is doing okay and if she needs something else," a deep voice said from the other side of the door.

"Sly, no! Let them be," Juniper tried, but the door burst open and Sly rushed forward, frantically searching for Aubry.

His eyes found her, and he stopped. His chest rose and fell rapidly, like he'd run up the stairs.

Liam looked back and forth between them.

Aubry blushed.

"Umm . . . can I help you?" Liam asked, trying to keep the annoyance out of his voice.

"I needed to see . . ." Sly trailed off as he took in Liam's face. "Oh, am I interrupting? I'm sorry, mate." He rubbed the back of his neck.

Was Sly *flustered*? Well, that was a first. Despite himself, Liam couldn't help but smile in amusement.

"It's alright. Liam was about to fill me in on what I missed and I'm sure it will be essential information you all need to know as well. Right, Liam?" Aubry looked at him expectantly.

"Uh, right . . ."

Sly dragged two wooden chairs over from the small round table under a window on the opposite wall.

"I guess it's story time then." Liam smiled sarcastically.

Sly planted his chair right next to Aubry's and reached for her hand. She grasped his back.

Liam narrowed his eyes at their intertwined hands.

What is happening?

"Aubry—" Liam started, staring at her like a deer in headlights.

"Liam, please update us. You may as well start over since I think Sly and Juniper should know what you just told me." Aubry smiled at him. She looked more alert and alive than a second ago.

Liam shook his head in minor annoyance.

"So, basically Milo told me that him and my mom were married and Conroy is their son." Liam dropped, eager to get a reaction.

Juniper and Sly exchanged glances.

After a second, Sly nodded.

"Why don't you seem more surprised?" Liam asked.

"Well, I—" Sly shifted in his seat.

"You knew?" Liam accused.

"I didn't know for sure, but I considered the possibility," Sly said cooly.

Cold hands of betrayal wrapped around Liam. "How long?" He gritted his teeth, anger rising.

"Liam—" Juniper said.

"I'll talk to you in a second." He glared at her, remembering her coldness from earlier. She looked offended, then sat back in her chair.

"How long have you *considered*?" Disdain dripped from Liam's words.

Sly studied him for a moment. "Since you told me your mum passed on her powers to you."

"All the way back at the hideout?" Liam shifted to the edge of his seat, voice rising.

Sly shrugged. "It wasn't hard to put together. I'd never heard of anyone having powers like yours. I'd seen Conroy manipulate the elements before and the fact that you could do the same thing made me wonder."

"And you—," Liam whipped his head to glare at Juniper. "You told me Milo was hiding something when it was you two hiding something all along!"

"Milo *was* hiding this, wasn't he?" Juniper raised an eyebrow.

"So that was your way of telling me?" Liam looked her up and down in disbelief.

She looked away. "I didn't tell you because you'd already tried to leave once. I didn't want you to give up again."

"Because you need me? You need me to defeat him, don't you?" Liam threw a hand in the air.

Sly swallowed but stayed silent.

"I can't believe this." Liam stood up and shook his head. "I can't believe I trusted you!" Liam paced again. Having run away once, he empathized with Sly's decision to keep that information to himself. But Sly knew how lost Liam felt here in Domhania. He could have at least shared his suspicions. Would it have mattered? Would Liam have even believed him?

Why did he feel so used? Liam knew from the beginning that they needed him to defeat Conroy. And Liam needed them to rescue his cousin. They had Aubry. Despite going off alone to be a hero, they still helped them. They stepped in and saved them when he and Aubry needed it most. Now wasn't it his turn to help them defeat Conroy so he wouldn't take down any more villages?

"Liam?" Aubry asked gently, on the edge of her seat, no longer holding Sly's hand. "What are you thinking?"

Liam huffed. "I'm thinking that I don't appreciate the way you kept information from me." He swallowed his pride. "But I also want to thank you for saving us."

Sly nodded, then Juniper.

"And if we're going to defeat Conroy and stop him from killing more people, we need to work together," Liam said. The truth of it hit him as he said it, extinguishing the anger and betrayal.

Aubry nodded, the corners of her mouth pulling up into a small smile.

Liam filled them in with all the missing pieces. He told them about the birthright ceremony his mom attempted with Conroy. Told them it cost her life, so she couldn't return. Shared how Milo saved Conroy but couldn't save Liam's mom. He explained what had happened on the training courtyard with all the elements, and how his powers worked off his thoughts and emotions.

"Hmm, so you can tap into what you feel, and that influences your powers?" Sly asked, chin in his hand, piecing everything together. "That's why when you thought of your mum in the courtyard, it was chaos? Because that's what you feel?"

Liam looked away, embarrassed to have his emotions on display so clearly, and a topic of conversation. Fatigue set in, giving way to annoyance. He grabbed his teacup and found it disappointingly empty.

Juniper stood up and poured him another cup before he had time to do it himself. She didn't make eye contact and sat down abruptly.

"I mean, it makes sense, mate. There is a lot there with you and your mum," Sly said.

Liam stared at the dark liquid in his cup and watched the white milk he poured in swirl and create a new color.

"Can Milo teach you how to control your powers?" Juniper asked.

"Yes. I need to train with him as soon as he's feeling ready to. We have to stop Conroy before he can destroy more villages. Before he absorbs more power." A weight settled on Liam's shoulders. He took a sip of tea.

"I saw what you did, Liam. The way you made his shadows wither away. No one else can even touch the shadows. You are the key to defeating Conroy," Sly said, staring at Liam.

Liam's mind raced with thoughts of the impending battle against Conroy. The weight of responsibility pressed heavily upon him. He took a breath to loosen his chest. He wouldn't make the same mistake of going at this alone.

"We need to gather allies," he said.

Aubry nodded, her expression resolute. "What about the fairies? They have a stake in this too. Conroy's darkness threatens their realm as well."

The three of them looked at Aubry skeptically.

"Willow told me when she was helping me." Aubry jutted her chin out.

Sly leaned back in his chair. "Conroy won't expect us to go after him so soon. We can use that element of surprise to our advantage. And we need all the help we can get." Sly nodded. "Even if it's from the fairies."

Aubry's eyes sparkled with determination. "I'll talk to Willow. From what she said, I think the fairies will be on our side."

Liam felt a surge of hope, knowing they had a plan forming. He stood up, a newfound resolve burning within him.

"I've also been reading about potions." Aubry looked over to a stack of books next to her Liam hadn't noticed when he first came in. Seven or eight tomes rose from the floor up to knee height.

"Potions?" Liam looked at her skeptically once again.

"Yes." She blinked at him. "Potions. After studying them for a while, I discovered books containing recipes that create items with negative effects on wizards."

"Hmm," Juniper mused looking into the distance. "I could see how that would work. Does it mention a way to make it work on one wizard without harming others?"

Aubry's eyebrows came together in thought. "I haven't come across anything yet."

"I wish Roya was here." Juniper sighed.

"Well, you can help me look and we can find a solution. I'm sure we can ask Milo to help," Aubry said.

Juniper nodded, lost in thought.

"Whenever you figure out how to make those potions, we should make loads of them so we're prepared when we go back," Sly said.

Aubry looked at Sly with dread-filled eyes.

Sly nodded. "Conroy will want to continue the birthright ceremony and now that we've gone to him, he'll want to come to us. We can't have him coming here, so we need to attack as soon as possible in order to catch him off guard."

Aubry looked worriedly at Liam, who chewed on the inside of his cheek.

"I better get on with training, then. We can't waste any time. Juniper, we need to reach out to the fairies and ask them to join the fight. Aubry, do you need anything before we leave you to rest?" Liam asked.

"Well, I hoped I could watch you train. I'd really like to see you use your powers." Aubry smiled at Liam.

Liam took in her healing body and shook his head. "I don't know if that's a good idea, Aub. Last time I hurt you, and you're still healing."

"She's actually due for another healing potion. I got her covered." Juniper stood and pulled out a vial with an earth green colored potion in it. "Bottoms up." She smiled, handing the vial to Aubry.

Aubry took it, unstoppered it, and tipped the whole thing into her mouth. After a couple of seconds, the bruises on her face lost some of their darkness. The cuts on her hairline closed up a little more, and she breathed a sigh of relief as Liam assumed the wounds he couldn't see knitted themselves back together.

"Thank you." Aubry smiled at Juniper, who looked back at her encouragingly. "See, I'm feeling much better. I'll just get dressed and meet you down in the training courtyard." Aubry pushed herself up from her seat and Sly was there in a flash, helping her stand.

"There you go," he whispered, his arms on either side of her.

Liam narrowed his eyes at them again. He had mixed feelings about what was going on between them.

Liam opened his mouth to talk to Juniper but Sly interrupted him.

"I can escort her down when she's ready and be there if you're worried about her?" Sly offered.

"Okay," Liam said hesitantly.

"You have to leave. She needs to change, Sly." Juniper crossed her arms and raised her eyebrows at her brother.

"Right, right." He blushed. "I'll, uh, leave you to it." Sly stared into Aubry's eyes for a beat before letting her go and heading out the door.

Liam shook his head as he watched Sly go. "I'll see you down there, Aub."

Aubry nodded, tugging on a piece of her hair, looking embarrassed. Liam stopped himself from groaning and headed to the training courtyard.

CHAPTER
THIRTY-THREE

———◆◇◆———

L iam and Sly's steps clicked on the marble floors in the hallway as they made their way through the castle. Liam sensed tension in the air, but didn't plan on breaking it. He liked the idea of Sly sweating it out for once instead of being so calm like he normally is.

"Aubry's healing quite well, it seems," Sly said awkwardly.

"Mhm," Liam responded, raising his eyebrows, wondering where Sly was going with this.

"She's uh, quite an extraordinary woman," Sly said, clasping his hands behind his back as they walked.

"Yes, she is." Liam glanced sideways at him.

"Listen." Sly stopped and turned to face Liam. "I've become rather taken with your cousin, and I wanted to be forthright about it." Sly stood up taller, his confidence seeming to build.

"Oh, I can assure you, you've definitely been forthright about it." Liam smothered a rising laugh.

"What do you mean?" Sly looked at him, confused.

"Seriously? It's pretty obvious you like her." Liam raised his eyebrows.

"I uh, well then." Sly shuffled uncomfortably and rubbed the back of his neck, eyes landing everywhere but Liam.

"And I can tell she likes you too." Liam smiled smugly. He was rather enjoying this more insecure side of Sly.

"She does?" Sly stared at Liam wide-eyed.

Liam laughed. "Of course. You two kinda wear your emotions on your sleeves, which is quite surprising because normally you're both very guarded with your expressions."

Sly smiled like a little boy in a candy shop. "Well, isn't that fantastic? But, are you alright with it?" His smile quickly melted into concern. "I don't want to overstep." He held up his hands.

Liam thought for a moment. Seeing them so smitten earlier was odd, but what right did he have to stop Aubry? It didn't happen very often. He wasn't about to get in the way. "If it's okay with her, it's okay with me. Thanks for asking though, mate." Liam smiled, amused, as he used Sly's term.

Sly chuckled. "Well, thank you." He held out his hand to shake Liam's.

Liam looked down at his hand, back up at Sly, and shook it, laughing to himself.

"Now, let's get to training shall we?" Sly turned on his heel and headed down the stairs, an obvious spring in his step.

Liam shook his head and followed.

"I wanted to thank you," Liam said in a low voice to Aubry when she'd joined them at the entrance to the training courtyard.

Aubry glanced at him. "For what?"

"Well, for one, coming with me."

"Yeah, well, you didn't leave me much choice." She bumped his shoulder, smiling. He smiled sadly back.

"And for . . . being here."

She looked at him curiously and waited for him to keep going.

"It's just that . . . I've always thought I had to do things alone."

Aubry tilted her head.

Liam pushed past the awkwardness rising in his chest. "It's just that, I always felt this..." He trailed off and looked at Aubry, hoping she would catch his meaning. He groaned. "You're really going to make me say it?"

"Say what?" Aubry looked at him in mocking ignorance.

Liam rolled his eyes.

"I've just felt this—this responsibility, I guess. That I had to do things on my own. And I see now that...that didn't work for my mom. I mean, look at the mess she left. I don't want to be like that." Liam stared straight ahead and let out a sigh. "I want to be different."

Aubry stared at Liam. "I'm proud of you, Liam. I'm sorry it took you so long to realize you aren't alone. But I'm glad we can do this together now." She grabbed his hand and squeezed. Liam squeezed back before she let go.

Sly followed them through the doorway and descended the stone steps to where Liam stood the last time. Liam pretended not to notice the way Sly and Aubry looked at one another when they thought he wasn't looking.

Once in the stone courtyard, Aubry took in the different areas with interest, her brows coming together. Someone had tidied up. The plants weren't limp and mangled anymore. The rocks were whole again, and everything seemed to be in its rightful place.

Milo stood in the center of the courtyard and turned to face Liam, today's navy robes swishing around him. "Okay, Liam. Here we are again. You *can* do this. You were *made* to do this." Milo nodded at him.

Liam took in his sea-blue eyes. He saw faith and confidence. He wanted that. Milo believed he could do this.

Am I really made for this? His mom told him to protect Domhania. He'd inherited her power. Therefore, this must be his destiny.

The fear buried in his stomach poked its head out and reminded him of the mess he'd made before. Reminded him of the pain, panic, and destruction he caused. Liam clenched his jaw, forcing the memories away.

"Before we start, I want you to clear your mind. Breathe in, and breathe out."

Liam closed his eyes. *Darkness lurks in you. You are broken. How can you do this?* the fear whispered. Cold bloomed in his stomach and anxiety pricked his chest.

He thought back to where he felt grounded. The garden with his mom. He recalled the sun. He reached out to the subtle hum under his skin and felt his power. He imagined green grass swaying in the wind, quiet waters flowing over smooth rocks. A willow tree's long branches riding on the breeze. Just him. Sitting. Being. He breathed deeply, then let it all out.

"Focus on your breath. In and out. Slow deep breaths," Milo said, and paused a few seconds. "Good. Now I want you to think of a happy memory. One of the strongest you have. A memory full of love."

A memory of love. He thought for a few moments. Fragments of a memory danced across his mind. Christmas morning. He saw the Christmas tree, lit up and casting twinkles of light on the walls. Garland, lights, and snowflakes hung cheerily from his grandparents' ceiling. Family tradition dictated that Liam's whole family would wake up on Christmas morning together. He saw his grandpa put the kettle on.

Do you really think this is a happy memory? a voice whispered in Liam's mind. Doubt poked at his memory and the image swirled and turned a muted shade of gray and it sounded like Liam was inside a bowl, unconnected to his memory.

Then Liam's parents flashed across his mind. Liam's dad suggested they listen to vintage Christmas music. His grandparents, parents, and Aubry started dancing, joy alight in their faces.

*Look how much fun they're having without you, t*he sinister voice whispered again. Liam clenched his jaw and tried to push against the fear and doubt. He felt the cold dregs of it pulling at him, threatening to wrap around his limbs and incapacitate him.

He commanded the memory to play out in his mind and felt his hands trembling with effort. The music played louder and Aubry's parents joined.

See, they don't need you. They don't even want you there.

"No," Liam murmured to the voice in his head. His memory played out in black and white, all the people he loved most laughing without him. Despair poked at his mind, eager to take control.

We could do great things together. Just let me in, it whispered.

"No," Liam said louder, pushing against the weight of darkness pressing on his mind.

We could bring her back. You could make better memories than this one.

Liam froze. He could bring his mom back? That was possible? He could relive this moment? And create more like it. Toying with the idea, he felt cold needle-like hands pry into his mind, and push against his golden power. He gasped as his lungs felt like he'd been plunged into ice.

It's not what she would want. Liam shook his head. He inhaled and pressed against the ice, melting it with his power.

His memory gained color, and he could hear the vintage Christmas music clearly. Hear his parents' laughter. Little Aubry tugged his arm and drug him downstairs to join in. The adults' faces lit up. Liam's mom wrapped him in a big hug. He went from his dad to his grandparents to his aunt and uncle, collecting hugs. Love and joy filled Liam's heart. He felt whole. He felt complete. He felt loved.

"That's great, Liam!" Milo's voice said, reminding Liam he wasn't in his grandparents' kitchen.

He opened his eyes and saw golden balls of light in his hands and felt their warmth.

Milo nodded at him.

"Now use that," he encouraged. Liam focused on the waterfall in the corner and willed it to flow out of its containment and dance, forming beautiful shapes through the air. He tapped into a little more of his power, letting it float up around him. The water twisted and turned like ballerinas performing en pointe.

Aubry gasped behind him. He kept going and pushed the water higher and higher. He made animals, different shapes, and then snowflakes that floated through the air. They showered down over the courtyard and turned into mist.

Milo laughed and flung his arms wide. "Liam, that was fantastic!"

Liam smiled proudly. He looked over at the plants and flicked a hand toward them. The leaves and vines woke up and danced when Liam stepped closer. The flowers bloomed bigger, and the leaves became lusher. He floated the blossoms off the stems and through the air to encircle Aubry, who stared at them open-mouthed. She plucked one out of the air and stuck her nose in it. Liam smiled and set the rest of the blooms on the ground in a circle.

Buzzing with light and magic, he turned to the rocks. He placed his hand above the stack, and they levitated one by one until he had six in the air. They moved in and out of each other in circles and figure eights. With a flick of his hand, he moved them high into the sky until they were small dots, then let them drop just before they crashed into the ground. Then, he assembled them neatly back into their pile. Milo nodded silently, watching him.

Next, Liam turned to the fire. As he stepped over to it, his anger, frustration, and resentment bubbled up in his chest.

Do you really think she loved you? the voice whispered. Liam thought back to his mom's late nights writing. Thought about the desperation on her face. She'd tried to get back to Domhania for years to see Conroy and Milo while he was right in front of her. Conroy was the Chosen One. Not him.

Flames from the fire crept out of the furnace and he felt a tingling sensation in his fingertips.

Your mom dumped you here with no plan. No explanation, the doubt said.

Did she? Liam had countless memories of him and his mom talking about Domhania, talking about stories. She'd made sure he knew about the pendant around Sly's neck. He looked at Milo, Sly, and Aubry. She hadn't left him here alone. He had a teacher, friends, and family. She entrusted him with her dying wish. Because she trusted *him*. She loved him and knew he could do this.

Liam latched onto his memory of his mom's hug at Christmas and let her joy, acceptance, and love replace his anger, frustration, and resentment.

He walked across the courtyard, boots clicking on the stones, and stood in front of the furnace. He raised his hands, palms out. Slowly, a small flame snake crept out the door of the furnace. He thought of his grandfather's twinkling eyes as they danced in the kitchen. Energy flowed from his heart, down his arms, and into the fire. He thought of the music and his family's laughter. The fire circled him calmly. He moved his arms through the air and crafted a phoenix of fire. It flew, dipping and diving, through the air as Liam watched it for a few moments. With a final swoop, it flew gracefully back into the furnace. Liam lowered his hands and let out a breath.

Inhale. Exhale.

He looked up at Milo to find him beaming. "Well done, Liam. Well done."

"Liam!" Aubry said from behind him. "That was so beautiful. I've never seen anything like that before." She had one of the flower buds tucked behind her ear and hands clasped under her chin.

"How did that feel, Liam?" Milo stepped toward him, a smile spreading across his face.

"Much better."

"That's how it's done," Milo said, nodding. He walked over to Liam and grabbed his shoulder. Liam looked up into his eyes and didn't feel resentment. Instead, appreciation bubbled in his chest.

"Do you think I can defeat Conroy with this power?" Liam asked.

Milo looked at him pensively. "This was a start."

"You and me together, do you think we can defeat Conroy? Stop him from destroying more villages? From absorbing more power?" Liam felt hope filling him for the first time in a while.

Milo took a long breath, and a look of sadness came across his expression. "If we keep training, and we work together with the fairies, along with the potions Aubry and Juniper are working on, I think we could stand a chance, yes."

"Isn't that a good thing?" Liam asked.

"Fighting is never a good thing. But sometimes necessary. And fighting my son . . . well . . ." Milo trailed off.

Of course. How could I not think about how hard that would be for Milo?

"Now, I'd like to move into the next stage of your training. You seem to be improving on controlling your power and learning how to siphon more and less as needed," Milo said, walking to the far side of the courtyard.

"What's the next stage?" Liam called.

Milo whipped around, a flash of power shining from his hand to the ground at Liam's feet.

"Combat," Milo said calmly.

CHAPTER
THIRTY-FOUR

———————◆○◆———————

L iam jumped to the side, heart pounding. *Did Milo just shoot lightning at me?*

"If you want to fight Conroy, you need to fight me first. I *am* the one who trained him." Milo smiled, amused.

"Liam, you got this!" Aubry encouraged from the back of the courtyard, safely behind the half wall outside the training area.

"C'mon mate, just remember what you did at Conroy's castle. You can do this!" Sly yelled.

Liam clenched his jaw and focused on Milo, who stood poised, hands clasped behind his back. He took a breath and nodded at his new teacher. Power trembled in Liam's hands, and he cracked a smile, eager for this opportunity to see what his power could do in a controlled environment.

With a thrust of his hands, Liam sent vines erupting from the ground and twisting around Milo's legs.

Milo was ready and unleashed a wave of scorching flames, quickly incinerating the vines that bound him.

Undeterred, Liam switched tactics and sent dozens of stones through the air at Milo. The wizard nimbly leaped backward, twisting a hand effortlessly to erect a shimmering force field.

"You can do better than that," Milo taunted, smiling.

Liam ducked and weaved, narrowly avoiding fiery blasts and sharp gusts of wind from Milo. With a quick flick of his wrist, Liam summoned a barrage of thorns and shot them at Milo, who deflected them with a shield of swirling flames. The courtyard filled with the sounds of clashing elements and the acrid scent of burned earth.

Gritting his teeth, Liam wove his fingers through the air, summoning gusts of wind that battered Milo's defenses. Cracks spread through Milo's magical barrier as loose objects whipped around them.

Then Liam changed patterns, his movements becoming tighter, more controlled. The winds coalesced into razor-sharp shards of ice raining from above. Milo's shield buckled under the onslaught until finally shattering in a glittering spray.

The elder wizard's eyebrows rose in surprise as Liam's ice volley forced him to raise his hands in a protective block. "Well played!"

Liam concentrated all his power into one final elemental torrent—water, air, earth, and fire twisting together into an unstoppable vortex. The maelstrom slammed into Milo, sending him off balance and driving him to his knees.

Liam stood motionless, chest heaving, shocked. Slowly, Milo climbed back to his feet, brushing dust and debris from his robes. A warm smile played across his lips as he raised his free hand. . .the hand he'd kept hidden behind his back during the duel.

With a simple flick of his fingers, Liam's energy vortex dissipated into nothingness. Milo's upraised palm now contained a small, glowing orb blazing with contained power.

"You wield the elements impressively for one so young," Milo said, eyes twinkling with pride. "But raw ability is only a fraction of a true wizard's arsenal."

The orb pulsed brighter, forcing Liam to squint against its brilliance. When the light faded, Liam gasped as it rushed towards him, engulfing him. He covered his eyes against the white light of power and the next moment, it was gone, dissipating into the crisp air.

Milo chuckled deeply. "That duel merely scratched the surface of your full potential. I think we've had a successful session. Why don't we go enjoy some of that tea and scones Sly was talking about, hm?" He winked at Liam and walked past him. He touched Aubry's shoulder and made his way up the stairs. Liam watched him, navy robes draped around him like a cloud of wisdom.

"Liam." Aubry ran over, enveloping him in a giant bear hug. He steadied himself and squeezed her back, smiling from ear to ear.

"That was amazing!" she said, pulling back and holding him at arms' length. "Liam, I don't know what to say."

"You don't have to say anything," he muttered. "Let's go get some tea."

They stopped in front of tall oak doors with twisted golden handles on the second floor. Liam froze in awe.

Milo chuckled. "I figured if you're anything like your mother, this would likely be your favorite room in the castle. Tea is waiting inside the library for us."

Liam gazed from Milo to the doors. He was going to see a castle library. He couldn't help but smile.

The door opened toward them and Sly popped his head out. "You coming?" He'd pushed the door open enough to reveal the extravagant inside and Liam's mouth dropped.

After a beat, he followed Sly inside, Aubry trailing behind him.

Books filled the walls from top to bottom. Wooden shelves held thousands of books with different colored spines, some brighter and some faded like they'd been there for years. Some books sat behind glass cabinets on the walls. Ladders hung along the bookcases. Smaller bookshelves with flat tops sat in the middle of the room holding map books. Several were open and lay flat on top of the cases. Comfy chairs and chaise lounges were interspersed throughout the room, tucked in between bookcases and corners. Rugs scattered the floor. Wooden and glass display cases showed off globes, magnifying glasses, hourglasses, and other trinkets unfamiliar to Liam.

There was a second level on each side of the library with spiral wooden staircases leading up to them, giving way to more books and display cases. Plants hung from windows, spilled out of pots on the ground, and draped over bookcases. It looked like a greenhouse had infested the library.

Directly in front of them, across the opposite wall, blazed a fireplace. The flame danced inside, inviting Liam to sit down, open a book, and maybe even fall asleep.

For the first time since Liam came into Domhania, he felt welcome. The entrance of the library opened onto a huge marble step. After descending two more steps, they were on the main floor covered in wood.

Liam's eyes wandered, trying to take it all in. Libraries were a topic he and his mom often talked about. Liam would get into the habit of looking at different libraries online from around the world and they'd admire them together. They talked about what their dream library would be like. Hers had lots of plants, natural light, and cozy corners to curl up in with beautifully carved bookcases.

Liam's had most of the same, in addition to a fireplace and a dog. The library he stood in now, he realized, was a combination of his and his mom's dream libraries.

He shook his head. *Did she create this for us?*

Sly led them further into the library, back to where the fireplace blazed. A pot of tea sat on a side table with cups filled, waiting for them.

Johnny sat in an overstuffed chair, carving something into a piece of wood. Fox snacked on biscuits with his tea. When he saw them he stood, spilling crumbs from his lap onto the rug.

"Hi," Fox said around a mouthful of biscuits, crumbs spraying out. He raised a hand in greeting.

"I thought you didn't like biscuits?" Sly smirked and plopped into a chair beside him, grabbing one of Fox's treats. Fox stared at him.

Looking around, Liam wondered how old his mom was when she first started coming to Domhania. She told him she started writing as a girl. Words would spill out of her, and she couldn't write fast enough to get them all down. Had she created this place as early as her childhood? She kept so much of her life a mystery and didn't provide many details when Liam was growing up. They had never visited Ireland. *What was so bad in the real world that she had to escape from and create a new life here?*

As he looked around the library, he felt maybe his mom had created some things with him in mind.

"Liam, it's Earl Gray," Aubry said from one of the green loveseats by the fireplace, where she sat sipping her tea as steam curled around her face.

"Perfect," Liam smiled. At least he could count on the comfort of Earl Gray tea. He grabbed the remaining teacup and saucer from the side table and sat down across from Aubry on a matching loveseat. Sly sat next to Aubry, looking unsure of himself as he glanced from Liam to Aubry.

Liam smiled into his tea.

"So, how was the training session?" Juniper walked up to them, boots clicking on the floor before she stepped onto the giant rug in front of the fireplace.

Startled by her appearance, Liam choked on his tea.

She turned to look at him, one dark eyebrow rising. It was the same look she'd given him at the Stream Side hideout when he'd challenged her. An almost amused expression that looked like she wanted to see more of this side of him. Why did he get the impression she enjoyed flustering him?

While Liam figured out how to breathe without tea in his throat, Aubry jumped in.

"It went amazingly well! You should have seen Liam." Aubry's green eyes gleamed with pride. "The way he used all the elements was beautiful. And then he practiced combat with Milo." Her eyes widened in excitement as she recounted the story. "And they went back and forth, countering one another." She moved to the edge of her seat. "And then we realized Milo was only using one hand."

Juniper smiled.

"And then Milo bested Liam, of course. It's only logical. He's been a wizard much longer and has more extensive training. It was incredible to watch. I couldn't believe it was real." Aubry sat back against the loveseat like she'd expended all her enthusiasm.

"Wow, what an accurate retelling." Sly laughed.

"Very accurate indeed," Milo said, gliding over to join them.

"Are you feeling okay?" Liam said. He hoped their session wasn't draining, especially with Milo still recovering.

"I'm doing alright, thank you, Liam." Milo smiled politely.

"Well, now that we're all here, we can talk about our strategy to stop Conroy and best him at his own game." Sly stood up and Liam could see his Stream Side leader hat was on. He paced in front of the fireplace, hands in front of him. Liam could see the wheels in Sly's mind turning, calculating, and strategizing.

"We know Conroy wants to take Liam's power because he believes it's his birthright," Sly said, turning to them. "All this time he hasn't had access to Liam's powers, he's been absorbing life forces from villages around the realm." Sly's jaw ticked. "And we will not let him continue that course. With Liam and Milo working together, they can stop Conroy. Juniper, what have you found about potions to weaken other wizards?"

Juniper straightened and put her hands on her weapons belt. "I found a blend that will supposedly siphon another wizard's power. I've also imbued said potion into a weapon." Slowly, she drew a dagger from her belt that glowed indigo.

Liam flinched.

"Don't worry, it won't hurt you unless I use it on you," Juniper assured him.

"Are those the same magically enhanced weapons Conroy's men are using?" Johnny asked, not taking his eyes off his carving project in his hands.

"I think so. Theirs seemed to have magic in them that weakens anyone they're used on. Each cut with that blade infects its victim with magic that locks up muscles and feels like Wizard's Fire, which it very well may be," Juniper explained.

"Will these weapons you made hurt anyone, or only wizards?" Johnny asked, still not looking up.

"Both. It will further injure non-magical beings than a normal blade would, but the potion I imbued it with will also weaken a wizard," Juniper said.

Johnny nodded.

"I have good news!" a bright voice called from the entrance, causing everyone to turn around. Willow flitted toward them, her chestnut-colored hair bouncing behind her like a long cape.

Her voice was enough for Johnny to look up from his whittling at last. He set his jaw and glared at her.

"I've talked to my brothers and sisters, the Winter Fairies, and they said they're with you in this fight against Conroy. But . . .the Summer Fairies, the ones you ran into earlier, are staying neutral." She stopped at the edge of the rug, looking at all of them, face flushed. She landed lightly, then bounced on the balls of her feet, waiting for someone to say something.

"Who asked you to invite them?" Johnny's nostrils flared as he stared at her.

"I did," Juniper said.

Johnny turned to face Juniper and gave her a look of disbelief. He stood up taller. "How could you do that after what happened? There is no way—"

"Yes, there is." Fox interrupted his older brother.

Johnny stopped, stunned.

"We need help. You know we do. It's time for you to get over your prejudices and see not everyone is the same. Not everyone is as bad as you think they are. Why can't you look for the good in people for once?" Fox said, chest rising and falling quickly. Liam stared at him, impressed. It wasn't easy to stand up to Johnny.

Johnny swallowed, maintaining his towering position. "When has anything ever gone right? When would assuming something positive have helped us? The world isn't built the way you think it is."

"Maybe it's not built how *you* think it is. What you want to see is what you will see," Fox said, stare unwavering.

Silence settled in the room for a few moments.

"So, you don't want our help?" Willow asked softly, looking around at everyone nervously.

"We want your help. Thank you for asking your family to support us," Juniper told her, smiling.

Johnny huffed, sat in his chair, and started carving with more force than before.

"Right." Sly nodded his head once. "So, with the support of the fairies, thanks to Willow"—she curtsied quickly— "Milo and Liam, and the potion-imbued weapons, we stand a chance to take down Conroy and stop him from further destroying villages. We can't let him get this pendant." Sly touched his chest. He looked at them, eyes gleaming. "And based on Liam's findings, we know a portal exists between Milo's castle and Conroy's. We'll enter through there. Fox, can you roll out the map for us?"

From his perch on the loveseat beside Aubry, Fox snatched a rolled-up parchment. Kneeling, he opened it on the floor, weighing down the edges with spare books. Liam joined everyone huddled around the map, ready to form a plan to take down Conroy.

CHAPTER THIRTY-FIVE

W illow circled them, delicate wings shimmering in the early afternoon light slowly turning gray as snow fell outside. After several minutes of talking and planning, Sly addressed them in his leader's tone again.

"Alright, we all know the plan. Johnny, Fox, you two will create a distraction at the front gates to draw attention there. Milo, Liam, Juniper, and I will sneak in through the portal room and around the back of the castle. Willow, you and your family will provide aerial support scouting for any surprises."

They nodded in agreement, faces set with determination.

"What about Conroy himself? How do we plan to take him out?" Willow asked.

"We'll need to split up once inside," Sly said. "Juniper and I will take the main hall while Milo and Liam confront Conroy in his chambers."

"What if he has wards or protection?" Aubry asked.

"Liam and I will take care of that. We'll handle the magical defenses while the rest of you keep the guards at bay," Milo said.

"Sounds like a plan. Let's hope it goes smoothly," Aubry said, worrying her lip.

"It won't be easy." Sly looked at Johnny, Fox, and Juniper. "Together, we can do this."

Everyone but Milo nodded.

"Be careful, everyone. We're counting on each other to make it through this," Juniper said.

With one last glance at the maps, Liam stood.

"Let's gather our gear, ensure we imbue the weapons, and then head out at nightfall in a few hours," Sly instructed.

"Sir, can we go over how to take down the wards?" Liam asked Milo.

"Certainly." Milo nodded quickly and looked away, his mind clearly on something else. "But first, I need to show you something. Meet me outside the library and I'll take you there." He turned and swept out of the room, navy robes billowing behind him.

Liam watched him walk away and saw Juniper in his peripheral.

"Hey." Liam stepped in front of her before she left with the others. "What's going on?" Staring in her eyes, he saw a war between frustration and composure.

Finally, she said, "You just left. How could you do that?" Juniper crossed her arms.

Liam sighed. "I just wanted to get Aubry out of here."

"And you thought you could do that yourself?" Her forehead creased in skepticism.

"Obviously I was wrong," Liam muttered, trying not to think about Milo's injury because of his botched rescue attempt.

Juniper chewed on his answer, then nodded curtly. "Just don't do it again."

"Wouldn't dream of it." Liam raised his hands. She eyed him for a moment like she was going to say something else but turned and walked away.

"Liam," Milo's soft voice called when Liam stepped out of the library and into the hall. Liam spun to face his teacher.

"Before we review the wards, I want to show you something." The tight smile on Milo's face didn't reach his eyes.

"Okay."

Milo stood in the hallway, waiting for Liam, looking like he was about to walk into a lion's den. His forehead crinkled, and he knotted his hands in front of him.

"Come with me." Milo turned and glided down a hallway to the left that Liam hadn't noticed before. As they walked, the overhead archway got smaller. The stone walls and floors trapped the cold wintry air inside, making Liam shiver. Small diamond-shaped windows lined the walls. Looking out, Liam noticed the snow on the mountain, but the valley below was green, like it was spring or summer. He would have to ask Milo about that. Yet another thing he hadn't had the chance to figure out.

"Oof," Liam uttered as he ran into something tall and strong.

Milo.

He had stopped right before a door and turned around to face Liam. His stony face made Liam stand straighter.

Sadness clouded Milo's eyes. "This room was your mother's workshop." He stared at Liam.

Looking past Milo, Liam saw a wooden door with a curved top and a brass handle decorated with vines and flowers. "She didn't bring me in here very often. Only she could open it. But I know she would have wanted you to see it. Maybe it will help you find the answers you're looking for."

His mother's workshop? Looking at the dark wooden door, Liam imagined what could be behind it. Could it be potions? Books? Journals filled with stories like her writing room back at home? What had she done here? Maybe there would be answers to help him use his powers and understand where they came from. Maybe there will would answers about how to stop Conroy.

"I think you should try to open it." Milo motioned to the door handle.

"Didn't you say only she could open it?" Liam chewed the inside of his lip.

"Yes. But since you're her son, I think maybe you'll be able to open it." Milo nodded at him.

Liam took a breath. Here it was—the parts of his mom he'd been wondering about. Could this fill in the holes of his knowledge? "Okay, I'll try." He traded places with Milo and stepped in front of the door. Reaching for the handle, he felt a tingle on his palm. He snatched it back and looked down at it.

"What happened? Did it hurt you?" Milo stepped closer to inspect his hand.

Liam shook his head. "No, I just . . . felt something." He squinted at the handle.

"Try again. I think that's a good sign." Milo half smiled.

Liam faced the door once again. He stuck his hand out and grabbed the vine-encrusted handle. Warmth burst from his palm, up his arm, and into his chest.

His mind flashed to his last conversation with his mom. Her small body lying in her bed. Limp brown hair falling over her shoulders.

"Liam, I have a special gift and once I . . . Once I'm not here anymore, the gift will pass on to you. I know the timing isn't ideal, but I must tell now." She shook her head, glassy gray eyes staring into blue-gray ones. *"I'm so sorry. I didn't think it would happen like this."*

"Mom, what are you saying? Are you feeling okay?" Liam felt her forehead for a fever. She felt normal. She grasped his hand gently and brought it back down.

"We don't have much time." His mom's words strained. *"You can't make the same mistakes I did."*

Liam pinched up his face in confusion. *"What do you mean?"*

"Don't get lost. Don't get lost like I did." She reached up to hold his face in her hands. They were like ice. The lines around her eyes looked like someone had taken a pencil and drawn them deeper. Her gray eyes weren't a vibrant deep-sea color,

but more like washed-out steely silver. Tightness crawled its way up Liam's throat
as he noticed these changes in his mom. How could he manage this alone?

"Liam, with this power, you hold a great amount of responsibility. It's up to you
to protect the storyworld and look after it for me."

The handle flew out of Liam's hand and the door banged open.

The door was open. He had opened it. His breath caught in his throat.

The room *felt* like his mom.

Candles decorated the room, scattered on tables, the desk, and in sconces on
the walls. A stained-glass window spilled colored light onto rolls of paper stacked
on a long table against the far wall. A wooden desk with a stack of drawers on
top sat in one corner of the room. Next to that, a high-backed green chair angled
toward the fireplace. Towers of teacups and saucers sat on a small table to the
right of the fire. Books lined the upper walls all around the room.

A rectangular table sat in the middle of the room, filled with pieces of parchment and journals. With tears in his eyes, Liam shuffled over to the table and
touched one of the leather-bound journals. He felt his mom's kiss on his cheek.
He jumped and slammed his hand to the side of his face. Looking to the side,
he saw nobody there.

What the heck was that? Was he imagining it? It felt so real. Heart thumping,
he looked around to make sure no one else was there.

"Often, a wizard leaves behind traces of themselves. Traces of their magic
in a place they once loved. Sometimes we can feel those traces," Milo quietly
commented from the doorway. He was on the other side of it, not in the room.

Liam squinted at him. "Why haven't you come in?"

"I—" Milo cleared his throat. "I cannot come in unless invited." His shoulders sagged.

This whole time, this room with traces of his mom, was here, and Milo
couldn't enter? He couldn't enter to feel close to his wife? To be reminded of
her? Something inside Liam broke. Here stood this man who had a life with his
mom. Created a family with her. Her leaving this world severed his connection

to her. Liam had been harboring jealously for Milo. But should he have been? Liam had been able to go into his mom's writing room. Been able to try to find answers. But Milo hadn't. Milo knew what it was like to lose Liam's mom. They had that in common. The weight of Liam's realization settled in his chest.

Which was better; building a life with someone, loving them, creating a family and then being immediately cut off from them? Or to have someone there, but constantly distracted and then search for pieces of them through their things, like trying to solve a puzzle to know them?

Tears leaked down Milo's face as he looked at the workroom from the doorway. He gasped and tried to cover it with his hand. His body trembled as his eyes trailed over all she'd left behind. Everything she'd written, researched, notes she'd taken that were stuck behind this door. Milo gripped the door jamb to hold himself up as sobs shook his body. Seeing Milo like this sent panic through Liam's chest. A man so cool, calm, and collected, stripped down in front of him.

Such pain. Such loss.

Don't battle the darkness alone.

"Milo. Please come in."

Milo stilled and stared at Liam, eyes wide and tired. He wiped his face, took a steadying breath, and slowly stepped over the threshold.

Liam's teacher clutched his chest and covered his mouth with his other hand, still trying to hold back his emotions. He stood there for a moment, letting the remnants of his wife surround him. Liam wondered what Milo was seeing while he was in this workshop. What memory was he thinking of?

Liam watched him. One of his hands curled like it was holding someone else's. The tenderness in Milo's gaze made Liam turn his head, leaving Milo in his memory.

After a moment, Milo shuffled over to the table and touched a journal.

"Nora," he breathed, caressing the cover of a navy leather-bound notebook. His sobs shook his shoulders. Liam placed a hand over Milo's. He clutched it back.

A boy and a wizard stood side by side, both mourning someone they loved. Someone that had left a gaping hole in their hearts with her absence. After a while, Milo finally looked over at Liam with red-rimmed eyes.

"Thank you," he said, squeezing Liam's hand. "You do not know what this means to me. Thank you." He let go and walked to the high-backed chair. He touched the top of it, then sat down and stared into the empty fireplace.

It was odd seeing Milo this way. He'd always been the strong, stoic wizard to Liam. Never betraying his emotions too much. Calm, cool, collected. Now looking at him in the chair, he looked spent. Tired. Exhausted. Flattened by the weight of loss. Liam knew that feeling well. He felt it tinge every moment and memory he had since his mom passed. Had Milo felt that way since she passed too? For almost two decades?

It had only been a few months, and Liam was exhausted. How could someone live this way for longer?

"I know what you're thinking," Milo said, still staring into the empty grate.

Liam raised his eyebrows.

"How is he such a mess?"

"I wasn't—"

Milo held up a hand. "You don't have to pretend on my account."

Liam crossed his arms.

"Remember I told you not to battle the darkness alone?"

Liam nodded.

"Well, I haven't exactly been following my advice very well," he huffed. "Until a couple of weeks ago, I have had no one here besides Willow since Conroy ran away." He turned his face to Liam, loneliness sitting in the shadows under his eyes, and the turned down edges of his mouth. "But since you all arrived, you've reminded me how important friendship is. How important it is to laugh, even when things are hard. How much we can learn from one another. I hadn't realized that I'd shut those things out. And yes, it breaks my heart to know that the reason you're here is that you lost your Nora, too." He pressed his lips into a flat line. "But I can't help but think that you were her last gift to me."

Liam tilted his head, trying to understand.

"You are what this world needs, Liam."

Liam shook his head.

"I know right now it seems like there isn't much you can do. But I promise you there is. You just haven't realized it yet. You're here for a reason. And you are going to make things better, just like your mom said you would. And I will keep telling you that and keep reminding you until you believe it. All of us will believe in you until you believe in yourself." Milo stood up, righted his robes, grasped his hands behind his back, and walked over to Liam.

"You can move through this and keep going. It's not always going to be like this. No, the pain will not go away. And some days will be harder than others, but you will grow and expand to hold more things in your heart than just grief. To endure more. And you will. But not alone. Never alone. Look around you. Lean on your friends. Lean on the love you have. And you will find the way through together. Promise me, Liam. Keep going." Milo gripped Liam's shoulder.

"I promise," Liam whispered.

Milo nodded and smiled, the tears clearing from his blue gaze.

"Thank you, Liam. I'm going to join the others. Take as much time as you need . . . this is your workshop now." Milo walked to the doorway and looked around the room again. Taking a deep breath, he smiled, turned, and glided away, leaving Liam with his mom's things.

CHAPTER THIRTY-SIX

L iam trailed his eyes around the workshop and landed on the rolls of parchment and journals in the corner. Maybe there was something here about the birthright ceremony. Something about how to stop Conroy.

He made his way over to them and sighed. How was he supposed to sort through all of this?

There has to be some rhyme and reason for everything, right? His mom's writing room at home hadn't been this chaotic.

He pushed through papers and the smell of years gone by and old ink engulfed him. After a moment, he deciphered that the papers on the desk all had to do with portals, fairies, and magical creatures. Nothing he needed now.

The sun slipped lower into the sky, sending colored light through the stained-glass window. He followed the light to the far wall where rolls of parchment and leather-bound journals laid packed into the leftmost corner of the wooden table mounted on the wall. Unfurling a couple of parchment papers, he saw they were maps. Some of Domhania, and some of other realms.

When he'd first arrived at the Stream Side hideout, they'd thrown around the idea of him being a Realm Jumper. Were these the other lands someone could travel to? His hand itched to unroll more of them and lose himself in the places available to him, but he told himself he would come back another time. The rest of the group would be waiting for him soon. He looked up, seeing it was almost sundown.

"C'mon, Mom. I know there's something here that can help." Liam sighed.

He felt a tug to his right and followed the long table down the wall a couple feet to where a leather journal quivered underneath a stack of others. Hesitantly, Liam pushed the stack off. The brown leather journal flipped open, fanning the pages until it stopped at a sketch of something. Taking a step closer, he sucked in a breath, hoping it was what he needed.

Narrowing his eyes, he saw a sketch of the pendant Sly wore around his neck. The same type of sketch his mom would draw over and over in her journals at home. The one she had him memorize. But this one looked different. The sketch clipped to the front of his mom's story journal had an engraving of a rose and snake connected by a figure eight. This sketch was missing the snake on it. The page the journal opened to looked like a diagram depicting how to remove the snake piece of the pendant, making it incomplete.

Liam's heart thumped in his chest. Could this mean something? Scanning the page for words, he saw a small note in the bottom corner that said, *While whole, the power is strong, but broken, the power is unattainable.*

Dropping the journal, Liam stared through the stained-glass window. Did this mean they had a chance? He had to see the back of Sly's pendant.

Hope thudded in his chest, and he ran out of his mom's workshop to find Sly.

"There he is!" Sly greeted Liam as he slid into the dining room, panting.

Juniper, Sly, Aubry, and Milo sat at the long wooden table in the middle of the room. They were gobbling their last meal before they went through the portal and ambushed Conroy's castle.

"We made a pot of Earl Grey. Seemed fitting for this evening." Sly motioned to the wide window behind him. The gray expanse of the cloud covered sky dumped snow on them, infusing the castle with a chill.

"Where are Johnny and Fox and Willow?" Liam asked, noticing their group was smaller.

"Out doing something for me. Should be back in time for our departure. You better eat before we head out." Sly nodded at Liam.

"Sly, I need to see the pendant." Liam rushed over to where Sly sat.

Sly gave him a puzzled look. "Everything okay, mate?"

"I need to make sure—" Liam tried to catch his breath.

"What was that?" Juniper clinked her teacup down and listened. A deep boom rattled the cups on the table, rippling the tea inside, creating rings like a pebble when thrown into a lake.

Liam's stomach dropped. He looked at Aubry across the table, whose face mirrored the fear he felt unfurling in him.

"It's Conroy." Milo's long stony face stared out the window. Liam saw no fear in his features. Only an eerie calm.

"How do you know? Maybe it's just a storm?" Aubry's eyes flitted back and forth between Liam and Milo.

Milo shook his head. "I can feel him. He wanted me to feel him. He didn't bother cloaking himself." He stood up slowly. "Make sure you are armed and prepared for battle. He isn't alone. The portal is enchanted to deposit portal users into the library. Meet me there, quickly."

"How was he able to find us? I thought you said the protection spells would drive them away?" Liam's heart beat harder in his chest.

Milo nodded solemnly. "Residue from the transport potions you drank must have remained in Conroy's castle. He must have taken a sample and magnified it to break down the wards keeping him out of my castle."

Dread pooled in Liam's limbs. Was this it? The moment he would face Conroy? He didn't think he was ready. He barely understood his powers and how to use them. What if he hurt someone? Or couldn't save them? His thoughts spiraled and anxiety fluttered in his chest. All he wanted was to enjoy some tea with his friends. Was that too much to ask?

Images of the last time he encountered Conroy flashed through his mind. Anger. Resentment. Destruction. Aubry's broken body. Conroy's shadows draining him. Milo's cry of pain. Blood.

Liam squeezed his eyes shut, pleading with the memories to go away.

"Ah!" something touched his forearm and pulled him back to the present moment. Juniper sat next to him; her brown velvet eyes anchored him.

"Liam, we can do this. Together." He couldn't tell if the confidence in her voice was genuine, or if she was trying to convince herself as much as Liam.

He stared at her and thought of Sly bleeding on the floor in the tree in the forest, life seeping out of him. Because of Conroy. He looked away, trying to hide his fear.

"Hey." She shook his arm. "We'll do this together. Okay?"

Looking back at her, he saw worry lines on her forehead. She *was* scared.

Liam studied her. They didn't really have a choice, did they? He wasn't going to let Conroy hurt anyone else. "Together." He nodded, staring into her eyes, desperately trying to take some of her confidence for himself.

Liam followed Juniper out to where the rest of the group waited by the archway between the dining room and living area. Sly bounced on the balls of his feet, looking like a bull ready to be let out of its holding bay. Aubry reached for Liam's hand. He squeezed and nodded, trying to give her some of the confidence Juniper had offered him.

"Where are Fox and Johnny?" Liam asked.

Sly dared to look a little worried. "They'll be here." He pulled out a sack of weapons he'd stashed behind a side table and passed them out. It felt all too familiar. He thought back to the weapons they strapped on when they left the Stream Side hideout to find Aubry and Milo's castle. So much had changed. So much hadn't.

Juniper strapped on her bow and arrow just as Fox and Johnny came running into the hallway.

"Really cutting it close." Juniper shot them a look.

"We're here, aren't we?" Johnny said stiffly, crossing his two axes on his back and attaching them. Fox restocked the leather pouch at his belt with his throwing stars. Sly grabbed a couple of knives for himself and slid them into sheaths on his leather vest. His long fighting sword sat snugly at his hip, handle gleaming in the candlelight from above. Liam grabbed himself a sword and tied the holder around his waist to sheath it. Aubry looked around at the weapons like she was going to throw up.

Sly noticed and reassured her. "Don't worry." He placed a gentle hand on her back. "Remember what we practiced with the long dagger?"

Aubry stared up at Sly, her forehead crinkling, and nodded slightly. Aubry hesitantly grabbed a dagger about the size of her forearm that had leaves engraved on its hilt and attached it to the weapons belt she wore on top of a leather chest piece.

Sly tilted his head to look more closely at Aubry. She met his gaze, and her breathing slowed.

He swallowed. "Well, you look lovely and ready for battle." A small smile crept up Sly's face as he admired the leather armor she wore on her torso, braided hair, and boots.

Cherry tones bloomed on Aubry's face. "Thank you," she managed, then grabbed his hand.

Johnny loudly cleared his throat and stared unamused at Sly, his hands lazily resting on the belt at his waist. Fox looked up at Sly and smirked.

"Everyone ready, then?" Sly looked around the circle at their crew and took a breath. "When we're out there, I want everyone to remember we're in this together. We have one another's backs. No matter what. Am I clear?" His intense stare bored through each person.

Everyone mumbled their own type of "yes."

"Good," Sly said. "Let's be on our way, then."

CHAPTER THIRTY-SEVEN

---◆◇◆---

B rushing past everyone, Sly seemed to glide across the floor down the hall as he led the way to the library. He had them travel against the walls for cover on their way. As they moved, the castle trembled more and more.

The six of them stood before the grand library doors. The tall oak structures loomed above them. For a moment, none of them moved. In a way, it seemed they all knew what waited for them behind these doors and delaying it made it a little less real. Liam looked up at them, took a breath, and said a prayer.

Sly stepped forward and pressed the doors open.

Holding his breath, Liam scanned the library, looking for Conroy and his men.

Silence.

"Fox, Johnny, cut around the back to distract them when I give you the signal," Sly ordered.

The two brothers nodded and moved to follow their orders, disappearing into the bookcases.

"You two stay in the shadows and watch our backs," Sly directed Aubry and Juniper, who nodded. Sly stepped closer to Juniper, putting his hand on her shoulder.

"Be careful," he commanded in a low voice. She nodded. Sly turned to Aubry and a soft expression filled his face. He placed a hand on her cheek and ran his thumb over it.

"Please, please, be careful," he breathed.

Aubry flushed and nodded. She reached up to cover his hand with hers and moved her head to place a kiss on his palm. "I will," she promised, emerald eyes locked on his russet-colored ones.

With a look at Liam, Aubry followed Juniper and jogged off into the maze of bookcases. Sly turned to Liam.

"Are you ready for this?" Sly's eyes looked concerned.

Liam nodded. "I think so," he said, confidence waning.

Knowing that Conroy was here again, he could feel his anger and resentment simmering. The fear in his stomach sent a chill through him. The magic under his skin tingled his arms and fingers.

He breathed deeply and thought again of his Christmas memory. Of being grounded in the golden power he knew lived in his blood. The power he'd inherited from his mom.

Suddenly, a bright blue light blasted into the library from the entrance, sending the doors flying. Sly and Liam ran for cover behind one of the waist-high bookcases.

"Oh, Daddy! I'm home," a voice called, contempt dripping from his words. Liam shuddered and slid his head out from his crouched position to get a glimpse. Conroy stood on the steps at the entrance to the library. His towering form oozed power. Blue magic glowed around him. His lips pulled tight over his teeth in a sneer as he scanned the expanse of the library before him. Dressed in black, he looked like a shadow himself. His gray eyes brooded like storm clouds. Instead of his usual fireballs glowing in his hands, he held a blue light that sparkled with power.

"What in the world is that?" Sly whispered to Liam. Liam shook his head. He had absolutely no idea. They hadn't gotten that far in his wizardry training yet.

From either side of Conroy, his men spilled into the room. Packs of men. More than Liam could count. They marched through the portal door, down into the library.

How are we going to fight against all of them? They were armed with weapons that glowed with the same blue power coming off Conroy. Had he given all of them magically enhanced weapons? Knives, swords, and bows and arrows all glowed blue in their hands.

"Find Liam and bring him to me. The pendant is of equal importance. You can dispose of the rest of them, but leave my *father* to me," Conroy said, like the word 'father' left a foul taste in his mouth.

Sly looked down and touched the pendant beneath his shirt.

The men spread out on either side of the library like ants invading new territory. Liam's heart slammed against this ribcage as he watched them disperse into the rows and rows of bookcases and hoped they didn't find Aubry.

"Oh Milo, come out, come out, wherever you are!" Conroy growled, surveying the library from the doorway. Liam made a move to confront Conroy, and Sly's grip tightened around his upper arm like steel. Liam widened his eyes at him.

Sly narrowed his and shook his head. He motioned for Liam to stay put and wait. Liam tensed his jaw in impatience.

"Were you looking for me, son?" Milo glided into the library in navy robes, cool, calm, and collected. A picture of peace. In contrast, Conroy stood taller than his father, emanating rage.

"You thought you could keep me out of here after all these years? I know your magic. I know your tricks. You aren't strong enough to keep me away. It was only a matter of time," Conroy gloated.

Milo nodded slowly, walking in a circle around his son. "I know." Milo stared at him, love in his gaze.

Conroy shifted uncomfortably.

"Well, if you knew I was coming, I hope you prepared well enough." Conroy raised his hand, and blue power glowed in his palm. Surprise flashed across Milo's face as he looked at it.

He raised his own hands and conjured purple swirling power for himself. Son and father stood at the ready, facing one another.

"I don't want to fight you, Conroy," Milo's voice pleaded.

"No. You never wanted to fight, did you?" Bitterness sharpened Conroy's voice. "You didn't want to fight, even when it mattered most."

Milo's calm face started to crack, hurt showing through. "I have always done my best by you."

"You let me grow up without a mother when you could have saved her, but you were too much of a coward." With each word, the power in his hands grew and dark smoke spirals emanated out from his chest like a secondary cape.

Not the shadows. Fear rose in Liam's stomach.

"You know why I couldn't use chaos magic. She wouldn't be the same," Milo said.

Conroy shook his head. "You just didn't know how to use it."

"Conroy, Zadamir is filling your head with *lies!*" Milo raised his voice. "Did he tell you why he wants to teach you to use this dark magic, fueled by rage and revenge?" He raised his eyebrows.

"Because he wants to help me! Help me the way you couldn't!"

Milo shook his head. "No, son. He wants to use it himself. You are just his vessel to get it."

"That's what Zadamir told me you'd say. And you know what, Father? He told me *you* were the one using *me*. You wanted to use me and take the birthright power for yourself. But it doesn't matter anymore because I'm going to take what's rightfully mine. The power that mother was meant to give me. I'm taking it all and you can't stop me."

Conroy threw up both hands and blasted Milo with his blue power. At the last second, Milo blocked it with his purple magic and spun out of the way, anticipating Conroy's next move.

"Hey!" Sly yelled. One of Conroy's pawns held him pressed up against the bookcase, putting pressure on his neck. Sly struggled under the weight of the giant guard. Liam unsheathed his potion-imbued sword and struck Sly's attacker hard in the face with the handle, knocking him off balance just long enough for Sly to wiggle out and face him, drawing his own sword. The man cried out and covered his face with one of his hands, blood seeping between his fingers. He lunged at Sly with his own blue, magic-imbued sword. Sly blocked and the swords sparked when they met. The guard came at Sly with a longer sweep of his sword. Sly blocked, ducked, and then swept his leg on the way up. The hitman fell onto his face and stayed on the floor, still.

Sly nodded at Liam. "I'm sure there are more not far behind. Let's move."

Turning to make it through the bookcases, they stopped short.

Five more men came around the corner and ran at Sly and Liam. One of Conroy's guards sliced Liam in the chest with his knives and kicked him hard. He fell back against a bookcase, sword clattering away. He clutched his sternum. The power from the blade sizzled through his bones and pain licked through his veins. It burned like the fireball that Conroy had first thrown at him outside of the Stream Side Kids' hideout weeks ago, but worse, like it had been amplified.

With his hands braced on the ground, he saw two pairs of feet move in on him. The first blow hit him in the back of the head, then the side of his ribs.

White-hot pain burst through him. He snapped his head up to look at the men advancing on him and summoned his power. He tried to start with light weights like Milo suggested in the training courtyard, but the burning pain from the imbued sword scattered his concentration. He blasted them with raw power. The men flew backward, giving himself time to painfully rise to his feet.

Sly moved in on one of Liam's attackers. Their swords sliced through the air, clanging against one another, but not slowing down. Sly drew his sword up as his opponent stepped back to take a swing. Shaking his head, Sly blocked his advances and swung his sword at him. Metal clanged on metal. They twisted and turned, glowing swords sparking. Conroy's guard sliced a cut on Sly's forearm. Sly didn't falter.

Liam watched, anxiety in his chest. Conroy's men had swords that simulated Wizard's Fire. It was only a matter of seconds before Sly started feeling the effects.

A quick movement from Sly sent the man's sword flying.

Flashing a grin at the man, Sly made to take a step forward, but stopped short, taking a breath, pain flashing across his face. His hesitation cost him. Sly's opponent rushed him while another got him from behind. Liam heard a sickening crack. The man behind Sly twisted his arm behind his back and broke it while pushing him onto his knees.

"No!" Sly's pain-laced voice cried. The man unsheathed a glowing knife and sliced Sly's neck where the pendant hung.

A red line appeared on Sly's neck. The man holding Sly's broken arm shoved him forward, and he fell onto his face. The guard with the knife snatched the pendant, eyes gleaming.

Sly! No. Not again. Liam shook, rejecting the thought. Shook with anger. Shook with fear.

Liam looked around, desperate to find something he could use. Books? Stone? *Fire? The candles!*

Could he use them like the fire in the training courtyard? He'd never tried it before. Would it work? What if he failed?

I've always had time to focus on a peaceful memory. What if this doesn't work? He had to try. For Sly.

He drew his hands together, pushing away the pain burning his chest, forcing himself to focus, and commanded fire from the candle chandeliers and sconces on the walls. He thought of Sly. Thought of his words to him, letting him know it was going to be okay. He thought of the laughs, the jokes. The friendship he had.

He willed the fire to move. The small flames from the candle chandeliers flickered and slowly elongated until they met one another, forming a big, long flame. The giant snake of fire rushed down on top of Conroy's men and encircled them, confining them. They slashed unsuccessfully at the fire with their weapons.

Taking the few precious seconds he had, Liam dove over to Sly's still body on the ground.

"Sly? C'mon, Sly. Please!" Liam lightly touched his back, not wanting to injure him further. Blood pooled on the floor from the cut on his neck. He turned Sly's head to check his breathing. His eyes fluttered open.

"Sly!" Liam tore a piece of cloth from his shirt and pressed it to Sly's neck wound.

"They took the pendant," Sly breathed, eyes rolling back.

"It's okay, I have them here," Liam said.

Just as he looked up to make sure they hadn't moved, the giant window against the back wall of the library exploded, sending glass and stone inward. The impact of the explosion knocked over bookcases, display cases, and furniture. It rumbled through the floor and rattled tables and stacks of books. The fireplace was destroyed. With nothing to hold it in, the fire gladly leaped over the rubble and caught on paper and wood. Flames rose higher and higher as they gathered paper for fuel.

The men Liam had contained were no longer stuck. He'd broken his concentration. They moved forward, drawing their blue glowing weapons.

"Stop!" Liam bellowed desperately.

They could not come closer and hurt Sly anymore. They would not fill him with the hot pain of their magical weapons. They'd come to the castle, ruining his mom's favorite place. This library. And now it laid in crumbles, because of them.

A surge of power shot out from him, directed at the intruders. All the men in his line of sight collapsed, unconscious.

A high-pitched scream echoed off the marble floors. Liam and Sly looked at one another.

"Here, unstopper this for me. It will help." Sly shakily pulled a vial with earthy green liquid in it from his pocket. He recognized it as the potion they'd given Milo after Conroy injured him.

Liam tore the stopper out and poured it into Sly's mouth. Sly groaned and clutched his side. Panic thrummed in Liam's chest, worried he'd made it worse, but Sly exhaled in relief.

Despite the slice on his neck slowing its bleeding, it didn't heal up. The magically enhanced weapons were powerful. Juniper and Aubry had supposedly altered the potion to combat the effects of Wizard's Fire more quickly than normal. Sly stopped shaking and Liam took that as a sign the potion was working. Thankfully a non-magical injury, Sly's broken arm slowly healed.

"Thanks, mate," Sly mumbled. He winced as Liam helped him into a sitting position.

Another high-pitched scream echoed off the stone floors. They looked at one another. Liam looped an arm around Sly, who was unsteady and injured, then ran off toward the scream. Well, Liam tried to run, but Sly was limping, slowing them down. They clumsily zigzagged through the maze of bookcases and found Conroy's men fighting Juniper and Aubry.

Juniper was up high on one of the bookcases, aiming an arrow at the guard trying to chase her down. Two more were making their way up the bookcases to go after Juniper. Aubry was backed into a corner and held out a shaking dagger in front of her as several men moved in on her.

"Stay back!" she commanded. Liam let go of Sly and made to run at Aubry the same time Sly did.

"Go help Juniper!" Liam pointed. "I got Aubry." Sly hesitated for an instant, then limped over to Juniper, drawing one of his knives from his vest.

One of the men knocked the knife out of Aubry's grip and lunged at her with a blue glowing sword. She dodged and countered with a knee to his stomach, and then an elbow to the back of his neck which sent him to the floor.

The second man used Aubry's takedown as an opportunity to rush her. He yanked her by the hair and pulled her to the ground. She yelped in pain as he stepped on one of her arms to pin her to the ground. He raised his knife.

Anger and dread simmered up and bubbled out of Liam.

Aubry, who'd been like a sister to him throughout his childhood. He thought about the plethora of times she'd run after him in their grandparents' garden. Consoling him when he fell. He would not let the men hurt her.

He pushed his hands out in front of him like he was going to shove the man off Aubry. His surge of electric power flung Aubry's attacker against a bookcase, knocking books down on top of him. Gasping, Aubry sat up, looking at Liam, her eyes wide.

Something slammed down hard on Liam's shoulder and sliced it open. He saw the glow of blue magic as he fell to the ground.

"Liam!" Aubry screamed.

Liam pushed his face up from the floor, pain sizzling through his shoulder, and saw five more of Conroy's men circling them. Then more on the right, the left, and from behind. They were surrounded.

"You better think hard about your next move, wizard boy." The man above him pointed the glowing sword at his throat.

CHAPTER
THIRTY-EIGHT

---◆○◆---

Thunk. A blade flew into the man's chest. Liam's attacker looked down, looked up confused, then crumpled to the ground, sword clattering.

Aubry stood, her arm extended from throwing the blade through the air and planting it in the man's chest.

Liam stared at his cousin for a beat, not believing what she'd just done. She killed a man. To save Liam's life.

Liam scrambled up, pain from his wound sizzling through him. He grabbed the magic-imbued sword and moved over to Aubry, fumbling to down the potion he had at his hip to stop the pain of Wizard's Fire in his veins.

"Aubry!" Sly said, slipping next to her and grabbing her hand. "Are you hurt?" He cupped her face and searched her for injuries.

"No." Tears filled her eyes. "But you are!" She gently touched his neck, hands shaking. He winced and pulled away from her touch, nearly tumbling back. She grabbed his waist and held him up, looking at him, terrified.

"It's not you, love." He took her hands in his, reassuring her. "The weapons Conroy's men are using are infused with magic. It leaves a worse injury."

Aubry looked up at Sly through her eyelashes, anguished.

"I'll be okay. It'll just take a little longer to heal. Your potion worked beautifully." He brushed a lock of auburn curls behind her ear.

He looked at the man on the ground and then raised his eyebrows at her. She nodded.

"Can we please do this later and pay attention to the crowd of men encircling us right now?" Juniper said.

"What do we do? What's the plan?" Aubry looked around at the men outnumbering them.

Liam took in the worried faces of his friends—Sly, crusted in blood; Juniper, sagging from fighting Conroy's men; Aubry, working to hold up Sly as she grimaced through her own injuries.

There was no way they could win. Not against all these men. He would not let his friends die trying, either. How could the world his mom created kill him and his friends? Maybe there was another way?

"Nothing," Liam said.

They stared at him.

"There is nothing we can do! We're outnumbered. Do you *want* to die?" Liam gestured to the thirty men surrounding them with glowing weapons.

"That's right, listen to the wise wizard boy," one of the men sneered.

"Where's Conroy?" Juniper asked.

Liam's eyes widened. "Fighting Milo."

Don't battle the darkness alone.

Liam closed his eyes.

"Liam?" Juniper's voice quivered.

Shouts and battle cries rang through the air.

Turning to the source, Liam saw the Stream Side Kids and dozens of fairies barreling in from the library's entrance led by Willow. Johnny and Fox came up around Conroy's men, encircling them. All the Stream Side teenagers who could wield a weapon stormed through the doors. They charged into the library, heading straight for Liam and his friends. Metal clanged on metal as the Stream Side Kids and fairies met Conroy's men. Chaos ensued as the battle raged on.

It wasn't over yet.

Thank God! The fairies were good on their word and helped the Stream Side Kids travel to Milo's castle in one day. With their magic, they could travel long distances in a matter of minutes.

Johnny twisted and turned, fighting with his axes. Fox lithely moved between the men, striking them down. Conroy's guards fell as the Stream Side Kids fought back. Hope sparked in Liam's chest. Maybe they could win this.

Picking up one of the glowing blue swords, Liam joined the fight, slashing at each guard that came at him. He grimaced past the pain in his shoulder, willing himself to keep going. Juniper made her way to the top of a bookcase and took aim with her bow and arrow. Sly and Aubry fought side by side, Sly slashing with his sword and Aubry with her dagger.

As Liam fought the men coming after him, he itched to use his powers, but doubt butted up against his desire. There were too many people. He could hurt someone. The last time he used his powers successfully, he was in a mostly empty training courtyard. It was too risky here. He swallowed his fear, gripped his sword tighter, and blocked a strike from a guard coming at him. The guard swung at Liam, aiming for his injured shoulder. Liam blocked, but not hard enough. His strength waned and his attacker's sword sliced deeper into his wound. He bit back a yell and breathed through the shock of electricity from the imbued weapon.

The guard raised his sword to strike again. Gritting his teeth, Liam lifted his uninjured arm, and summoned air to fling his attacker off his feet. The guard knocked over two others as he flailed backward into a bookcase, then slumped to the ground.

Liam took a shaky breath, trying to steady his body as he felt the Wizard's Fire start to burn in his veins.

He looked around, and, despite himself, he smiled. They were winning. It looked like they were going to overpower the guards. The odds had shifted.

Conroy's men were falling one by one, leaving the Stream Side Kids and fairies standing.

Then more guards rushed out of the portal and came at them from all sides, driving the Stream Side Kids into a circle.

Seconds felt like minutes as the Stream Side Kids and fairies struggled to hold their ground and fight off Conroy's army. A Stream Side Kid fell. Then another. One by one, their numbers dwindled. Overpowered.

A pang of grief hit Liam. They'd come and given their lives to defend him and the others. He didn't deserve their sacrifice. This battle was because of him. Their deaths were on his hands.

His grief burst through him, and he used it to conjure wind to blast some men off their feet, giving the remaining Stream Side Kids enough time to catch a breath before the next wave of attacks.

His use of power cost him. Remembering the potions, he snatched a vial from his hip and sucked it down. The earthy taste bloomed on his tongue. At first, he didn't feel anything except the hot burning of Wizard's Fire in his veins threatening to bring him to the ground.

A second later, it felt like a breeze passed over him, brushing away the pain. He took a cleansing breath, and the burning dissipated. The fire died down into a throbbing ache. He felt the bleeding slow in his shoulder.

Liam turned to see Johnny and Fox fighting back-to-back, blood streaked across their faces. Two men who made it to the top of the bookcase Juniper had perched on pursued her. She leaped from bookcase to bookcase, but two more cut her off. She looked around, panicked.

Liam's heart thudded.

Guards forced Aubry and Sly to their knees, holding blades to their throats. They were losing.

Conroy's men moved in, holding swords and daggers to throats, ready to kill more of them. More Stream Side Kids fell. Blood pooled in the center of the library, looking like a red rug on the floor.

A place that was meant for peace, learning, and comfort, now tainted with blood. Tainted with death. Tainted with darkness.

Liam shook with rage.

The fire in the library burned hotter and moved in on them from the back of the room. The chandeliers shot up with flames.

Burning everyone alive won't help!

But he couldn't find something to hold on to. His vision filled with falling Stream Side Kids and blood. The people he loved were injured and bloody. It was over. How were they going to come out of this? He was supposed to *save this world*, his mom said. Protect it. All he'd done was plunge the Stream Side Kids into battle. He'd brought Conroy out of his dark corner which led to them being pursued and almost killed multiple times.

This can't be the end of the story.

The chaos inside Liam manifested in the room. The roaring fire crept closer, wrapping itself around the tall bookcases, glass display cases, and books.

Glass exploded from the heat, sending shards flying. The candle chandeliers shot flames toward the ceiling. The floor shook. Snow flew in from the pane-less window, soaking everyone in the vicinity.

"Liam, be stronger than I was," his mom's voice rang through his mind.

Be stronger than her? How?

Looking at his friends' faces, he saw the terror in their eyes as he plunged the room into elemental chaos.

"Liam!" Aubry's shrill voice called out to him. The man holding the knife to her throat yanked her hair. "You can do this! I know you can!" she screamed. The man behind her knocked her out with a blow to the head. Hot anger ripped through Liam. Sly struggled against the men holding him to get to her.

Liam forced his mind to a memory.

Snow ran across his mind. The snowball fight before they'd made their way up to the castle took form in his thoughts. He thought about the fun they'd had being with one another. Laughing together. Juniper's confident, velvet brown eyes flashed across his mind. Sly's reassurance that everything would be okay. Johnny's strong countenance. Fox's playful one. Aubry's hand on his shoulder. He held those moments in his heart and called upon them for strength.

Warmth bloomed from his chest, down his arms, and into his feet. He crackled with power.

He reached out his energy, looking for something to use. From the decimated window, a breeze blew in and across his face. He snapped his head to look out the window and see snow.

The snow!

Reaching out with his senses, he latched onto the snow and willed it to obey him.

A blizzard spun and slashed through the air. It twisted and turned into a cyclone, taking books, debris, and stone with it.

Liam pulled it toward them, putting them in the blizzard's eye. It whipped around them, lifting Conroy's men off their feet, sending them hurtling through the air like black flies caught in the wind. Ice shards sliced through their clothes. Weapons flew from their hands.

A blizzard of evil men, stone, snow, ice, and books ripped through the library.

A blizzard of emotion. Good, bad. Angry, joyful, painful.

Focus. Breathe. He heard Milo's voice in his mind. He let the power flow through him and used his emotions to direct it.

People hurtled through the air, shouting.

Liam slammed them down, forcing grunts from the guards.

Ice slowly encased each of them where they lay on the library floor, frozen in time. Unable to move.

Unable to hurt them anymore.

CHAPTER
THIRTY-NINE

A cry of pain echoed through the debris-strewn library.

Milo!

Liam took off to the entrance. He rounded a corner and then another before coming head-to-head with one of Conroy's goons. How had he not gotten all of them? Frustration burned in his stomach.

This one had a sword. Fatigue from his giant blizzard had set in, so Liam took that as an invitation to pull out *his* sword.

An enemy sword swooped at Liam and instinct took over as he blocked and sidestepped. He stepped in to jab the man, who moved out of the way and slashed at Liam's good arm, drawing blood. Liam inhaled and felt the sting of the cut and the warmth of the blood oozing from it, but he kept a grip on the sword and pushed the pain away.

He arched his sword, aiming for the man's shoulder, who parried his strike and knocked Liam's sword out of his hand. It clattered away behind a bookcase and pain sparked in his arm. Liam made to go after it, but the man stepped in front of him, holding his sword pointed at his chest. He took a few steps toward Liam.

The whistle of something sailing through the air grabbed Liam's attention. A second later, an arrow planted itself in the man's chest. The guard crumpled to his knees.

Looking up at a bookcase, Liam saw Juniper with her empty bow raised. She lowered it and nodded at him. Liam returned her nod and ran toward Milo's voice.

He finally made it out of the bookcase maze and found Conroy and Milo still fighting on the marble steps at the entrance. Conroy's back was to Liam, and Milo looked exhausted. Fear bloomed in Liam's chest and he ran over to them.

He would not let Conroy take Milo.

Milo glanced at Liam and swiftly moved his wrist, deflecting Liam to conceal him behind a bookcase.

What is he doing? I'm trying to help!

"Are you tired yet, Father? Ready to give up?" Conroy's voice rang out.

"I will never be ready to give up trying to stop you from going down this dark path," Milo said.

"So be it," Conroy said.

Liam poked his head out.

Conroy shot his blue power at his father. Milo retaliated. They pushed against one another, locked in a stalemate.

C'mon. Liam clenched his fists.

After a few seconds, Conroy's power grew, devouring his father's.

"If you want to get in the way, then I will gladly let you. And I'll take your power too." Conroy stepped forward. His blue power moved closer to Milo, who looked more haggard by the second, his face more and more sunken.

Liam burst from behind the bookcase and tapped into his own power. He coaxed it to the surface and threw rubble at Conroy to get his attention off Milo.

"Oh, little brother, coming to join the party? You're exactly who I've been looking for." Conroy slowly turned his head.

"Leave him alone!" Liam moved more debris from the ground, sending them raining down on Conroy.

Conroy created a shield over himself that broke the rocks into dust. "Would you rather I take your power first?" Blue sparks flickered from Conroy's hand. "I can arrange that," he said, and flung his power at Liam.

Liam focused on it and deflected Conroy's attack. Before Liam could retaliate, purple knocked Conroy's blue power out of the way.

Conroy yelled in frustration. "You just can't help getting in the way, can you?" Conroy turned on Milo.

"This is between you and me, son. Leave Liam out of this." Milo stepped toward his son.

Conroy flung a powerful blast at Milo, knocking him to the ground. The wizard landed with a grunt.

"This has everything to do with Liam! He's the one who stole my power. How does a boy from another realm inherit what's mine? So naïve, so small, so weak. He could never be worthy of such power." Conroy glowered at Liam.

Liam seethed. For too long, Clive and his friends at school would tell him the same thing. He was too weak and could never amount to anything worthy. For a long time, he'd believed them. But now, he realized it was a lie.

Yes, he'd been thrown into a world he knew nothing about, and people got hurt because of him. He'd also learned the strength that came from letting others help him.

He wasn't alone.

He'd learned how to use his powers and not let his emotions control him. His actions *mattered*. They affected everyone around him. It was time to save his friends in the way they were expecting him to. It was up to him to do his part now.

"It's not yours to take," Liam said.

Conroy scoffed. "You don't seem to understand the breadth of my power, little brother."

"You don't seem to understand the power of the birthright ceremony."

Conroy's eyes flashed in anger. "How dare you tell me what I do and don't understand about magic." He stepped toward Liam, blue power balling in both hands, smoky shadows moving with him along the floor like snakes, waiting to strike.

Liam thought back to when he'd opened the ground to swallow Conroy whole. The same rage scratched at the edge of his senses, begging him to use it.

He took a breath.

He couldn't let his anger take over this time. There was too much at stake. Too many who could get hurt.

Conroy moved closer still and Liam felt a chill coming with him. Magic buzzed in his own veins, and he opened himself up to it.

Shadows reared at Liam, aiming for his throat. Liam jumped to the side and shot them with a blast of air, dissolving them.

Conroy brought fire surging at Liam from the chandeliers and sconces around the room. Acting fast, Liam reached out for the chill and snow outside the window as a shield, creating a wall of water in front of him.

Conroy laughed as the fire danced on the surface of the water, hissing and steaming. Heat pressed in on Liam, flames burning through the shield. Sweat dripped down his face, and his skin screamed at the heat. Liam pulled more power from his veins and created a solid wall of ice to block the flames before they could burn him.

That was a bit too close. He panted, eyeing Conroy for his next move.

Conroy shifted his focus to the marble ground beneath their feet. The ground trembled and sharp spikes of marble and rock erupted from the floor, aiming to impale Liam.

He conjured the air to propel him further away.

As he landed, Liam felt a chill up his spine. Conroy had summoned his shadows again and tendrils of darkness snaked toward him, hungry for his life force and power.

Liam conjured a whirlwind of air, the gusts momentarily scattering the shadows before they came together again.

Conroy raised his hands, and the shadows coalesced into a dark vortex, drawing life from everything around it. Liam felt his strength waning. His power was in place, but his human strength was fading, weakening his body. The surrounding plants shriveled up and turned gray. Liam saw Milo struggling to stand, strength draining from him as well.

Desperation surged through Liam, and he grounded himself, looking for the golden power he'd used in the dungeon when they saved Aubry. Latching onto it and his connection to the elements, he brought on an assault of ice spears, fire, wind, and sharp spikes from the ground, all aimed at Conroy. Calling forth more power, Liam held his ground, catching Conroy off guard.

"Get off me," a voice called from behind him, threatening to break his concentration. Hearing a scream of pain, Liam turned to find Aubry now conscious and forced to her knees. A guard held a blade at her throat and blood gushed from her side.

"Maybe you want to stop so we can talk?" Conroy stared down Liam.

"Let her go!" Liam yelled, air whipping through his hair, buzzing with power.

"Gladly. You're the one who determines that," Conroy yelled over the sound of flying wreckage and debris.

With a grunt, Liam let go of his power and stumbled backward in exhaustion.

"Good boy. Now, let's discuss this birthright we're talking about." Conroy brushed himself off, stepped around a spike protruding from the ground and walked closer to Liam and Aubry.

Liam stepped toward Aubry, body heavy, panic rising in his chest as he looked in horror at her bleeding side.

Not again.

Conroy would *not* make her suffer like this again! Determination bubbled into his hands, golden power glowing from them.

"Ah ah," Conroy wagged his finger, sending tendrils of shadows snaking around Liam's feet, holding him in place. They moved up his legs and wrapped around him, pinning his arms to his side. "Like you said, little Liam, the power you have is not mine to take. You were right there, unfortunately." Conroy clenched his jaw in annoyance. "It's something that has to be given."

Liam froze, trepidation speeding up his breathing as he looked back and forth from Conroy to Aubry.

"So." Conroy stopped a couple feet from them, smiling coldly. "You're going to give me *my* birthright or your cousin dies."

"No!" Liam struggled against the shadows, but they gripped him tighter and chilled him to the bone.

"Liam, you can't give it to him. You can't." Aubry locked eyes with him and winced in pain. She looked like she was barely holding on. Her body shook as his had when he was blasted by Wizard's Fire. If one of Conroy's men had stabbed her with one of the magically enhanced swords, she would die even quicker. He had to get a healing potion to her.

Liam looked behind Conroy to see if Milo was okay. He didn't see him. He was alone. He swallowed and squared his shoulders to Conroy.

"Okay. Just don't hurt her anymore. I'll give you what you want." Desperation and defeat settled in Liam's chest.

"Liam, no," Aubry pleaded.

"Quiet!" The guard holding her shoved her forward, and she sprawled face-down on the floor.

Liam fought against the shadows, calling forth his power. Focusing on the thrum of power in his blood, he directed it at the shadows so they would loosen around him.

Conroy flinched and released Liam.

Stumbling forward, Liam caught himself and glared at Conroy.

"You ready for the ceremony, then?" One of Conroy's dark, greasy brows rose.

"Just let me help her first."

"You get to help her after I have what I want."

Aubry's gaze met his from the floor where she lay sprawled. She shook her head slightly and grimaced in pain. If he argued, he would waste precious time. He couldn't risk it.

Liam clenched his jaw and nodded curtly.

"Excellent," Conroy said as he stepped up to Liam.

Liam had read a little about the birthright ceremony one night when he couldn't sleep after Milo told him about it. Liam extended his hands in front of him, palms down. A few inches below his, Conroy held his palms up, eager to receive Liam's power.

The ceremony had to start with one party willingly giving power to the other. Liam closed his eyes.

I don't know if this is what you had in mind, Mom. But I'm doing this so save Aubry, Liam thought, trying to connect with his mom the way he had in her workshop. He knew she was counting on him to make things right. To save the world and stop Conroy. But he couldn't sacrifice his cousin. He wouldn't lose her.

He summoned the power that thrummed in his veins. He felt it holding onto him, not wanting to leave. Not wanting to be given up.

I'm sorry. Liam pushed forward and willed the power to his palms. He felt warmth pooling in his hands. Slowly, he pushed it from his palms to Conroy's. As soon as he did, he heard Conroy inhale and knew it was working. Liam focused on the golden power that grounded him. The warm sun, the memories of love, and pushed it out of his palms.

Conroy winced. Liam opened an eye to see why. Confusion came over Conroy's face as he watched Liam transfer his power. Dark smoke shot out of Conroy's chest and swirled around his ankles. It slinked along the floor for a moment then turned a golden color.

"No! What's happening?" Conroy looked around frantically at his shadows that were turning gold and melting into the ground like they'd never existed. "What are you doing to me?" he growled.

Liam kept going, pushing his power into Conroy, and as he did, Conroy started shaking. His arms trembled and Liam realized he was trying to break their connection. He couldn't stand to hold Liam's power. It was hurting him.

A yell ripped through Conroy and he tore his hands away from Liam's, shadows shooting from Conroy's chest to push Liam away from him. Both shot backward, a flash of power blasting them away from each other.

"What have you done?" Conroy coughed on the ground, propped up on an elbow.

Dazed, Liam pushed himself up to sit, gasping for air after getting the wind knocked out of him from the blast. His vision had gone blurry, and he looked around for an auburn blob somewhere to his left. He crawled to Aubry, still lying on the ground, and shoved his hand into his pocket, bringing out a healing potion.

"Aubry, here." Liam's voice trembled as he brought the vial to her lips, gently tilting her head up to drink. "Drink this, please. C'mon, Aubry."

She groaned but drank the potion.

"Thank God. Now, please work," Liam begged, waiting for her wounds to stop bleeding.

A sudden pain shot through Liam's chest, and he cried out. Cold, hollow breathlessness followed. It felt like someone was stealing the air out of his lungs. His limbs burned like he'd been blasted with Wizard's Fire.

What was happening?

"Look what you've done to us!" Conroy weakly shouted from a couple feet away, still holding himself up on his elbow, looking haggard. "Not finishing the birthright ceremony will kill us both," he breathed.

Liam looked down at his hands and saw his veins darken like they were being filled with ink. Burning, aching ink. He breathed through the pain and looked up just in time to see Milo stagger out of the rubble, robes torn, face long and pale. Conroy saw him too and quickly summoned his shadows to curl around himself. "Good luck, little Liam."

He vanished in a swirl of smoke.

CHAPTER FORTY

M ilo made his way to Liam.

"She'll be okay. Just give her more of the healing potions for the next twenty-four hours," Milo said, blue eyes skating over her injuries and assessing the damage.

"You're sure?" Liam looked up at his mentor, blinking back tears.

Milo nodded. He looked at Liam and grimaced. "You stopped the birthright ceremony?"

"Conroy pulled away," Liam said, trying to catch his breath. "What's going to happen to me?"

Milo stared at him, emotion welling up in his eyes. "Nothing. You're going to be okay."

"How is that possible?" Liam shook his head. "You said before it was killing my mom and Conroy. Isn't it doing the same to Conroy and me now?"

"It can be stopped," Milo said.

"How?"

"Come with me over here, please. If you can." Milo offered Liam a hand. Liam turned to look at Aubry again.

"She will be okay. I sense the potion working already," Milo said.

Liam swallowed and turned to take Milo's hand, which he was thankful for. His legs felt like they were on fire. He struggled to stand. Milo steadied him, taking his elbow.

Milo walked them around a row of bookcases to an unassuming display case. Miraculously, it was still intact. He let go of Liam, making sure he could steady himself against a bookcase. Milo slid open the display case, then moved his hand to open a false back.

Liam stared and gripped the bookcase as another wave of pain washed through him.

Milo pulled out a small black journal, an ancient-looking key, and a gold ring.

"This"—Milo held up the journal—"holds important information that I believe will be of great value to you. It's my journal. It holds all I know about Conroy, and magic, which I think will help you master your powers, and anything else about Domhania you won't find in these books." Milo glanced around at the library. He handed Liam the journal.

"Why are you giving this to me?" Liam shook his head, utterly confused.

"This"—Milo held up the key so Liam could see the handle stamped with what looked like a comet and the moon—"is the key to the castle. Take good care of her." Emotion rose in Milo's voice as he handed the key to Liam.

"Take care? Where are you—" Liam looked up at Milo, finally realizing what he was doing. "No. No." Liam shook his head hard and pain shot through his neck. In the next breath, it felt like a knife was being pushed through his chest. He tried to breathe through the pain. "You're not going anywhere. You can't go. You can't leave me here alone. I need a mentor. I need—" Liam's voice was thin and desperate. "I need you."

Milo reached out and grabbed Liam's arm and held up the golden ring with his other hand and looked him in the eyes. "And this—" Milo swallowed. "This was your mother's ring. I thought you should keep it."

Liam's nostrils flared, and his throat ached.

"It's time . . . time to say goodbye." Tears filled Milo's eyes.

"No! No, not yet. It's *not* time yet." Liam's throat tightened. He remembered Milo's calm and inviting face when they first found the castle. He remembered the mysterious sparkle in his eyes, the wisdom he'd shared. The emotions Liam got to see in his mother's workshop. Everything Milo had taught him about his powers. Who would he be without Milo's help?

"Liam." Milo held his gaze. His voice held an air of wisdom and resolve. "Liam." Milo reached for his arms. "You have done so well. I'm very proud of you and what you've learned. You've grown so much and I'm confident you will continue to do so. Know that I believe in you. And I always will."

Liam stared into Milo's sea-blue eyes and felt his warmth. His confidence in him. "But how can I do this without you?"

"Your friends and family will support you. Remember, you are not alone. No matter what the darkness may whisper. You are not alone." Milo smiled weakly at Liam. "Keep going, Liam. It's been my pleasure to see you this far." With a last squeeze, Milo's grip loosened, and he stepped back. "Now, please let me do this one last thing before I leave you. For you. For Domhania. For your mother. She would have wanted this. Let me honor her in this way."

Liam blinked away tears. He nodded, then put everything Milo had given him in his pockets.

Milo stepped closer to Liam. "You're supposed to be here. You're meant to save this world. I know you'll make your mother proud. You've already made me proud." Milo's blue eyes glistened with tears.

Milo raised Liam's hands, palms up, a couple of inches below his own, palms down. "Just breathe, Liam. You'll be okay in a minute."

Liam wheezed. His lungs felt like they were filling with fluid. He commanded his body not to collapse. To fight through this.

Milo looked into Liam's eyes and summoned his power. For a moment, Liam felt nothing different. Just felt the scorching agony of the broken ceremony.

Then he saw white power flow from Milo's palms into his. Liam felt a cool, tranquil feeling push against the hollow, life-sucking sickness of the broken birthright ceremony. He felt it start in his palms, work its way up his forearms, his neck, chest, torso, arms, and legs, until his entire body felt like it was floating in a cool body of water.

Watching Milo, he saw his eyes become sunken, his hair dull, his skin lose its flush.

Liam watched Milo give his very life to him. Saw it seeping out of Milo and into himself. He couldn't let him do this. He couldn't.

"Yes, you can. I want to do this for you. Accept my gift, please," Milo pleaded weakly.

Liam clenched his jaw and stared into Milo's calm sea-blue eyes.

"They need you," Milo said.

Agony tore through Liam.

Milo wobbled. Liam held him by the elbows, and they sunk to their knees.

"What's happening?" Juniper's voice broke through Liam's fog of grief and he saw Juniper, Sly holding Aubry, Johnny, and Fox watching them from several feet away.

A lump stuck in Liam's throat. He tore his eyes away from the group and watched Milo. He had to. He understood the weight of this decision. He was living because of Milo's sacrifice for him.

"Thank you," Liam choked out.

Milo nodded, his body sagging, breathing shallow. Liam saw it coming. The life dimmed in Milo's eyes and he leaned forward. Liam guided him onto the ground, holding his head in his lap.

Milo smiled one last time, then closed his eyes.

"No," Liam whispered.

He crumpled over on top of Milo. A dull ache started in his chest and grew into a sharp pain. A hollowness. Agony. Grief.

He felt so alone.

A hand and then an arm came around him.

A sea of grief washed over him, pulling him under.

CHAPTER FORTY-ONE

———◆○◆———

A fter the battle was over, the library lay in shambles before Liam and his friends. Bodies scattered the floor, making Liam want to retch. He stood there thinking how much easier it would be if Milo were with him.

Milo.

He was the priority right now.

The rest of the Stream Side Kids and fairies could handle the library.

Liam, Aubry, Sly, Johnny, Fox, and Juniper stood in a semicircle around the grave Liam dug for Milo. They stood in a clearing on the mountainside behind Milo's castle. This spot looked over the rich, green valley.

After burying Milo, Liam waved his hand to sprout tulips on top of him. They all stared, quiet for a few minutes.

"Milo was— "Aubry started, but choked on her words and took a few breaths.

"Milo was a wise and strong wizard who, in his kindness, welcomed a group of six teenagers in their time of need," Sly finished for her. He reached down and laced his fingers through hers.

"Milo loved sharing stories to make other people laugh," Juniper added through tears.

"He encouraged you when you didn't fully believe in yourself yet," Aubry added.

"Milo gave people a chance to prove themselves and didn't judge them by what others might think," Fox said.

"Milo didn't give up on me. I'm—" Liam stopped, unable to go on for a moment. Aubry grabbed his hand.

Liam swallowed.

"I'm standing here today because of him. He showed me what sacrifice looks like." Liam bowed his head. "Even his last words were an encouragement and love for another person. Thank you, Milo, for blessing us with your presence. You will be missed." A tear ran down his face, and he roughly wiped it away. The hollow ache in his chest hadn't gone away since he watched Milo take his last breath.

They all came around Liam. Aubry put her arm around his shoulder while Juniper, Fox, and Sly touched his other shoulder in support. Johnny nodded in solidarity. They stayed like that until a light snow fell.

One by one, they went inside.

Liam stayed.

He stayed until snow covered his boots.

Stayed until he couldn't feel his fingers.

Stayed until he felt tears freeze on his face.

He stayed until Aubry came to usher him inside, out of the snowstorm.

CHAPTER
FORTY-TWO

S unlight streamed through the bedroom window, waking Liam. He rolled over to face the wall and stared at the stone.

He felt raw.

Like a shell of a person.

He didn't know how it was possible to hurt this much and still be alive.

He didn't want to move. Didn't want to do anything.

What's the point? What's it all for?

He heard muffled voices from the other side of the door.

"Do you think we should go in and check on him?"

"Maybe we should just let him get his rest?"

"But he hasn't eaten anything in two days. He's probably starving."

"If he was hungry, he would come out, wouldn't he?"

Liam rolled over and pretended not to hear them. He wanted to be alone. He closed his eyes and drifted off.

When Liam woke next, the sun was still shining. He had slept for a full twenty-four hours.

I guess I should get up now. If only because my stomach is very upset with me.

He pushed himself up in bed and groaned at the stiffness of his body. Lying in bed for a few days took its toll. He heaved a sigh and kicked his feet onto the rug.

After getting dressed, he headed downstairs to fill the emptiness in his stomach that was now hunger. Lumbering down the staircase, he thought of the last meal they'd had at the table together with Milo. The last teatime they enjoyed. His throat tightened, and he pushed the memory away.

"Liam," Aubry said, surprised. She sat at the table with a piece of toast halfway to her mouth. "You're up!" She stared at him, openmouthed.

"So it seems," he said, and plopped down at the table full of toast, jam, potatoes, fruit, eggs, and bacon. And of course, tea. He reached for the tea. Sly, Juniper, and Aubry glanced at him between bites. He raised his gaze to meet theirs. Sighing, he went about buttering his toast.

They ate in silence for a few minutes.

"Is there anything you want to talk about, Liam?" Aubry asked quietly.

"No." He swallowed.

"Okay," she said and went back to eating breakfast.

"I'm going to go on a walk." Liam brushed crumbs from his hands and stood.

"Do you want someone to come with you?" Aubry asked.

"No thank you," he replied.

Liam walked through the hallway and into the main sitting room where Milo first told him about his mom and her life in Domhania. He remembered the pain in Milo's face when he recalled how she died. Maybe her life here wasn't as amazing as she thought it would be. Her life was cut short, and she left a mess behind. It seemed the same was true in his world as well.

Liam shook his head, not knowing what to think, and pulled the heavy castle door open.

The biting cold shocked his system.

Just what he'd been hoping for.

He trudged through the front courtyard and out the white iron gates, down the mountain. The walk down was a lot faster than he remembered the hike up being. As he walked, the snow thinned and became nonexistent. He narrowed his eyes at the oddity of it and followed the path to a small lake at the bottom of the mountain. Standing for a moment, he breathed in the crisp air. He spotted a boulder on the edge of the lake and sat down, admiring the glassy surface.

And then he yelled.

Frustration, anger, sadness, and anguish rolled through him. He didn't want this pain inside anymore. He yelled into the lake, into the woods, and into the sky. How could everything around him be so beautiful when things were so wrong?

Milo was gone.

His mom was gone.

He had no teacher, no direction.

Conroy was still out there, and he was supposed to protect Domhania somehow. What a sick joke.

Maybe none of it even mattered. All his presence had accomplished was getting people killed. Guilt settled in his stomach.

What was the point of letting people in and giving them a chance if they were going to die?

Why did I even come here? Domhania had been one disaster after another. He didn't ask for his mom's mess. He wished he could forget it all. Go home and pretend like none of it ever happened. What good had come out of this, anyway?

He let out a breath.

Well, maybe not everything was bad. He thought about Sly, Juniper, Johnny, and Fox. The friends he'd made. The laughs they'd shared. He'd been more honest with Sly than he'd been with himself since his mom died. And Sly had opened up to help Liam not feel alone. To help him keep going. To help him not battle the darkness alone.

He and Aubry had gotten closer than they'd ever been.

She hadn't given up on him.

He thought about his mom.

He'd found more pieces of her than he thought he ever would. A whole workshop. Stacks of her notebooks, waiting for him to read them. Waiting for him to get to know her.

Domhania. His powers. His inheritance.

His mom had left him with this world, the people in it, and this magic.

He stretched an arm out, palm up, and golden power swirled into a ball.

Maybe all of this was the greatest gift she could have given him?

"How you holding up, mate?"

Liam looked over his shoulder and saw Sly standing there, arms crossed, head tilted, surveying him.

Liam shrugged.

Sly walked over to the giant bolder and joined him.

"Why did I let him die for me?" Liam clenched his jaw and stared at the tall pine trees on the other side of the lake.

"This isn't your fault. It was his choice to sacrifice himself for you. Now it's your choice whether you're going to going to honor his sacrifice or not," Sly's low voice consoled.

"Then why does it feel like it's my fault?" Liam clenched his jaw harder.

"We can't control who comes and who goes, or when. It's not up to us. What we *can* do is choose to love one another or not. The degree to which you feel the pain of loss is the degree to which you loved," Sly said, looking at Liam.

Liam stared out across the lake, chewing on what Sly said. He thought about how Sly and Juniper watched their parents die. He remembered the love in their voices when they'd told stories about them around the campfire.

"How did you move through the grief when your parents passed?" He glued his gaze to Sly, watching for his reaction.

"As you know, it can be a dark road to get to the light at the end of the tunnel," Sly said.

Liam nodded, knowing the darkness well. He felt it settle around his shoulders like a cloak.

"And the journey through grief is different for everyone. It's times of ups and downs. And the only way to heal"—Sly paused and stared seriously at Liam—"is to go through it."

Liam blew out a breath. Not exactly what he wanted to hear. He didn't know how much more exhaustion he could carry. Fear burrowed deeper into his stomach. The soreness of grief set into his joints.

Sly looked at him over his still steepled fingers. "The key is to not battle the darkness alone."

Liam blinked. "Did you talk to Milo about this?"

"What?" Sly narrowed his eyes.

"Never mind." Liam shook his head.

"None of us are strangers to grief," Sly said. "And some of us have tried to go through it alone, and it didn't work out so well."

"What do you mean?"

Sly let out a breath and rubbed his jaw. His russet eyes shone with the pain of a memory. "After our parents died I—" The words caught in his throat. He swallowed and his voice scraped out the next words, "I thought I could handle things on my own. I wanted to be strong for Juniper. I wanted to be strong for all the Stream Side Kids." He stared across the lake. "I didn't talk about it much. I let Juniper talk to me, but I didn't reciprocate. Until one day, I couldn't hold the weight of everything anymore and I broke." Sly's hands balled into fists.

"I took some rum with me to one of the cliff sides by a waterfall." He rolled his lips and kept going. "I drank more than I ever had. I started punching trees, throwing rocks, and bloodied myself up.

"I stood on the edge of the cliff and let the breeze blow across my face. I looked down at the water flowing, so calm, so steady. I wanted that. I didn't know how to keep going. I stepped my foot off into the air. I was ready to jump. To fall. To let it all go and be free." A muscle in his jaw jumped. "Then I heard Juniper call my name. I turned and slipped. I was holding on to the edge with one hand. Juniper dived to the ground and grabbed my other hand. For a second, I didn't think I would make it. I was halfway gone." He hung his head. "But Juniper's grip was like iron. She wasn't letting go. She hauled me up, and I helped as much as my inebriated self could. Once she got me up—" He shook his head. "We cried. Cried for our parents, for all the parents at Stream Side, for us, for our friends. For the burden we had to bear. She told me I couldn't bear it alone anymore. And I didn't want to."

Liam watched Sly, mouth slightly ajar.

"That day I learned that what I thought was strength, was weakness. I kept my pain hidden from everyone out of fear and shame. And that's not strength." He looked at Liam. "True strength is letting others in. It's being vulnerable. Being honest. Letting loved ones help you bear the burden. It's not battling the darkness alone."

Liam sat in Sly's words.

True strength was letting others into the pain? Being vulnerable? Not trying to sort it out himself? To not keep it down, out of the way of others?

"I don't know—" Liam's throat tightened. "I don't know how to do that." Liam turned to look at Sly.

"I didn't know how either," Sly said. "Juniper and I figured it out together. And it's not like she was perfect and knew all the right things to say." Sly chuckled. "Many times she said the wrong thing, or didn't speak when she should have, or vice versa. Many apologies were said. But we did it together. We're not meant to go through life's challenges alone. We need people to help us through. To hold us up on either side when we can't walk ourselves.

"And we're here for you in what you're going through, Liam." Sly's open gaze made Liam believe it. Believe that these people he found could help him through this. "And so is Aubry," Sly added.

Liam nodded, the knot of fear in his stomach slowly loosening.

"Thank you," he breathed. "I mean it. Thank you." He stared Sly in the eye to bring home the sincerity of his words. In his gaze, he saw safety, honesty, and strength. All things he wanted for himself. "I'm sorry," Liam said.

"For what?"

"For not realizing how much pain you and Juniper still hold. For thinking that I'm the only one hurting and hurting the most. You've both lost so much, too."

Aubry had lost her aunt. She watched her slowly die with Liam. Milo, the sole beacon in Domhania's confusing darkness, was gone. They'd all lost him.

Liam exhaled loudly.

"I know I've been trying to figure this all out, mostly on my own. Be the hero. It's just that, for so long, I've been told I can't do it. That I'm not strong enough and I thought—" Liam hung his head, then looked at Sly. "I thought that meant handling things on my own. Sometimes it's easier to put up a wall and tell yourself you're alone and no one knows what you're going through than it is to invite someone into your mess."

Sly gave Liam a small, knowing smile.

"And you let me in," Liam said hoarsely.

He'd been so focused on being someone his mom would be proud of, being a hero, proving Clive and the bullies wrong, thinking he had to accomplish it all on his own, he hadn't considered how he was affecting the people around him. Regret washed over Liam. His mom's grief had caused her to disconnect and put up a wall around herself. He didn't want to do the same thing.

He didn't want it to take hold of him and prevent him from living. To turn him into something dark the way Conroy did. He had to break the cycle.

"Thank you," Liam said.

Sly dipped his head.

"Don't battle the darkness alone, mate."

His words struck Liam's heart. The same words Milo had told him.

Liam nodded, and Sly reached out a hand to grasp his shoulder and squeezed. He let go, and they both stared out at the lake until the sun rose to the middle of the sky, sending sparkles along its surface.

CHAPTER FORTY-THREE

———◦———

S ly and Liam walked back up the mountain trail, the bitter air biting at their cheeks. Dark clouds rolled in, and snowflakes drifted down as they approached the looming white iron gates.

Liam shoved the gate open with a protesting screech of metal on metal. They crossed the courtyard in silence, fresh snow crunching under their boots.

Milo didn't appear to greet them this time.

Once inside the entrance hall, Liam paused, nostrils flaring as he drew in a breath of stale castle air—equal parts musty and familiar. He shrugged off his snow-dusted coat and toed off his boots, leaving them in an unceremonious heap.

Distant voices echoed from the dining hall, pulling him further into the castle. He realized, with a pang, that the others had already gathered for lunch. Liam ran a hand through his windswept hair and forced himself to continue down the corridor, Sly's steps shuffling behind him.

As he entered the hall, the conversation ceased. All eyes swiveled to him—a mixture of concern, curiosity, and something else he couldn't quite identify.

"Don't mind me," Liam muttered, digging his hands into his pockets as he slunk toward an empty chair. "Just in time for lunch?"

He dropped into the seat next to Aubry, very aware of her studiously avoiding his gaze. An awkward silence hung in the air, thick as molasses.

Finally, Liam couldn't take it anymore. "Look, I . . ." He sighed, squeezing his eyes shut. "While I was out there, I did a lot of thinking . . ."

Slowly, he forced the words out—apologizing for being distant, for taking them for granted, for selfishly shouldering burdens he had no right to bear alone. With each admission, he felt a weight lifted. "I wanted to apologize. I'm not sure what to do now. And I know my mom said I was supposed to take care of Domhania, but I need your help. I can't do this alone. I really need all of you. If we're going to stop Conroy and save Domhania, we need to work together. You've held me up before when I didn't know what to do." Liam locked eyes with each of them for a beat. "If it weren't for you, I don't know where I'd be . . ." He let out a breath and waited for someone to say something.

When he finally trailed off, Juniper reached across the table to give his hand a reassuring squeeze. The others joined in with murmurs of understanding.

Aubry was the last to respond, but her red-rimmed eyes and watery smile made his heart clench. "We're with you until the end, Liam. Whatever it takes."

As if on cue, a sumptuous spread materialized before them—roast beef sandwiches, greens, several different rolls and bread, roasted vegetables, colorful fruits, and sticky toffee pudding for dessert. For the first time in days, Liam felt a spark of genuine hunger.

Aubry shot him a sly wink as she snagged the first sandwich. "Well? What are you waiting for? We've got a world to save...and a wizard can't fight on an empty stomach."

CHAPTER FORTY-FOUR

A week later, Liam stepped into the castle and a flutter of voices and movement. Sly slid up next to him, welcoming him home.

"How were they today?" Sly asked.

"Quite obedient, actually." Liam smiled. "The more I use them, the easier it gets."

"Proud of you, mate. Milo would be too," Sly said.

"Thank you." Liam smiled sadly.

"Hey, listen, I wanted to thank you." Sly motioned around the room. "This place has been such a blessing to the Stream Side Kids. As much as our hideout was a magical place, it means a lot to them to have a semblance of a proper house. And a castle at that. Thank you for suggesting it. And thank you for repairing the wards." Sly shook Liam's hand.

"I wouldn't want it any other way. This place is big enough, and I know Milo would like the fact it's getting so much use and serving others. And I couldn't have repaired them without Willow's help." Liam smiled and took in the back and forth of the Stream Side Kids, tidying up and making things their own. They had set up a map table in the back of the sitting room, added blankets and pillows to the couches, and even helped Roya move into the infirmary and Alchemy Lab downstairs next to Willow.

"We might need another dinner table, but other than that, we have all we could ever need here," Sly said. There were about twenty of them all together, and the dining table fit about half. So far, it hadn't been a tremendous problem since some of them enjoyed eating their dinner on the couches and in front of the fire. Something they hadn't been able to do for two years.

"The castle will take care of it for us. It knows what we need when we need it." Liam smiled and glanced around at the stone walls.

Aubry sidled up between Liam and Sly.

"Hey, are you two, uh, going to go back home? I know that's why you wanted to find Milo in the first place." Sly shifted on his feet and cleared his throat.

Liam sighed. "Well, full moon does happen *every* month. So . . ."

Aubry beamed at him. "So we're going to stay for a little bit?"

The hope in her eyes made him chuckle. "Yes, I think that would be a good idea," Liam said.

"Thank you!" She lunged at Liam and grabbed his neck, pulling him in for a hug. Then she turned to Sly and gave him an even more enthusiastic hug.

Sly pulled back, took in her hope-filled face, and kissed her.

"Aaaand that's my cue to leave." Liam hurried away, trying not to gag.

Roya also appreciated the space upgrade when she moved in. "Oh my goodness, this is the place of my dreams!" she said when Liam had walked her to her new workspace.

"There is one condition," Liam said.

Roya raised an eyebrow.

"Teach Aubry everything you know about potions."

Roya puckered her lips. "I think I can make that happen."

He nodded, and the side of his mouth ticked up.

When Liam told Aubry the news, after she finished celebrating with Sly, her jaw dropped for a few seconds.

"You're kidding? I get to learn from a real potions master?"

"You do. Might want to head over. She's getting set up and could use some help."

"Okay!" She took off.

Liam smiled.

He walked around the castle until he made it to the weapons training room downstairs. Juniper was teaching a class on how to string a bow and care for arrows. Since the Stream Side Kids had moved in, they invited people from the neighboring village, Sagewood, to join them. Kids, parents, and adults hiked to the castle each day for classes. Watching the parents and kids learn together, Liam felt a pang of loss and sadness at the realization he would never get to train with his mom.

He knew the Stream Side Kids grieved the loss of their parents too, so Liam had invited childless couples to take a Stream Side Kid under their wing. The couples had longed for children, and the Stream Side Kids longed for love and mentorship.

Of course, no one could take the place of their parents, but the beauty of the arrangement drew a smile from Liam whenever he thought about it.

Juniper clicked around the room in her knee-high boots, teaching the class with enthusiasm and warmth, pulling him from his thoughts.

Liam leaned in the doorway and watched her. She was so animated and present with whomever she taught. Her coils bobbed happily as she nodded to her students.

After a few minutes, she looked up at Liam and smiled. He smiled and lifted his hand in hello.

"Miss Juniper!" One of the younger girls called.

"Scarlet, I told you, you don't have to call me that." Juniper laughed, and she walked over to help her.

Liam made his way down the hall and out into the training courtyard, where he trained every morning before anyone else got up. The still silence helped him focus.

Rising early became a new habit, as he'd never quite enjoyed getting up early. But it had proven to be his favorite part of the day. He'd been working on recalling joyful memories, as Milo had advised him to. His control had grown the past week, and he was proud of his progress. He wondered where he would be now if Milo was still mentoring him.

He'd been flipping through Milo's journal and found many entries about training and refining powers. Using those, Liam had created a semblance of a training schedule for himself. He also spent time in his mom's workshop—*his* workshop now—hoping to connect more with her and uncover things about her he'd longed to know. He hoped it would be enough.

As Liam had studied his mothers stacks of journals, he came across entries filled with grief, hope, and a recurring word, *Inkbound*. He'd found it in several different journals and hadn't pieced together its meaning yet. One of his mother's entries that had caught his attention referred to herself as *Inkbound*. What did *Inkbound* mean? Was he now *Inkbound* since he'd inherited his mothers' powers? And where did she get her powers from?

He took a breath through the flutter of anxiety in his chest. All this would be so much easier if Milo or his mom were here to answer his questions.

For now, he focused on his breathing and began another training session. They weren't sure if Conroy had survived the broken birthright ceremony. If not, Liam needed to be ready for Zadimus, Conroy's teacher, who he knew little about.

In a few days, they'd send out a group to gather information to see if Conroy was still out there or not. Either way, he needed to be ready.

"Did you recover it, Conroy?" The master of shadows held out his stiff hand.

"Yes, sir." Conroy's voice wobbled. He carefully placed the sapphire pendant in Zadimus's hand. Wrapping his fingers around it, Zadimus smiled, an evil glint growing in his dark eyes.

"Let them try and stop us now."

THE JOURNEY CONTINUES

In Book 2...

ACKNOWLEDGEMENTS

Writing this book took a lot longer than I thought it would and has changed shape many times. I can't believe we're finally here. My goal with this book was to write something that spoke to young adults in a time of grief and hardship. I wrote a book that I wish I had when I was younger. My hope is that this book has brought you some comfort and that you feel seen. I'm rooting for you.

Bringing a book into the world takes many hands. I'm deeply grateful to everyone who helped me bring this book to fruition. My gratitude is overflowing, and if I were to write about it, this part would be pages long. Here is my attempt to thank the people that helped get me here.

Thank you to my copy editor Andi L. Gregory for diving into this book and pruning it into a better version. I'm grateful for all your help and time! Thank you to Mary Weber, my developmental editor, for helping me refine the characters and shape of my story. I look up to you in so many ways.

Thank you, My Lan, for a gorgeous book cover design. I'm in awe of your work and commitment to excellence.

Thank you to my friends and business team, Cheryl Cummings and Evan Gallagher. Cheryl, thank you for making a beautiful website, taking breathtaking photos, and making me look good in so many ways. Evan, thank you for your videography work, marketing help, and constant encouragement. My author business would be non-existent without you two.

My Pen Pals writing group. Thank you for your feedback on parts of my novel and for creating a space for creativity. It's been a joy to write with you all these past few years.

My very early beta readers, Ashley Jones, Abigail Dengler, Helya Kargosha, Evan Gallagher. Thank you for marching through an early and clunky version of this book and helping it shine.

My author friends in the Red Herrings Society. Thank you for answering all my questions, being willing to help and support me on this journey, and giving me a community to grow with.

My parents Randy and Vicki. Thank you for instilling a love of reading in me at a young age. I'm fond of my plethora of memories of you reading to me before bed every night. Thank you for giving me space to let my imagination grow.

My in-laws Tim and Debbie. Thank you for sending me to my very first writing conference. You helped put wind in my sails and kick-start my publishing journey.

My siblings, grandmas, aunts, and uncles for constantly telling me I could do it.

Thank you to my beloved husband, Tyler. You gave me a chance to make this dream a reality. I wouldn't be here were it not for you. Thank you for the many late nights, encouragements, for reading my novel and suggesting I add "more cool stuff." Thank you for not letting me throw my manuscript out the window the fifty-two thousand times I wanted to. Thank you for taking our baby boy on walks so I could work on my book. You believed in me when I didn't believe in myself. You've stood by me and loved me in a way that leaves me in tears when I think about it. I'll never be able to say thank you enough. Know that this book wouldn't exist without you. Thank you for making my dreams come true and helping me flourish. I love you.

And thank you to my Lord and Savior, Jesus, for being my rock, sustaining me, and leading me through this entire process. I hope this book honors you.

I stand on the shoulders of all of you listed and not. As well as you, dear reader. Thank you for going on this journey with me, Liam, Aubry, and the Stream Side Kids. Let's see what's next.

ABOUT THE AUTHOR

A Southern California native, K.T. Jay loves to spend the occasional rainy day curled up in a wingback chair by the fire with a good book and a cup of tea. When she's not writing, she enjoys spending time with her husband and son, going on walks, visiting botanical gardens, and feeding her pet tortoise hibiscus flowers.

Sign up for her newsletter to stay up to date on publishing news at ktjayauthor.com.